For *Grit & Grace: Portraits of a Woman's Life*

A
TANGLED
MERCY

ALSO BY JOY JORDAN-LAKE

Blue Hole Back Home: A Novel

Whitewashing Uncle Tom's Cabin: Nineteenth-Century Women Novelists Respond to Stowe

Working Families: Navigating the Demands and Delights of Marriage, Parenting, and Career

Why Jesus Makes Me Nervous: Ten Alarming Words of Faith

Grit & Grace: Portraits of a Woman's Life

A TANGLED MERCY

A Novel

JOY JORDAN-LAKE

LAKE UNION
PUBLISHING

Text copyright © 2017 by Joy Jordan-Lake

Published by Lake Union Publishing, Seattle

www.apub.com

Amazon, the Amazon logo, and Lake Union Publishing are trademarks of Amazon.com, Inc., or its affiliates.

ISBN-13: 9781477823668
ISBN-10: 1477823662

Cover design by Kimberly Glyder

Printed in the United States of America

*For the people of Charleston, South Carolina,
whose reply to a violent hate was love and unity, and
particularly to all those connected with Emanuel
African Methodist Episcopal Church, whose strength,
courage, forgiveness, insistence on justice, and
unflagging hope have inspired so many others to action
and faith for two hundred years. And for my family,
who never gave up.*

Chapter 1

Charleston, South Carolina

April 9, 1822

Later, Tom Russell would wonder if the very boards of that place—splintered, unpainted, unlovely—had leaked some sort of lethal courage into his blood and made him see things that could not be true. Could never be true.

Tom sprang away from where he'd been leaning into its side. Even here in the wee hours of morning, even shuttered tight on a weed-strangled lot, the church still thrummed with movement and sound: deep, grieving chords struck through with a raw and dangerous power. Maybe it was only the dark and the mist of predawn, or maybe it was Tom's state of mind, but the clapboards themselves seemed to throb.

This was insanity. He would not wait. This meeting, that person, and this place could mean nothing but trouble. Time to walk away. Now. Before it was too late.

Through the dark, Tom slipped toward the seawall that bounded East Battery. Out on the harbor, square sails sliced through the scrim of fog, and for a moment unhinged from the present, a moment swung open too wide, Tom Russell pictured himself there at the bow. His face, at least. And his build. But no copper disc hung from his neck to label him what Charleston insisted he was: a blacksmith. Who ran a shop on East Bay. And who was the possession of one Widow Russell.

Instead, the man Tom Russell pictured leaned hard over the ship's starboard railing, as if by sheer force of will he could make the ship clear the harbor still faster. Before they could follow. Before he'd be shot.

Tom could see himself standing tall, with shoulders that might have been hammered from iron and a shirt that was unstained with soot or with sweat—whiter than the canvas swelling four stories up. His head was lowering now to a woman who lifted her face to the wind and let her eyes shut—in what he knew was relief. Immense and total relief. In the sure knowledge that they were safe. The two of them. *Safe.*

Leaping up onto the bouldered seawall, Tom landed with a jolt that was meant to shake clean from his head that image: two figures, safe, at the bow of a ship sailing toward freedom.

Delusion, that's what it was. As deadly as any bullet or noose.

Chapter 2

Charleston, South Carolina

April 9, 2015

Gripping her coffee and feeling her way through the mist that clung to the water and to the mansions beside it, Kate climbed the steps of the seawall. A thousand miles of asphalt had made her stiff and bleary-eyed, but this view, her first of Charleston Harbor since she'd left as a child, was nothing like she'd remembered.

Left, Kate thought. Or been dragged away—that was more like it.

Where she'd recalled sunshine that was searing and gold and houses in a paint box of pastels and roses that spilled in reds and yellows so bright they hurt the eyes, here was a haunted gray silence. Spanish moss swayed from long-armed live oaks that seemed to be reaching and reaching for something they could not quite touch. Brick crafted by slaves walled off the gardens, broken only by wrought iron gates. And low-growing palmettos spiked upward like swords.

Kate looked out over the water, as dark here before dawn as her coffee. Beneath her, low waves hissed over a strip of pebbles and sand. And for the first time since she'd walked out so bravely on her life in New England—how stupid she'd been to think she was brave, how incredibly, terribly stupid—nausea and doubt rose together. A thousand miles south she'd driven, all afternoon and all night, thinking that finally, after so many years, she was on a journey to answers.

But this. These tragic oaks and high walls and wrought iron gates.

This was like coming stumbling back to some faintly remembered but much longed for home, only to find that no one remembered you here—and they'd locked every door.

Kate threw back her head for one last long swig of coffee. Time to face facts.

She checked her phone. No call back yet from the one man still living who might, just might, have some answers.

She dialed the number for her father's attorney again—*My late father,* she corrected herself. The lawyer had often appeared in her dreams as a little girl, his tarantula body with its crooked legs and its scuttling walk. "I'm here on behalf of your father," the spider-lawyer would spit at her in her sleep, "who sends, of course, his regrets."

It was a phrase she'd heard often enough in her waking hours growing up: *Your father sends his regrets.* Often enough it seeped into her sleep.

Even now, as a grown woman—a graduate student, for God's sake, in one of the top history programs in the country—Kate found herself holding her breath like a small, frightened child as she waited for the attorney to answer.

"Botts here," snapped a voice at the other end of the line. And before Kate could gather her words, he went on, his small, sniveling voice sounding tighter—angrier, too—than ever. "Katherine, I was planning on calling you back first thing this morning—although I generally refrain from making or receiving calls before six a.m."

Kate glanced at the time on her phone: five forty-five. Awake all through the night, she'd lost track of when the rest of the world would be waking up. "Oh. Sorry. I—"

"I hope you won't consider for one more moment the outlandish idea of driving down to Charleston. Rank foolishness. Let me reiterate that while attorney-client privilege, which extends beyond the grave, prohibits me from disclosing my client's reasoning on his testamentary dispositions, I can assure you that there was no provision in the will for you but the modest amount you have already received." And then he added, an afterthought, "Which I regret—again—to say."

Kate sighed. "And I regret to have to repeat that my calling you is not about money. I told my father for years I wanted none of his money—since apparently I was worth none of his time. Look, I'd just like to talk with you, Mr. Botts. I've waited my whole life to ask questions, and now, it would appear, I may have waited too long."

A silence followed.

And when Botts spoke again, his voice had deepened to nearly a croak. "My sincere sympathies, Katherine, on the recent loss of your mother. She was . . ." He took several seconds to sort through possible words. "A lovely woman."

"She was. Although I don't recall you or my father expressing that sentiment very well or very often before." Another silence, only the cry of a gull as it flew in an arc around Kate. "And as to my driving to Charleston, I'm sorry to hear you think it's a foolish idea, but as it happens, I'm already here. And I'm looking forward to meeting with you. Soon, I would hope."

I came, she could have added, *because of that lovely woman, my mother.*

That, Kate had to admit—though not out loud to Botts—was the truth that had hounded her here.

~

Kate had stood midlecture in Robinson Hall. It had been her first official chance to impress a vast hall full of first-year students and the head of the History Department. She'd arrived with slush inside her black pumps from a frantic, last-minute dash across the Yard. The pants of her power suit sopping from the knees down, she'd dripped icy water across the wood floor as she'd paced at the front of the room and tried to pretend she wasn't a wreck from the past weeks of grief.

Approaching the lecture's climax, she'd faced the hall's screen to click through a series of daguerreotypes of slaves, their bodies seeming to float above the silver-coated plates of the pictures, their eyes meeting the onlooker's stare.

"Could individual players in that late spring of 1822 have known, do you think," she asked the class without turning, "that in laying plans for revolt they might be changing not just the course of their own lives, not just of the Low Country or even of the South, but the entire course of the nation?"

And then she'd clicked to the next slide, that picture she'd snapped of an old Polaroid, imported at the last minute into the presentation as an image of the Low Country. This image, grainy and faded, showed a young white woman in a long, billowing dress, a magnolia blooming to her right and a live oak towering on her left. It was Kate's own mother, Sarah Grace, with satin and lace falling clear to her feet, in a photo that before had seemed simply fitting for this point in the presentation. Now, though, enlarged like this on the screen, it looked downright alarming: the stark white glare of the magnolia blossoms and the billowing dress against the deep shadow of the oak—something alarming, too, in Sarah Grace's expression, her mouth an attempt at a smile but her eyes stormy and desperate and dark.

Kate had turned to look out over that sea of undergraduate faces, their sleep-deprived pallor, their eyes deadened by stress to wax-figure expressions.

In that flash of a moment, her staring up at the screen, it had seemed like a revelation, a brainstorm: rather than slogging on through the flood of guilt and unanswered questions since her mother's death three weeks ago, Kate could fight back. She could toss a few duffels of clothes into her Jeep, along with the last boxes of her mother's possessions she had yet to sort through, and she could drive the thousand miles south to the last place Kate remembered her mother as happy. Kate could demand answers from anyone there who might know, and from Charleston itself—with the kind of research she'd been trained to do. The kind of answers she knew how to find in musty old books and archival papers but had never known how to ask for from her own family, while there was still time.

It had struck her in that terrible, irresistibly beautiful moment that she could go there herself. Today. Right now. That there was no longer any reason to hold off on digging through whys. Not anymore.

Which was when Kate was sure—so stupidly, utterly sure—what she had to do. And where she had to go.

"Are you certain," came Botts's creaking hinge of a voice from the other end of the line, "that you aren't simply . . . running away?"

"Running away?" Kate repeated, incredulous. "From a whole year of loss, you mean?" *And from a truckload of guilt,* she nearly added out loud, but she could not say that to Botts—him, of all people. "Believe me, I'd run away if I could. Instead I came here. Which is where my meeting with you comes in."

Kate drew a breath, her mother's voice in her ear: *A lady knows how to be strong, Kate—and is also smart enough to be sweet, for when just being strong won't roll the stone.*

Ironic, Kate thought. Poor Sarah Grace. She'd wielded sweetness and smarts expertly. But being strong—she'd struggled as long as Kate could remember with that.

A pause. The dark harbor water was turning silver as morning broke.

"If," Kate made herself add, "you would be good enough to fit me into your busy schedule."

Botts seemed to be weighing his words. "I cite for you the 1998 Supreme Court ruling *Swidler and Berlin versus the United States*. Let me make myself perfectly clear: When we meet, I cannot legally discuss anything that pertains to your father as my client. Or to your mother, in regard to my client."

When we meet. Not if *but* when. He'd already conceded that much.

"I understand that, yes. Still, I'd be grateful for your time."

"Perhaps you're not aware, Katherine, that I no longer live in Charleston but in a coastal town to the north. As I work very few days in the firm's central office now that I am mostly retired, I come back to the city only as needed. I will see what I can do about making a trip soon. How long do you expect to be there?"

Kate scanned the scene before her: the mansions, the harbor, the cannons that seemed just now to be pointing at her. "I need to speak with my academic adviser." *If he's still taking my calls.* She cleared her throat. "He may have some specific recommendations." *Like my withdrawing from the History Department and taking up waitressing.* "Regarding my research, that is. So it's hard to say yet."

"I'll be in touch," Botts said. And with that, the line went dead.

Loosing her hair now from its ponytail holder and letting the sea breeze buffet it, Kate passed a hand over her aching forehead—as if she could shut out for the moment what kind of damage she may have done to her life. What was left of her life.

Even now as the early morning dark was beginning to fade, the shore of Charleston Harbor still lay swaddled in thin bands of white. Nothing moved but a ship gliding silently out toward Fort Sumter and, beyond that, the sea.

Kate scanned Charleston's harbor, its edging of historic mansions with white piazzas soaring out from each floor like gulls lifting into the sky. Toward the mansions, a carriage was clattering out from the fog.

Its blinkered draft horse arched his black neck against its weight and tossed his white mane as the carriage rolled past.

Even Kate's clearest memories had not prepared her for the undertow feel of this place, like being sucked back not just to her own childhood but two hundred years backward in time.

From her jeans pocket, Kate plucked the pen and scrap of paper she always carried. With a few swift slashes of ink, she blocked in the carriage, the palmettos, the cannons, the ship, the live oaks—and a runner, just now leaping up onto the seawall and stretching his calves.

The runner's entrance into the scene was out of place, jarringly so, but also strangely fitting somehow: something strong and graceful— ancient, even—in his movement that linked him with the ripple of the horse's shoulder and flank, the surge of the ship.

The runner glanced her way then. For a long moment—too long.

But she shook off his stare and focused back on her scrap of paper, her pen.

Sketching a scene had always helped her sort the chaos of life one line at a time: the world at its core, shadow and light. She'd sketched her mother sometimes during Mass, those rare and shining moments when Sarah Grace seemed almost at peace.

Kate had sketched her father, too, though not nearly as often, his being all but gone from her life once she and her mother left Charleston. After each of the handful of times since age four that she'd seen him, she'd sat down to sketch what she could recall of his face—her way of decoding the man underneath: the broad, intellectual forehead, the jawline that was strong and firm and square, the mouth that was a straight, unreadable line but that could, without warning, curl into a sneer.

Just once, she'd tried mailing a sketch to her father—a kind of apology after he'd shown up unannounced just in time for the first round of a national spelling bee where she'd earned a place. Watching his face, Kate had heard the word that was hers to spell—fittingly, the word *annihilation*—and known that she'd spelled it wrong not by the judge's *I'm sorry, that's incorrect* but by the disgust on her father's face. He'd sent back her sketch by return mail. Over the pastel lines that she'd labored so long to get right, their proportion and tone and expression, he'd scrawled in red ink:

Thank you for this, but as I assume you and your mother do not wish to expose yourselves to yet more public scorn, you, Katherine, might wish to spend your time studying in the future.

Sarah Grace had turned away. "He means that for me, Katie. Not you."

But Kate had kept the note tucked in the flimsy pine desk where she'd done her homework, and she'd often pulled it back out in the wee morning hours before major exams when she thought she could not study one minute more. She would never, she'd promised herself—not even if she had to study in place of sleepovers and ball games and dances and dates—be that stupid again.

Running a hand back through her hair, tangled and windblown by the drive down and now by the sea breeze, Kate squinted at her sketch of the shoreline.

"So this," she murmured, "is Charleston."

"Yep," came a voice from below.

Soft and small as it was, the voice nearly knocked Kate from her edge of seawall.

Scrambling up on top of the wall from a thin strip of beach below, a child looked up at her through a fringe of long lashes, with brown eyes too big for his face. "Never was a city more sweet on itself than Charleston."

He stood there with a mop of black curls on his head, baggy gym shorts over spindly brown legs, and a man's sweatshirt flopping too long on his wrists. "It's what my daddy says about Charleston."

Kate found her balance again on the seawall. It was hard enough to sort through her own thoughts, the jumble and mess of them, without some random child showing up—perfectly nice, probably, as kids went, but wanting to jabber just when she most needed to think. She tried not to sound annoyed. "I bet your dad's pretty smart. Listen, I don't mean to be rude, but shouldn't you be in school?"

"Since my last birthday, my daddy trusts me to go out for a run in the mornings—me and my uncle, we're runners, the both of us—long as I give a shout back through the door 'fore I hop on the bus, even if I am sweaty going to school. My daddy says it's no shame to work sweaty, so long as the work's good. Just now, I stopped to snag me this shell from below." He held out his palm.

Only half listening to the boy's scattershot thoughts, Kate nodded, not looking at him. "Good for you." Then, to be sure he went sweetly along on his way, she glanced toward his palm. "That's nice." She stopped. Turning back toward the child, she slid a finger over the stippled brown shell in his palm. "Wow, kid. A knobbed whelk. A really large one."

He brightened. "You know its name?"

A wave slapped the seawall below. Then another.

Kate could see her mother beside her, the two of them kneeling in the surf as it dropped away from high tide, Kate's short, chubby legs covered in sand. *And there,* Sarah Grace was saying, *is one worth adding to our collection: a knobbed whelk. How clever of you to find it. And here, this stripy one is a lightning whelk. See the difference?*

That must have been on the Isle of Palms, just off the coast here, where they'd sometimes walked as a young family. And later, after she and her mother had fled whatever it was they had fled, Kate had sat on the cold linoleum floor of their duplex with the starfish and sand dollars and scallops and oyster shells all mounded around her, clutching a conch to her chest and sobbing, *I want to go home! Why can't we go home?*

And then the seashell collection had disappeared entirely. Like everything else—without explanations that made any sense.

Because it makes you cry, Katie, her mother had said. *My poor, sweet little Kate. It makes us want to go back.*

11

She'd hugged Kate so tightly then that her chest hurt. *I'm so sorry, my Katie. So sorry,* she'd cried. *But, please. No questions. For your momma's sake.*

"Whelk," the boy on the seawall was saying, relishing the sound of the word. "A big awesome brown *whelk.*"

"Yep," Kate said. "I know a few names of some shells. That one's worth stopping a run for, I'd say. Nice find. Now, if you don't mind, I really need to be—"

The boy cocked his head at her. "You know, lady, wherever you're from, they gabble fine—talk fast as hell. Hope it's not bad I said *hell.* Gave up my *goddamn*s last year when Mrs. Buckshorn—she was my teacher for third, and I didn't have to repeat—charged us a quarter per cuss. Only *hell,* she said, didn't count if you're meaning the real actual place, which I mostly do."

Kate turned back, nearly startled into a laugh—but caught it in time, the boy's brown eyes round and earnest. She cleared her throat instead. "I can see where that could get pricey."

"So you wouldn't be from around here?"

"Me? No. That is . . ." She returned his gaze, which was steady and waiting, as he cocked his head to the opposite side. This ought not to be a hard question, and yet here she was with no answer. And too many. "My family was from here—at least, both of my parents were. But home for me . . ." She frowned at the boy.

Maybe it wasn't his fault. But he'd asked the question.

Kate plucked at the front of her sweatshirt, a deep crimson, and pointed with one finger to the white crest at its center, the word *Veritas* inside the shield and the all-uppercase word *HARVARD*, like a royal pronouncement, beneath it. "I'm from somewhere else. Up north. Far away."

The boy crossed his arms over his chest, the sleeves of his runner's pullover too long and flopping. He shook his head.

Kate had wanted a few moments of quiet to take all this in—this vortex of feelings stirred up by coming back here—to weigh whether she'd screwed up her life beyond hope, but this kid with the curls in his face couldn't leave her alone. "Can't you read, little guy?"

"Read fine. But you can't be raised by any kind of a college. Can't come from there."

Kate looked from the boy to the crest on her sweatshirt and back.

"And 'little guy,'" he added, "wouldn't be what you'd want to call me."

"You know, for a kid who's no bigger—"

"Than the thick of a rice sickle?" he suggested. "How my daddy says it. But I'm older than my looks might deceive me to be."

"Is that right?"

He blinked long lashes back at her. "And I sure as smack hate to say it, but you . . ."

"What about me?"

"You got some kind of slippery grip on your stack of nice."

Kate stared at the child. Her mouth dropping open, she crossed her arms to match his. *My stack of nice?*

"But my daddy says we make exceptions for folks that got too much lonely on them."

"That's not—"

"Says it's the folks say they're not lonely who'd be the saddest of all. 'Cause they hadn't grown the insides big enough yet to admit it."

"Is that right?" Kate could hear the irritation ridging her voice. "Well, with all due respect to your dad, he doesn't know me." She meant to walk on then. Instead she stared down at the boy's face, the cheekbones high and strong, carved sharp under the soft spill of black curls. Striking in that way that pain sometimes chisels a face into beauty that hurts to look at—pain etched on the raw of your heart.

"You," she said softly, "know about lonely, too. Is that it?"

Brown eyes lifted to her and did not blink.

A pelican dove into the water behind them, but neither one of them turned.

The boy stepped closer and reached for the scrap of paper that Kate held. His brow furrowed as he studied it. "You draw this your ownself?"

"I sketch," Kate explained before he could ask, "wherever I go—like other people take pictures." She plucked the pen from her pocket to show him. "Kind of an old habit."

He ran a dark finger over the lines of the horse with an earnestness, almost a reverence, that made Kate take another look at his face. He was assessing her sketch line by line.

"A habit," she admitted quietly, "that's kind of important to me."

"You got it down good—perfect, even, I'd say—the boat and the buggy and trees. But how come you got ropes coming down all out of the trees, like folks about to get hanged?"

"What? No." Kate peered over the child's shoulder. "No, see, that's just the Spanish moss dangling there, and wisteria vines." But the kid was right: the drape and loop of the moss and the vines did suggest something like nooses.

"Maybe I've been reading too much about hangings lately," she said. "For my studies. My work."

The boy's eyes popped wide. "Must be some kind of work. How come they let a girl do it?"

"A *girl*? How old are you? You look—"

"Like the milk hadn't dried good off my mouth yet? I know. But recollect I said I wouldn't be near so young as I look. You hung any pirates?"

"*Pirates?*"

"The hangings. Your work."

"Oh. Nope. No pirates. That I recall."

Deflated, the boy dropped his shell in one pocket of the gym shorts, then dug in the pocket on the other side. "Here's what I keep with me alltime, like you do that pen. Calms me down good if I'm getting

14

worked up. If the mad's coming on." On his palm now sat a cube of bright-colored squares.

"A Rubik's Cube?"

"Something crosswise about that? I like things I can sort into straight. How things ought to stand." His fingers flew over the cube, spinning each side into one ordered color within seconds.

Kate touched the cube with one finger. "No. I don't suppose there's anything crosswise about that. Maybe that's why I sketch, you know? Trying to sort life into straight. Only I think it takes me a lot longer to sort things to straight than it does you."

"Algorithms. That's what you're needing." Dropping the Rubik's Cube back in his pocket, he knelt for a stone and with one snap of his wrist sent it skipping over the water. The arm jutting out from the too-long cuff was nothing but bone and a tight swath of dark skin.

Kate frowned. "You need to go home, don't you think? Before catching your bus. Get something to eat."

He shrugged. "Had a rice waffle with syrup. And I'm fine right here, talking with you."

"You need a second waffle, for sure. And I've got things I have to do. Adult stuff."

"I know about adult stuff," he said. And something hard—glinting and sharp as tin torn into bits—reflected in his eyes.

"Look, I don't mean to be rude, but maybe you shouldn't talk to strangers."

The boy pitched back his head. "And maybe *you* oughta learn how to make friends when you're fresh-new in town."

Kate's hands went to her hips, but the boy's eyes shone up at her. Sighing, she let her hands drop. "Okay. You win. But I drove all the way down from Boston last night, so I'm pretty worn out. And I've got a whole lot of things to . . . sort through, you might say."

"Yeah? Like what?"

Like my whole life, she wanted to say. *Like what shattered my family. Like why both my mother and father loved Charleston and both of them left, separately, and did not come back. Like why my father, who died last year all alone, avoided seeing me at all costs—except for a handful of visits that came too late and the one time he tried to summon me and I shut him down because I was mad and hurt and bitter, and I didn't know he was sick. Like wanting to know where things went wrong for us all and why.*

But there were things, Kate knew all too well, you did not say to a child. There were things that were too much for them to understand, much less to carry.

Her gaze out on the water, she crossed her arms over the crest on her sweatshirt and shivered, suddenly cold. "Like, I wouldn't even know where to start."

The boy checked the man's oversized watch on his wrist. "I still got a whole ten minutes at least. So we got time for you telling why you came down here to Charleston from"—he nodded to her sweatshirt—"off. How we say it down here: *from off.*"

"I really don't . . ." *Want to* was the end of that sentence.

Because I don't trust anyone. That was the truth, wasn't it? The truth behind why she'd rather ignore a sweet random kid who had time to kill before catching his bus than simply tell him one true thing about her life. It was the truth behind every friendship she'd ever attempted and every man she'd tried to date and then found a reason to dump—there was always a reason if you looked hard enough. Because if you didn't end things soon after they started, a friendship or a romance, either one, then you were setting yourself up for hurt. For learning once more what you'd already learned, sitting all afternoon and into the night alone on the curb, waiting for your father's headlights that never came, or believing your mom would stick to her promise and stay sober through your high school awards dinner. The truth was that there was no end to the people you could not count on. Safer, then, to trust no one.

But the kid's curls were tumbling over big, innocent eyes. And he'd have to leave soon for his bus.

Slowly, watching his face for signs of boredom—people could lose interest in you any moment—Kate plucked out two old Polaroids from her back jeans pocket. One of these was the photo that had started her down this road—quite literally—to ending up here in Charleston today, the photo that she'd adapted for her presentation, then let herself be overwhelmed by midlecture.

The boy peered over her arm. The first photo showed her mother in the long, flowing satin beside the live oaks. More than anything, those ropes of dangling moss gave the scene an otherworldly quality, as if the young woman with the distant expression had only floated there for an instant—had no real tie to that moment or to the man holding the camera. In the second photo, Sarah Grace, this time in cutoff jean shorts, sat on top of a massive white pediment, like some historic site, high above the ground.

"That you in the pictures?"

"That was"—Kate took a breath at the gut punch of the past tense—"my mother."

The boy spoke in a whisper. "Your momma's crossed over, too?"

It was a phrase—from the Low Country maybe—that Kate remembered her mother using, and hearing it now, Sarah Grace's death washed over her in a wave. A full moment swept by before Kate realized what else the child had said.

She bent toward him. "Too?"

He leaned into her side and slipped a small hand into hers. The two of them faced into the breeze and stood for a time there, letting low waves lap at the seawall beneath them. Kate's eyes spilled over, and she batted the tears from her cheeks with the sweatshirt cuff above her left hand, which held the photos, rather than pull her right hand from the child's.

Other people, Kate realized, would have hurried to ask either of them—out of a socially expected concern—how long ago the loss had been and from what and how things were going. Other people would have babbled well-intentioned comforts and platitudes.

But the two of them only stood there, side by side, saying nothing at all. Just watching the roll of the sea. And, strangely, that was just right.

It was the child who finally broke the silence as he reached across her to gesture toward the two Polaroids. "A partner's what you'd be needing."

Kate pulled gently away. "That's a nice offer. Really. But these pictures aren't even the official research I'm supposed to be working on. I'm sorry, but I don't have time for a partner."

The boy bent closer to study the photos. "Why?" he asked suddenly.

"Well, because partners take time to train."

He shook his head. "That's the wrong slice of why. What I'm meaning is, why's your momma so extra big smiling in this one"—he pointed to the photo of the tanned girl in cutoffs, perched high above the ground on the edge of some historic pediment, her head thrown back, laughing for the camera—"like she wanted to make people think she was happy?" His finger moved to the other photo, Kate's mother in the long, flowing satin, and gazing off into the distance. "Your momma was pretty. But her face got all kind of sad behind the eyes."

"She was," Kate agreed. "And it did."

"That why you're here?"

"I'm here mostly for my work." Kate almost said it with conviction. Almost as if it were true.

He nodded. "The hangings."

She managed a smile. "Yeah. The hangings. It's my research on a slave revolt that was planned in Charleston. There are documents here in some archives that I can't access online. Guess I want to understand what *really* happened one particular summer two hundred years ago. Who did what and what motivated them to do it. And why my mother—she loved history, too, and majored in it in college—made lots of notes about some of the main players of that revolt. It was like she was obsessed with reading about it."

Kate stopped. "So, yeah. I'm mostly here for my work. My academic research."

The child's face had the same patient, utterly unconvinced look of Kate's academic adviser. And probably of Botts, if she could have seen his expression at the other end of the line.

"Okay, and also to figure out a whole lot of things from my personal life. Like—you're totally right—like why there's sad behind the eyes in both of these two pictures. You're pretty smart, you know that?"

Receiving the compliment like an old center fielder shagging a pop fly he's caught hundreds of times, the boy nodded. "I know."

Kate raised an eyebrow at him. "Really? Wow. Good for you. That's something I've never been good at saying about myself."

The boy nodded toward the sweatshirt. "So you tell folks that's where you're from so other people can say it for you."

Kate stared at him before answering. "A little *too* smart maybe."

His brow furrowed again. "I stomp on your feelings any? Didn't calculate to."

"You're okay." Refusing to meet his eye—*Ridiculous to be called out by a kid and, worse, for the kid to be right*—Kate swung back her hair. "Listen, I need to go. And you need to catch a school bus, right?" She gave his hand a quick squeeze. "Anyway, it was nice to meet you. Maybe I'll see you around."

The boy was inching away. "Okay if I'm your very first friend here in Charleston?"

Already turning, Kate stopped. "You look to me like just the kind of friend I need. And you know what? I'm sorry I was a little crabby to you there at first."

"*Real* crabby's more like it."

"*Real* crabby, then."

"It's okay." The boy leaned in. "And I got your back. No sweet-mouthin'. I mean it."

Impulsively, Kate gave his shoulders a hug—long enough to feel the bones beneath the flop of the shirt. "I believe you," she said. "And I'll return the favor someday. I promise."

A glib thing to say. A promise she couldn't keep.

And no one, she of all people knew, ought to make promises that couldn't be kept to a child.

Clambering down the seawall, she glanced toward the harbor, where the ship was sliding back out toward sea. And there sat the cannons, poised and waiting for whatever invasion might dare disrupt the city again. There, too, still sharing the scene with the ship and the cannons, the runner stood on the seawall, cell phone to his ear. And here came the carriage again, approaching from up East Battery, the clip-clop of the hooves, the rattle of the harness and spoked wooden wheels.

It unsteadied her, present and past bleeding together like that, and she paused in the middle of the street to take it all in.

The sun at the horizon was just burning through mist and spilling red out from the edge of the earth.

Kate's hand went to her neck. "Like blood," she murmured aloud, glad the boy wasn't there any longer to hear. "My God. It's like watching blood rolling in."

Chapter 3

1822

Dawn over Charleston Harbor had always calmed him—and calm was something he could use these days. But this morning, the air felt taut and already hot, and the sun's first rays were staining the water an eerie red.

A clipper's bow cut the water soundlessly as the ship sailed into port.

Far down the harbor, stevedores and slaves swarmed the wharf, distant shouts in waves of sound, a jumble of Gullah and Ibo, Portuguese and Dutch, as the men began unloading the ship's hold.

Soon, suspended crates swung high above the wharf. Some of them might have held silks or laces. Fine porcelain or coffee or tea. Madeira. Or sugar, if the ship had come from a Caribbean port. Pineapples. Or mangoes.

Dark arms and backs strained at the ship's ropes. A white man, shouting profanities in mostly incoherent torrents of sound, swaggered through their midst with one arm raised over his head, a pistol pointing straight to the sky. Every fifty or so paces he paused to lower the pistol beside a slave's head, the gun's mouth pointing upward but its barrel along the slave's ear. From this distance, Tom could not hear exactly what the white man was saying or what sort of responses he got, but those who must not have said what he wanted to hear, or those whose dark, bare backs must not have seemed bent hard enough into the work, heard the pistol's report smack up against their ears. Howling, these men lurched to the boards of the wharf, holding the sides of their heads. Then, jerked back up to their feet, they bent again to the ropes and the crates.

Fourteen years ago the United States had outlawed the importation of slaves by ship. So now, here in the city that saw the greatest amount of human chattel brought into its port, the most valuable of former cargo handled the incoming goods.

All of it, all of them—*all of us,* Tom corrected himself—bought and sold at a whim.

Near the wharves, just behind the Custom House, a crowd had gathered around a low platform, where a white man in a battered top hat—it looked badly moth-eaten and crumpled even from here—was announcing something Tom could not make out. The man flung both arms over his head as he spoke and pointed into the crowd as white hands raised one by one in response.

Beside him on the platform, a young woman stood trembling, her dress ripped at the neck, one hand grasping the hand of a child who could have been no more than ten. Pulling the boy's hand to her waist, where she clutched on to it still harder, she seemed to be locking her arms, bracing herself, as if to say to the crowd of men gathered below that no earthly power could part her from her son.

But the man in the battered hat thrust both hands overhead as he bellowed a *"Sold"* that carried over the water. Stepping between the mother and child, he wrenched the boy's arm so that the boy stumbled to his knees.

Ignoring the auctioneer's arm blocking her way, the woman dodged past him and reached for her boy. From the back of the platform, a burly man in a stained, coarse linen shirt, reddened jowls hanging low onto his collar, leapt forward and pinioned her arms behind her back.

Kicking and flailing, the child, panicked and sobbing, strained for his mother. *"No,"* he screamed. *"Momma, no. Momma, don't let them take me. Momma, help!"*

The mother lunged for her child with such force she nearly broke free.

At the auctioneer's nod, a third white man stepped forward, slapping the boy with the whole force of a well-muscled arm. The child staggered back, dazed.

"Don't you move a damn muscle, boy," the auctioneer bellowed.

Don't move, Tom willed the child. *Don't do it.*

But, whimpering, the boy lifted one arm for his mother.

And she lifted hers to him.

For a moment, their eyes locked. For a moment, their fingertips touched. And, for a moment, the auctioneer hesitated.

Instinctively, as if he might intervene even from this distance, Tom stepped toward what had to come next. And in the next moment, it did: a backhand to each of them with a viciousness that lifted the child's feet from the pine boards beneath him and knocked the mother to her back. The man who delivered the blows swung the boy's skinny frame down from the platform and onto a waiting buckboard.

The mother's *"No, no, nooo!"* as she twisted and fought swelled out over the harbor, and a flock of gulls lifted, crying, up from the seawall, as if joining in.

The auctioneer, turning back cheerfully to the crowd, raised his voice over the mother's screams. "Nothing but a little adjustment period needed—a day or two should do fine—and this little gal, she'll have forgotten this here ever happened, be ready to serve any need you got. Now what am I bid?"

Hands over her face, the mother collapsed to the platform, and Tom could feel her racking sobs as if they were surging inside him.

"No!" she cried, lifting an arm once more in the buckboard's direction. *"No!"*

Tom squeezed his eyes shut to keep back the tears welling up fast.

How many hundreds of times had he witnessed this same scene before?

A routine occurrence, that's what slave auctions were, as much a part of the fabric of this city as the unloading of silks at the wharves. Most auctioneers took a more subtle approach than this one—not for the sake of the people they sold but because bruises or cuts or any reprimand of defiance in public made buyers skittish. But every time, it was the cries of the mothers that pierced through Tom's will not to see, not to hear, not to feel—their cries that made the horror of every auction brand-new.

Behind him, he heard a crunch of footsteps on the crushed shell. Tom stiffened but did not turn his head toward the steps. "I got no reason for talking with you."

But the footsteps did not retreat.

With another rough swipe at his eyes, Tom sniffed the air, red swells of water lapping the low rise of the seawall, then shook his head, scowling. "Fish, what it smell like every morning at dayclean. And mudflats at candlelighting. But all through the day when you come around, Vesey, trouble."

"*Bom dia*, Tom," boomed a man's voice behind him. "*Goedemorgen.*"

"You can't never be like anyone else, can you?" Tom said, still without turning. He knew without looking the figure that went with the voice: dark hair gone the color of ash these past couple of years, eyes too full of powder and spark—like they'd fire at any wrong word. "Didn't reckon I'd have to tell you but once. But I'll say it again if I got to."

"*Buenos días.*"

"Stay the hell away from me, Vesey."

"And *bonjour*."

"You speaking a whole ocean of languages might impress a pack of ignorant field hands that you and those lunatic lieutenants of yours go out to recruit." Tom dropped his voice to a harsh whisper. "But not me."

Glancing quickly over both shoulders, Denmark Vesey cocked his head back as he spoke. "Nine thousand we're counting now, Tom. Nine thousand recruits. An army, that's what we got, and it's building day by day. Got some weapons already from the outlying farms. Some been disappearing real quiet from owners too old or too gone from town or too stupid to notice anything much, like their daddy's old musket gone missing or, say, a sack of paper and cartridge just disappeared. But we're needing more. Fast."

Frantic, Tom turned toward him. "Can't you understand what would happen if someone—*anyone*—even start in to hear you? My question's not whether you're smart. It's whether you lost your damn mind."

Vesey stepped closer, his mouth nearly to Tom's ear. "There's only one thing we need to make this the day that changes the whole course of this country. Wanna know what that is? The finest blacksmith in Charleston."

"I can't be bought with your flattery, Vesey. You know why I didn't stay at that splintered woodpile of a church to meet you and that Peter Poyas? Because I knew what you'd be wanting to say. Knew any man who signs on is a damn fool that can't count who in this city got all the"—Tom glanced behind him and lowered his voice—"guns. All the powder. All the cannons. All the balls. And us? Let's see, we got us some shackles and a whole lot of hoes."

Unfazed, Vesey nodded. "Which is how we chose the date: half the city sailed to Newport or Europe by summer to miss the yellow fever and heat. What we need . . ."

Tom kept his face rigidly fixed on the harbor. If passersby glanced toward the seawall, they did not need to see rage contorting a slave's features. "The word's spread already, Vesey, all this you been planning: You trying to enlist Haiti. You ghosting around Bulkley's Farm and the river plantations, getting hope stirred up to a frenzy. You"—this last he dropped to just the slip of a sound—"needing weapons made."

Vesey opened his mouth to speak, but Tom's fury was not finished. "You think for one single minute, just one, the word's not gonna find its way to somewhere it shouldn't? My God, Vesey! What do you see when you look around in this city, huh? Here's what I see: no way out except playing by the buckruh's rules. Lay low. Work hard. Don't let on the hunger you got to get loose. Everyone got to look for they own chance: every man for himself." He turned his back.

"Every woman, too, Tom? I'd value hearing your answer to that."

Tom's head snapped toward Vesey. His words, though, came slowly, measured out and examined. "Here's what I say: Leave my business to me. And go find yourself some free man to recruit."

Vesey sauntered a few steps down the seawall, as if to show his indifference, then strolled back to stand close beside Tom. "Free black's the last person I'd trust, that whole Brown Fellowship crowd licking the boots of whoever they figure they got to." He spit to one side. "Last person I'd trust next to a house slave. Both got too much to lose to the whites. Too much reason to grovel. And tell what they know."

"Exactly my point. *Someone* will tell what they know. And the graves will start getting dug."

"But a man, a craftsman like you, well now, he'd be different."

"You don't listen real good, do you?"

"No point getting worked into a vex, Tom. Reckon I know you better than your customers do—the ones call you docile and sweet. Been watching you, and here's what I know: you're a man believes in what we're planning."

"What I believe is no horde of field hands"—Tom's voice had risen to nearly a shout, and, glancing both ways, he dropped it again to a whisper—"with nothing but rice sickles and big sticks can raid a city arsenal in the Neck or a gun shop across from St. Michael's while the guards ask real polite just how they can help: *Here now, Mr. Vesey, sir, you take yourself another armful of muskets, how 'bout? Don't go forgetting them bayonets you'll be wanting to fit on the ends.*" Tom shook his head.

"What I believe in is facing the truth—and not getting strung up by the neck for a cause bound to fail."

On the wharf, bales of Sea Island cotton twined together were lofted up and out toward a waiting ship, stevedores on the wharf throwing their weight against the ropes, dark hand over hand, the cotton swinging now side to side like a clock's pendulum.

"We ain't got much time, Tom Russell. You know that. Not much time at all before the whole powder keg of this city explodes."

Shouts from the wharf. A crack, echoing over the water, of splitting wood. The arm of the structure holding the pulley crashed to the wharf, the cotton bale plummeting thirty feet from the sky. Screams. Stevedores and sailors and slaves all running.

A thundering smash.

Then silence.

A pair of dark legs jutting out from below the fallen bale.

Tom turned away, stomach roiling.

But Vesey looked on. "Bound to be pieces of Negro all over them planks. Take upwards of hours to clean good."

"You make a poor fist of man, Vesey. You know that?"

"On the contrary, I got a heart as full up of feeling as the next man, including a brute of a blacksmith like you."

Tom's right arm cocked back. Released.

A white man driving a phaeton up East Battery reined in his trotter. "You there! Boy!"

Tom checked his swing just before it made contact. "Mayor Hamilton."

Vesey waved to the mayor. *"Bon matin!"* he called cheerfully. "My friend here's just showing off the right jab he's practiced."

"Get on off there, hear? And don't *ever* let me catch your type back up on that seawall again!" Mayor Hamilton gave the reins a sharp snap and drove on.

Jaw clenched, Tom dropped himself off the wall to street level.

Vesey waved again to the phaeton as it rounded the corner and slowly, pointedly taking his time, swung down. "Thought cocky ole James Hamilton'd fix your flint good—slave like you fighting in public."

"That's exactly what I'm talking about, Vesey. Man like Hamilton's looking for any reason to get himself better known. The man gonna keep climbing—if he's got to use you or me or Governor Bennett or the whole city here to help him to more power, he'll do it and never look back. But are you careful around him? Do you so much as keep your voice down? No. You got to be the strong man that take chances, and to hell with whoever get hurt."

But Vesey, one hand snatching at the coarse cotton sleeve of Tom's arm, held a newspaper up with the other. "You read, Tom Russell, blacksmith?"

Tom shook him off. "Damn it, Vesey! Will you put that thing away?" Tom swatted at Vesey's arm.

Shrugging, Vesey slowly folded the paper, but rather than tuck it under his arm again, he let the rectangle of it rest in his hands, held in front of his waist.

Tom glanced both ways up and down East Bay. "If I *could* read, you think I'd be fool enough to be caught doing it on a public street? It's different for you—free man don't got to hide what he know."

Vesey shook his head here, his mock-jovial smile gone hard now. "Don't be deluding yourself that *free* for the black man in Charleston means actually free."

"So if it's risky for *you*, how long you think it'd take for somebody to haul me into the workhouse? Five minutes? Ten? Been sent to that place just once in my life. Took me four months, *four months* just to stand up straight again at my own forge."

"*Your* forge, Tom?"

Tom's shoulders squared, the muscles in his neck pulsing. "There's not a soul in this city old enough to open a gate can't point out my work."

"Mm-hmm, that's right. I agree. Don't nobody twirl iron like you, make it bend to some grand design you got in your head. But here you are, straining and sweating all the day long, making some of the best wrought iron this city ever saw—ever will see—then handing over your whole pay to that Sarah Russell, and her all fat and fine."

"She give me back part, if that's what you're getting at."

"Part. A tiny, pitiful part. For day after day of swinging that hammer over your fire, you sweating blood to line an old white woman's purse. And for what?"

"Same as you did."

"Buying your freedom?" Vesey scoffed, then spit to one side. "When I won the lottery—you should've seen the kind of riled that clerk got when he had to hand that stack of bills to a slave—the captain and missus sold me to myself 'cause I'd always been more trouble than help. Made sure of that. But you . . ." Vesey leaned in. "Kind of work you do? No chance in the world old Widow Russell'd be letting a gold mine like you get out of her grasp."

Tom did not answer.

"And meanwhile, any old time your owner or *somebody else's*"—he paused—"gets a mind to sell one of you off to pay a debt, there's not a thing in the world you can do. You go on trying to save every penny you can from the handful Mistress Russell tosses your way like scraps to a dog. You go on ordering Gullah Jack out of your shop like you been doing every time he come whispering in your ear that we won't be standing for this much longer."

Tom turned his back. Fixed his eyes on the harbor and the tide glinting red. "Plan you're spreading can't end no place but one."

"Still, you hadn't walked away yet—not even with all my provoking, now, have you? 'Cause part of you wants to know more. Has *got* to know more."

Vesey leaned closer. "What if you could play inside the buckruh's rules and still work it your own way? What if you and me called it just a business transaction? Treat you different from all the rest. What if we *paid* for the weapons you'd make? Starting with three hundred bayonet heads."

Vesey waited, then lowered his voice to add, "What if I knew you got somebody you'd be looking to protect? And that you been thinking somebody's bound to get hurt. Soon."

Snapping around, Tom glared at Vesey.

"Dangerous thing"—Vesey looked up at the blacksmith—"for a man like you to ignore somebody he loves, somebody who needs to get free of what's hunting her." He let his words fall like a hammer. "Every. Damn. Day."

Tom stiffened. But did not speak.

"And someday, Tom, someday real soon, I'm visioning you'll be joining us. Because you're too smart not to know just what the future might hold for you if you don't."

Vesey lifted the *Charleston Courier* and spread it before Tom's eyes. Just below and to the right of the masthead was an ad in bold print. "Since you like to pretend you can't read a damn word, though I just happen to know you learned letters from the white smithy who taught you iron, I'll read it for you, an ad that, one day, might be pitching the sale of somebody you'd maybe like to protect: AT PRIVATE SALE—A VALUABLE NEGRO. ONE PRIME, HEALTHY WENCH."

"*Enough*, Vesey."

"EXCELLENT HOUSE SERVANT, A MEAT AND PASTRY CHEF, GOOD TEETH, TO BE SOLD FOR NO FAULT BUT BREEDING."

"*Damn* it. *Enough!* For the last time, don't come round me asking again. *Stay the hell away.*"

Tom Russell broke into a run.

Chapter 4

In the news clip being played and replayed on the screen of her motel room's TV, a man was running away.

Cringing, Kate sat down on the bed with the box she'd hauled from her Jeep. In the video, graphic and unedited, the man ran across an empty lot, then collapsed, shot in the back by a police officer. Kate gripped the edges of the box as she counted the gun's reports: *One. Two. Three. Four.* The shots kept coming. The man facedown in the dirt was black. The police officer, white.

She turned up the volume, the commentator's voice blurting into the room: *And in the death last week of the unarmed black man stopped for a broken taillight six miles north of Charleston, South Carolina . . .*

Kate drew a sharp breath. She'd been so deep in her own grief and the upheaval of her own life she must've missed this.

A video captured on a bystander's cell phone has emerged and appears to show a story counter to the police officer's filed report . . .

Right here, north of Charleston.

Cranking the volume to its highest level, Kate lugged another half dozen boxes from her Jeep into the motel room and lined them up on the spare bed. The news anchor finished gleaning insights on the North

Charleston shooting from three analysts, then shifted topics. With a sigh, Kate shut off the TV.

The nonsmoking room with a "property view," which meant that it overlooked the parking lot, retained the scent of stale cigarettes and a cloyingly sweet floral air freshener meant to cover it. Green carpet circa the 1980s crawled leprous from door to bathroom sink, its stains forming a pattern of splotches and swirls.

But this was the only low-cost motel within walking distance of the historic district. So it would have to do.

Long enough, maybe, for the History Department to make its decision about her future. After which she might need to camp out on the street.

Closing the curtains, Kate dumped the contents of the next of her mother's boxes on the slick paisley of the spare double bed. She'd already been through closets and drawers and cabinets until her head hurt, already plowed through several boxes of valentines from Kate's kindergarten years, dog collars from three rescue mutts back, and ancient bank statements on which Sarah Grace's handwriting had totaled up tilting columns of numbers and scratched through them and totaled still more, as if trying to make the math bend more in her favor by reworking the same numbers.

None of the half dozen boxes so far had yielded anything but memorabilia and out-of-date bills, and Kate surveyed the remaining batch of cardboard with an overpowering urge to pitch all the rest and spare herself the pain of reliving the past.

Sarah Grace must have saved every last sketch Kate had ever drawn. Each charcoal and pastel had been created with a single goal, one Kate had approached doggedly as a child: to make her mother smile. This one of the horse rearing, the proportions of his body just right—Kate had labored over the point of his hocks and the musculature of his neck all afternoon. Or this one of the sunrise over the water. Maybe *this one* would do it.

"You'll be an artist someday, my Kate," Sarah Grace used to say.

And Kate would sit up straighter, beaming.

Sarah Grace would nod and display the sketch or watercolor or oil on the refrigerator or safety pin it to the curtains above the kitchen sink or prop it up as the sole centerpiece on their Formica breakfast table. "You make sure you do something good with your life, you hear? Something that puts more beauty and more kindness into the world. And be a person of courage, my Kate. With a tender heart but a lot tougher hide." Gently, almost fearfully—as if her daughter might disappear if Sarah Grace made the wrong move—she'd run a hand over Kate's braid. But she often turned away at this point. "That last part's important—the tough hide. I want you to hear me. Don't turn out like your momma, Katie. It's not safe."

Kate had to squeeze shut her eyes now at the memory. And the image of a Ford Taurus slamming into a tree.

Rising to pace the room and twist up her long hair into a ponytail, Kate plunged back into the boxes: what had to be done. No avoiding the sound of her mother's voice with every layer of paper.

Here was a stack of what must have been cards from wedding guests, their glossy white now yellowed and soiled. Kate flipped through a hum of names that sounded only vaguely familiar from her childhood, like the call of the bullfrogs late at night near their house on that leafy, lantern-lit street in Charleston: Manigaults and Middletons, Ravenels and Rhetts, Pinckneys and Petigrus and Poinsetts, but no Draytons that Kate noticed. Sarah Grace's own parents had passed away when she was young, and Kate couldn't recall her ever mentioning other relatives in the Low Country—or anywhere else. Or maybe she'd thrown out any Drayton cards when she and the dashing young Drayton she'd married had learned to despise the sound of each other's names.

Here was the hairbrush with the soft bristles—too soft to do any good in Kate's thick mane of hair—and the sterling handle. It had sat in a place of honor on Sarah Grace's chest of drawers, though Kate had never seen her mother use it. She ran her fingers over its molded silver fleur-de-lis: so unlike anything else her mother had owned.

"All that sterling we got for our wedding," Sarah Grace had confessed one night, her words soft and slurred, "I had to sell it, you know, Katie. Every last thing but this one. Just as well. Anything that expects a polish just for sitting there is a mite too high on itself."

In the next box, Kate sifted through reams of crayoned art she'd made for her mom and a paper-plate tambourine and a cardboard Thanksgiving turkey, its feathers traced from Kate's first-grade hand. Here was her parents' marriage certificate, dated June 9, 1990, just after Sarah Grace's graduation from the College of Charleston.

And there beneath a cotton ball snowman was Kate's birth certificate. Paper-clipped to it was an old postcard of a motel—nothing picturesque or charming about it that would suggest a reason for having saved it, just a one-story ramble of sagging doors and crooked clapboard in need of paint. Kate flipped it to its backside: the Wayside Inn in Wadesboro, North Carolina. It certainly wasn't the sort of place Heyward Drayton would have stayed—ever. And why attach it to Kate's birth certificate? Had she and her mother been there at some point together—possibly on their flight north from Charleston? Had it been some sort of happy memory of freedom that Sarah Grace had saved?

Kate googled the motel, but it had gone out of business. An article from the local paper announced Wayside's demise: its earlier days as a picturesque family accommodation for motoring holidays in the 1950s, followed by its steady decline and a more recent history of "suspicious activity, drug deals, abandoned children, and sordid assignations." Cringing, Kate wedged the postcard into her own motel room's mirror at eye level. Maybe something else would spark a connection. She'd come back to it later.

Farther down into the box were pages of something else . . . photocopies. Some from microfiche, some from books, the shadow of the binding showing at one side of the copy. Housing records, it looked like, and a government census from Charleston, circa 1820. Personal letters and lists of inventory—also from early nineteenth-century Charleston. A tattered brown copy of a small book, *The Trial Record of Denmark Vesey*.

And a 1991 booklet entitled *Places with a Past* from an exhibit during Charleston's Spoleto Festival—some of the booklet's pages dog-eared.

Sifting these items out from the crayoned art, Kate inspected each piece. She remembered these sorts of pages splayed over their kitchen table. And this tattered brown book, Sarah Grace hunched over it with a highlighter and a pen.

But, Momma, you finished college, Kate had protested once, swinging her braids to her back with a toss of her head. *You said you read all this already. For your senior thing.*

Sarah Grace had hardly glanced up. *Thesis. My senior thesis. I read this already all right. And they gave me a diploma. But I didn't finish. I didn't.*

Never an explanation for why the search was important. Never any signs that she might be closer to solving whatever mystery she must have seen there.

Kate flipped through the yellowed pages. Its bibliographic note explained that the book, published in 1970, was basically a reprinting— with the addition of a scholarly introduction—of a rare copy of "An Official Report of the Trials of Sundry Negroes, Charged with an Attempt to Raise an Insurrection in the State of South Carolina," discovered in 1862 in the garret of a Hilton Head Island home. Almost all the original copies had been destroyed, the note continued, because the court document was thought dangerous for slaves to find.

Scanning the pages, Kate paused at her mother's underlinings and highlights. On pages 81 and 82, she'd highlighted in bright green the name Tom Russell, a blacksmith. On page 140, the book listed the court's verdicts, and again Sarah Grace had highlighted and this time also circled Tom Russell's name.

"Right," Kate murmured, nodding to the book as if she were having a conversation with her mother's notes. "The weapon maker of the revolt. But why this revolt? And why did you especially focus on him?"

She squinted at the notes her mother had scrawled in the margin next to Tom's name in a list of men condemned to death:

But Tom Russell
SURVIVED

Kate shook her head. "Not according to the court records."

Sighing, she stacked each of her mother's photocopies and notes, together with the little brown book, and slipped them inside her own laptop case. She would come back to this later, too, once she'd dug through more boxes.

Toward one box's bottom, in a sealed envelope with a stamp but no address, Kate found a raveled blue ribbon strung through a small silver key—too small for a house or a car. And taped with yellowed cellophane to the dingy blue ribbon was a scrap of paper penned in her mother's handwriting:

Palmetto 8-

The paper was torn on its right end, so whatever had followed the eight was gone now, except a stray mark.

Kate flipped open her laptop and googled *Palmetto 8* along with *Charleston*. The search brought up a craft brewery, a condominium development, a bank, a hotel . . . she scanned the first couple of pages. Nothing that suggested a match for Sarah Grace's tiny key. An idea niggled at the back of her mind but then slipped away. She slipped the key and its scrap into her wallet.

At the bottom of the same box was a Polaroid similar to the second one Kate had in her jeans pocket, her mother in cutoffs, sitting on the pediment high above the ground. Only on the back of this photo was Sarah Grace's distinctive scrawl:

I'm glad for the happiness of your life now—or I should be. The truth will need to be known someday: that I have been a coward in every way. But for now, I beg you to hold close what only the three of us know—and I wish to God it weren't even three. For Kate's sake, and yours, I'm leaving Charleston.

> *God bless and keep you,*
> *SG*

And just beneath those initials, at the very bottom edge—as if Sarah Grace had added this last bit impulsively, almost afraid to include it in the same thought:

(*TR lives on.*)

Had this been intended for Kate's father and never mailed? The *I'm glad for the happiness of your life now* didn't fit, though. Not the word *happiness*, and not Sarah Grace's wishing it for him.

And what about the *TR*? Surely not Tom Russell again. *Lives on* wasn't quite the same thing as *SURVIVED*—was it? Maybe *TR* here referred to something entirely different. What possible sense could a reference to Sarah Grace's research as a history major make in a note to Heyward Drayton?

Shaking her head again as she set aside the Polaroid, Kate sifted through other loose photos. Here was an early one of her father. *Senior year*, Sarah Grace had scribbled in blue ink on the back. Heyward Drayton was striking as a young man, the face all contradiction: a cleft in his chin suggested sweetness, and over it rode a hard mouth. His hair waved in abundance, and that topped a broad, arrogant forehead, a span of sharp angles and pride. It was a study of what ought not to exist together in the same moment, much less in the same face.

His eyes were a color Kate had never been able to name. Maybe just the gray glint of a blade.

She did not have his eyes. Anyone could see that.

Kate fanned out three more photos, apparently taken no more than seconds apart. A young Heyward Drayton held a swaddled infant and bent his face to hers—stiffly, holding the bundle a little out from his body as if he feared the baby might break.

On the photograph's back in her mother's hand:
Heyward and Kate

In the second picture, he nuzzled the child. In the third, the baby was laughing. The young Heyward had lifted his eyes from the child, the camera recording an expression of startled rapture. A hard, polished man, it appeared, who'd been ambushed by joy, eyes wide with wonder, a glint of wet on one cheek catching the camera's flash.

Kate had never seen these before. She sat down heavily on the bed. When she could stand again, she dumped the whole of the next box onto the bedspread. Nothing in this one but strands of colored Christmas lights—Sarah Grace had never embraced the demure white lights of her New England neighbors. From the box's absolute bottom, though, tumbled a small blue velvet case.

Until that moment, Kate had forgotten it existed. And now her heart leapt. Not for the money it had to be worth, Kate would have told Botts—and been ferocious about it—but for what this little box represented.

The money, though, for a young woman suddenly now without any family and possibly soon without a job or any prospects . . . the money wouldn't be such an unwelcome thing.

She circled the room twice before touching the box.

Inside, of course, would be her mother's engagement and wedding rings, the diamond gleaming incongruously—only the lives it united having turned ugly. Kate remembered it vaguely from her childhood, not so much on her mother's finger as sitting on Sarah Grace's dresser in its blue velvet box. The diamond blinked enormous and clear in Kate's memory.

The one material thing of real value I own, Sarah Grace had said. *And I can't stand the sight of it.* After which she'd stuffed it in her sock drawer.

It was so like her to toss valuables into that sock drawer—or later, apparently, into a cardboard box with strands of colored Christmas lights.

Kate took a deep breath. Reached for the blue velvet. But as she opened it, two silver earrings tumbled onto the bedspread. She checked under the box's lining. No rings.

Probably sold at some point along with the sterling to keep a roof over their heads.

She fought back a wave of rage at her father, who'd never bothered to contribute financially to their lives.

Lifting the earrings to the motel room's dim lamp, Kate squinted at the dangling birds—herons, she realized, with their long slender necks and beaks, heads raised against the wind and lifting their wings, just ready to soar. The earrings glittered bright even beneath the sputtering motel bulb, as shiny as if they'd hardly been worn.

Slipping their wire hooks into her ears, she rose to view herself in the mirror, cracked in one corner and spotted at its edges but still giving back the flash of silver on either side of her face. Kate gave her head a quick shake, her mother's silver birds nearly coming to life—as sparkling and free as Sarah Grace had been broken and trapped.

Closing her eyes, Kate felt the contours of the earrings and tried to remember ever seeing her mother wear them—but couldn't. Sarah Grace must have put them away for good when she took off her rings, all painful reminders, no doubt, of the Low Country and the giver of the gifts, the man who had walked out of their lives.

Kate could still see him as he stood at the door of their Charleston house for the last time, the home she and her mother had also walked out of within days.

Kate had been huddled close to a low fire in the fireplace—so it must have been winter. Too little to reach the mantel, she'd asked her momma that evening to set a framed picture close to the edge where Kate could see it, and she'd plopped down and dug out a handful of crayons and begun drawing the little family inside the frame.

Mommy, Daddy, me, she'd murmured over and over again as she'd lined out three figures building sand castles at the beach.

Mommy, Daddy, me, she'd insisted to no one who was listening, her little voice steady but scared against the rising shouts from her parents' bedroom.

Her father's tall frame was rigid as he stalked away, the door slamming so hard behind him it sent the picture set too close to the edge crashing to the floor.

There in the midst of the shattered glass, her mother still in the bedroom and sobbing, Kate had looked at the door. And at the crackling fire. And at the three smiling picture-people there in her chubby hand.

But now she remembered something she'd forgotten: her father turning at the front window. His face, handsome and square, distorted now. And wet.

Daddy's so angry, Kate had thought at the time. *Daddy's so sad.*

It was the sadness that she'd forgotten. The way he'd lifted a hand to her and froze there a moment, looking at her. Then turned his back and strode away into the night, the screech of his tires shredding the quiet of their leafy, gas lantern–lit street.

What she hadn't forgotten was this: glass shards dropping from her lap to the ground as she rose, stepped to the fireplace, and let go of her drawing, its swooping flight over the smoke and then down, down into the flame, where the three smiling faces began to burn.

Chapter 5

1822

Sparks flew upward, arcing, raining down on the circle of stone.

Again the bellows blasted air in great gushes. Again the sparks.

Tom Russell looked up once from the forge but let his hands speak first. Eyes fixed on the anvil, he swung down the hammer to make the whole shop shudder again.

"*No,*" he said. "For the last time."

His chest, as black as the coal he bent over, swelled and rolled and glistened above a low flame, as if the inside of him glowed—as if the blacksmith himself stood ready for forging.

Denmark Vesey lifted a ball-peen hammer and used it to stir the coals. "Bayonets and spears'd come first," he said. "And remember, we're willing to pay for the weapons."

The words were not out of his mouth when a rattling at the side door that led into the alley and then a pounding made both of them jump.

The two men exchanged glances over the fire.

"*Damn it*, Vesey! If somebody's heard . . . !"

Tom stepped softly to the side door, one finger over his lips, and was easing the bolt sideways when the East Bay–facing front door of the shop flew open, slamming against the interior wall.

Three skirts swept into the shop, two of them billows of silk, one of them—the one lagging behind—hanging in coarse blue tow cloth.

Two voices chattered at the same time. Then stilled.

"I'm Miss Emily Pinckney," one of the two white women called, "as you are likely aware."

Lifting his hammer, Tom Russell kept his eyes down. "Yes, ma'am." He could have guessed she was a Pinckney; that much was true—although her haughtiness, her presuming that of course he kept careful track of the ruling white families and each of their individual names made his jaw clench and his fingers tighten around his hammer.

Emily Pinckney had her father's broad forehead, and her eyes, the color of ice over blue water, surveyed the blacksmith shop just as he had, with their family's stiff superiority. But something else flickered there as the girl scanned the walls: a startled kind of wonder, it seemed.

As if snapping herself from her own reverie, she gestured impatiently. "We've been trying for some time now to access your shop from the side door."

"No, ma'am. Made it so it don't open inward from the street. Need it dark back here in my forge to see."

"*Dark* to see?"

"Iron got to be just the right color for crafting. Need dark to see."

The second white girl swept toward the forge—closer, in fact, than any white woman ought really to come. "That's extraordinary. Imagine my being seventeen and never knowing that."

Tom did not say what he thought: that no white woman here needed to know such a thing.

He let himself look—but only once—at the figure in the blue skirt, the third. Her neck like a dancer's, long and slender and graceful, skin the light beige of Low Country sand. A head she kept high. Always kept high.

Dinah raised her eyes—just once—to meet his.

A jolt ran through his body. Tom fumbled his hammer.

Vesey's head cocked, as if he'd seen this. He looked hard at the implement Tom was now fishing out of the coals with tongs. "I best be getting on. Got plenty of carpentry work to finish on up 'fore we call this day done." Vesey put a hand to his hat but did not lift it to the ladies, and his smile had more mockery than friendliness to it. He paused at the threshold. "Time to take action, I'd say."

The blacksmith held his breath and glanced toward the white women's faces as Vesey sauntered out the front door of the shop.

The Pinckney girl's face had gone even stiffer, as if she were determined to ignore Vesey's self-assured exit. "My father asks me to inquire if you have his gates completed quite yet. The sheaf of rice. The family crest with a thread of damascened gold?"

"Be another day, maybe two." Tom hauled on the bellows to keep himself from adding this next: that he'd never forgotten an order in all the years he'd bent over the forge. "Deliver it myself by the end of the week."

"Well," she said, "that should suffice." She gathered her skirts as if she would go, but her companion who'd walked too close to the forge was waving her forward.

"Come see this!"

"Angelina, land's sakes, you'll catch yourself on fire leaning so close."

"Emily, *look* at the detail on this bird he's making. I've never seen anything like it. Not outside of the real living thing, anyway."

"You'll get ash all over that pretty lace. Your momma won't let you out of the house with me ever again."

"The heron's just lifting up, don't you see? But one leg—"

"Don't say *leg*, Angelina!" the Pinckney girl whispered. "It's vulgar."

"It's a bird. A magnificent bird. I refuse to say *limb* for a bird. But just look what Tom's done here. Dinah"—she motioned to the woman in blue—"you've got to see, too. But one leg looks like maybe it's mangled." She addressed the blacksmith. "Was that a mistake? Or did you mean it to be?"

As if it were an answer, Tom lifted the bird, its wingspan nearly three feet across.

"A heron just taking flight," the girl Angelina remarked. "And these stalks here would be rice. Ripe. Just readied for the blade." She paused there, as if something disturbed her, though she wasn't sure what.

Drawing the heron back through the coals and then to the anvil, Tom smashed down the hammer, metal fanning to feathers, then reached for the tongs and a tapered pick.

Back into the fire it went, the metal quivering. The flames of the forge curled down into coals, the iron wings glowing red at their tips as if the bird were flying through fire.

Tom raised his hammer in its next arc. But did not raise his eyes.

"I wish," the one called Angelina murmured, "the leg weren't hurt like that. Although I suppose the point is it's flying now. It's gotten free."

Dinah's eyes, wide and frightened, darted to Tom's, then away.

Angelina stared past them all into the fire. "That it's gotten free would be good."

Emily linked her arm through her friend's. "It's not proper, our coming in here more than to check on Father's order. He'd have my hide if he saw. We must leave now."

And they did, three skirts sweeping back toward the shop's door, the last, the blue one, pausing at the threshold.

"Your purse, Miss Emily!" the blue-skirted woman called out toward the street. "I believe you left it inside."

Dinah turned back, cheeks flushing. She shut the door nearly closed.

Tom was around the stone counter and across the shop's floor in an instant, one arm cinching her waist.

One eye on the street, she ran a finger from his temple down to the edge of his mouth. "Things got to change." Her voice was so low he could barely make out the sounds. "Got to cut loose all my tomorrows from what's already past."

"Vesey came back today."

She shook her head. "That can't end nowhere that'd get us two free. Don't you go join up. We got to keep alive, you and me. And we got to get out."

"Dinah!" Emily Pinckney's voice carried in from the street. "I have my purse here!"

Tom brushed two of his fingers, dark and calloused, to the silk of her neck. His words came choked. "For you I would risk the wide world."

But Dinah, one hand on her middle, slipped from his arms.

The door shut softly behind her.

Chapter 6

2015

The morning sun gaining strength, Kate strained to make out the tiny font on her laptop's screen and shifted the computer's position on the café table. Rubbing her forehead, beginning to ache now, she bent closer to the screen. As the next 1822 *Charleston Courier* masthead slid by, she paused. Squinted at the date, its numbers blurred. Too much ink here on some apprentice's part—and not enough sleep on hers.

She picked up her phone. Dialed the office of the chair of the History Department again and this time left a message: "Hi, Dr. Ammons. Kate Drayton here. I think I owe you an . . ." *Apology* was the word he deserved. But that might remind him of her train wreck of a lecture, and maybe that memory had faded already for him. "An explanation," she supplied instead. "I'm down here in Charleston doing research, just pulled in this morning, and already reading old *Courier*s from the weeks just before the revolt."

Kate let her left hand drop to the keyboard, as if he could see proof of her working. "And I'll be visiting the archives here soon, of course. Today, in fact. Probably. I expect it to be incredibly worthwhile—the research here in person, I mean." She swallowed. "About my deciding to come down so abruptly, I realize I'll need to have someone cover the grading for your Early American seminar for a couple of days. Or . . ."

Or maybe longer. Or maybe forever, if I've already dug my own grave.

"At any rate, Dr. Ammons, I wonder if you'd be good enough to call me back. Just so we can be sure we're on the same page."

On the same page? She cringed. Like she thought they were equals. Which graduate students and full professors were decidedly not.

"And so I can get your expert feedback on my latest research here." There, that sounded more like she knew her place. "Thank you so much for your valuable time." She gave her cell number and signed off.

But who was she kidding that he'd believe she'd bolted down here with no notice at all, just walked out midlecture, because of a burning, urgent, clock-ticking desire to begin archival research on the Denmark Vesey revolt?

Kate rubbed the heel of her hand across her forehead. She'd better have something new to tell him about her findings on the revolt by the time he called back. She'd better read fast.

Her fingers flew over the keys, calling up the Charleston County Public Library's South Carolina Room. She skimmed down its holdings. And the South Carolina Historical Society's archives, housed at the College of Charleston's Addlestone Library. Both definitely worth visiting soon.

Then again, maybe Dr. Ammons would never call back. Maybe her name had already been deleted from all departmental records. Her transcript dropped into a file labeled *Mistakes Made in Admittance.*

Maybe she was already fired from her teaching assistantship, her name scrubbed from the door of the office she shared with two other grad students who, even if they weren't actual friends, had brought her Dunkin' Donuts coffee and three Boston Kremes the day after she'd learned her mother had died. They'd stood there, mute but well meaning, looking as if they desperately wished they knew what to say. Kate, who knew better than anyone that there was nothing to say, had been grateful for the coffee and doughnuts but especially for their silence.

She reached now, shakily, for more coffee to calm her nerves. *Which is how bad things have gotten—coffee to calm my nerves.*

From where she sat, she could see a fountain, its spray a pearly pink under an early morning sun nearly smothered in storm clouds hanging low over the harbor. A runner was pounding past—the same runner, in fact, from the seawall, the Nike swoosh over his chest. Kate ignored the face but cocked her head at the form, the force of each foot hitting the pavement and launching, the sheer reach and grace of his stride.

She'd once been a runner—up until this past year, in fact, when running or anything else she'd done in ritual fashion didn't seem to make sense anymore. Not after her father had called last summer to summon her to DC to see him and she'd refused—because what right did he have to demand her presence like some sort of feudal serf before the king?—and he'd died the next week, just when she was thinking of relenting. He'd known he was sick, as it turned out, three months at the most to live, and maybe he'd wanted to say good-bye. Or tell her how she still wasn't measuring up one last time. She'd never know now.

And then three weeks ago, her mother—one slip of a tire, one slick spot on a curve on a road in their little town in the Berkshires out the Mass Pike from Boston. Sarah Grace's Ford Taurus had accordioned into a sugar maple. And, just like that, Kate's family was finished.

The simple cruelty, the senselessness of the whole year, the chance at some sliver of reconciliation stolen from her. The car wreck that could have happened to anyone but happened with Sarah Grace at the wheel: Sarah Grace, who was depressed, who needed her daughter to check weekly on her—and Kate mostly did, but sometimes, like that time, she could not make it back to Great Barrington for the weekend. Sarah Grace, who drank too much when she was alone. Who'd tried bravely for years to battle the darkness that crashed down on her without warning. Some days she was stronger than others. But that weekend when Kate could not come home was especially dark. The car might have slid on the ice toward the tree. Cars sometimes did that. Or—and here was what bore down on Kate as if the car had landed on top of her chest—Sarah Grace, at the end of her strength, might have been steering directly toward it.

~

Last summer, after word of her father's death—the phone call that came in even as she was searching online the Greyhound bus schedule to DC—Kate had given up going to Mass, her way of shaking her fist at the divine. If God were that capricious to keep her father alive all those years to torment her, then take him out just as he might have been ready to offer her some sort of peace or ask forgiveness, then Kate wanted no part.

She'd given up running at daybreak, too, or sleeping at predictable times. More shaking her fist at God or whatever pretended to order the chaos of the world—and clearly did a despicable job. She embraced strange hours, spent evenings, and sometimes more, with men she'd only just met, then refused to see them again.

Since her mother's death, she'd kept no real schedule at all. Returned no phone calls or e-mails. Graded stacks of research papers from Dr. Ammons's Early American seminar—anything to keep herself distracted—but had no idea what they'd said even moments after she'd read each of them. She took long walks by the Charles River alone and wondered what would have happened if she'd made it back to Great Barrington that weekend to check on her mom.

A breeze from the harbor wafted its way to her, and Kate lifted the weight of her hair. She took a long swig of coffee.

At the table to her left, two seagulls squawked over the remains of a chocolate croissant. To her right sat an elderly woman, thick silver hair rolled into a perfect chignon, her spine the straight of those raised to believe the world was waiting for them to order its chaos. But Kate was a believer in the first commandment of Boston street etiquette: never make eye contact with strangers.

Kate stretched and lifted her coffee, the scent of baked bread hanging here in the mist.

A waitress was approaching the table of the elderly woman, the server's greeting a running chatter: "Why if it isn't my favorite customer come awful early this morning."

Kate included them both in the sweep of her frown.

Behind her, from the shop across the alley from this café, came the clangs of metal on metal and metal on wood. Someone was hammering something, and each hit was echoing inside her head.

After unloading her boxes, she'd returned to the southern tip of the city where she'd stood with the boy, then walked north on East Battery, which turned into East Bay, historic mansions giving way to a march of rectangular houses and shops, all in pastels. Then came the phalanx of art galleries and restaurants where she sat now, beneath a brass sign that announced **PENINA MOISE: SERVING THE FINEST BAKED GOODS AND COFFEES**.

After the café came an alley, cobblestoned and shadowed.

And just past the alley, a wooden shingle hung from scrolled iron brackets over the sidewalk: **CYPRESS & FIRE**, it read.

It was an intriguing shop, antique brick with paned windows and upscale sculptures just visible through the wavy glass of its window display. From the narrow two-story shop, smoke curled out a crooked brick chimney, its mortar mostly crumbled away—as if it had stood leaning forward to watch the invasions and victory marches and funeral processions of two, maybe three hundred years.

Curling back into her chair now, Kate tried to ignore the elderly woman and the waitress who kept glancing Kate's way.

"Mm-hmm. From somewheres up north," the waitress attempted to whisper and smoothed a hand over a platinum helmet of hair.

"Dear Lord," said the elderly woman, newspaper lowering. "Incredible, really."

Startled, Kate turned to find the woman staring directly at her. And quite unashamed to be caught.

Kate sat like that, twisted around, for several seconds, returning the stare.

She opened her mouth to ask what, exactly, happened to be *incredible, really.*

But maybe it was nothing to do with her after all. Nothing but the out-loud musings of an old but still beautiful woman staring off into the distance and simply distracted by Kate's sitting there in her line of sight to the palmettos and bay beyond.

Turning back, Kate knocked bagel crumbs from the scarf that fell in a loop from her neck and brushed still more from her faded jeans. Sitting up straight, she returned, pointedly, to squinting at the archived *Charleston Courier* on her screen.

"And, Miz Rose, were you wanting cream with your coffee this morning?"

The elderly woman surveyed the waitress from under half-lowered lids.

"No coffee worth drinking requires cream."

"Well, now, if I didn't up and forget." The waitress turned to Kate with her pot. "You getting good and ready for a warm-up yet?" She stepped closer and whispered, "More cream?"

Kate shook her head. "I'm all set." Rifling through her backpack, she pulled out the booklet from the 1991 Spoleto exhibit *Places with a Past*, something Sarah Grace might have saved because she saved everything— or might have kept because it had added to some sort of case she was trying to build. On one of the dog-eared pages, she'd circled a picture of a newly created sculpture in black marble, four children gazing innocently out, two of them with their chins resting on one hand, and two of them with their heads resting on crossed arms—the effect very much like Raphael's cherubs replicated on valentines and mugs.

The sculpture of the four children seemed somehow related to the Vesey revolt, though Kate would have to read this page more carefully later—when she wasn't being scrutinized from the side. And a long string of numbers scribbled at the bottom caught her eye, too, with one too many digits for a Social Security number—so a phone number, perhaps?—beneath a name that began with *Ch* but was hard to read: *Chris, maybe, or . . . ?*

Was this someone related to the exhibit somehow or possibly someone who studied the Vesey revolt, or both? Or maybe it was just the phone number of a friend, and Sarah Grace had simply jotted it there.

To her right, the elderly woman's silver chignon was bobbing, as if she were already agreeing with what she was about to say. "I swan. Incredible. That's what it is."

Poor muddled woman.

Muzzied, that's what Sarah Grace would have called her. *Bless her sweet, muzzied heart.*

The older lady was rising now and sweeping toward the café's door. She was precisely what Kate's mother had described these Charleston types as: sleek and perfectly pressed—and with one eyebrow that seemed perpetually raised.

From behind her, an arm reached for the door. The runner guy from the seawall. Nike T-shirt wet through with sweat. He held the door farther open.

The elderly lady looked the young man up and down, a sizing-up stare that would've been rude in a person less far along in years. Or wearing less pink.

As she swept forward, he gave a small bow.

At that, she paused with a nod, deliberate and regal, to acknowledge his service.

"I've not seen a man bow in years—not since my debutante ball in '51, when the world looked to be set right-side up once again." She nodded, agreeing with herself. "Rubber, and lots of it, and gabardine and gasoline and handsome young men who weren't being shipped off from my very harbor to war."

War. Pronounced *wah.* The old lady spoke like Kate's mother had: soft syllables, anchored deep into iron. Only this was a Low Country woman born into money. Generations of money.

Kate could hear her mother's voice—with that accent, too. Sarah Grace reeling off old Charleston family names as part of her bedtime stories: Rutledge. Rhett. Huger. Manigault. Middleton . . .

Understand, Katie, her mother had said, brushing Kate's curls from her eyes and onto the pillow. *These sorts only mate within their own pedigreed club. Like royalty. Or registered dogs.*

But what about Drayton, Mommy? You told me the Draytons were part of that club. Can you tell me a story about that? Kate had pulled the plastic tiara from her bedside table, clutched it tight in both hands on top of her chest, and snuggled deeper into the blankets.

Once upon a time, Sarah Grace had whispered, *a handsome but very proud prince fell in love with a chimney sweep girl.*

Little Kate had clapped her hands. *That's good, Mommy! Did she love him, too?*

Sarah Grace's voice had come back slow through the dark. *At first, maybe she fell in love with the idea of being a princess. He brought her gifts. He was dashing.*

What kind of gifts?

Oh, princess gifts, pretty white dresses and fountains and flowers.

Chocolate, too?

Oceans and oceans of chocolate, right outside her door.

So what happened? Did she learn to love him at last? Did they live happily ever after?

She did learn to love him, yes. Sarah Grace ran a hand through Kate's curls. *Happily ever after, though . . . no, they did not.*

But, Mommy . . .

Her mother had kissed Kate on the forehead—too hard—and hauled the bedroom door all the way shut, even though it swelled and jammed in its frame in summer.

Kate would lie on the fold-out couch that was her bed, springs poking her back, and wonder about Charleston. About why her mother had fled that place but in her mind seemed never to have gotten away.

Her mother still checked out books from the library about Low Country Carolina history—not exactly in abundance where they lived in Great Barrington, Massachusetts—and snagged them from yard sales when she made the rare find. She looked up from these books, her face a mask, if Kate ventured a question about what Sarah Grace was reading and why, since they lived in the North now—and the North had some history, too.

Kate had learned early not to press too hard for answers. Sarah Grace rarely got angry at her daughter when Kate wanted to know about Charleston or about her father or about their life before they'd left. Instead, she would take Kate in her arms, hold her close, and stroke her long hair.

I'm so sorry, she'd murmur. *I'm no excuse for a momma. I'm sorry.*

And then, oblivious to anything Kate might say after that, Sarah Grace would send her to bed.

The bump and scrape of the stool on the kitchen's linoleum floor meant she was dragging the stool to reach where she kept the bottles—*the strongest stuff* was all Kate knew to call it back then—that she sometimes, on a good day, did not want to reach . . . but could not bring herself to throw out.

On these nights that Kate had asked too many questions, she would clutch her covers up to her nose and pray for a miracle—that maybe the stool would somehow have shrunk, would not help her mother reach that top shelf. Or that the bottles all would have been drained since the last time. That there'd be nothing left to sweep her mother someplace far away from where she would come back when she woke up sadder than ever.

So Kate had learned early not to ask questions about her father or Low Country history or present-day Charleston or whether, perhaps, they had aunts or uncles or cousins left there. But she learned early, too, that there were questions that cried out to be asked.

~

But now the silver head dipped. "You, young man, possess gracious manners."

"My pleasure, ma'am."

"Surprisingly so," the lady added. And swept through the door to the café's interior.

The runner guy stood there a moment, holding the door open with one hand and touching a stubbled jaw with the other, his neck dripping with sweat. He shot a glance sideways at Kate—and she could see that he also recognized her. One eye crinkled in a flicker of a smile. But Kate looked away.

Which might be rude here in the South, but better to trust no men at all than to trust the wrong ones. And weren't they all the wrong ones in some way or another?

Which was when Kate's phone rang.

As soon as she saw the caller ID, she spoke before she'd gotten the cell fully up to her mouth: "Dr. Ammons, this place is a gold mine for research. I'm linked in right now, as a matter of fact, with the online archives of the South Carolina Historical Society." Maybe if she spoke fast enough, he would not have time to give her bad news. "And I'll drop by there in person later today."

"Ms. Drayton. We appear to have a problem." Ammons was speaking—as he did when the issue at hand was a delicate one— through teeth set lightly together: Katharine Hepburn in a bow tie.

In the pause that followed, Ammons allowing her time for the storm clouds of panic to gather, Kate could picture him at his mahogany desk, dark hand stroking a brindled beard. Decades ago when he'd been hired, he'd been the only African American in the History Department. A handful of others had joined him over the years. But he remained its token, and mostly closeted, Southerner, a product of Alabama who'd tutored himself years ago out of all trace of a Birmingham accent.

"If it helps to know that I'm working hard here, I'm up to late April of 1822 now in the library's old *Courier*s online, and no sign city leaders had any inkling yet of a revolt being planned—at least not before May." With her free hand, she scrolled through the next issue. "There's one participant in the revolt I'd like to pursue particularly: Tom Russell."

"Blacksmith," Ammons offered. "Weapon maker."

"Exactly. I'm surprised you know about him. He's pretty obscure."

A pause.

"A historian's task, Ms. Drayton, is to seek the obscure."

She cringed.

"However, I will add that my knowledge of him ends there. Do enlighten me further."

"Tom Russell's name appears nowhere so far, by the way, for any reason."

"No," he said.

Kate set down her coffee. "No . . . what?"

"It wouldn't, of course. The blacksmith's name. It wouldn't appear." Ammons's voice deepened and slowed: a grandfather's voice for a not-very-bright toddler. "A black artisan slave, no matter how accomplished at his trade, would hardly be advertising his shop, now would he?"

In the background Kate could hear the crunch of footsteps on snow, the blare of a car horn, the distant rumble of the train underground. Which meant Julian Ammons was where he went every morning before office hours: to the Au Bon Pain in Harvard Square to sit with his coffee outside—especially on the days he expected would be difficult.

Best not to think about that in relation to this phone call.

Kate sank lower still in her seat. "I don't suppose so. But, Dr. Ammons, I think you'll be pleased with the progress I've made in plowing through pages."

Plowing. Bad word choice—too much like she viewed research as a chore. As opposed to a privilege. A delight. Her reason for living. You didn't say *plowing* to the head of the department. "That is, I'm getting to uncover all sorts of intriguing new angles on the revolt."

Sweat trickled between Kate's shoulder blades, and she uncoiled the scarf from her neck, letting it drop to the table. Stomach clenching, she dug frantically in her jeans pocket for loose bills. Whatever this conversation was going to be, since it could herald the end of her world as she knew it, she didn't want to have this particular chat in public.

Leaving a pile of crumpled cash she didn't bother to count on her table, she stuffed her laptop into her backpack and turned toward the street. Waiting to cross East Bay, a crowd had gathered, heads bowed in a row over phones clutched in cupped hands like communicants at the altar rail.

"Dr. Ammons, thank you so much for the opportunity to lecture to your seminar."

She paused for him to say something—perhaps that everybody gets nervous and it hadn't been the unqualified disaster she'd thought.

But only silence came from his end of the line.

"I'm not sure," she went on, "that it went as well as we'd both hoped."

"Ms. Drayton, I really must ask: Were you quite sober?"

Kate covered her eyes with one hand. "So it was the complete, surround-sound failure that I think it was?"

"Cataclysmic, I'm afraid."

"So I really did . . . just walk out."

"With the parting line 'It's time, past time, I got to the truth.' I'd wager it's a closing line my students won't hear again during their years at Harvard."

Closing her eyes, Kate let this sink in a moment.

"Ms. Drayton, I must be honest with you. Would it be fair to say you have missed appointments with senior faculty members who might once have been candidates for your dissertation committee?"

Kate hesitated. "That . . . might be fair."

"And that there have been times you failed even to make an appearance to lead undergraduate sections? Or to grade papers on time? Or include any kind of meaningful comments on those papers that a first-year student might use to improve?"

Kate slumped against the nearest brick wall. At other schools she might have bought silence with the grades she'd tossed out: far higher than the papers deserved. But Harvard first-years wanted notes in the margin to explain any minus to the right of an A. She'd been ratted out.

The clatter and bang of something falling inside the shop next door made everyone outside the café jump. Kate had to cover one ear to hear Ammons's voice.

"What on earth was that, Ms. Drayton?"

"Given the direction of this conversation, it could be the sound of my future falling down around my ears." *And my present,* Kate had to bite her lip to keep from adding.

She wanted to beg. She wanted to tell Dr. Ammons that modest as her grad assistant stipend was, it paid her bills for her closet of a studio apartment and groceries heavy on ramen noodles. And while she might not have genuine friends in Cambridge, she had colleagues, at least. People who knew her name. Who noticed if she did not show up. Who assumed she was smart—perhaps not smarter than they were but smart enough to have worked her way there.

As opposed to this—her hitting this wall. The mangled mess she'd made of her life. She managed just enough of a voice to choke out, "Is there a final chance?"

"I've no intention of being utterly heartless. Yours has been a most difficult year." He sighed. "I am trying to be on your side here. I just need to know that *you* are on your side."

"You mean . . . wait. I'm not already kicked to the curb?"

He ignored the question. "The truth is, Ms. Drayton, I shall remember your disastrous closing long after I have forgotten yet another demonstration of self-satisfied brilliance."

Her back turned to the café, Kate jumped when something brushed her shoulder.

And there was the elderly woman, who'd just re-emerged from inside the café. She stood with one hand stretched out—Kate's scarf coiled over a veined, delicate hand. "I think," she drawled, "this might be yours."

"Oh." Kate let the phone drop a few inches. "I hadn't noticed I'd left it."

"I am Mrs. Lila Rose Manigault Pinckney."

Pinckney. One of the Pinckneys from the jumble of wedding-gift tags in the boxes? Maybe. Although there might be scores of people here with that name.

Kate shook the woman's hand quickly. "Kate Drayton."

"I thought so. Yes. Dear Lord in heaven."

"Excuse me? Wait. How—"

"But how rude of me, sugar. Here you are on the phone." The woman was already sweeping back toward her table. "I do hope that you cotton to Charleston." The city's name came rolling soft off her tongue, the *r* opened out to the breeze of an *h*: *Chahlston.*

"Cotton to?" Kate murmured. From the hand she'd dropped to her side came a voice through the phone: *"Ms. Drayton."*

Kate jerked the phone to her ear.

A door was groaning open in the background. Heels echoed on a wood floor. Which must have meant Dr. Ammons had reached his office.

And now, like every time she'd seen Ammons enter his office, he would be skirting its perimeter, one finger running absently over the spines of leather-bound books.

"Sorry. I'm sorry. Which is all I seem to be saying to you this morning."

"Did someone there just say the name Pinckney?"

"What? Oh. Yes. A fairly strange interaction."

"An old name there, Pinckney. At any rate, Ms. Drayton, there was a time when I might have soft-pedaled the truth for a young woman struggling to make her way in the academy. Now, thanks to the triumphs of feminism, I am free to tell a student, female or male, when that student's work merits abject despair."

"Despair?" She echoed the word in a squeak.

Ammons's tone softened. "I assume for the near future, you'll be staying in Charleston."

"For a few days, yes. But the semester's not over yet. There's the discussion group I'm the TA for. I couldn't sabotage my standing in the department."

"Allow me, then, to put your concerns to rest. So far as this department is concerned, you are in a very deep hole."

Kate leaned against the brick wall of the shop where the hammering had finally ceased. "That was putting my concerns to rest?"

"Sugarcoating the truth is no favor to you. The good news of your new status, academic probation, is that you can hardly hurt yourself more at this point by taking some time away. So stay in Charleston. Find some of the answers you need."

"So my standing in the department is . . ."

"Dire, Ms. Drayton. And probably, though not assuredly, irredeemable. But do stay in touch. Should you happen to unearth something utterly new regarding the Vesey revolt and should you write about it in scintillating language, thoroughly documented, and should that research be publishable in one of our discipline's leading journals . . ."

Kate stepped away from the wall but found her knees had gone rubbery, her head fuzzy. She had to put out a hand to steady herself.

She knew what *stay in Charleston* meant from her academic adviser: the door of her future in academics—all she knew how to do, all she'd made plans for, the only place she belonged—swinging shut.

The alleyway here that crossed East Bay Street shot a block toward the harbor and turned into a pier. Out over the water, the clouds had gained bulk. They muscled against a weak morning sun.

All up and down East Bay, palmettos stood straight and unbending, only their fronds clattering in the growing breeze. Yet the ground lurched underfoot, Kate was sure. Like she'd stopped somehow on a roundhouse, her whole life switching track and direction—and she was only on board to watch.

Kate bit her lip hard and was glad he could not see the tears welling up in her eyes. "I understand."

"I am conducting research of my own in June not far from you, my needing to respond to some revisionist scholarly work—polysyllabic claptrap, but requiring a coherent response—on the siege at Fort Wagner, or where it once stood, on Morris Island, close to Charleston. I may be able to check in with you while I'm in the environs."

She faced the harbor—into the wind. Rain began falling now in silvered streaks through the palmettos and glossed the cobblestones of the alley. Kate backed under the eaves of the shop Cypress & Fire. In the rain, the firm lines of the world—the brick of the buildings, the trunks of the palms—had all come unmoored and floated now in the mist that rose from the street and over the harbor.

"And, Ms. Drayton, at the risk of crossing professional boundaries, I feel I should add one more thing."

She braced herself for one final blow.

"I am rooting for you. Whatever you may find there."

She pressed her mouth into a line until she could trust herself to speak. "Thank you."

From her jeans pocket, Kate tugged out the sketch she'd scribbled there on the seawall: the mansions, the buggy, the cannons, the ship. And the ropes that she'd drawn—the tendrils of moss hanging like so many nooses. All blurring now in the rain whipping under the eaves where she huddled.

"You know," she said into her phone, "I'd not realized what it would be like coming back. It's like somebody left a camera shutter open for two hundred years, like old sepia shots bleeding into the new."

"That," said Julian Ammons, "would be Charleston."

Chapter 7

1822

Another gust shook the carriage, the horses shifting uneasily in their harness traces under the deluge, then stomping, brass rings jangling. Emily Pinckney pulled her skirts clear of the carriage's wheel and its elliptical springs and ducked under the roof formed by the landau's folding top. But mud from the horses' rear hooves splattered the front of her dress, white silk suddenly speckled in brown.

The gentleman who reached to assist her bowed low. "My humblest apologies. I fear even with both ends of the landau's hoods raised, ladies, you'll not arrive entirely dry."

Emily produced her most winsome smile. "I don't care a fig about the mud, really."

Handing her in, he bowed again. "We'll follow behind and look for you there."

Emily lifted a gloved hand as he mounted his horse and cantered away through the rain.

"You don't care a fig," groused Angelina, as she shifted in the seat across from her, "because Dinah's the one who just washed it and has the hands to show for the lye and the lemon juice and the boiling water, then sewed every button back on. And now will wash it again."

"Angelina, can you not just enjoy the evening?"

"You know, you and my mother both call me Nina only when you're feeling pleased with my behavior. Which means I hear 'Angelina' from both of you most of the time."

Emily ignored this. "Dinner at Governor Bennett's. A house full of Charleston's first families. And us just out in society. How *can* you be so gloomy?"

Angelina tugged absently at her dress. "Gloomy is not what I am."

"What, then? Generally taciturn and irritable?" Emily rearranged her skirts carefully. "Perhaps—and I should have been more sensitive to your feelings as my oldest friend—perhaps you're not happy with John Aiken's attentions to me." She tried to meet her friend's eyes. "If there is any understanding between you—"

Angelina waved this away. "It's not that. Not at all." The landau's wheels rattled over the crushed shell and slogged through long puddles. "Emily, how much did you hear when we were in the alley the other day—trying to get in the side door of the blacksmith shop on East Bay?"

"Oh. That." Emily turned her face toward the open window, storm clouds like tattered black and gray quilts, thunder rolling across the bay at the same pitch as the carriage wheels. "I wondered when we'd get around to discussing that. I was beginning to guess you'd pretend you'd heard nothing. That I'd imagined the whole thing."

Angelina leaned so far forward she was hardly still seated at all. "What did you hear?" She reached for Emily's hand.

Emily huffed and jerked away. "What I heard, I'd like to forget. Until this moment, in fact, I'd convinced myself I'd misheard the words."

Angelina pressed her lips into a line. "Tell me just one word, then."

Emily stared out at the water, the harbor in seizures now as the wind battered down.

"I can't." She drew a long breath. "I won't say it aloud."

They rode for a time with only the rhythm of the wheels over the street's sand smoothing the jagged-edged silence.

Emily kept her eyes on the street through the crack in the landau's two hoods. "There's Penina Moise. Poor woman."

Nina, sulking, only grunted from across the carriage.

"She must be headed to their temple on Hasell—and here in this rain, of all things. All those brothers and sisters to care for, and her father dying when she was twelve, and a sick mother, all the household duties falling to her. I asked her once—"

"I *know*," Nina said, rousing, "that you're changing the subject."

"I'll have you know that Penina Moise is a friend. Even if she is a Jewess." Emily pointed with a gloved hand out the window, the set of her jaw announcing she would persist in the distraction of chatter. "And, look, there is that ridiculous Quaker couple, the last in Charleston, so far as I know. Although someone seems to keep their meetinghouse standing, even run-down as it is. Heavens, could that bonnet be becoming on any woman? I admit I'm surprised any Quakers would stay on here, what with the stridency of their views."

Emily stopped there. "I'm sorry. Your sister's move last year to Philadelphia . . . people say she's become one of them. I wasn't thinking."

"They are against slavery. I'm not sure, however, that I'd call them strident."

Emily shrugged this away. "At any rate, that couple's horse appears lame. Which would explain, I suppose, the reason they are knocking at the door of the blacksmith."

At this last word, the girls exchanged glances, and Emily pressed her lips hard together.

Nina leaned forward. "What was it you heard in the blacksmith's shop?"

But Emily, jaw set, only turned her face back toward the street.

∾

Emily stationed herself near the serving tables draped in white linen and heaped with platters of creamed oysters, bacon, shrimp, cakes, and steamed mullet, along with pedestaled compotes holding pistachios and dried apricots and fresh pineapple and baked apples, the sterling reflecting the candles' glow. A tall, lanky servant in white gloves dished almond ice next to a stack of blue Canton porcelain with scenes of pagodas and arched bridges.

Angelina, still shaking water from the hem of her skirts, followed her there. "Julius," she whispered.

Emily tried turning her back, pretending she didn't hear.

But Nina would not be ignored. "It's his name, you know."

Emily scanned the ballroom as couples began to form their squares for the next quadrille. "Who on earth do you mean?"

"The servant serving the ices. His name is Julius. One of the Bennetts' footmen."

"All right, Nina. You won't leave me be until I ask. So I'll ask: What is it? Why on earth should I care what the name of the Bennetts' footman should happen to be?"

"Naming a slave after a Roman ruler." She blinked. "You see it, too, don't you? The irony of it?"

Emily set her plate down so hard its sterling spoon jumped. "No, Angelina. I don't. No one ever sees what you see, not even me. My lands, you can be so peculiar."

Now a strong waft of bourbon and mint passed by: the juleps on a platter balanced high on a dark hand, the slave tiptoeing his way through a landscape of bright gowns.

Walking their way, James Hamilton swirled the claret that half filled his glass.

"The mayor," Nina whispered, "is talking with your father. And Governor Bennett."

Emily put a finger to her lips.

"Nothing," Hamilton was saying, "but grave concern for you, Governor, and your interests. It's only that there is reason to think the servants in your very household—and possibly yours, too, Jackson, have been exposed to all sorts of abolitionist outrage."

The servants spooning the oysters and ices did not move. No more of a flinch than the parian busts that sat between windows—one each of Presidents Jefferson and Washington and one of King Charles II of England.

"You and I, Governor, each have our own reasons for knowing the man to be a menace. Quite possibly a dangerous one."

Bennett scoffed. "Vesey is a nuisance, I'll grant you. But not dangerous. As for my own household, Rolla and Ned there"—he nodded toward the footman behind the steamed mullet—"would no more see me harmed than they would their own flesh and blood."

The footman Ned, towering over the petticoat clouds and dark coats floating by, might not have heard. He stared straight ahead, the red of the claret and the gold of the champagne and the pale green of the juleps making rainbows in crystal that sparkled and shifted their arcs.

"Miss Pinckney," came a man's voice.

Turning in time to greet John Aiken, dry and impeccably groomed now after standing in the downpour to help her into the carriage, Emily curtsied. "Why, Mr. Aiken. How gallant of you, your behavior this evening. Miss Grimké and I . . ." A flicker of disapproval passed over his face as she said her friend's name. "We were most grateful."

Without looking back, she let herself be washed into the swirl of skirts, the brass sconces along the walls blurring into a single ribbon of gold.

~

The last dance of the night, nearly dawn now, brought the girls into the same quadrille diagonally from one another.

"I'm sorry," Emily whispered as they glided past one another the first time. "I'll tell you," she added at the next pass, "what I heard in the shop."

Nina's face turned from her partner.

"I heard," Emily said as she spun back, "only one word clearly."

But the violins plunged to a halt. The dance had ended. Couples bowed to one another, then joined the other guests moving as a river toward the cascade of staircase to wait for carriages below.

Once inside the landau they said nothing at first, both of their faces turned toward the harbor. The rain had stopped, but the wind still gusted hard. Nina leaned out over the edge of the open landau, let the wind whip at her hair, which was coming loose from its pins. At the opposite side of the carriage, Emily closed her eyes against the gale.

"Weapons," she said at last, her voice barely rising above the force of the wind. "The word I heard them say in the shop was *weapons*."

The wheels splashed forward, the horses' iron shoes crunching wet sand.

Harness rings jangled.

At last, Angelina eased back in her seat, long strands of hair in her face, down her neck: "Em, look at me. This is what happened: we both misheard. We had to have. If we told this, what we misheard, to your father or mine—to anyone—it would mean disaster. To lots of innocent people. Not just now but for years. Decades, even. Emily. Please. Look at me. We will repeat this—what we misunderstood—to no one. Ever. *Promise me that*."

Chapter 8

2015

Kate turned from the harbor, the wind whipping her hair into her face so she could hardly see. A block down East Bay, she could make out the form of the elderly woman walking away with the straightest of spines, not even hunching into the gale. *Mrs. Lila Rose Manigault Pinckney*— was that what she'd said? What a name. The smell of magnolia practically wafted from it.

Miz Rose, the waitress had called her.

She had somehow spotted Kate as a Drayton—her father's daughter. Which was a jolt. All Kate's life, people had commented on her favoring her mother—even convenience store clerks in the Berkshires who never exchanged pleasantries with the customers would grin at Sarah Grace and ask whether she or her sister—they generally winked here—was the oldest. But Kate's being picked out as her father's daughter by a complete stranger had never happened before.

Kate pressed herself closer to the outer walls of the shop Cypress & Fire. Its old paned windows, thick and dimpled, reflected the sky, a mottled gray and black now. Past the shop's window display of freestanding sculptures, modern and gleaming, sat furniture: chess tables and nightstands, headboards and mirrors, all of them embellished in ceramic with copper inlays and bright, swirling colors. Clearly, this gallery was one she could not afford.

Huddled under the eaves, Kate dialed the office for Botts's firm again, and this time was sent by a receptionist—"I'm afraid he's out of the office today"—to his personal voice mail. Something cold and brittle in the slow-moving sounds of his Low Country accent, like an echo rebounding off ice: "You have reached Percival Botts, founding partner of Rutledge, Wragg, Roper & Botts, Attorneys at Law. I will return your call"—a pause—"as time allows."

"Just following up," Kate said. "To set a specific time for when we'd meet here in Charleston." Kate left her cell number—again.

As she hung up, something about the number she'd just called made her wonder . . . she tapped "Recent Calls" to scan the digits again, the Charleston prefix: 843.

Swinging her backpack around to her front, she dug for the *Places with a Past* brochure with the string of numbers scrawled at the bottom of the Vesey memorial page—it began, in fact, with 843. A phone number, then. But the chances of the number still belonging to the same person—even if it was still a landline, as it must have been in 1991—had to be minuscule.

Still, holding her breath, Kate dialed.

One ring. Then two.

Kate turned to peer into the gallery behind her as she waited through another ring. And another.

Deep at the shop's back, something glowed inside a cavelike structure. And a dark figure bent near the glow, examined what looked like a tray full of tiles, and closed the door on the fire.

So the shop was part gallery—elite, handcrafted art—at its front and part working kiln at its back. And wood shop, too, it seemed. Very appealing, really, letting the high-dollar clients see just how their art and their furnishings were being made.

The dark figure turned and bent his substantial frame over a long table.

The phone had rung now probably twelve times or more with no answer. Kate hung up. Another dead end. Still, though, there'd been no out-of-service message, no fourteen-year-old letting her know it was a wrong number. So maybe worth calling again.

And meanwhile, it was time she ducked in out of the wind.

Bracing herself against the next gust, Kate slipped through the front door of the gallery, the wind slamming the wooden door behind her.

Suddenly, from behind the stone counter, something flew at her, cuffs flapping just past his little hands.

The boy from the seawall threw himself at Kate for a hug.

Laughing, Kate pulled him off after a moment. "Didn't you ever make it to school?"

"Made it. But my stomach went to pinching again like it does, which the nurse said was maybe me feeling sad as much as me being regular sick but she was sending me home just in case of the sick."

"I'm sorry about the sick. And the sad. But it's really good to see you again, little guy."

"Recollect now: that's not what you'd be wanting to call me." He grinned, then cocked his head. "And you look like hell."

Kate put a hand to her hair—the windblown mess of it. "Yeah, well." She flattened her palm. "A quarter a cuss."

His brow crinkled, and he patted both pockets. "Ain't got nothing on me today."

"You can owe me, then. But I do collect. What's this great place you found here?"

"Look." He grabbed her hand and pulled her to the opening at one end of the stacked-stone counter. "Dirt floor!" he announced, pointing exultantly to the ground and kicking off his own shoes, toes wriggling now in dirt mixed with coarse sand and crushed shell. "Hardwood out there in the gallery. Dirt floor back here in the shop."

Straightening, the craftsman at the back stepped forward. "Can I help you?"

"I was admiring your gallery," Kate said. "And didn't expect to be finding my very first friend in this city hanging out here."

The boy nodded importantly. "That'd be me."

The craftsman held out a hand covered in sawdust and clay—which he quickly withdrew, wiping both hands in quick swipes on his khaki shorts. On his left hand, the gold of a wedding band flashed. And there was something about the man's manner, too, that suggested clear lines—polite, but just distant enough to announce there were boundaries. Like a fence whose sturdiness let you know it was safe to lean on. Kate felt herself relax.

The craftsman nodded toward the boy. "He mentioned meeting someone on the seawall." He offered his hand, wiped clean of clay now, to Kate. "Name's Daniel. Welcome to our gallery."

"And I'm Kate. Hold on. Did you say *our*?"

His arm swung back to rest an elbow on top of the boy's head. "This guy's and mine. Though my son here's mostly in charge."

The boy nodded earnestly.

"That I can believe." Kate's gaze swept from sculpture to dresser to table to kiln. She tried not to let her eyes rest on the father and son, who shared the same smile, which broke over their faces at the same time—a little mischievous, a little surprising. "A working craftsman in the middle of the city. Amazing."

Daniel winked at the boy. "Artisans, that's what they call us in the tourist brochures. Half the town'd like to run us out for being a fire hazard—which is when the tourist-brochure makers and the wood-fired-pizza-place owners are our best friends. Other half'd like to run us out for a profession that makes a man sweat like even a horse isn't allowed to here South of Broad—which would be when the Historic Charleston Foundation and Preservation Society folks become our best friends."

"Your son helped me out just when I needed it." She turned back to the boy. "But I don't believe we exchanged names."

She waited.

"It's okay, big guy," said his father.

"My momma says I shouldn't ought to give out my name to strangers." The boy wiped his mouth on the shirt cuffs that shot past his hands, curls falling into his face.

My momma says. Kate hesitated at the child's use of the present tense. Hadn't he told her up on the seawall that his mother had died? Something in his father's face looked pained.

The boy crossed his arms petulantly.

"And she would be right," Kate agreed. "But you and I met already, remember? You were the brave one between us."

"No kind of coward."

Daniel reached gently for him. "Don't recollect anybody saying you were, Son."

But the boy jerked away. "Just last fall I knocked a boy over—good twice my size—and took out his front teeth."

The man nodded. "Reckon you did. And I reckon your momma would allow you telling this newcomer your name."

The boy hesitated, then thrust out his hand. "The name's Gabriel."

Kate gave him her hand and shook his hard. "Nice. Like the angel."

"'Cept I wouldn't be one of them." The boy's feet shifted in the crushed shell. "Gabriel Ray," he added and smiled—like he was pleased with the beat of it, the way its sound circled back: aggressive, angelic, and plenty dramatic.

Kate tilted her head, hearing something behind or beside what he'd said, something else tucked there in the scallop of sound.

"My momma named me. And I'm the fastest and smartest boy in the city."

Studying his son's face, his own flinching in pain again, the crafts-man turned. Stepping back to his worktable, he began arranging ceramic tiles at the edge of a chess table, its wood grain glowing golden.

Kate addressed the child. "So . . . Gabriel Ray. Anybody ever call you Gabe?"

"My momma, she stuck to the whole full smack of the thing. But you can."

"All right then. Gabe."

"We good enough friends you can give out yours—with its tail end?"

"You were my very first friend here, remember? Drayton's the tail end of mine."

The craftsman paused in reaching for his tongs. Not looking up, he lifted a bottled Coke off the counter. "Old family name here, Drayton."

"So I'm learning. Although I'm not sure whether that's a good or bad thing."

He adjusted more tiles. "Depends. Draytons built a rice plantation out on the Ashley River. Owned hundreds of slaves. Made themselves a fortune on the backs of those slaves."

Kate squirmed but didn't try to respond.

Daniel arranged more tiles. "Another Drayton, this one named Charles, a slave, testified against some of the other participants in a slave rebellion planned here."

"The Vesey revolt," Kate blurted out.

Daniel looked up. Nodded. "Good for you." With a rubber mal-let, he tapped several tiles in place. "Another Charles Drayton, this one white, built himself a fancy place down the street on what we call Battery Row. When you walk down East Battery, notice the mansion that's got a whole different architectural style, with geometric railings, number twenty-five—the change thanks to some Union shelling."

Gabe piped in, "It's my favorite on the Row. 'Cause it's the differentest."

"Impressive," Kate said. "You two know your stuff."

Father and son exchanged knowing smiles.

Gabe nodded earnestly. "It's our job."

"I wonder," Kate asked, "since I'm gathering Charleston's not such a big place—the historic district, at least—if you know a woman named Lila Rose Pinckney. Another old family name, I believe."

The craftsman glanced up again. Nodded.

Gabe reared back on his stool. "That's our preacher's name, Pinckney. Got two daughters, for the folks that like girls, which wouldn't be me. Real nice family, the Pinckneys. They—"

The man shook his head at his son. "Different Pinckney. The one our friend here is meaning, she's white."

Gabe bounced on his stool. "Didn't know there was a white kind. They cousins?"

But the craftsman addressed Kate. "Miz Rose's been a customer of mine for years. Just yesterday mentioned a project she's wanting to bring by. Heirloom she's wanting adjusted."

"I know which customer you're meaning now," Gabe said. "One with the silver corkscrew hair. Real strong pocket."

"Strong pocket?" Kate asked.

"How we say it in Gullah. Means rich."

As Kate watched, Daniel donned two padded gloves, plucked several tiles from the kiln, laid them in a metal trash can padded with newspaper, set the can in the fireplace, adjusted the chimney's flue, lit the newspaper on fire, then covered the can.

Kate gawked.

The boy tiptoed closer. To Kate, he whispered, "The fire and smoke work with the copper and glaze. Raku's what it's called. Never know what pattern you'll get." To his father, he added, "Can I watch some stretch of longer?"

"You finished up calc for the day?"

"*Calculus?*" Kate turned to Gabe. "At your age?"

"I was finding a little trouble at school."

"What happens when you go *looking* for it," his father suggested.

Gabe shot a glance at his father and ducked his head. "I was too gifted to teach easy, they said. *Too dang gifted,* they said, only they didn't say *dang.* We're trying putting me ahead in math to see does that help with the trouble—me looking for it."

"My question, Son, was did you finish your homework?"

Gabe pitched his head philosophically toward the beamed ceiling, the curls tumbling back from his face. "The day, you know, is just an arm long. You can reach clear across it."

"I take it that means *no*," said Daniel.

Gabe tipped his head back toward Kate. "That's Gullah, too. My daddy, he knows it best. Means you can handle what you got to in a day. Or like when I saw you this morning early up there on the seawall, you looking sad. In Gullah, my daddy would say, 'Look like she lived in sorrow's kitchen and licked the pots clean.'"

"Wait. Do I really look sad?"

Gabe nodded gravely. "For folks who know you well as I do, yep. You stand up real tall—tall as you can for not being tall—and whip back that hair, and you smile pretty brave. But you got some kind of sad behind the eyes."

"You don't miss much, do you?"

Gabe padded up to his father's arm. "Kate here's likely needing a walk-through of a real working artisan shop."

Carefully Daniel removed the lid from the can, smoke billowing up the brick chimney. Then he poured water into the can, steam hissing from the tiles below. Watching as the steam cleared, Daniel fingered a leather cord at his neck.

The boy popped himself up onto a three-legged stool. "So we got fire here, Kate. And we got water."

"That much I see."

"And we got wood. Cypress. Got to be cypress—the furniture and the sculptures both. Watch now what the fire's gone and made."

With long wooden tongs, Daniel lifted a tile from inside the swill of ash. Copper glinted in swirls over an emerald-green background. The next tile was copper swirled over blue.

"Okay, that's gorgeous." Kate studied the tiles. "So you two make all this yourselves? And sell it yourselves?"

Daniel laid down his hammer. "With plenty of sales help on the floor of the gallery—since Gabe and I don't just run this place." He propped open the gallery's side door. Stepping into the alley, Daniel ran a hand down the glossy flank of a black draft horse with a broad white blaze down his nose, a white mane and tail, and thick skirts of white feathering that fell from his knees and hocks a good twelve inches down to his hooves.

"So you knew there was a giant horse just out your side door?"

"His stable's on Anson, but we bring him here now and then for a break," Daniel said—as if that explained everything.

"There can't be two like him in the city. He was pulling a buggy this morning. Don't tell me you're also running one of the carriage-tour companies."

"Let's just say that more than one income stream is a good thing in our situation. Got some bills we got to pay. And we—me and Gabe both—got tired of hearing the other companies' pick of what stories they tell to the tourists."

"The history's wrong?"

"Not wrong so much as what's missing from lots of them. Like if you don't mention the ugly—the slave auctions, for instance, held on this very street—it didn't exist."

Kate's hand dropped to the laptop in her backpack. "You know, it would probably be a little rude—the three of us just meeting today—if I started taking notes right now. But the stories the two of you probably know. I'd like to ask questions—if you don't mind."

She saw wariness flicker in Daniel's eyes.

"I don't mean today. Just . . . sometime. If you're okay with that. I'm interested in history, too."

Gabe lowered his voice to an admiring whisper. "The work she does is *hangings*."

From where he'd bent over a front hoof, Daniel glanced back. "That right?"

Kate laughed. "I might need to explain."

But Gabe had already slid off his stool, Kate following him, and slipped through the alley door to rest a hand on the horse—whose head appeared nearly half as big as the whole of the boy. She ran a hand down the animal's neck, then back to the velvet of his muzzle. "Looks like a warhorse to me."

Daniel let out the headpiece of the halter a notch. "Bred for war is right—way back. But Beecher here pulls a buggy full of people paying good money to get swept back in time."

"And, Gabe, do you ride along?"

"Alltime after school and on weekends. The buggy business, he can't do it too good alone, me being the one who lets him know when he goes talking too long and boring."

Daniel chuckled. "My son speaks the truth."

"My daddy mixes it up, though, fits songs to the stories and talk. Goes to sites nobody else even goes near. Best carriage tour in the city, that's us: Gullah Buggy."

"I'm sold." Kate turned to glance back out the front window that opened onto East Bay.

A dark-skinned man—remarkably tall—in a suit stood facing the shop, his face livid, neck swelling above his tie like the whole top of him might blow apart.

From the window, obstructed by an outcropping of old brick, Kate couldn't see who the man was addressing.

But stepping closer, she could hear most of what he was saying. Behind her in the alley, Daniel and Gabe were engrossed in inspecting a shoe of Beecher's that was coming loose.

One of the voices outside the front window rose. "What possessed me to think that even after all these years you had one ounce, one *ounce* of compassion—or even good sense?"

A tangle of two voices. One of them possibly familiar—though it was hard to tell in the snarl of sound.

Kate moved closer to the front window.

The man she could see, his voice rising above the other, said, "I swear I don't know why I didn't just take the whole thing into my own hands back then. Or why I don't now. You never were anything but his messenger pigeon, you know that? You never were."

Kate leaned out farther through the open window.

His features contorted, fists clenched, the man in the suit might have caught sight of Kate watching him as he spun on one heel and stalked away.

Embarrassed, Kate leaned back, but then forward again as the second man, the one she'd not been able to see, scuttled out of the alley and onto East Bay, his head hunched down into the points of his shoulders.

Percival Botts.

"Wait!" she called from inside the shop. "Mr. Botts!" Bolting for the front door, she lifted a hand to the craftsman and boy in the alley and ducked out into the drizzle that remained from the fast-moving storm.

Botts had already disappeared somewhere down East Bay.

If he no longer lived here in Charleston, then he must just have driven in soon after they'd talked earlier this morning. So had he driven in solely to meet with her—and simply hadn't yet returned her call? Or could it be he didn't want her to know he was here?

Her laptop inside her backpack slapping her back as she ran, Kate jogged south on East Bay, the direction she'd seen Botts disappear. Becoming East Battery, the left side of the street turned from shops and houses to harbor. Kate bent to catch her breath.

Maybe it was idiocy, chasing him like this if they were going to meet soon. But nothing about her past memories of Percival Botts told her she could trust him.

Botts crawling out of his rental car, parked in front of their New England duplex, then scuttling in his black suit over their unshoveled walk—his spider legs jerking across the snow. Botts scowling at the cracks in their front window. Botts thrusting forward the divorce papers for her mother to sign. Botts refusing to meet Sarah Grace's eye as she sank to the kitchen table . . .

Kate had lost track of him now. Unless that was Botts up ahead, turning right onto South Battery. Kate broke back into a run, reaching White Point Gardens in time to see him slipping through the gate of a sprawling white Victorian house—an inn, its sign announced—with a broad porch skirting its base and a turret above its left side.

So there. She knew where he was staying. She could even try to demand that he see her right now.

Suddenly nervous—Botts did that to people—Kate squared her shoulders and smoothed the jeans and top, badly wrinkled, that she'd plucked from one of her duffels back in the motel room.

A shadow winged close to her.

A great blue heron, its neck stretched long, swooped over the harbor, the tips of its wings skimming the surface as it arced right. Leaning into its flight, wings wimpled and poised for the next downbeat, the bird mounted the wind. Kate stopped to watch as it lofted, current to current, out toward the open sea. Then circled back toward Charleston.

As the heron arced back, the sun just edging out from behind the clouds caught the wet tips of its wings, now glowing gold. Kate shielded her eyes to watch.

It seemed not bound to this world—not to worries or death or distress. Not to falling-in families or nose-diving careers. It just flew. And reveled in that.

Something, Kate thought as she forced herself to walk toward the inn, *I've never, not ever, known how to do.*

Chapter 9

Walking beside the mule that pulled his cart, the creature's nose bumping companionably against his side, Tom delivered the wrought iron heron to the mansion on Meeting Street three back from the water.

Something decorative for the garden, Tom—and large had been the extent of the order from this customer, one of his regulars. So he'd crafted the vision inside his head. And prayed the older couple who lived here would not see what that white girl Angelina had seen in his iron heron: the longing, the ferocity, the flight.

Leaving the order with the footman at the back entrance, Tom walked slowly up Meeting and, in front of the Pinckney house, pretended to inspect the mule's front left leg. But he could see nothing of Dinah. He'd been hoping for a glimpse of her shaking out rugs on a piazza. Or stepping down into the garden to clip roses for the Pinckneys' table.

Wanting to wait but aware of the sun's sinking fast into the harbor—and the curfew bells that would be sounding soon—he hoisted the mule's hoof to search for an imbedded pebble causing a limp the animal did not have.

Still no sign of Dinah.

On the piazza of the first floor, something fluttered. Two white girls, their skirts swishing around them, settled themselves into chairs: the girls who'd come to his shop to see about the damascened gate—breezed in like they owned the city and the whole of his shop, or the Pinckney girl had. And beside her, the Grimké—the one whose sister up north had been all but disowned by the family, people here whispered. Angelina, her friend had called her. Who'd looked at his heron and shuddered. This one, glancing both ways, opened a newspaper.

Tom scanned the length and height of the Pinckney house and its gardens. No Dinah.

The Pinckney girl batted the back of her friend's *Courier*. "You know Father insists that real ladies do not read newspapers—that ladies have only to trust the governing of the world to men."

"Which is one more reason your father doesn't care much for me—the influence he thinks my sister might be having on me, Sarah and the Quakers she's taken up with, and the influence I could be having on you. That's right, isn't it, Em? He'd had a bit too much of his bourbon last night, and I could see it there in his eyes at dinner, his dislike of me." The Grimké girl lowered her voice to the pitch of a man's. "'Your inattention,' your father said at one point, 'to good Southern breeding. To our way of life.'"

The girls laughed—thin, brittle notes that had nothing to do with mirth.

They drifted from the piazza inside through the door flung open wide to the night breeze. From inside came the crashing crescendo of a pianoforte. Beethoven—Tom recognized it. The widow Russell had once played the pianoforte, and Tom had shod many a horse to the notes of a concerto, badly performed. Tonight Emily Pinckney, the top of her head visible through the first-floor parlor windows, banged out Beethoven as if the hammer and speed of it could catapult her free from the house.

Dropping the mule's hoof, Tom was just standing, just turning to walk on up the street, when he caught sight of blue toward the top of the house that maybe wasn't just the shreds of sky left as dark overtook it.

And there Dinah was in the cupola, where she stood with a blue head rag over the black spill of hair that fell to her shoulders. Only now one hand was to her throat and her mouth twisted into what must be a scream, her head thrashing backward in panic.

A man's hand slapped over her mouth. The tumbler he held sloshed amber liquid onto her neck and her chest, and then it shattered against the frame of the cupola window, the man brushing its jagged glass across her neck. No sound came from the cupola, just a terrible, twisting silence above the crash of Beethoven below.

And Tom standing there. Staring up. Able to do exactly nothing to help.

The strength drained from his head down through his torso and out of his legs so that only his locked knees were holding him upright.

The back of Dinah's head was pressed to the glass now, her hair blending with the black of the night. Behind her, the man, his upper lip curling as he looked down into her face, then pressed his mouth onto hers, his hands pulling at something and ripping and tearing. Then the bare of one of her shoulders.

Both of Pinckney's arms circling her.

Wrenching her back. Wrenching her down.

Both their heads disappeared then. Nothing in the yellow glow of the cupola but the flicker of candlelit shadows.

Nausea shot up Tom's middle, scorching his throat. It cut off his air. It swallowed him whole.

Closing his eyes, he tried to shut out the sight of her face twisted with fear. Or himself, the sinewed mass of him, unmoving there on the street, like a shorn Samson roped to one single spot where he was helpless to fight.

Helpless even to move.

Beethoven pounding around him, Tom stood there, dizzy and sick, still hoping to hear something. See something. Know anything other than the too much he already did.

Two levels below, Emily Pinckney came sweeping back out onto the piazza, holding a thick leather-bound book. "*Clarissa*. By that long-winded Samuel Richardson, who would *not* get to the point. This was the giant block of a novel we slipped from your mother's parlor as little girls, remember? The one she was horrified to find that we'd read. Imagine if she'd known how we loved acting it out: you and me taking turns as the sweet, flawless damsel and the blackguard Lovelace who took Clarissa's innocence from her—and Dinah in all the supporting roles. Dinah asked once, I recall, to play the virtuous lady Clarissa—before her ruin at the hands of Lovelace."

"And you would not let her," Nina mused. "I remember."

The Grimké girl might have said something more or not—Tom had to bend double now, his head nearly touching his knees.

"And, Nina, remind me to tell Dinah she must have me dressed early tomorrow for the Ravenels' picnic. Where has she gotten to, by the way? Honestly, these past several months she can just disappear. Shamefully inconsiderate of her when she knows it's getting late."

Two levels below the cupola, Emily Pinckney leaned on the first-floor piazza's balustrade and sighed. "The truth is I'm in no mood to care about ladylike conduct and good Southern breeding tonight." She snapped open the newspaper and handed half its pages to Angelina. "See what a baneful influence you are. What would Father say if he knew?"

A few yards away, in the cavernous dark of an ancient magnolia, Tom Russell had dropped to his knees and was beginning to retch.

Chapter 10

2015

Pausing at the entrance of the inn's garden, Kate ran a hand over the shape of a lyre crafted into the gate's elaborate design. She'd read only just this morning that one clue to the quality—and often the age—of Charleston's ironwork was the craft of its curls. This gate's wrought iron wound in tight, perfectly tapered spirals. And for a moment she held on to it, as if its age and its strength might transfer some sort of courage to her.

At the inn's sign requesting that only registered guests pass through its gardens, Kate did not stop. Out on South Battery, just a few yards away, a tourist carriage was clattering past, its driver sporting Confederate gray. Just beyond the gazebo and cannons, the land spilled into sea.

Through pink and purple clouds of azaleas, she skirted right, not toward the inn's main entrance but instead toward the far side for a view of its vast wraparound porch. From here in the garden below, myrtle and magnolia rising around her, she could see two sets of high-heeled sandals as they clattered past on the porch. Except for an older couple sipping coffee at the far end, the porch was empty now of guests.

She'd seen Botts come straight toward the inn, so he must be either here on the porch or inside.

"Mr. Botts?" a man's voice called.

No answer.

Kate ducked back into the shade of the magnolia.

Footfalls sounded over the boards—not the sharp click of an attorney's dress shoes but heavy and dull. Construction boots, she could make out from below.

"Mr. Botts?" the man called again.

Again, no answer.

A scratch of wood on wood, and Kate could see a man's arm moving one of the wicker chairs closer to the edge of the porch and the construction boots propped on the porch's lower railing.

Then the rhythmic strum of a guitar. And a bass voice on a mournful melody line—a song Kate knew. Knew well, in fact.

Summertime, and the livin' is easy.

She could see her mother bending to push her in a tire swing—the one they'd strung up together from a silver maple in the yard in front of their duplex one bleak Christmas Day in New England, to the neighbors' horror—the eighteen-wheeler's tire and a fraying rope visible from the street, where, on both sides of the town square, colonial saltbox two-stories marched stiffly, dutifully, their original wooden shutters intact, their original iron boot scrapers still affixed to front stoops. All but Kate and Sarah Grace's house, which sat small and low and unkempt, like a whispered apology. Kate could see her mother ignoring the neighbor walking his schnauzer, both master and dog cocking their heads, dubious, disapproving, as Sarah Grace shoved at the tire as it swung past and sang in time to its swing:

Fish are jumpin', and the cotton is high.

Sarah Grace's voice keened over the notes, sorrowing, sliding. The words that followed rang eerily true, Kate sensed even as a small child: the daddy who was rich, the momma who was good-looking—and something deeply, elementally tragic about that pairing, like a fault line that assured some future catastrophic collapse.

At some point, the song had come to an end, the sway of the rope had stilled, Kate laughing up at her mother—only to find her mother staring out and away, her fingers on the spiral and fall of Kate's curls, but her eyes not seeming to see them.

Sarah Grace bent then, cinching her arms around her daughter and kissing the top of Kate's head—and held her like that for so long Kate wondered if her mother had forgotten again where they were: outdoors. In front of their little house, the smallest by far on the square. The neighbor shaking his head.

"It provokes one," said the neighbor—perhaps to his dog or perhaps to no one at all, "to wonder about the South."

~

The guitar landed a final D minor—this one mangled, discordant. A rumble and scrape then, like boots scuffling as someone stood up.

A low rasp of a voice came from around the far curve of the porch. "You are early, Mr. Lambeth."

"I try to break the stereotype of the slow-showing contractor at every chance, Mr. Botts," the voice of the young man who'd been singing replied.

Kate crept closer.

"And?" Botts again. Curt. Impatient.

"I'll cut right to the chase."

"By all means do. I have a meeting soon. And my time is immensely valuable."

The toe of the work boot tapped once, then twice, as if the contractor were making himself pause before answering. "I'm here to advocate for the family."

"And which family, might I ask, would that be?"

"Let's not play games, Botts. I believe you know."

They'd moved closer, just a few feet away from her now. Kate tried to quiet her breathing.

She saw a square jaw, a hand raking hair back from the face, and eyes that widened, blinked once, as the younger man—the runner guy from the seawall—caught sight of Kate hiding there.

A cell phone rang.

Botts's voice: "I need to get this. I assume you are willing to wait."

A series of thuds as he walked a few steps away from the runner—and toward Kate. "Yes," he muttered into the phone, "I've talked with the lab."

A pause. He stepped farther away from the contractor. And still closer to Kate. The toes of Percival Botts's wing tips, polished to an ebony gloss, poked to the edge of the porch.

He lowered his voice. "They received the follicle and root samples, some antique items of clothing—including the handkerchief, yes—their usefulness for DNA purposes yet to be determined. And, of course," he uttered this last with distaste, "the buccal swabs."

A pause. Then he said, "Like you, they told me it might or might not be enough for a determinative result." A pause. "Yes, I can meet for lunch, but . . ." He shot out his breath in annoyance. "I'll see you there."

A muffled beep as he hung up without signing off.

Kate could see up to the knees of Botts's trousers.

He did not move. Which might mean he'd heard her there, only inches away. Breathing. Or shifting her weight.

The contractor guy's voice edged into the silence. "Everything okay?"

The wing tips pivoted left. A pause. "What was it you were attempting to say, Mr. Lambeth, when I was unavoidably interrupted?"

The contractor's eyes darted down toward her, and for a moment Kate thought he might give her away. Instead, he tromped down the porch in the opposite direction. A wicker chair scraped across wood. "Mr. Botts, I wonder if you and I could chat for a moment."

Hesitating only an instant, Kate rounded back through the garden, mounted the porch stairs, and stood before them. "So," she said. "Hello."

Botts froze. The attorney had not changed in all these years: the black trench coat, the small head between pointed shoulders, the jerk of limbs strung too loosely together. Percival Botts was as much the tarantula of her nightmares as ever.

Kate braced herself. She knew what kind of pain Percival Botts left in his wake. Hadn't she seen Sarah Grace pale when they were expecting a visit from Kate's father and they opened the door on Botts standing there, his tiny eyes hard and glaring?

Kate had watched her mother struggle—to find a job, to find them housing, to help Kate feel secure in their new life even when Sarah Grace herself clearly did not—back as far as their flight to New England. In Kate's mind as a girl, Botts represented all that had conspired to make her mother always short on money—and even shorter on resilience. So Kate learned long ago, you didn't take your attention off Percival Botts for two shreds of an instant—not unless you'd already abandoned all hope and were prepared for surrender, a white flag poled through your heart.

She could guess what he must see, looking at her. Long hair frizzed by sea air, clothes rumpled, face pale—the very picture of what her father thought she would become: a failure.

He stood a full moment, unspeaking. Then, stiffly, extended his hand. "Katherine. I was planning on contacting you to apprise you of my arrival." Botts pulled his briefcase up his side and in front of his middle as if he were drawing a sword.

"I thought I'd save you the trouble by just showing up."

The whetted gray of his eyes held steady on hers. "I was assuming you had research you could pursue in the meantime. Assuming, that is, you've managed to retain your position in the department. I understand there have been . . . issues."

Kate took a moment to absorb this. "That's more about my life than I would have guessed you knew. I didn't realize that in addition to attorney-client privilege, attorney-client spying also extends beyond death."

The contractor's gaze, uneasy, circled from Kate to Botts and back.

"My adviser's been encouraging me for some time to travel to visit some archives, but leaving Massachusetts wasn't something I could do in good conscience . . . before."

"Sarah Grace," Botts said, as if forcing himself to form the words.

"Yes. But since my circumstances have obviously changed, it occurred to me now might be a good time to pursue that research. For my work. And also some questions I've had for a very long time about my family. As it turned out, I left Cambridge without a lot of advance planning." *To say the least.*

This fell leadenly into the silence.

So Kate continued. "Since her funeral, I've been going through boxes. With all sorts of papers and . . . memorabilia. And also a good bit of research."

Botts's eyes widened over his craggy outcropping of nose. Cautiously, he nodded. "Sarah Grace . . . your mother had no gift for order."

"There's a reason," Kate persisted, "that Sarah Grace never let go of Charleston."

Botts jerked back his head. A small gesture. Still, he'd been startled.

But he regained his composure quickly. "And you assume, Katherine, that somehow your mother's nostalgia ought to mean something? Perhaps you've been reading more novels than scholarly works."

Kate leaned forward, one elbow resting on the opposite arm, which was crossing her chest. "The reading material I'm most excited about now, actually, is going through Sarah Grace's belongings in all those boxes."

Botts tensed—no hiding that. "If by *belongings* you mean deeds to cars that broke down decades ago, then all best of luck to you."

"Still, I'm guessing it might be worthwhile, my reading all the way down through. Don't you think?"

Here he seemed to visibly pale. Something like fear flashed through his eyes—before they hardened again. "Your mother and father's marriage was stormy, it is fair to say. Perhaps she felt she needed to put some distance between herself and the Low Country. But if you're assuming there are inheritance issues that concern you, then you would be unequivocally mistaken."

Kate studied his face, the ragged angles of his features going, if anything, sharper as he avoided meeting her eye. "I didn't say a word about inheritance. What makes you bring that up, Mr. Botts?"

Small eyes narrowed to what Kate could have drawn with two slashes of pencil. She wanted to give him time. But the words, years of them, tumbled from her. "With my mother gone, all the things I always thought she'd tell me someday feel urgent now to understand. I thought maybe you could explain what happened. Why both of them came from Charleston and both of them—separately—left. Or why, for all her running away from this place, she never stopped talking about the Low Country, reading its history—dreaming about it even, I think."

Vaguely, she was aware of the contractor still standing there, his eyes on the porch planks and his weight shifting from one foot to the next. But all her focus now was on the attorney and the expression she could not read on his profile, the twitch of his eye and the pressed line of his lips.

Botts remained facing the harbor. "*Reading its history,*" he repeated, each word chopped to a dull chunk of sound. His hands went deep in the pockets of his trousers, arms stiff, his body a wall—but his face in profile contorted. "She should have . . . told you herself."

Kate touched his arm. "Please. What was it that shattered her?"

In Botts's eyes, she could see something newly wedged open, something newly exposed.

"*What,*" she whispered, already wishing she wouldn't say it, already regretting the words as they formed, "did my father—and you—do to her?"

He rounded on her. The moment of seeing into his eyes was over. That wedged-open shaft had slammed shut once again, his face all contempt.

"Look," she said, "I'm sorry. That didn't come out like I—"

But it was too late.

"If she'd listened to me . . . ," he hissed.

The contractor, Lambeth, edged a step back.

"I'm sorry to air all this in front of you," Kate told him. "But Mr. Botts here has a track record of not returning my calls when he has something to hide." It was only a guess, a stab in the dark. But the lawyer flinched at that last phrase—she was sure of it.

She spun back to him. "Then what, Mr. Botts? What more damaging could you have possibly done? You and my father had already arranged it so we got nothing financially. You managed to wound her all over again every time you showed up in Great Barrington with some new excuse of my father's to ignore us—and all along, you pretended that your client's conduct was okay."

He stepped back as if he'd been struck and took a moment to gather himself before speaking. "Let me ask you this, Katherine: Did your mother never give you specifics of her earlier life in the Low Country? Did she never divulge anything while, for example, she was . . ." He glanced away and then met her eye. "Drinking?"

Kate pushed the words past a throat that had closed. "*That* is enough, Mr. Botts."

It seemed like betrayal somehow, Sarah Grace so recently gone and the image that Botts conjured up from Kate's childhood so vivid: Sarah Grace with the light from the hallway behind her, leaning hard into the door's frame—clutching at it. Sarah Grace groping for something solid as she made her way to Kate's bed. Her kneeling. A garble of sounds. A prayer, perhaps, or a confession or both, sodden and murky with no proper end—just a finishing swamp of *sorry so sorry, I'm sorry.* Sarah Grace's face buried in her little girl's thick, wavy hair, the hair going wet through with tears, as Kate lay curled there, afraid to breathe.

"You," Kate told Botts, trying to steady the shake in her voice, "have no idea what you're talking about."

"We may as well be honest with each other about that, Katherine, if nothing else. Yours was not the only life her drinking impacted."

Kate shook her head—and knew she was shaking her head at the truth of her past. But she would not expose her mother like this, her kind, gentle, too-fragile mother, for whom life was often so dark. Kate would not let Botts see the raw place he'd hit.

With a jerk of both arms, Botts's grip on his briefcase tightened, his hands like white claws holding their prey.

Kate could not bear to look at his face, his eyes boring into hers to see if he'd been right. So she focused instead on his hands. "All I want is to ask a few questions. Or maybe *demand* is the word I want. Sarah Grace raised me to be nice at all costs—to never demand. But that didn't work out too well for her, did it?"

Botts stepped toward her. "While we're asking questions, Katherine, perhaps I might ask some of my own, as a kind of surrogate of my client, your father. It would appear that you've made some rather injudicious decisions just lately."

"Seriously? Even a year after my father's death, you're still, on his behalf, the all-seeing firm of Rutledge, Wragg, Roper & Botts, Attorneys at Law and Observers of Wayward Daughters?"

"Having observed the . . . obstacles faced by both of your parents in their separate ways, I could imagine, Katherine, that you might very well—" He stopped himself there.

"Go careening off course, just like my mother? Is that what you meant? Look, you want the truth? Here's the truth. The clock's ticking for me. Even if my doctoral program gives me one final shot, I'd better research and write and submit for publication something arresting and original and meticulously documented—incredibly fast. If not, I've wasted a whole lot of years of education—blood, sweat, and tears—with no fallback plan, no practical skills, and no real savings to speak of."

"Your father's testamentary dispositions—"

"*Enough* already with his money! If he couldn't be troubled to help when my mother was barely keeping the two of us fed, and she never wanted to take him to court to *make* him trouble himself, then why would I want his money now? I was simply catching you up, Mr. Botts, on the loveliness of my situation." Hearing herself describe her life out loud made it seem more real than ever, and Kate's chest tightened as if giant clamps were crushing her lungs. "Let me save you some of the time you've always spent poking around my life to report back to my father: I've really screwed up this past stretch of road. But you know what? It's not been my best year."

Botts's eyes stayed narrowed on Kate. His jaw worked forward and back.

"Maybe, Mr. Botts, you'll tell me this. What did my father mean when he tried to warn me away from choosing the early nineteenth-century Low Country to study for my dissertation, picking up where my mother left off? He told me it was"—she made quotes with her fingers—"'a history that can only hurt you.'"

Botts straightened to rigid, his face guarded again and hard. On his breath she caught the bitter edge of the coffee he must have drunk before coming. "That, Katherine, is part of what I am bound not to discuss."

She had hit some sort of target. Her mother's research—and now Kate's own—was somehow connected with their family history, fragmented and shrouded in secrets. And her late father's lawyer knew more than he was willing to say. "So, then . . ."

Botts, though, was already checking his watch and scuttling across the porch. "I have a meeting scheduled, a prior commitment. And I *never*"—he briefly turned his head back toward her—"go back on prior commitments. I'll thank you to keep that in mind. I will be in contact."

"Do *not* walk away from me!"

He flung one arm high as if batting away her protest, and his trench coat flapped beneath climbing jasmine as he hurried away up Meeting Street.

Arms hugged tightly over her chest, Kate turned. The live oaks at the front of the inn stretched toward its porch, their arms impossibly long and graceful, Spanish moss like gauzy gray scarves draped from the bend of each joint—reaching as if there were something they wanted, desperately wanted.

All through the oaks' branches, wisteria vines looped and fell like twisted hemp.

Like nooses, she thought, remembering the boy's reaction to her drawing of them.

From the pocket of her jeans, she dug out the sketch, crumpled now, that she'd scribbled there on the seawall: the mansions, the buggy, the cannons, the ship. And the nooses.

Kate let the southern sea breeze—stronger now but too warm, too thick with the past—whip hard at her hair. Botts's voice echoed in her head.

Did she never divulge anything while, for example, she was drinking?

Eyes down as she spun around, she smacked into a Nike T-shirt. She'd forgotten about the contractor guy. Lambeth.

"I didn't know which was worse," he confessed. "To leave or to stay. I wasn't planning on mentioning your hiding back there, you know. You didn't have to come out."

Bristling at being caught in a weak moment, Kate kept her voice chilly. "It was time I confronted the weasel myself. Not that it did any good."

"Looks to me like maybe—"

"I'm *fine*."

He nodded. But still didn't leave. "You know, when I saw you sitting there, back at Penina Moise, I couldn't help but wonder if—"

"*No.*"

"I'm sorry . . . no?"

Kate hugged her arms tighter over her chest as if she could hold in the hurt that she'd held so close for so long and that Botts's words had kicked the lid off. "Look. I don't mean to be rude. But *no*."

"To . . . ?"

"To whatever it is you wanted to ask. The answer is *no*."

A grin started at one corner of his mouth but stopped only halfway. His face—a handsome one, if you liked the rugged, inscrutable type, which Kate did not—was sunburned and sweaty and in need of a shave. His T-shirt stretched across a muscular chest, and a scar cut across his left cheek. He was the kind of man that women made fools of themselves chasing after in action-adventure movies—directed by men. But in real life, a smart woman learned who to trust, which was no one. And a smart woman knew how to maintain her walls against precisely his type.

He raked a hand through his hair. "Looks like I dove in this pond from the wrong end. I wasn't actually hitting on you."

Kate straightened, arms still crossed over her chest. "Oh. Well. It . . . had all the markings."

"I apologize, then, for the markings." He raked his hand through his hair again, making it stand nearly on end. He stepped toward her, his face only inches from hers, that almost grin hanging there.

She stood her ground.

But he brushed past her. Bent. Turned with a crumple of white in one hand. "This yours?"

"Oh." She took the scarf. Looped its length once around her neck. "Second time today I've dropped it. It was my mother's—her favorite. It would kill me to lose it."

"Listen, I got no interest in sticking my nose in where it doesn't belong, but if that Botts fellow was your father's lawyer—"

Kate held up her hand. "Look, if I had any answers, I wouldn't be here. Sorry, but I've got to go." She turned—just a notch. "I didn't say thanks. For your finding this. And sorry for interrupting the talk you were trying to have with Botts."

He studied her for a moment, and his hint of a smile disappeared. "There'll be time for that yet." With a nod, he strode diagonally across Meeting Street to the sprawl of a historic home. At the upward sweep of a twin pair of brick steps, he paused to tighten the screws at the base of its railing, then hoisted a ladder propped there to one shoulder.

But just before he ducked into its garden, he swung back toward Kate, who was still leaning against a porch railing at the inn.

"Is it important?" he called from across the street.

"Is . . . what important?"

"You finding Botts again today and trying to get him to talk?"

Kate hurried down the inn's steps toward the street. "It is, yes."

"The client he's meeting today over lunch has an old friend who owns a café, and she's there all the time—kind of holds court. In fact, you know the place." One hand holding the ladder, he gestured north with the other. "Penina Moise."

Before Kate could thank him, he'd disappeared behind a wall covered in climbing jasmine.

Chapter 11

1822

Tom Russell swung his hammer once more.

On the walls leaned wrought iron gates with damascened crests—gold highlighting the design—and balcony railings with fleurs-de-lis and lyres and crossed swords and all manner of swirls. Works of art, fearsome and graceful and strong, some so massive they had to be walked, four men to a gate, out from the shop.

His shop. *His.*

Tom strode out the front of his shop, letting its door slam behind him. A few dozen paces and he was onto North Adger's Wharf, his eyes darting right, then left.

From St. Philip's and St. Michael's, the church bells tolled curfew. Behind him, from all sides of the street, slaves raced through the dusk, bare skin slapping the pavers.

Tom felt for the copper badge at his neck, its imprinted block letters all too familiar to the touch of his forefinger and thumb.

CHARLESTON
422
BLACKSMITH
1822

A badge of his being an urban slave, complete with a number tied to his owner.

But tonight he'd use the badge as his ticket for ignoring curfew.

Denmark Vesey was right about one thing, at least: Tom Russell was known. And was trusted. *Tom Russell, yep, he's real docile*—it was what people said.

A spatter of a ship's lanterns lit a spotty path down Adger's Wharf.

Tom skirted the light, though, keeping well into the shadows of stacked cotton bales and towers of crates. Darkness was settling over the harbor, its surface holding fast to the last glimmers of day.

A lantern swung into the shadows just ahead: a patrolman marching the length of the wharf.

Tom ducked low behind a stash of empty crates reeking of fish.

Back and forth swung the lantern. Back and forth.

Leg muscles protesting from the position he'd crouched himself in, Tom shifted his weight to his knees. A board creaked.

The light swung right toward the sound. Toward the crate blocking Tom. Footsteps echoed as the patroller approached.

"You! Boy!"

Tom waited for the lantern to blaze in his face. Caught.

Instead it plunged forward. Onto another face.

"Ain't nobody but me, George Wilson, here, sir."

Tom knew the voice. A house slave. He'd been often to the blacksmith shop on East Bay, sometimes with a horse of Major Wilson's who'd thrown a shoe. Sometimes with orders for kitchen tools or shutter guards. Just recently with the entire payment clutched in his hand for an elaborate sword gate.

"Just going home with a sack full of fruit—see these here mangoes and pineapples—for the major. But now it's gotten so near to dark. Major, he had a hankering, and he begged me to go." George Wilson's voice quaked.

Tom didn't blame the little man for his terror. You couldn't live in Charleston more than a week without passing by the workhouse and hearing the shrieks and the moans of a slave caught out past curfew, and today's drums would be sounding soon with the final warning.

"Well, now. Is that so, George?"

"Oh, yes, sir, yes, sir. You come on along with me, if you like, and see can you find Major Wilson at home to ask him your ownself."

For a moment, the light stayed where it was. Then, with a lurch, it floated left down East Bay with the trembling George Wilson.

Tom let out his breath.

That meant the wharf was probably clear of a patroller, at least for a few moments.

Keeping low, he leapt from shadow to shadow along the wharves toward the Neck.

At first, all he could hear was the shushing of marsh grass, the call of gulls over the water. The occasional jump of a fish.

Just as the mansions gave way to tenements and the broad piazzas shrank to a few square feet of porch covered in drying linens, Tom slipped left, inland. At King Street, the only road that cut through the Lines, a jagged wall built during the War of 1812 to defend Charleston from any British troops approaching from land, a guard checked Tom's neck badge.

A good head shorter than Tom, the guard yanked on the badge, jerking Tom down and over. The guard's mouth moved as he seemed to sound out the word *blacksmith*, and Tom realized the man could probably only just make out the word. With a grunt, the guard waved Tom aside, and he passed through into the Neck.

How exactly, Tom wondered, *will Vesey and his lieutenants deal with this problem, this one road, King Street, that could so easily be shut off—which would block access for recruits from outlying farms and plantations coming to fight in the city?*

Some recruits were scheduled to arrive by canoe from the coastal islands, but that wouldn't account for the droves who would be arriving by land.

Several blocks up ahead was the church where Vesey had asked to meet him but Tom had not waited. Would not be sucked into this dance with death.

But now, standing outside its glassless window, Tom could make out a handful of words, whispered—if whispers could shout: "Like the Hebrews in bondage in Egypt, where God saw fit to make the waters run red with blood, our day of liberty and brotherhood and equality—I tell you, of safety and happiness—is coming. Do not grow weary of striving. No, not yet. Our day of redemption and release is in the hand of the one Judge, the only one, who hears our cries. Yes, even now . . ."

Typical of Vesey, it was a sermon that was part Declaration of Independence, part Old and New Testament, and part current events—especially from the French Revolution and the newly established Haiti, which had thrown off white rule less than two decades ago. And typical of Vesey, his preaching, like the songs from the rice fields, carried just enough of the promise of some future world that he could argue he was speaking of heaven—Vesey could assure some angry white passerby who might overhear, despite the remoteness of the location here in the Neck, *Goodness knows, why no, sir, 'course I wasn't speaking of* this *life—no, not me.*

But then afterward, Vesey's lieutenants would speak one by one with potential recruits, who would then tell others one at a time: *July 14. Our own Bastille Day. Our own independence.* Vesey might preach to whole groups, but he was adamant that the rest of the rebels spread the word quietly and directly so that each new recruit had no idea who else was involved in the revolt—and therefore could not inform on anyone except the one person who'd approached that recruit with the plan.

But Tom hadn't come to listen to Vesey's sermon or anyone else's whispered persuasion.

Crossing his arms, he reminded himself why he'd come: the image of Dinah's head lurching back up in the cupola of the Pinckney mansion, her soundless scream. And Tom, more than six feet of muscle and utterly helpless, had doubled up there on the street and vomited until dry heaves were all he had left.

Now, the drums from the city limits warning the last chance for slaves to be off the streets before curfew, figures flitted past Tom, their footsteps echoing, frantic and stumbling, into the dusk. But he kept to the shadows, crouching. Even in front of the faithful disciples of Vesey, Tom would not link himself to the cause.

Only when the last of the small crowd had dispersed did Tom step into a pale pool of light from the moon, finding Denmark Vesey alone outside the front door of the church, his eyes on the stars.

Vesey did not jump when Tom appeared. Hardly, in fact, seemed startled at all.

"I thought you would come," he began.

"Haven't come like you think. Not like them." Tom's head jerked in the direction the crowd had dispersed.

Vesey lowered his face from the stars. "What then?"

"With conditions. Only with these conditions. That you commission me to make what you want me to make."

"Weapons."

"A word I don't want used again. That you pay me well for my work. That all payment get sent to Widow Russell. I'll be telling her it's rice-harvest equipment—new planter in town, him needing trunks to block up the water, scythes for the rice, hoes and shovels. All paid direct to her."

Vesey's eyebrow arched high. But Tom ignored this.

"That my part of the payment get settled between me and her. That it's a dealing of business. That's all."

Vesey nodded slowly. "A business transaction you're hoping that, even after Widow Russell takes her lion's share, might be enough to earn you your freedom. Or, more to the point in your case, earn someone else's."

Tom merely looked back at the old man.

"You realize, don't you," Vesey demanded, "how rare it is now for a white owner to be able, even if they wish it, to grant a slave freedom?"

"Willing to take that gamble."

Vesey examined the stars. "Any more conditions?"

"That my name *never* get included on any of the lists you, Peter Poyas, Mingo Harth, Gullah Jack, Ned Bennett, and Rolla Bennett keep. No matter how careful you guard those lists."

Again, Vesey's eyebrow shot up. "You do know things."

"When you run a shop on East Bay, you got the pulse of the town. Not much happen in this city I don't know about before."

"A shop *you* run. That's right, Tom. That's more the spirit I've been looking to hear out of you."

"Can you do it or not? Keep my name out of it?"

Vesey considered a moment. "It can be done. And I'll tell you this: your joining us makes me more sure than ever we will succeed."

"Reckon you didn't hear me too good. I'm not joining you."

"Making the rest of our . . . *implements*, then. And let me promise you this: your name will go with me to the very grave." He held out his hand.

Tom shook it but pulled his own hand quickly away. "That rabbit George Wilson, he one of your new recruits? He was headed out here like he might be wondering what was happening—and scared half to death."

Vesey's brow furrowed. "With the exception of Ned and Rolla Bennett at the governor's, there's not a house slave in the whole army. Can't be trusted. Pull the trigger on my own head before I tried to recruit the likes of George Wilson."

Tom disappeared into the dark, leaving Vesey behind to stare at the stars.

~

Back in the shop, Tom shoveled ash over the last of the glowing coals. But stopped.

On the far wall of the forge, where he'd mounted a piece of chipped slate he'd found on the street, he'd chalked up with soft rock the next several months of orders. Just four grids for this month, April, and the following three, May, June, and July. Instead of words or numbers, he'd sketched rough pictures—a gate with lyres or a fence with damascened gold at its tips—positioned as many squares away as days until the projects were due.

Only one white man had examined it well, that wall. He'd gazed up at the sketches and squares. But after a moment, Colonel Drayton had only shaken his head and laughed.

"I'm impressed, Tom," he'd said. "I am impressed."

Tom let one finger count forward now to the month of July and day fourteen.

He marked the day with only a picture: a gate.

An open one.

Returning to the forge, he hauled on the rope to the bellows and fanned up the flame.

Then thrust iron rods into the fire.

The quarter hour of warning drums would be stopping soon, even here in the Neck, the northern part of the peninsula that housed scores of free blacks and slaves hired out for their skills by their owners. He'd been given permission two years ago to move from the quarters behind the Russell home and into a room in the Neck shared by four other artisan slaves. They were still watched and patrolled and told when to be in for the night and how many could congregate where. But it had been a small taste of freedom, a taste he knew better than to risk by ignoring curfew.

But he'd just signed on for a rebellion that, if it went according to plan and fanned the spirit of liberty and hope, could sweep the Low Country—could free slaves across the South.

And if it failed . . . then being hauled to the workhouse for breaking curfew would be the least of his worries.

Tom lifted his hammer and brought it down in a shattering blow.

Chapter 12

Kate stood in the alley that ran between Penina Moise and the gallery that Gabe and his father owned and listened a moment to the clatter of cookware from the back of the café on one side and the clanging of something metal from the gallery on the other—as if one of the sculptures might have toppled. Something in the racket on both sides helped focus her mind.

As humiliating as it might be, she'd come here to confront Botts again—and if she had to make a scene in a public place, so be it. Whatever he knew—or did not—about the implosion of her parents' marriage or about her mother's compulsion to study a nineteenth-century slave revolt, it had to be more than Kate did.

I beg you to hold close what only the three of us know, her mother had written to someone on the back of that photo.

Could one of the three have been Percival Botts?

Meanwhile, she had to keep trying every path she could find to possible answers.

Pausing outside the door, Kate redialed the phone number her mother had scribbled at the bottom of the *Places with a Past* booklet. A ring. And then two.

And then a clatter—someone picking up finally?

But it was only the kitchen of the café again. More rings—and no answer. Frustrated, Kate tossed the booklet and her phone into her backpack.

Stepping inside the café, Kate wound through shelves of Low Country cookbooks and Sea Island blackberry scone mix and sweetgrass baskets. The platinum-haired waitress chirped at her to follow.

"For folks by their ownself," the waitress tossed back, "we got a table off to the corner can't fit even two very good. 'Cause in Charleston, nobody much eats alone."

Guess that makes me nobody much, Kate opened her mouth to say but instead ordered an iced coffee. Not only was she not officially meeting anyone here, she didn't even know what time the person she'd come to ambush might be seeing his client for lunch. Just wait till this waitress had to watch this *nobody much* eat alone for the next couple of hours.

On the cover of the café's menu, an oval daguerreotype featured a woman with dark hair looped on both sides of her head to a bun at the back. Inside, the menu described the talents of Penina Moise, an antebellum Jewish poet and hymn writer, a faithful member of Charleston's own Kahal Kadosh Beth Elohim, the first Sephardic synagogue in the nation.

Arranging her laptop, Kate called up the website of the Historic Charleston Foundation—which, it turned out, owned several of the house museums in town, including the mansion on Meeting Street where Nathaniel and Sarah Russell had lived—and presumably the blacksmith Tom, too, unless he was one of the small class of urban slaves allowed to "live out" in separate quarters. Kate shot the archivist at the foundation an e-mail with several questions, including whether they had any information on Tom, such as where his shop might have been or any indication that he might indeed have survived the summer of 1822. Kate included a request for an in-person meeting.

She scanned the café again for Botts. And kept an eye on the door.

A short, bearded man was moving from table to table. He bent for hugs, spun to greet an old friend, swept up an infant and swayed with the baby as he beamed at another table of guests. Servers dodged and busboys pirouetted out of his way. But he—with his beard, his scraggled hair, and his squat, solid form—was the center of a kind of graceful, if precarious, dance.

"I came to my senses," he roared to one table, his head thrown back in a laugh, "in New York as a young man and freed all future generations of Greenbergs from the cold. As a young man, I discovered what few people know: that a Jew does not, after all, shrivel up in the sun like a grape. My people suffered the pogroms. Kristallnacht. The Holocaust. Must we also always suffer the cold?"

The table of diners laughed with him.

"Your daughters, then?" one diner asked. "How are they?"

The owner shook his leonine head. "A child learns nothing that comes from the lips of her father. This is wise, to ignore such advice?" He hit his forehead with the heel of one hand. "But this is the way of the young. Not one, I tell you, but both, *both*, my daughters have moved to New York. Lawyers, the two of them. This contributes, I ask, to the good of the world?"

A short man in a dark suit entered the café and turned his face to the street. Kate held her breath.

But the man, who turned again and took a seat, was not Botts.

A female diner dressed all in linen—that elderly lady Lila Rose Pinckney from the table outside this morning, Kate realized—lifted her wineglass to the bearded man. "I must say, Mordecai, and you may tell your lovely girls I said so, that I fail to see any point in drawing breath anywhere outside the Low Country."

"Ah, well said, well said. They will come home someday and settle here, when their bones grow brittle and break to splinters from all that cold. I tell them this."

And now he was spinning toward Kate.

"Welcome!" he thundered, arms up and open. "Welcome to Penina Moise!"

In front of Kate landed a box of steaming Sea Island blackberry scones.

"My gift," said Mordecai Greenberg, "to the stranger in a strange land."

"These smell amazing. Thank you."

He nodded to the books she'd unloaded from her backpack onto the table. "This is why a young lady such as yourself must eat alone?" He read off a few titles: "*He Shall Go Out Free: The Lives of Denmark Vesey. Deliver Us from Evil. The Trial Record of . . .* this is the reading that takes the place of a lunch companion?"

"It's for my work. A working lunch." Why was she apologizing now to someone she didn't even know for how she wanted to spend her time? And why did people down here assume they had the right to comment on her life?

As if responding to what she'd been thinking, he patted her hand. "My own girls would tell me I must sometimes keep my thoughts to myself. I say only that you and your books are most welcome here. Only don't eat too often alone. Books can be like friends, yes. But do they keep you warm at night when you grow old? I ask you."

The older woman Kate had met this morning was holding up something for the platinum-haired waitress to see: a *New York Times*, apparently left by a previous diner on a chair at her table.

The waitress reached to clear it away.

But Rose did not relinquish the paper. "I do not purchase these. Ever. If left in my path, however, I feel it my duty to keep apprised of those scurrilous scalawags to the north."

The woman's accent was an absolute river, soft on the consonants, long on the vowels, gentle on flow.

Cautiously, Kate slid from her seat and approached the woman. "Forgive me, Mrs. Pinckney, but I believe we met briefly earlier today. I'm Kate Drayton." She held out her hand.

The older woman nodded, one silver eyebrow still hovering high in its arch. "Of course, dear. I'm hardly likely to forget."

"I don't mean to bother you if you're waiting on someone, but I was curious this morning that you seemed—and maybe I had the wrong impression—that you seemed to know who I was. Before, I mean, I'd told you my name."

"I'd have picked you for Heyward's daughter anywhere."

"Then you knew my father?"

A pause, infinitesimally short but enough to suggest that whatever she'd known of Heyward Drayton might have been complicated.

"Why, yes. I did. And please allow me to convey my sympathies on the passing of both your father and mother—in such a short span of time, too. I declare, what a sad . . . state of affairs."

And again, that odd, constrained look. As if she were speaking more broadly than of only their deaths.

"You knew, then? About their deaths? Word traveled back here?"

"*All* word travels through Charleston, I assure you. All word worth hearing."

"Mrs. Pinckney, I wonder if I could ask—"

"Please, do call me Rose. Not Miz Rose, as half the town does, or Mrs. Harold Pinckney, as the lesser half does."

"I'm a graduate student in history, specializing in the early nineteenth-century Low Country, and I've come to Charleston to further my research." Even if she were on academic probation, teetering on the edge of final dismissal, at least it still served as a reason for being here—without drawing questions that she had no answers for.

The waitress set a glass on Rose's table. "Here's your Chardonnay, Miz Rose. 'Bout ready to order that shrimp and grits, light on the andouille sausage?"

Rose raised a hand. "Do give us a moment, won't you?" It was more command than request.

The platinum helmet snapped right, and the waitress flounced three tables away.

"Katherine Drayton, I had heard through various reliable sources that you were in this field."

Kate blinked. "You'd heard that?"

"Charleston is a small town in many ways, at least for those of us whose families have known one another for generations. I must say that I wondered when you would be coming down."

Not *if*, Rose had said. But *when*.

"Mrs. Pinckney—Rose, I wonder if I might talk with you sometime."

Rose stiffened a little. Guarded. "Talk with me, dear?"

"About what you knew of my father—and my mother, too, if you knew her. Honestly, I'd love to hear anything you'd like to tell me."

Rose appeared to be gazing out the window and took a moment to answer. "Naturally," she said at last, "you would have questions." Her gaze drifted back to Kate, and Rose seemed almost startled to find her still there. "How would tomorrow be, sugar, at, let us say, half past ten? My home, if you'd like to write the address down, is—"

Scrambling to her table for a pen and hurrying back, Kate sent a wine goblet near Rose flying, and it shattered on the floor.

The waitress came running, with a comforting chatter of "Hon, now you don't worry yourself none at all, you hear?"

Kate knelt to pluck shards from the floor.

Rose, unfazed, only nodded absently. "Good. Yes. That's good."

From where she crouched, Kate lifted her head. "I'm sorry, *good*?"

But Rose was not looking at her. "Sometimes things get broken when you go after the truth. And sometimes people get hurt."

"The truth? I'm not sure . . ."

Rose's gaze swung to meet Kate's. "What's that, dear?"

"You said something about the truth. Things getting broken when you go after the truth."

"Did I?" Rose asked. "Well now. Sometimes I do slip and say what I mean, instead of what ought to be said." She smoothed the linen pleats of her skirt as if she were realigning her thoughts. "Let us hope that you are one of those who falls helplessly under Charleston's spell. I wonder if perhaps in your studies you have heard of a certain Angelina Grimké."

Just standing up as she scanned the restaurant again for Botts, Kate turned, startled. "Angelina Grimké? Of the Grimké sisters from here in Charleston? Of course. That's my era."

"I understand the old girls are rather well known outside Charleston. Their ancestral home here on East Bay has only just received its own marker. And high time, I might add."

Kate sank back into the chair across from Rose. "You'll be glad to know that the Grimké sisters have become better known lately. They get trundled out as the sort of antebellum American South counterparts to the few people in Paris who hid Jews during the Vélodrome d'Hiver roundup—as people who could somehow see past the culture around them. To me, Angelina and Sarah Grimké are endlessly intriguing: raised in a slaveholding family, but both the girls growing up to question the whole system—and then fight against it as abolitionists. I've always wondered what they saw or heard or read growing up that made them that way—different, I mean."

Rose tapped a white forefinger against deeply lined lips. "Yes," she said. "What they saw that made them different."

Kate leaned in toward her. "Rose, you mentioned Angelina specifically."

"Yes." Rose hedged, wavering on a decision. "Yes, I did."

"Most people seem to know more of Sarah Grimké—if they've even heard of either of them. Was there a reason that you mentioned Angelina?"

Rose pursed her lips. Then offered, "I have in my possession a few . . . let us call them family papers. From what you have called, I believe, your era."

"Family papers? You mean . . . letters?"

"Some, yes. And in particular a journal. One of my ancestors, it seems, was a particular friend of Angelina Grimké's. Perhaps you might like to have a brief look."

Kate stared. "Rose, you realize, surely, that your family papers might be incredibly valuable to historians' understanding of the early nineteenth-century South."

Mrs. Lila Rose Manigault Pinckney gazed back. "I should hope so. They are incredibly valuable just now to me in my understanding of it. For my own reasons, I've chosen to keep these family documents to myself for the time being. I am, however, intrigued with the idea of allowing you, given your interests, to peruse them along with me. A trial run, perhaps, would be in order."

"Rose, I would absolutely love to see whatever it is you have. But these papers eventually belong somewhere that could be monitored, climate controlled."

"So I understand. People from the Southern Historical Collection from Chapel Hill have more than once prostrated themselves on my doorstep. But, oh my Lord, those white gloves of inferior cotton they use."

Kate did not volunteer that some archives used worse: disposable plastic surgical gloves.

"My ancestors, Katherine, that great cloud of witnesses, would not approve of just *anyone* peering into their lives."

Mordecai Greenberg appeared by Rose's side, his cheeks flushed a deep red above the scraggle of his beard. He laid a hand on her shoulder. "My dear friend, it falls to me to inform you—why it falls to me and not him, I don't know—that your lunch meeting must be postponed."

Kate said the name before she'd fully registered who Rose Pinckney's lunch companion was supposed to have been. "Botts."

"Why, yes." Rose studied Kate's face an instant. "You would know him, I suppose, through your father."

Greenberg shook his head. "The *schmendrick*. He shows up at the door. I greet him. He is not polite. He starts this direction. Then he orders me—not asks but orders—to come and tell my good friend that her lunch has been postponed. And is a reason of medical emergency given?" He shook his head again. "Your wine, my friend, is on the house today. Are you ready to order?"

Botts must have taken one look at the young woman sitting at his client's table—*so Rose Pinckney is also a client of Percival Botts?*—concluded that Kate was there to confront him again, and fled.

As if she were thinking the same thing, Rose's eyes flitted from the front door of the café, where no one but two businesswomen stood, waiting for a table, to Kate. Stiffly, she stood and squeezed the café owner's hand. "Fortunately, Mordy, I was not particularly hungry, having been here only a few hours ago." Turning back to Kate, she added, "I am glad, Katherine, that you will be able to join me at my home tomorrow. I believe you and I have a great deal to discuss."

Biting her lip, Kate had to restrain herself from bombarding Rose with questions right there.

"Tomorrow," Rose said, as if responding to what Kate was thinking.

"Yes. Tomorrow. I can't tell you how much I'm looking forward to it. Telling me anything you remember about my parents and allowing me to see your family papers, Rose . . . you won't be sorry. I promise."

Rose's head cocked sideways, the chignon like a crown sliding to the back of her head. "Can any of us promise that, truly?"

Rose swept from the café, leaving the scent of lavender in her wake.

What was it she'd said about going after the truth?

Sometimes people get hurt.

Chapter 13

It was a nightmare that woke Emily Pinckney, an image—lively and lurid—of Angelina and Dinah and herself leaning over the blacksmith's forge, Nina reaching into the coals. Bare-handed, she held up a glowing ember for them to see. But it was Dinah who screamed and covered her face.

Shaking her head as if she could loose the image from its hold in her head, Emily bolted up to a sitting position. The whole bed jostled; the rice sheaves carved into her bedpost seemed to shift and sway. Emily pressed a hand over her eyes.

As the door of her bedroom opened and she heard light footsteps across the wood planks, Emily sat huddled in her bedclothes, knees to her chest, hand still over her eyes.

When at last she dropped her hand, Dinah was standing in front of the fireplace and holding a washbasin—and looking quizzically at her.

Emily shook off the bedclothes and rose. "I had a most unpleasant dream. Nina was . . ." She stopped there. "Never mind. Set the basin down. I'll attend to it in a . . ." Her voice trailed off as Dinah did as she'd been commanded, the washbasin dropping just below her middle as she lowered it to the stand, the front of her skirts smoothing for a moment over a rounded bulge at her belly.

Emily's whole body went stiff. Slowly, she raised her eyes to meet Dinah's, which were flinty and cold.

"So. Dinah. Which blackguard of your fellow servants is to blame for this?"

But Dinah merely looked back at her. And said nothing.

"You realize, of course, that eventually you must tell me." Emily's hand shook as she reached for the bedcover and pulled it up over herself like a buffer between herself and whatever Dinah might say.

Again, no answer, except for Dinah's raising her chin a bit higher— and it was already too high above a long, slender beige neck. She turned to reposition the basin. Drew a pale-green watered-silk morning dress from the armoire and stood holding it ready, her face a mask. Her eyes, though . . .

Emily Pinckney looked quickly away from the smoldering there. And asked nothing more.

~

In the formal dining room, Jackson Pinckney was drinking his coffee in silence, his leather-bound ledger propped open to form a black wall, behind which he was muttering a string of observations, most of them blessedly incoherent, about the latest indigo exports. Emily settled herself across the table from him and, her hand shaking a little from her own most recent observation, stirred the sugar into her own cup.

From behind his ledger, her father observed, "A millstone around the neck of the South. That's what it is."

Emily knew this speech from her father but humored him by providing his next line. "The South has trapped itself in an economic system that cannot be sustained indefinitely."

Slamming his ledger shut, he looked up, glowering. "Exactly. Northern radicals accuse the South of oppressing our slaves for the sake of profit, but they have no idea what a burden we bear, supporting

116

the people who work for us even into a slave's old age. I don't know but what the slaveholder is more oppressed than the slave. In fact, I recently wrote . . ."

Glancing toward the front entrance, Emily was relieved to see that Nina had not yet arrived. Much as she should have known her place, raised as she'd been in the respectable Grimké household, Nina rarely let such a comment from anyone, even a man, pass without a rejoinder.

Emily, on the other hand, responded to the last buffeting winds of the rant simply by rising to pour herself more coffee from the urn on the sideboard.

By the time she was sitting back down, he had switched subjects and made no attempt to lower his voice. "Have you noticed nothing of Dinah's behavior lately? Her impudence toward you? I assume you have addressed this with her."

Before Emily could answer, Dinah herself entered, carrying a steaming tureen directly in front of her middle.

Emily hurried to fill the silence. "And what would you have for us there, Dinah? I smell mace. And caramelized onions. And cloves."

"Turtle soup."

"I thought so, yes. But for breakfast?"

"Prue said to tell Miss Emily that it was fresh-made this morning, and it might as well be eaten fresh-made."

Jackson Pinckney's gaze shot to his daughter. "You see?" he demanded. "Exactly as I was just saying."

"I will address it, Father. After breakfast, when you retire to your office." Unsteadily, watching out of the corner of her eye to see if the bulge at Dinah's middle could be detected—probably not just now with her hands linked like that in front of her—Emily leaned toward the steam and sniffed: cloves, yes. And Madeira. Cayenne pepper. Onions. Brown sugar. And thyme.

She cleared her throat and scrambled for something to say. "Dinah, do you recall when Prue taught us to make turtle soup, you and I, when we were girls? We'd balance on that one rickety stool. And, you recall, you never wanted anyone to touch the knife to the turtle?"

"Long time ago," Dinah said. "Not scared of knives now." And she swept from the room, slender ankles and small feet moving across the just-polished oak floors.

Emily swallowed and glanced toward her father. But if he'd heard anything in that last response, he showed no sign. He'd raised the wall of his ledger again.

"Father, I don't know if I mentioned it, but Angelina Grimké will be paying us a visit this morning."

"*You*," he corrected. "Paying *you* a visit. That girl may be from a good family here, but she's growing too much like her sister Sarah, an odd bird if there ever was one—reading her brother's law books. Woman's mind isn't made for that kind of strain—look what happened. And homely, my God. The face of a horse, both of them. And not a horse bred with attention to looks."

"Father, please!"

"But the worst of it is the ideas your young friend Nina might have picked up from her sister. You know she's in Philadelphia now, the sister Sarah."

"With the Quakers. Yes. I know that."

"Imbibing God only knows what dangerous ideas. There's a reason all the Quakers have left Charleston. If they don't value the Southern way of life, if they must constantly rail against our economic obligations here, then they did well to remove themselves."

"I think they would argue those economic obligations are choices we've made."

Her father's eyes narrowed at her. "You make my point for me: their baneful influence."

Emily was finding herself combative this morning. "Not all are gone, Father. The Quakers, I mean. From Charleston. I saw a couple just the other day, having their horse reshod at . . ." She stopped short of naming the blacksmith's shop on East Bay. "And someone must be keeping up their meetinghouse on King."

"Almost all gone, then, and good riddance to the last of them. Their traitorous, abolitionist rantings are not welcome here. Both those Grimké girls have the feminine gentleness and finesse of a locomotive. Amazons, that's what they are."

"Miss Grimké," announced the footman at the door of the dining room, "to see Miss Pinckney, sir." The girl herself stood just behind the footman.

"Speak of the devil in skirts," Jackson Pinckney muttered.

"Nina." Emily hurried from the table to greet her. "Father was just remarking about some recent articles in the *Courier*. We're so glad you've come."

Pinckney stood, extended his hand to the girl, and seemed to be on the point of speaking.

But the footman appeared again at the door of the dining room. "Colonel William Drayton to see you, Mr. Pinckney."

Emily and her father both turned to greet his old friend.

"Jackson, forgive me for paying you a call so early in the day. I decided to presume upon both our family relations and our friendship."

"Something urgent?"

"Not *urgent*, exactly. Not yet, at least. Only a conversation over-heard by a house slave—a servant, however, in this case, who is known for enjoying dramatic effect. I merely thought what he claimed to have overheard was worth mentioning to you, Jack, for your insights." Sweeping the top hat from his head, he dusted its sides with a flick of a forefinger, then handed the hat to Dinah.

She lowered her eyes to the hat she balanced in the palms of both hands and backed up a step. But did not leave the room.

Colonel Drayton bowed to Emily and Angelina. "Ladies, I do hope you'll excuse us. We don't wish to bore the fairer sex with the details of keeping our lovely city secure."

~

"Just what was this nightmare that distressed you so much?" Nina asked. She seated herself on the edge of the bed.

Emily held up a hand to her maid. "Dinah, the curls nearest my face don't look as they should. And the top could be smoother. I was too . . . distracted before breakfast by other matters to notice." She and Dinah exchanged glances in the looking glass.

Slowly, as if registering the fact that they both knew Emily's hair had been perfectly coiffed in the latest fashion, not a hair out of place, Dinah reached for the brush.

Nina flopped to her side on the bed, an elbow bracing her head.

The brush, a slender sterling affair, reflected the morning light from the east-facing door to the piazza as Dinah smoothed the hair.

Emily's gaze shifted from Nina back to the mirror—to Dinah's face, contorted somehow at the top of the glass, and beneath it Emily's thick, flowing hair and pale skin. And a knife held to her neck.

Emily gasped. Unable to move.

Then let out her breath. "Oh. *Lands*. It was only the brush."

Dinah stood where she'd paused in midstroke, one hand strangling silver.

Nina joined them by the looking glass, the three of them staring at their reflections.

"What did you *think* it was?" asked Nina.

Dinah's eyes smoldered again. Only for an instant, but Emily was certain she'd seen it.

The three of them stared into the glass as if they were each daring the others to look away first.

"What else would it be?" Nina persisted.

Emily opened her mouth. Closed it again.

She swept to the door that led to the piazza. "Dinah, I don't know why you can't ever remember not to close this while it's still cool enough in the day."

Throwing it open, she stepped out and breathed. "Wisteria," she said. "It's in bloom."

Nina joined her on the piazza and lowered her voice. "Does your skittishness have anything at all to do with what you and I *misheard* the other day on East Bay? At the blacksmith's shop?"

A thought suddenly occurred to Emily, and it rocked her back a step. But it was a welcome replacement for what she'd been thinking before, and she latched on to it hard. "He must be the father. Of course." Her eyes darting to where Dinah stood at the window, her back to them, Emily dropped her whisper still lower. "Of the baby Dinah is carrying."

Looking unfazed, Nina nodded. "I saw the bump last time I was here. Are you just now discovering she's pregnant?"

"*Hush*, Nina! It's not proper to speak directly of such things."

"You sound like my mother, who will not allow that kind of talk—and who's given birth to more babies than the whole Left Bank of Paris."

Emily shifted uncomfortably. "I'm not sure a mention of the French is at all relevant in any discussion of proper behavior."

"The thing is, Em, women in Dinah's condition can be irritable. But you're skittish as a colt—and seeing things that aren't there. There is *nothing* to fear."

"Hush! Do you want her to hear you? If there's really nothing to fear, why do you assure me each time we meet that there's nothing to fear? 'The lady doth protest too much,' wrote Shakespeare."

Ignoring this, Nina hooked her arm through Emily's and led her back through the door. "Now, then. Why don't you let Dinah finish brushing your hair so we can go for our walk?"

Shakily, Emily Pinckney sat down.

Returning to the dressing table to stand behind Emily's chair, Dinah raised her arm.

Catching the rays of the sunrise from the open door, the polished sterling back of the brush flashed red as Dinah brushed. All three of them stared straight ahead at the mirror, watching the lift and slash of Dinah's arm as she worked the brush, its sterling gone crimson.

Like fire, Emily thought. *Or blood.*

Chapter 14

Kate paused outside the windows of Cypress & Fire, Daniel bending to open the door to the fire and, with giant pads on his hands and arms, extracting a vase. He plunged it into the bucket of water, steam rising from the back of the shop.

Leaning against the old brick, Kate dialed Botts's number. Took a deep breath. And, just as she'd suspected, was sent straight to voice mail.

"So," she said, "it seems we just missed bumping into each other at Penina Moise over lunch. What a shame. I know you said we'd meet soon, so I do look forward to your calling back so we can set a time in the next couple of days for that." She left her cell number again—as if he couldn't simply tap "Call Back" if he weren't trying so hard to avoid her.

Frowning at her phone, she googled the College of Charleston's History Department, scanned through the faces of the professors, pausing at the few who had white hair or were balding. Then she hit "Call."

An administrative assistant purred into the phone, "History Department. May I help you?"

Kate made herself straighten and tried to sound more professional than pleading. "Yes, my name is Katherine Drayton"—*Is it helpful or harmful to emphasize that last name here?*—"and I'm a graduate student from Harvard"—*Surely* that *name couldn't hurt*—"here in town conducting some research for my doctoral dissertation. And I wonder . . ." Here was the part that would make no sense to anyone else. "I wonder if I might make an appointment with a member of your department who might have been teaching there in, say, the late '80s. Possibly Dr. Sutpen?"

The name on that page of the website had sounded familiar. And maybe Kate was only convincing herself out of desperation, but she had a vague recollection of her mother sauntering around their tiny living room while pretending to smoke a pipe and describing what she was preparing for dinner with an exaggerated Southern drawl: *Why, mah deah, we must begin with the thawing of the bird, you know. The propah thawing of the bird will separate the truly fine minds from the merely mediocre, don't you see?*

Kate would collapse in giggles, and Sarah Grace would pull her up from the floor. "Katie, you should have met my college thesis adviser. What a hoot. Ole Sutpen."

Had it been Sutpen?

Kate held her breath. This had to sound strange, not asking for a scholar famed for a particular area of research. Just someone who had been there when her mother would have been a student.

"Ms. Drayton, I am sorry to say most of our professors take the summers off . . . that is, for research. And I'd recommend e-mailing anyone you'd like to reach, too. But let me just suggest that you're patient for a response. It could be a good while. And he may not check his voice mail for a while, hon, but would you like me to send you to it?"

Discouraged, Kate was about to agree. "Forgive me if I'm being pushy, but I don't know how long I'll be in town, and it's urgent."

"Oh my," said the administrative assistant, sounding politely unconvinced.

"I wonder if you could tell me if there's any particular place in town that Dr. Sutpen might typically go for research in the summers."

A pause. "Hon, I don't think that's the kind of information I can share. You understand."

An answer that told Kate at least that Sutpen was doing research in town, rather than some far-flung sabbatical location: one small step forward to finding someone else who might have known her mother. But Sutpen could be at any number of libraries or archives or museums or preservation sites in Charleston—the city was teeming with them.

What would Sarah Grace have done in this situation to get her way?

Kate drew a breath and tried to think not like the young woman from Boston she was but like her Southern momma. "I absolutely understand, yes. And the College of Charleston is wise to trust you with faculty members' privacy. Thank you for that. Could I just inquire, though, and forgive me for asking a personal question, but you sound like you might be a mother of young children?"

It was a risk. The woman might be offended by the assumption and hang up—or she might be flattered.

"Why, yes. As a matter of fact, I have a three-year-old." Kate could hear in her voice that the woman was beaming.

"Oh, how wonderful. Almost exactly the age I was when my momma and I had to leave Charleston. I have so many questions about what happened to her before that, bless her heart. For years, I've wanted to understand more about her life. And now that she's recently passed"—Kate slowed to let that sink in—"I'm more eager than ever to talk with anyone I can find who might have known her. I think Dr. Sutpen might have been her thesis adviser. So you can imagine how much I'm wanting to talk with him face-to-face. So recently after my momma's death."

Another pause. The administrative assistant lowered her voice. "I tell you what. It's not like I'm sending you to a private club or something. Dr. Sutpen's been working on a project that will have him at the South Carolina Historical Society—it's housed at our Addlestone

Library up on Calhoun." Her voice dropped here to a whisper. "And he likes mornings best."

～

Hanging up, Kate sighed and leaned again against the brick wall. She'd taken one more tiny step.

Perched inside on his stool, Gabe glanced up toward the front window from a textbook splayed on the counter. He darted to the front door. "Kate!" Taking her by the wrist, he tugged her inside.

"So tell me the truth, Gabe: Is it me you ran to welcome, or did you spot what I had in my hand?"

She cracked open the box of Sea Island blackberry scones. "Could I interest my very first friend in this city in sharing the wealth?"

Daniel set down his tongs. "Let me guess: the owner of Penina Moise found out you were new in town. Mordecai Greenberg pays a manager to keep him in line. Left to himself, he'd give away half the meals, then throw a party for the other half."

"Is that something that needs keeping in line?"

"Only if you want to keep the doors of your café open."

"Oh. Right."

Gabe reached for a scone.

Kate paused to watch a mouth so small making crumbs of a bite so large. "I've got to go sequester myself in some archives, but these smelled too good not to share." She turned to Gabe. "So that stomachache of yours is a little better, I guess? And your daddy doesn't mind your having several of those?"

Gabe shook his head. "Better, mm-hmm. And we don't generally eat dinner till right about candlelighting."

"About *when*?"

"It's Gullah for *dusk*," Daniel put in. He glanced up from the planks of cypress he was staining, then straightened to an exaggerated tour-guide pose, complete with hands miming holding the reins. "The term *Gullah* refers—"

But Gabe stepped forward, small hands also holding invisible reins, posing for the memorized speech. He tucked his chin far back into his neck as he pitched his voice low. "Refers to the people, culture, and creole language created with the coming of West African folks brought against their will to the coast here in the seventeen and eighteen hundreds."

Laughing, his father tag-teamed with him to continue the speech. "While the majority of Gullah's words might be English derived, its intonation, stress, sentence structure, and changes in the sounds of particular letters show its connection . . ."

"With African languages such as Krio," Gabe concluded triumphantly. He glanced at his father, who gave a thumbs-up.

Kate applauded. "*Candlelighting.* Nice. I like that. I've read about the Gullah culture down here, of course."

The *of course* sounded pretentious, and the *down here* condescending, which she heard for herself—and saw in the upward twitch of Daniel's mouth. "But that's probably different, reading about it, I mean, than actually learning about it. In person. From experts."

Gabe beamed, and Daniel gave her a single nod. For all the hard edge to his eyes and square of his jaw, there was a softness in him and a warmth. The quiet burn of kindness deep down inside.

From the dirt floor at the back, Daniel lifted a length of cypress trunk onto his counter, arms bulging with the strain. Watching, Gabe clenched one hand like calipers around his opposite arm, nearly as thin as one of the planks his father had just been staining. He squinted at his father's upper arm. Then back at his own. And frowned.

His father winked at him. "You keep pushing that currycomb in circles like I showed you all over our friend Beecher's big ole haunches, and pretty soon there won't be shirtsleeves enough in the Low Country to hold in the muscle of you."

Satisfied, Gabe turned to Kate. "Every day we're up before dayclean, me and my daddy, so we can get Beecher all set together—days I'm not running. And see to the couple of folks keeping the shop when we're out on the buggy."

"Up before dayclean," Kate echoed.

"*Dayclean*'s something my daddy says alltime."

"Alltime?" Kate pulled out the scrap of paper she'd used for her last sketch and jotted these down: *Candlelighting. Dayclean. Alltime.* Then she dropped the scrap beside the art-exhibit booklet she'd been inspecting at Penina Moise when Lila Rose Pinckney had made herself felt.

Tentatively, not sure she'd earned the right to ask too many more questions, Kate held up the booklet. "At the risk of sounding like the kind of idiot who thinks all sculptors know all other sculptors around the world, could I ask you about something?"

Warily, Daniel lifted his head from the cypress table legs he'd been sanding. Kate slid from her stool at the counter and brought the photograph of the four children in black marble closer.

Immediately, Daniel's face lit. And even Gabe skittered closer from his few feet away.

"Mother E!" Gabe exclaimed.

Kate shook her head. "Mother E?"

"Where that sculpture is located—I'll let Gabe explain about that." Daniel took the brochure and ran a finger over the page as he scanned it. "Not a bad summation of the work. It was brand new at this time, in '91."

"Exactly. I found it in some things of my mother's. I'm guessing she went to the exhibit herself, since it would have been maybe a year after she finished college here but before she left to . . ." Kate stopped there. To what? Escape from a painful marriage? Hide from something here in this city? "Before she moved away from Charleston. The sculpture seems to commemorate the Vesey revolt?"

"Right. The sculptor, Ronald Jones—he was born in the South but lives in New York, I believe—based his work on a stereoscopic photograph, a duplicate photo of the same thing that, when you view them at the same time, appears kind of three-dimensional, called *South Carolina Cherubs* by George Barnard. And Barnard was basing his on Raphael's cherubs—"

Kate's hands shot up. "I knew it! Actually remembered something from an elective in college."

Daniel nodded. "From the painting *The Sistine Madonna*, only Barnard's stereoscope depicts the cherubic innocence of African American children in Reconstruction South Carolina. All that to say, the sculpture here has a rich and complex history—"

"I'll say."

"And in their innocent gaze, the four black angelic children are meant to represent a kind of cloud of witnesses of the Denmark Vesey revolt that was planned in this city."

"Kate here," Gabe piped up, "knows all about that. Since her work is in hangings."

Kate exchanged looks with Daniel and did not contradict the child. "This is all exactly what I needed to know. But where is Mother E?" She addressed this to Gabe. "The booklet says it was installed at a chur—"

Gabe puffed out his chest. "Mother E's what I call her. Mother Emanuel to everyone else."

Kate's brow puckered, then relaxed. She skimmed her booklet. "Emanuel African Methodist Episcopal Church. Installed in some sort of entryway." She glanced up. "Really? So just anybody could go see it, then?"

Daniel blew sawdust from the table legs. "Just anybody'd be welcome." He stepped to a homemade kiln, fireproof insulation leaking out one edge of its door. "And if you want to understand the history of Charleston, you'll want to get by Emanuel soon."

Kate jotted the name in her notebook. Put a star by it. And then, because Gabe was watching, circled the star. The child nodded in approval.

"Son, it's time we took that break of ours," Daniel said to Gabe. "Just after this next step for the new sculpture."

Letting the smoke escape up the chimney, he doused the can with water, then used the long wooden tongs to lift a ceramic disc a good foot across, a hole in its middle, from the water. Copper gleamed in a background of teal and brown. "Kate . . . Drayton," he added, voice tight—and Kate heard the way he paused before her last name, as if needing a running start to form it. "You'll excuse us, I hope." He picked up his cell and shot a quick text.

Leaping from his stool, Gabe grabbed his father's arm. "Can Kate come?"

The pause again here. "I don't know if . . ."

Kate was quick to shake her head. "Oh, thanks, but I couldn't. I ought to get some research done."

Daniel shot a look at his son. "Just in case any ten-year-old boys present are paying attention, our friend Kate here is prioritizing her homework—even if it means leaving off fun early."

Gabe gazed up at Kate with a warmth that shook her. "Daddy's using you as a did-good-in-school role model for me," he whispered. "Hope you don't mind the pressure." And he slipped his hand into Kate's. Daniel winked at her over Gabe's head.

Our friend Kate here.

It was only a phrase a father had thrown out to his son to make a parenting point, and the son had only looked at her with a child's instinctive affection and taken her hand, but a lump swelled in Kate's throat. Little Gabe had insisted in drawing her—a near stranger, a woman who kept her walls firmly in place—into their circle of friends. She blinked hard to hold back the tears that would be too hard to explain.

Daniel hooked a **BACK SOON** sign on the front door of the shop and locked it behind them.

Gabe jumped ahead. "Come with us one more block, please?" He tugged on her hand. "Just as far as the fountain?"

Across East Bay was a small street only a block long—**VENDUE RANGE**, the sign said—and beyond it the pier. At the end of Vendue and just before the start of the pier sat a fountain splashing silver streamers of water high in the air, children cavorting into and out of its spray.

In the west, over Kate's shoulder, the sun sprawled, sending trickles of red between buildings and across the harbor, a swath of indigo blue that was fast going black. The pier reached into the harbor as if it were trying to catch hold of the horizon.

Kate nodded. "Just that far."

Near the fountain, a man stood with his back to them, hands hooked behind his head, bent arms on either side like two wings. When he raked both hands through his hair, Kate recognized him.

She whipped the sunglasses on the top of her head down onto her face and ducked to Daniel's far side. "That guy over there keeps popping up everywhere I go in this town. It's getting a little creepy."

"Who?"

Kate motioned with her head toward the contractor's back just as he turned, searching the crowd, at a right angle to them.

Daniel lowered his voice. "I know that guy. And believe me, if he's stalking you, you got reason to be concerned."

"Wait. You're serious?"

"Got a violent past."

Kate swallowed. "I saw the scar on his cheek."

Gabe was just completing his lope around the fountain's circumference and now broke into a dead sprint. Head down, he plowed full speed into the contractor, who braced just in time.

And wrapped the boy in a bear hug.

Kate covered her face with one hand. "Friend of yours, Dan?"

"Best friend." He chuckled. "Since first grade. Name's Scudder Lambeth."

"Mm-hmm. Violent past?"

"That part"—his voice grew serious here—"was true."

With Gabe on his shoulders, the man approached and wordlessly shook Daniel's hand. One side of his mouth twitched as he turned to Kate. "If I say it's a nice sunset, will you think I'm coming on to you now?"

"Sorry if I was a little jumpy before. You just looked—"

"Like I was asking you out. So you said."

Daniel looked from one of them to the other, apparently enjoying Kate's discomfort. "So. You two have met."

"She tried to make a pass at me by dropping her scarf," Scudder said. "But I was stupid and slow and failed to recognize a clearly flirtatious gesture for what it was."

"That was not . . . ," Kate protested.

"Sadly, I seem to have missed my chance."

Gabe beat his legs on Scudder's chest. "Run through the fountain, Uncle Scuds! Run through the fountain with me!"

Scudder Lambeth bowed then, nearly unseating his rider, and galloped away into the fountain's spray. Water pounding the top of his head, a wig of silver fanning out from both sides, he turned and waved and, as a bare heel landed in his side, resumed his gallop.

Laughing at her, Daniel shook his head. "That's more words than my buddy Scuds has spoken to a woman in months—usually gets all tongue-tied and stupid."

"Men are always so supportive of each other. It's touching."

"Smart of you to take the hard-to-get route, if you don't mind me saying. Took him clean by surprise."

"Oh no." Kate held up a hand. "You got it all wrong. I'm just here for research, and then I'm out. I'm not good with attachments—last thing I need right now."

Daniel lifted a shoulder and let it drop. "Good call. It'd take Scudder a month at least to ask you out—and I'm being generous. By then you'd be gone and he'd be calling a number in . . . where'd you tell Gabe—Boston? Anyway"—he nodded out toward his son, who was leaping and spinning through the spray—"you got a very first friend in town. And he'll hold you to it."

Kate smiled out at the child, who spun just then and smiled back, lifting an arm to his father and her before Scudder scooped him away by the waist. "You've got a great kid there."

His eyes on his son, Daniel nodded. Then glanced her way. "Listen, Kate, this is a little awkward . . ."

Bracing herself, she turned to him. He was going to tell her to steer clear of his son and their shop.

"I want you to understand what I'm about to say. The thing is, I'm not interested in women." Hearing himself, he chuckled. "That is, I was . . . or am . . . or may be again someday. What I'm trying to say is . . ."

Kate pointed to his wedding band and said quietly, "You're not looking."

"Exactly."

"You make that clear. In all the best ways."

"I just wanted to say that my son likes you. And he doesn't have many friends. Lots of gifted students like him have trouble with kids their own age. So, listen, any time you want to hang around Cypress & Fire when we're there, you're more than welcome. I didn't want it to feel weird, you know?"

Kate examined his face, the gentleness of his eyes. "I bet you're a really good dad."

He shrugged again. "Lots of us out there."

"No," she said—softly, not even meaning to say it out loud. "I'm not sure there are." She shook off Daniel's look of concern. "Listen, thanks for the welcome—best invitation I've had in a long time. And now I'm just going to step over there by the bench swings and leave you guys to it."

"Sure you don't want to join us?" She could see that he meant it this time. He yanked off his T-shirt, slowing as he maneuvered it past the leather cord at his neck. As he jogged into the spray with his son and their friend, Kate noted the medallion he wore—hard to see from this distance but unusual looking. This was their time together, though. So she stopped herself from running after him to inspect the medallion more closely.

"I'm all set," she called back, though she doubted they heard her, the three of them splashing and yelling and dodging.

Mesmerized by the bond between them and annoyed at herself for not moving on to where she couldn't be seen, Kate lifted her face to the mist that blew in gusts from the fountain's spray. She wanted to turn and walk far up the pier. But she could not stop watching.

The whole inside of her ached, and she crossed both arms tightly over her chest.

Chapter 15

Weaving her way through the dusk that fell over the pier like a slow rain of ash, Dinah clutched the bouquet of yellow tansies to her chest—clutched it hard enough she nearly stilled the shake in her hands. She'd picked more than the old lady had said she needed to make the tea. But she had to be sure it was strong enough to empty her body of horror, of fear. And if that meant she emptied it of life, her own included, then that was simply the price she was willing to pay.

Passing the dark fingers of wharves, each pointing to the sea as if taunting her, Dinah kept her head down. Another block covered and no one had stopped her. And another. But she should not be out this close to the tolling of the bells.

At the African Methodist Episcopal Church, its lot infested with weeds, the old lady emerged wraithlike from behind a palmetto, the gray of her skirts and the gray of her skin blending in with the mist that drifted now from the wharves as evening fell. A free black, the woman would be mostly ignored by the patrollers if she appeared to be minding her own business here just before curfew. But slipping some sort of potion to a female slave and meeting here with her at twilight . . . they could not afford to be seen.

Gripping in her left hand a ceramic cup with a broken handle and steam rising from its center, the old lady wasted no time. Snatching the yellow heads of the flowers from Dinah, she turned her back—whatever potion she was brewing a secret.

Then she turned but kept the cup locked in two gnarled interlaced hands. "Too much of the tansy," the old lady whispered, "and you'll bleed to death. Ain't no way for me to be sure how strong a batch this come out. Too little make you and the baby both sick as hell, but don't do nothing you say you want. Too much, the both of you poison to death. Even if the tansy just right in the tea, you bound to cramp up and vomit and bleed. Even then, no certain thing to it. You understand?"

Dinah dropped a hand to her middle and spread her palm over the roundness there.

The old lady leaned forward, one finger raised. "And if you too far along . . ."

"I understand." Dinah took the cup from her. Pressed a coin in the old woman's palm.

But the woman handed back the coin. "Child, you listen to me. You think now, 'fore you do this. One more dead body tossed on the pile of this world don't change none of the ugly, don't shift none of the pain. You hear? More ways to be free than this."

Dinah had already looped out of her way, East Bay not the closest path back to Meeting Street from the market. But walking a few blocks east, assuming she could still make it back before the tolling of the curfew bells, meant she might catch a glimpse of Tom inside the shop. To stop and talk would be too much to hope. But even just to make out his form through the glass, she would risk the bells.

Turning as if to inspect a barrel of rice and holding the cup and its contents steady, Dinah lingered outside the shop on East Bay where smoke curled from a crooked brick chimney. The windows dusted with soot, she could just see to the back of the forge.

Tom looked up just then from the fire. Dropped his hammer on the floor as he flew to meet her.

Looking both ways and careful to balance the cup in her right hand, she slipped through the door. "You should be in the Neck by now."

He pressed his lips hard to her forehead and his body hard against hers. "And you should be back at Meeting Street." He was nearly choking on the last words. "What's this?" He ran his hand down the bare of her arm all the way to the cup.

She shook her head. Knowing a thing could be awful enough, a knife deep past the skin. But putting a thing into words was lye in the raw of the wound. *His,* she wanted to cry, *this thing inside me, it could be his.*

His hand ran gently down her side, across her waist. Then stopped at her middle.

Eyes on hers, he rested his palm on the rounded bulge there and drew her closer.

Only once did she see something flicker across his face—a question. And a storm behind it.

"Ours," he whispered into her ear. And then more fiercely, as if the strength of the word might assure that it would be true. *"Ours."*

Dinah shuddered in his arms but did not pull away. And waited until she could raise her face back up to his and smile.

"Ours," she agreed. "Ours."

God, if only she could know for sure that was true. If only.

Her right hand still grasping the cup by her side, she gripped it harder, its contents sloshing only a little.

Tom covered her mouth in a kiss, and she sank against him for one final moment. "You got to go," he said hoarsely.

She ran a finger down the strong line of his jaw. "You too."

He caught the finger, wrapped it in his. *"Ours."*

With a final brush of his cheek, she flung herself back into the dusk of East Bay, and with one jerk of her right arm, she hurled the cup across the cobbles as she ran, even as a carriage careened toward her down the street.

Chapter 16

2015

With the jangling of its harness and the clopping echo of its Clydesdale's hooves, the carriage rolling to the curb pulled Kate's attention from the two men and Gabe chasing one another in and out of the fountain.

"Rebellion has often found root in this city," the carriage driver was saying. Kate stepped back from the fountain to hear as he formed his words tentatively, perhaps not firm enough yet in his memory for airing. "During the American Revolution by the patriots who chafed under British rule. Before the Civil War by the slaves who dreamed of freedom."

He stopped to take a question from one of his passengers.

"These bolts in our houses she's asking about," he repeated for the group. "Earthquake bolts they're called, and they held Charleston's buildings together when the city was too poor to tear anything down after the Civil War and for decades following. While Boston and New York demolished the old and erected the new, Charleston had no choice but to keep, by whatever means, its structures standing. Which is how, ladies and gentlemen, our former poverty gave us the largest and architecturally richest historic district in the United States."

The driver pointed back up Vendue.

"And if you can see back up the street to the corner, it was a joiner's shop next door to a blacksmith, both shops run by slaves hired out by their white owners. And the crates and coffins that the joiner made . . ."

Something about what the guide said before the carriage rolled forward caught Kate's attention—some link in a chain she couldn't quite see. She drew out her scrap paper and scribbled:

Next door, a joiner—made crates, coffins.

Passing the fountain, where Scudder, Daniel, and Gabe were playing leapfrog at the edge of the spray, Kate pried off the heel of each of her Keds with the toe of her other shoe and felt the pier's boards warm and smooth beneath her bare feet.

Every thirty feet or so on the pier hung bench swings long enough for six people. A family of five sprawled, squealing and crawling over one another, on the swing just up ahead. Two teenagers on a swing at the end of the pier fit themselves to each other's bony angles. Clumps of people wandered hand in hand, the last of the sun's glow slipping past the wharf pilings.

Two police officers strolled the length of the wharf, one of them redheaded and round-faced, grinning and nodding at every person they passed—and calling several by name. The other was built in hard, muscular squares, like a tower of concrete blocks. Even his head, with his hair flat across in a crew cut, was a square that sat directly on top of his shoulders.

At the edge of the very center of Waterfront Park, a short balding man, a green Celtics T-shirt hanging loose from his frame, had set up a tripod and camera and was photographing the harbor, pelicans balanced on the wharf pilings and gulls swooping low over the harbor, its ripples tipped with gold. Every minute or so, the photographer shifted a bag at his feet that was exploding with lenses and at least one other camera.

Not sure she should stay, but with no reason but a tall stack of books in an empty motel room to convince her to go, Kate dug again in her pocket for the scrap of paper and this time turned it to its back, to the blank side. Twilight fuzzed the lines of the pier and the sea. But the boardwalk was lit nicely by lanterns, and the fountain glowed in the gaslight, the last of the children coaxed out of the water by mothers holding towels open to wrap shivering forms. Daniel and Scudder and Gabe dropped, winded, in a pile on the ground, one on top of the other, like puppies, the spray of the fountain glistening on their skin.

Kate roughed out the fountain, the figures, the sheer play of the scene. Her chest ached again.

Gabe abruptly leapt up and ran full speed at a tall figure in a dark suit, the white of his clerical collar bright against the dark of the man's skin, a young girl on either side of him, holding his hand. Daniel and Scudder jogged to meet the clergyman and the girls, the group of them exchanging hugs and handshakes. Kate included that, too, the way the rounding out of the clergyman's cheeks pushed his wire-rimmed glasses up on his nose when he smiled.

The sketching had begun when she was small. Her mother would scour ball-field grime off Kate's cheeks on Saturday evenings. Up the steps to Mass she hauled Kate, Sarah Grace's face still pretty, but strained now, caved in under the cheeks by the big-fisted hardness of life.

But inside the nave, Sarah Grace's stooped shoulders straightened, her head lifting as she collapsed to the kneeler. Kate had wanted to draw her mother's face at these times, preserve the look of the woman she didn't know, the one not eaten away by despair and regret.

Afterward they would return to the house, where Kate would curl up with a sketch pad while her mother dozed on the couch, splinters of the liturgy cutting through the thin skin of her sleep. Ink pen in one hand, her pad clutched in the other, Kate let her fingers teach her about life: the shadows and sharp, unlovely angles of even the kindest, gentlest figure. The lines of a face that spoke loudly of pain, even with the mouth still. As a child, Kate had first sketched the truth in charcoal before she'd let herself actually see it: her mother collapsed on the couch, one hand flopped with its fingertips just brushing the floor.

"You're really good," said a voice over Kate's shoulder, making her jump.

Leaning farther forward, Scudder Lambeth dripped water from his hair onto her shoulder. "You're actually *very* good."

Gabe sprinted past, laughing, his father in hot pursuit.

"No, I—"

He held up his hand. "I hate false modesty in anyone, but especially women. You always give your sketches Latin captions? *Pacem*," he read.

"What?" Kate held up the sketch to the glow of the lamppost. Sure enough, she'd penciled in the word she'd been remembering her mother whisper those nights after Mass, *Pacem*—sometimes with longing or hope but more often like a frightened child's question: *Peace?*

Scudder Lambeth tilted his head at her. "Have you always liked to draw?"

Looking down at the sketch, Kate nodded. She could see her mother asleep after Mass on the couch, with Kate sketching on through the night and lining out what she had seen so far of the world: most of it more dark than light, more pain than peace.

"So is this what you do, Kate? For a living, I mean."

"No. Oh, no. I mean, I guess I thought about that sometimes as a kid. I had a fifth-grade teacher who thought that's what I should be— the marvelous Mrs. Saucie, who wore black Converse high-tops with all her skirts." Kate smiled at the memory. "And my mom thought I'd be an artist when I grew up. But she wasn't a very practical soul. Never very focused on minor details like paying the bills."

Glancing up now to the father and son chasing each other, Kate turned to say something to Scudder.

But Daniel had flipped Gabe upside down by the ankles. And Gabe, the tips of his fingers and the ends of his curls brushing the boards of the pier, was laughing and waving at them both to come play.

Scudder gave a little salute. "Good seeing you, Kate. I am, however, being summoned by a higher authority."

"Hey, before you go, sorry, it's probably none of my business, but sometimes Gabe mentions his mom—seems like a lot, in fact. But I thought he told me she'd . . ."

Scudder frowned. "Talking about her in the present tense?"

"Well, yeah."

"He started that lately, talking like she's around. And he's taken to running off sometimes out of the blue, days he's missing her extra. She died two years ago this fall, from cancer."

Daniel was twirling his son by the wrists now, Gabe's little legs splayed out as he spun.

"I'm so sorry," Kate said.

"That's where Gullah Buggy came from. She was always telling Dan he ought to go on the road with his stories and songs, and then for her funeral he hired a horse and old-fashioned rig to carry the casket, and all of us mourners walking behind—like the old days. With all the medical bills that piled up, Dan's been working two jobs and going to school and raising Gabe. Had his hands full."

Kate nodded, picturing Beecher pulling a coffin, little Gabe's head hanging low, his daddy holding his hand, Scudder beside them, and a river of mourners marching slowly behind.

"I guess I should be getting back," she said at last. "Pages to go before I sleep and all that." Reluctantly, she turned away.

"Hey. Kate."

She half turned back.

"You've got the advantage on me. You know what Daniel—and Gabe—do for a living, and me. I'm not sure I know what you do. Since it's not art."

"I'm here researching . . ."

Her words trailed off as her gaze rested on Gabe, who'd wandered away from his father several yards. Daniel had answered a cell call, and Kate could make out the strained patience in his voice: "Yes, and we will

143

certainly check on the shipping confirmation. I can assure you, though, that I did mail your order on the date we agreed . . ."

Gabe, meanwhile, had cocked his head at the photographer's bag of lenses. Little by little, the child was inching closer.

∽

The man with the camera hanging down his front like a big necklace and a camera on a silver tripod had his back to them. On the ground a few yards away sat a bag full of gadgets and lenses and all sorts of things the man fit on his cameras and spun and clicked like puzzles you had to line up just right. Gabe took a step closer to see better. He could make out the man's arms jutting out on either side of the tripod, scrawny and white as birch sticks. The man's head ticked back, his eyes narrowing on Gabe.

"Don't even *think* about stealing that bag, boy," the man growled.

Ignoring him—Gabe knew you didn't pay a man any mind when he called you *boy* in that tone—he thought of his own daddy's arms, thick and strong as the steel cables they tied up the cruise ships to the wharf with. Gabe's arms might be on the stick side themselves for now, but he was his daddy's boy, everyone said. He'd be a big man like his daddy one day, and not long from now. And a good man, that's what he'd be. A strong man and a good one, both like his daddy—but also one who liked to do math. Even someday when he'd be topping six five, he'd keep a Rubik's Cube in his pocket.

Even if he was mayor of Charleston, he'd keep the cube in his pocket, Gabe promised himself. Or leader of the Free World. You could do that now with brown skin. Or whatever color you had. So long as you knew whole mountains of facts about any ole thing somebody might ask, like how many euros went to the dollar today or how many hours of math more every week kids in China did than kids in the

United States—although you didn't see China sending kids to the NFL draft, now, did you?

No matter what he became when he grew up, a Rubik's Cube would stay in his pocket to help him stay calm. Help him sort out the mess people caused themselves.

Lord, Pastor Clem would say from the carved wooden block of a pulpit the boy loved to study from down below, *the mess people can cause themselves.* And he'd smile at them with affection, with tenderness, too, all his flock fanning themselves in their pews, but he'd wipe his forehead right clear across, like even the thought of the mess people caused was wearing his good-shepherd self out.

"The *mess,*" the boy said aloud in his best basement voice, "people cause."

A hand on his shoulder made the boy jump.

"Now wouldn't that be the truth, Gabe."

The boy pitched back his head to stare up into the clergyman's. "Hey again."

Clementa Pinckney smiled—the kind of smile that blew a warm wind over whatever it was you were thinking, making some of the grit and the grudge of your thoughts spin away.

"What," Pastor Clem wanted to know, "did I catch you in the middle of thinking?"

Gabe tipped his head in the direction of the photographer, who turned to glower every few moments. "Thinking how some people are real hard to think holy about."

Pastor Pinckney's own eyes followed Gabe's and then crinkled into a smile. "You know, people over the age of thirteen, if a preacher asks what they're thinking, they make up something extra special sanctified sounding—right out of thin air. It can wear on a man."

"What if I said I don't much like the looks of some people?"

The hand Clem Pinckney had placed on his shoulder grew heavier now. "Then I'd say that I see what you mean."

"You do?"

"And I'd tell you that changes nothing about how we should treat him if he came to us for help. We welcome the stranger. That's what we do."

Gabe crossed his arms but made himself look back up at Clem Pinckney's face. Even the mustache that dusted the man's lip was gentle, and so was the warmth in his eye. His voice went booming from the pulpit and smacked you up straight in your pew to listen—a little scared, too. In the statehouse also, they said, his voice could go crashing big. And make whatever senators napping that day bolt upright, ready to vote—even before they'd woken up good enough to think for themselves—vote with the nice, gentle man with the big boom of a voice.

"Yes, sir," Gabe said. But he didn't much mean it. He liked keeping hold of the feeling of not liking the photographer man with the cue ball for a head.

"I'll see you soon, son. You tell your granddaddy hello."

Gabe hugged the preacher hard around the waist. Pulling the Rubik's Cube from his pocket again, he twirled the lines of squares on their axes, his fingers flying. Then stuffed it back in his pocket.

The bag of lenses and gadgets was wide open on the ground. And the photographer man's back was turned. So it probably wouldn't hurt just to step closer. Gabe knew not to touch, but a step closer would mean he could maybe make out how they worked.

"Hey! You!"

Bent over the bag, Gabe lifted his head at the shout.

"Get the *hell* away from my bag, you little thief!" the man roared and ran straight at Gabe.

Gabe's heart stopped.

Panicked, he reached in his pocket for what always helped him calm down.

"Gun!" the bald photographer guy was screaming. *"Police! He's got a gun!"*

More shouts and the cops running and Gabe's daddy leaping and a terrible bang.

~

Kate screamed as Daniel dove in front of his son, the balding man lunging for Gabe, and there was some sort of crash.

Gabe hit the brick pavers, his father falling on top of him. The photographer's dash past his tripod had unbalanced it, and a long-lensed camera lay in hundreds of glass and black shards.

The cops arrived panting, gripping their Tasers. "Where's the gun?" the younger, stockier one demanded.

"Yanked the damn thing out just now!" the balding man screeched.

The older cop spun to the boy, who was still on the ground. A plastic cube of colored squares tumbled from Gabe's hand.

For several seconds stretched long, everyone stared.

Fist on one hip, the older cop reached out a hand to help Gabe to his feet and rounded on the balding man. "Is *this* the weapon you saw?"

"A kid slinks over to steal my gear and then goes for his weapon, I'm gonna kick his black ass."

Daniel sprang from the ground. "A *ten-year-old* got within two feet of your stuff and then reached into his pocket for a *toy!*"

Clem Pinckney laid a restraining hand on Daniel's arm. Slowly, carefully, the clergyman pulled off his glasses, dusted the lenses with the cuff of his shirt, and returned them to his nose as the rest of them watched. "Officer Mulligan," he addressed the older cop, then the younger: "Officer Hale. Thank you for coming so quickly." He nodded at the guns in their holsters. "And for your restraint in not utilizing your firearms. I wonder if you two gentlemen would be good enough to attend to our friend here and what's left of his camera."

One hand on Daniel's shoulder, the other taking Gabe's hand, the clergyman steered them to the side, back toward the fountain. In angry jerks, Daniel tugged his T-shirt back over his head and wrapped Gabe tightly in a striped towel.

Kate was still trembling. "What was *that*?"

Daniel spun toward her, fury still sparking in his eyes and landing on her. "What was that, you want to know? What was *that*? I'll tell you, Kate Drayton. *That* is the world I live in—the one I'm raising a son in!"

Stricken, Kate backed up a step and opened her mouth, but no sound came out.

"It's the world you live in, too, but when you're white and female and just popping down for a quick visit from your ivory tower, you don't have to know that, do you?"

Kate swallowed.

Gabe spun his Rubik's Cube frantically and kept his head down, Pastor Clem's hand on his shoulder.

"I think . . . ," Scudder began after a moment.

Daniel let out a long breath through his nose. "I didn't mean to lash out at you, Kate. What I was trying to say—"

"Was that our world's not always a fair place," she suggested quietly. "Less fair and less safe for some people than others. And sometimes, some of us need reminding of that. Like maybe I did tonight."

The line of his jaw softening, Daniel nodded. Then held up a fist to bump Kate's.

Daniel walked on ahead with Gabe and Clem, Kate lingering behind as they passed the fountain, the lights of East Bay set back a block from the park.

Something was shifting around in her memory—some fact that wouldn't yet move to the front or some pairing of thoughts that would not yet link.

∾

Kate could see Sarah Grace bending over her little daughter's birthday-party guest list, Kate proud of being able to spell out the names for herself in large block letters. Sarah Grace had read the list aloud in a pleasant, distracted way: "Kay, Greg, Benita, Ginger, Milton, Beth, Davey, Lib, Jason, Paula, Suzanne, James, Alan, Tiffany, Susan, Walter, Joyce . . ."

But then she'd looked up. "These are all the children in your class except T. J."

"I'm not inviting T. J." Kate had tossed back her braids.

Sarah Grace's eyes had blazed. "You're telling me you're not inviting the only little boy in your class who is black?"

Kate had been startled by her momma's eyes—Sarah Grace rarely got mad. But Kate crossed her arms and planted her feet. "He's just not my friend."

"Has he done anything mean to you?"

"Nope. He's all right, I guess. Just not my friend. Not inviting him to my party."

Sarah Grace's eyes filled then—for no reason that Kate could make out.

"Did it ever occur to you, Katie, it might be your fault, his not being your friend?"

Kate flipped back her braids again. "Don't care. Not inviting T. J. to my party."

Hand shaking, Sarah Grace reached for the list. "Then you're not having a party." She ripped the list down the middle.

Sarah Grace stalked to the other side of the kitchen, then turned. And Kate was relieved, her momma likely to say she was sorry now for losing her temper for no reason at all.

Instead, Kate's momma put her hands—which were still shaking—onto her hips. "It ever occur to you, Katie, how T. J. might feel?" she demanded—almost a shout. "And T. J.'s momma?"

Kate stormed into their tiny living room and yanked out a paper and pen to calm herself down. "Don't know why I'm supposed to give a *damn*"—she shrieked that last word so her momma could hear her first grader's fury—"about T. J.'s momma."

It was a memory out of nowhere, not something she'd thought of for years. And even now, there was something that needed linking together.

If she could only figure out what.

She dug out the scene she'd sketched earlier from her pocket and flipped it to its backside—to the words she'd jotted down when the carriage driver was giving his tour.

"*Coffins,*" she read out loud. "Oh my God. *Coffins.*"

Just a half pace ahead, Scudder turned back. "Did I miss something?"

"A carriage driver who passed a minute ago was telling his group that in the early nineteenth century, a maker of coffins used to operate there beside a blacksmith. Coffins. Next door to the blacksmith. Just in case you had things or people or weapons, in addition to corpses, you needed to move. In secret. With your life depending on the secret."

Chapter 17

By the light of only one candle, the forge's single window smudged with soot, Tom eased the pikes five at a time into the coffin. Here in the wee hours of morning, the sun long from up, he could afford to make no sound at all. Not while the city still slept.

Twenty-five. Thirty. Thirty-five.

Rumbling outside on East Bay. Tom's heart stopped.

But the wagon rolled on. Firewood delivery maybe.

Forty. Forty-five. Fifty.

Fifty would be all for now. Half of the pikes Vesey had already paid for. Money that Tom had passed along to the widow Russell, with a story about a young farmer up past the Neck just starting out with ready cash but no tools. She'd been glad enough to see the unexpected income, gave him a small portion back, and asked no questions at all.

Greed, it turned out, could be made to work in one's favor.

Carefully, Tom closed the coffin's pine lid on the hinges he'd crafted but did not nail it shut. He paced the floor of the forge. Peered out the windows at the front of his shop.

At first, nothing.

Then, from far north on East Bay, came the sway of a single lantern in the dark.

Tom opened the door a crack to listen.

Wooden wheels across the East Bay cobbles. A thin clatter of iron on stone: a single horse, not a team.

Suddenly the lantern rose higher, then plunged downward, then left, then right in a cross.

Tom unbolted the door at the side of the forge leading into Unity Alley.

The lantern went black as the wagon reached the mouth of the alley. Tom felt the horse's muzzle against his hand the same instant he could make out its shape.

Feeling their way, two men slid from the seat of the wagon. One of them hauled a barrel off the buckboard and pried its lid open to expose rice—that reeked. Plunging his hand down into the rice, he pulled out the limp, bloody form of a dead chicken.

Now both men slipped through the forge door behind Tom. By the light of the one candle, they circled the coffin.

Tom covered his nose and mouth with one hand and stepped back from the stench.

"Got to be done," said the man who'd opened the barrel. Lifting the lid of the coffin a few inches, he tossed in the carcass.

Tom held his breath against the nausea that rose from his stomach up to his throat. "How long that old hen been dead?"

"Long enough to do what we need it to do." He lifted his end of the coffin and grunted.

The second man smirked. "Few pokers too heavy for you, Mingo?"

"You wait 'til you feel it."

The second man lifted his end of the coffin and grunted.

"What'd I tell you?"

"What'd you pack in here, Tom? Whole armory?"

"Be dayclean by the time we get this thing to the wagon, you keep moving like that."

With Tom hoisting the center of the box onto his left shoulder, the three of them slid the coffin onto the wagon.

The first man shook his head. "Smell it from here."

"Mm-hmm. Lord Almighty give it a powerful stench. As a gift."

"Some gift."

"Shhh!"

The three men did not move as they listened for footsteps on the street. For voices too close. Anything.

The man called Mingo hissed the next words. "We either get this nag backing up this heap of a cart or our little play's up."

One step, then two, the horse backed up, harness straining.

The shells of the alley crunched beneath the wagon's wheels.

Then hoofbeats on the cobbles. A trot. Brisk. Official.

A horse and rider, a lantern clutched in one hand, the other holding his reins, appeared at the corner of East Bay and Unity Alley.

Tom braced. This could be the end of their planning right here. The end of them.

"Well, now." From his perch on the horse, the patroller spit tobacco at Tom's feet. "I got to tell you, I don't much like the looks of this here kind of secretlike meeting."

Tom's hands closed in a vise on the harness traces, every muscle in him tensed. He did not breathe.

The buggy creaked as someone stepped down from it in the dark. "Yes, sir." It was Ned, adopting his most lowly, servile tone, the role he played to reassure nervous whites. "That's surely right now. But course, we do got the allowance of burying. And a real faithful servant of Governor Bennett—you know how faithful us in Governor Bennett's house is—he cross over three days done gone. Lord say it time to bury." A scuffling of feet on the crushed shell.

"Hold it right there, boy. Can't you people tell time?"

Ned's voice became still softer, gentler, his Gullah accent deepening. "Us working people most ways. Up before dayclean and past candle-lighting. Can't be grave-burying just any time we'd be wanting."

Tom Russell understood why Vesey had picked this Ned. Not for his physical strength, which wasn't impressive, but for his theatrical skills, his ability to manipulate his accent, his word choice—no doubt his face, too, if Tom could see it. The man was a born actor.

The patroller shifted in his saddle, its leather creaking, and he spit. "At three thirty in the damn morning?"

"Got buckruh to serve breakfast. Got firewood for delivering. Got to bury them what cross over on we own time."

"Hell, let the dead bury their own dead." The rider snorted at his own joke. No one else spoke. "Any of you boys heard of what gets called the African Methodist Episcopal Church?" The rider exaggerated his pronunciation of these last words, like a language that was foreign and strange but amused him.

A pause. Then Ned's voice again. "Reverend Morris Brown be a fine, God-fearin' man of the cloth."

"Mm-hmm. Well, I don't much care for his church. Hotbed of trouble, you and your type"—he spit tobacco to one side—"off there in the Neck with nobody overseeing."

Nobody white, Tom thought. That's what the patroller meant.

"Ain't allowed's what I'm saying. This preacher Brown, he the one leading this funeral of yours? 'Cause I know you ain't holdin' no funeral without no preacher man."

"Reverend Morris, he don't know our friend here's died yet."

"Thought you'd said it'd been three days."

"Oh, yes, sir. It has. But Reverend Morris, he didn't know. Old hen"—Ned cleared his throat—"Old Henry here, he wasn't the most churchgoing creature you ever met."

With a great heaving noise, the patroller spit again. "Well, then, I reckon you boys'd be on your way to wake up the preacher man for this funeral of yours."

"Oh, yes, sir. That's right where we's headed."

"Then you won't mind if I come along to watch, now, will you?"

"Well, now. Glad to have you."

Tom's blood surged inside his chest, his neck throbbing.

The light from the marshal's lantern suddenly swung in a broad half circle. "You. Blacksmith. I never heard you was part of Brown's church. I keep an eye on who is and who ain't. Nothin' but a tinderbox waitin' to blow, you people thinking you can meet separate."

Ned spoke up quickly, a hand on Tom's shoulder. "Tom Russell here, he's what you might call under conviction. We been welcoming him into our fellowship just lately."

A pause. "How come you ain't got no more people'n these here for this funeral?" the patroller demanded.

Mingo's voice lacked the soothing molasses of Ned's. "How many folk you reckon come to your funeral?"

"Boy, I sure would hate anything real tragic to happen to you. Built a whole workhouse in the city for just that kind of uppity attitude."

Ned's voice eased in again, the Gullah accent he'd put on thicker than ever and soothingly soft. "You got to excuse Mingo here, him agonize he bone—terrible weary. When Old Henry cross over, it 'bout broke Mingo's heart. Now we got to tend to the dead 'fore the buckruh crack they teeth."

"Reckon Mingo here'd appreciate me coming along then. Wouldn't you, Mingo, boy? Add to the number of mourners. Let's go wake us up a preacher man. Reckon I'd like to see for myself how you people bury one of your own kind."

A slap of the buggy reins on the horse's hide. The creak and jangle and clank of the buggy rolling forward.

Heart pounding, allowing himself to think of nothing but the road directly ahead, Tom fell into step with Mingo behind the wagon, its jangle and clank jolting the stillness.

～

Morris Brown was still buttoning his shirt as the buggy's lanterns rocked wildly, its wheels bumping into the pitted terrain of Potter's Field.

Ned adjusted the reins. "Sorry we had to go dragging you out of bed for this funeral, Reverend."

"You did right. I'm sorry I cannot say I recollect this Henry you've described. I thought I knew my flock better. It's worrisome to have one whose name I don't even recall."

Ned Bennett cleared his throat. Lowered his voice. "Didn't much darken the door of your church. But sure thought highly of you. Dying words was 'Get me that remarkable Reverend Brown. There's a man acquainted with mercy.'"

Morris Brown studied Ned's face by the jumping light of the lanterns. "I see. This Henry was an articulate man, was he?"

The patroller riding alongside them reined in his horse. "Damn well better get a move on."

Mingo Harth skirted the front of the wagon. Snatched a lantern from its hook and two shovels from its bed.

By the lantern light, Tom saw Morris Brown's gaze rest on him.

"Tom here," Ned offered, "was especial close to the deceased."

Morris Brown held out his hand. "You are most welcome, Tom Russell," he said, as if it were the most natural thing in the world for the blacksmith to be there.

But Tom took his hand and was grateful for the steady calm in Morris Brown's eyes.

The patroller spit tobacco at Morris Brown's feet. "How about we get movin' here, Preacher? I got me better things to be doing with my time than listen to you jabber to thin air."

Ned in the lead, they marched ten paces through the field infested with weeds toward a scrub pine, where Mingo set the lantern down. "Right here's good as any. Best dig it shallow, or we'll be here, all us, slam to sun-lean."

The patroller slumped deeper into his saddle, his jawbone swallowed in fat. "Just get it done."

~

The four men, including Tom and the reverend, took turns digging the grave, a cloud of white dust rising from the desiccated ground—and Tom's pulse rising with the dust. Moment by moment, they were growing closer to having to bury the coffin—and with it, the weapons.

Ned placed a hand on Morris Brown's, which was gripping the shovel. "You commence preaching, Reverend. We'll finish the hole."

Dusting off his shirtsleeves, Morris Brown glanced toward the mounted patrolman a few yards away. "O Lord of mercy as broad as the sea. And of justice that rolls down like rivers."

The deep current of the clergyman's voice swept on, eddies of sound forming themselves into words.

"We grieve this night, Lord, the loss of our brother."

The patroller's eyelids were beginning to drop.

"But let us not grieve as those who have no comfort. Let us not grieve as those without hope."

The patroller's chin sank toward his chest.

"For it's not death, Lord, you say we ought to be fearing."

Mingo and Ned, their eyes on the patroller, lowered the coffin slowly, slowly into the hole, both of them straining to keep their grip.

Suddenly slipping from Mingo's hands, one end of the coffin fell.

With a heavy metallic crash.

The patroller snapped his head up.

And thrust the mouth of his gun toward Tom's gut.

Chapter 18

Checking her watch to be sure there was still time to read on before appearing at Rose Pinckney's, Kate scanned the archives' inventory of the Russell household's belongings, written sometime before 1820, the year Nathaniel Russell died: the delftware, the sideboards and armoires and dining table and sterling, the rugs and commissioned portraits and two carriages . . . and name after name of women and children and men.

There was Tom Russell's name. Bottom of the second page. In elaborate handwriting more appropriate for an invitation to a grand ball than a household property list.

Tom, capable, docile, quiet, in good health, not yet twenty-five years, already a skilled blacksmith.

Kate's pulse sped up. Something about seeing his name handwritten there made him seem more real somehow than merely reading it in a published history. Here, someone, probably Nathaniel but possibly Sarah Russell, had penned his name. Would have added the "docile, quiet" with no inkling of what the young Tom was actually feeling—that by the spring of 1822, he would be crafting weapons for a slave revolt that, if all plans went well, would be the most far-reaching in American history.

Jotting notes, Kate turned the page.

On the fourth sheet, Tom's name appeared again.

Mary, mother of Tom, sold in private sale to Drayton Hall. Insubordination.

Kate sat back hard in her chair. Drayton Hall. Her family name. Coupled there with the severing of a slave mother from her son.

Nathaniel Russell, a native of Rhode Island, Kate had just read, had made his fortune as a shipping merchant, trading all sorts of consumer goods, including slaves. In the language of a ship's captain, he had found Tom's mother's behavior unacceptable, *insubordinate*, and had relegated her to . . . what? The fields?

Kate's stomach churned.

On her laptop, Kate called up the website for Drayton Hall: a former rice plantation built in the eighteenth century on the banks of the Ashley River. Open to the public—with a still-tended slave burying ground.

Kate made a note of Drayton Hall's location just a few miles out from town, scanned the last page of the Russell family's folder, adjusted the gloves she was required to wear, and shifted to a letter, written in 1822, from a family close to the Russells. The mistress of the house appeared to be the author, the size of her handwriting growing, engorged, the words spilling over with both bile and regret as her hand covered the page.

> *A curse—to master and slave. Or shall I say more accurately, mistress and slave. God help us. Can we not all see the light skin of the servants in our neighbors' homes, yet are blind to the selfsame thing in our own?*

Kate paused to rub her eyes, which were beginning to blur, with the back of her wrist. Wearing the white gloves the archives required had its challenges. And hours of trying to decipher the smudged ink on yellowed paper of several dozen unfamiliar hands was taking its toll.

> *Will not the Divine Judge, who has made all men*
> *of one blood to dwell on the face of the earth, burn away*
> *the evils?*

Typical, Kate thought. Another white woman from the slaveholding class who was fairly clear-eyed about the horrors of slavery for everyone concerned—and could throw in a biblical quote like this to back up her sense of revulsion and wrong. But would not say a word—except in privacy, to a trusted correspondent or a diary.

Kate stopped there and, making notes for the next day's research on where she'd stopped, closed the folder.

A creak just outside the door of the South Carolina Room made her jump.

The processing archivist poked her head through the door. "Gone cross-eyed yet?"

"Two hours ago."

"Happy to hear it. Means you'd not be wasting your time here. Or mine. Didn't you tell me this morning when you came in—you and the Starbucks you were trying to hide behind the backpack . . . oh yes, I did see—that you had a meeting with Rose Pinckney set up for this morning at ten thirty?"

Checking the time again, Kate rose and stretched. "Think it'll take me longer than ten minutes to walk from here to the south tip of Meeting Street?"

"Mm-hmm. And let me tell you, that is one woman I would not be late for. Except for the rich and the white, Miz Rose reminds me of my own momma: got honey in the voice and steel in the eye."

∼

Following the walking map on her phone, Kate jogged, sometimes slowing to speed-walk some of the dozen or so city blocks. At the last stretch of Meeting Street before the Battery, and beyond it the ocean, she stopped to yank off her sandals, their straps cutting into her skin. She finished the journey barefoot, sandals in hand.

At Rose's address, a pair of brick staircases curved up like two arms to its front portico, rounded and plump. The piazzas on its left side were stacked one on top of the other, its cupola top like a tiny beret. With a start, she recognized the house as the one Scudder Lambeth had walked across from the inn to work on. So he must be connected with Rose Pinckney, too, just like Daniel Russell had mentioned her as a longtime customer. Everyone here seemed linked somehow to everyone else.

Except for me, Kate couldn't help but add—and hated how pathetic it sounded in her head. *Always on the outside of the circle, looking in.*

She mounted one side of the paired stairs. The beige clapboard frame sat quiet—a stark contrast to the hubbub of tourists in gold-fringed carriages and the occasional sightseeing van that rounded from the harbor, passengers gasping over the gardens and mansions.

Mrs. Lila Rose Manigault Pinckney herself flung open the door before Kate could knock. "I've always said Charleston appears at her best just after a rain, and today she's all dolled up in glitter. I am *so* glad you've come."

Rose's gaze dropped once, but only once, to the sandals Kate clutched and to her bare feet. One silver eyebrow arched high, Rose led the way without comment up a graceful sweep of broad stairs as Kate, ramming the sandals back on, stumbled after her. Just past the stairs' landing, French doors opened onto a porch clustered with white wicker beneath hanging ferns.

"Rose, you have a beautiful home."

"Built in 1809, dear. My husband, God rest his soul, insisted on only the finest preservation work. If I'd had as many parts guarded against age as this house, I'd be carded when buying my bourbon. Do be seated."

Kate hesitated at the long backless bench, painted black, with rocking bases at both ends.

"It's called a joggling board, sugar, and every home—*of any import*—here in Charleston has one on its piazza that was passed down at least five generations. They're part of a game, a mating ritual here. One lowers oneself onto the board—gracefully, of course, and with poise—in such a way as to joggle oneself closer to whichever beau one has strategically arranged to sit nearest."

Rose motioned to a white wicker table spilling over with pastries and breads. "A kind of midmorning repast, all from here in the Low Country: Carolina rice scones—with watermelon-rind preserves and just-the-right-kind-of-sour crab-apple jelly. And here we have homemade granola with benne seeds and pecans and Charleston-grown tea." Rose motioned with a wrinkled hand, her long fingers still delicate, graceful. "I assume you've had a good many?"

Kate lowered herself onto a white wicker love seat and tugged at her sundress, crumpled beneath her. "Many . . . ?"

"Beaux, dear. Suitors. You're not lacking in beauty. Though admittedly, your manners—no doubt owing to your being raised in the North—can be rather abrupt, you know. The want of good manners, however, can be easily tweaked; the want of a good chin cannot."

Kate's mouth twitched. "No one in particular. Unless you count some guys along the way with a string of graduate degrees apiece but no income."

"Lines, my dear, must be drawn." Rose poured the tea. "So you are not—how do the young people say it these days?—*talking* with anyone? The term makes no sense at all in this usage, you know."

Kate bit into a scone. "Truth is, I have no interest in *talking* with anyone at this stage of my life." She paused, little Gabe's face flashing into her mind: the curls that fell over his eyes, the thick of his lashes as he looked up into her eyes. "Unless he's younger than twelve and it's actually talking." She lifted a china saucer with a blue-and-white pagoda on it. "This is nice."

"It's come down in the family, sugar. The whole set has been buried twice in the backyard. Once from the British and once from the Yankees." Rose eyed Kate a moment as if she just might abscond with a plate.

The porch doors groaned at the entrance of a housekeeper balancing a tray with two sterling tumblers at its center.

"Ah, the juleps. Thank you, Marguerite."

"Rose, I was wondering . . ."

Rose Pinckney waited, brow raised, as Kate lifted the sterling to her lips.

"Oh!" Kate fought back a grimace. "They are . . . *wow.*"

"Criminally sweet?"

"Yes. Actually."

"Breathtakingly strong?"

"Well . . ."

"Perfectly vile?"

Kate laughed. *"Yes."*

Rose nodded. "I could not agree more. And this after a lifetime of trying to stomach the things. They're nothing but pulverized mint, crushed ice, a stultifying shower of sugar, and enough bourbon to submerge the *Hunley* again—our Civil War submarine, of which we are unreasonably proud." She raised a tumbler. "So, Katherine Drayton . . ."

"I go by Kate."

"So what *do* you think of Charleston?"

"It's gorgeous. Honestly, I'm enchanted and appalled at the same time."

"*Appalled*, dear?"

"You know, because of the history. And even . . ." Kate saw again Gabe by the fountain that night, the boy reaching into his pocket for his Rubik's Cube—and nearly flattened for supposedly having a gun. But Charleston was hardly the only city where this kind of thing happened. Far from it, which was part of Daniel's point. Maybe you just felt the weight of it more, standing in the port city where a good half of the slaves brought into the country had entered. Maybe it felt like layers and layers of something slow to peel off. Kate considered a moment and went on. "But the architecture! Those funny little false doors that lead to these porches: as charming as anything I've ever seen."

Rose held up a hand. "*Single houses*, my dear. Architecture imported from Barbados to maximize the sea breezes on the *piazzas*—*not* porches—and still keep a front door facing the street. Your father, of course"—Rose was watching her face—"would have encouraged every twist and turn of your research about Charleston."

"He wasn't exactly around to be telling me stories." She watched Rose's face in return. "As you may be aware."

But Rose's smile, static as an oil portrait, betrayed nothing.

"If anything, my father actively discouraged my research on the Low Country." Kate could still see him so clearly, the way he'd sat ramrod straight in Legal Sea Foods in Boston—preferring to take her to a public place the handful of times they'd met over the years, as if fearing what sort of scene she might make in private. That day at Legal, her first fall as a graduate student at Harvard, he'd asked her perfunctory questions: How did she like Cambridge? Was her apartment close to Harvard Square? What would her research emphasis be, or did she know yet?

He'd watched her warily throughout the dinner, as if any break in the conversation might allow her to go rogue and offer something he did not want to hear, like how Sarah Grace was doing.

In response to his last question, Kate had tried for a personal connection with him. "Early nineteenth-century Low Country Carolina is what I'm thinking—in part thanks to your side of the family, the Draytons of Charleston. And I feel like the Denmark Vesey revolt— all the people swept up in it, all that it represented—was *the* pivotal moment for Charleston. In a way, for the whole South. For the whole nation."

He'd listened, lips pressed hard together, the blue vein in the middle of his forehead beginning to pulse.

"This, I assume, is thanks to your mother," he'd spat. "Her obsession with reading about it. Let me assure you of this, Katherine: it's a history that can only hurt you."

Why? She wished now she'd demanded to know at the time. Longed now to shout at him: *Why did it hurt you so badly? And why did it destroy Sarah Grace?*

But Heyward DeSaussure Drayton did not tolerate misaligned thoughts, and Kate had never sat long enough in his presence to sort out the right words to ask. The few hours she'd spent with him in the past several years, she'd wanted to be the amiable daughter. The one he might want to see more of. Not the stubbornly independent offspring he'd always preferred to forget. Besides, she'd assumed she had time—decades of it—for sorting through words and demanding to know.

Frowning at the memory, Kate lifted her eyes to find Rose Pinckney studying her. Disconcerted, Kate asked the first question that popped into her head. "How was it exactly that you knew my father?"

"First and foremost, you should know that Charleston is a small town—of international fame—but a small town just the same, in which every house cat's name is known, at least in what we call South of Broad. Home to the oldest families. Do have another scone."

Kate's mouth full—too full, she realized too late—of the scone slathered in crab-apple jelly, she nodded.

"Our family trees are more vines, looping back into each other. I married a Pinckney, of course, but my maternal grandmother was also a Pinckney. Like the royalty of Europe, we've encouraged aristocratic inbreeding."

"To tell you the truth, Rose, in being here I feel a little disloyal to my mother, her having left. It always seemed she felt she *had* to leave, for some reason."

"Yes. Yes, of course, dear." Rose's eyes drifted out toward the harbor. Kate waited.

But Rose shifted abruptly in her wicker chair—and her train of thought. "This house predates the Late Unpleasantness. The War of Northern Aggression. You'll see, if you look straight through the French doors, that portrait that hangs over the sideboard. Emily is the lady's name."

Kate opened her mouth to try asking about her father again. But Rose had fixed her eyes determinedly on the portrait.

Rose gestured toward the painting. "She lived here, I should probably add. Do have a closer look, Katherine."

Kate stood and stepped through the doors. In a full-length portrait, a young woman's blue satin gown flowed in torrents from her waist to the floor. "Emily looks like she'd have some stories to tell."

"This was Emily's bedroom at the time, here on the second story, where the sea breezes could blow through in summer. A woman of 'surprising opinions,' they called her—the ones who did not say worse things of her."

"They?"

"Emily's diary reflects varying opinions about her from others. Particularly regarding her friendship with Angelina Grimké. Although I regret to say I only seem to have three-fourths of the volume here, the latter portion ripped away."

"Rose, do you have any idea what this journal—even if it is only three-fourths of one—would be worth to researchers? Primary source material on Angelina Grimké? She was such a prominent abolitionist, an early advocate of women's rights—the first woman to speak to a legislative body in the United States."

"But for our purpose here," Rose returned calmly, "she is merely a girl—about seventeen, I believe—and the confidante of Emily, whose story this is."

Sitting, Rose lifted a sheaf of letters from the table and ran her fingers over the twine that held them. On the table lay a small volume, its leather binding ragged with loose threads.

"Rose, I don't think these should be out here in the open air."

"Of course they shouldn't be, sugar."

Kate leaned forward conspiratorially. "But I'm grateful—*wicked grateful*, as we say in Boston—for the chance you're giving me to look at them."

"It may be that you are just the person with whom I might share some choice passages. I could read to you, as we both have time, over the next several weeks."

Kate hesitated. How long exactly would she be here? She'd tried saying *days* to Dr. Ammons, but he'd acted like that was nonsense. Told her to stay. Find some answers.

She itched to snatch up the journal and begin reading. Instead, she tried smiling. "I cannot wait to get started. If you're ready."

Unhurriedly, Rose reached for the small volume with the tattered binding, its back cover missing entirely. As she lifted the journal, she knocked a small stack of papers onto the piazza floor, these pages not yellowed like the rest, and with no words on them, only one long waving line changing color from black to blue to red to green on one page. And on another, a spiraling ladder of capital letters, like alphabet soup caught in a downward vortex.

Rose snatched up the pages. One silver eyebrow arched high like she was asking a question—whether Kate had been watching, perhaps.

Whatever the papers were, it was clear she did not want Kate to see them.

"The facts," Rose said, "are inconclusive at present. Until further work is done."

"Facts?"

"Are slippery things."

The pages with the spiraling ladder of capital letters disappeared in Rose's rolltop desk, which sat just inside the French doors. But what Kate had glimpsed looked strikingly like the illustrations she recalled from high school biology—textbook chapters on genetics: Mendel the clever monk and his peas.

Imperiously, Rose lifted one shoulder in a hint of a shrug. "I'm having my genetic code mapped." She paused, stiff and alert, as if preparing to fend off some unseen opposition.

"I think that's fairly common these days, actually."

"No." Rose's vehemence seemed to startle them both. She regained her composure. "This situation is less . . . usual, you might say. Some careful examination, however, becomes needful at a certain age, when one is faced with one's own not-too-distant demise and the disbursement of one's worldly goods. No small task, you know, sugar, to get it right: who is deserving of what. I am more sympathetic now with the pressures on the Almighty."

Kate lifted the mint julep to her mouth to hide a smile.

Rose flicked a blue-veined hand as if shooing away an annoyance, then settled herself back down into her wicker chair. "At any rate, you'd be amazed what an old silk cravat on which an ancestor perspired heavily can tell us." She propped the journal open on the wicker table. "If I may read, then, from the diary entry I was perusing when you arrived . . ."

A large florid script covered the journal's yellowed pages edge to frayed edge, as if its writer's thoughts were spilling faster than she could turn pages.

"Twenty-ninth of April, year of our Lord 1822," Rose read aloud.

"Today's month," Kate murmured, "nearly two hundred years ago."

"I've made a habit lately of reading the entry for the same date, or close thereabouts, in 1822." Rose's gaze flitted once to Kate before she read on:

Nina and I have agreed never to speak of what we overheard—may have overheard—in the blacksmith's shop on East Bay.

Yet I sometimes lie awake and wonder, What if even now we're plotted against, our throats about to be slit in our very beds?

Kate and Rose exchanged glances over the journal.

"Oh my God," Kate said.

Nonsense, Nina assures me. We simply misheard.

She has seen, she says, the way her mother makes the family servants regret the slightest word out of place—their legs and backs, even their mouths torn to shreds. On that, Nina is right. I myself was served tea by a Grimké servant whose iron headpiece included a bit such as I would not place on my horse. The servant had attempted escape.

Yet, I see a look in Dinah's eyes now that I've not seen before—full of fury, I think, and sometimes even contempt. Why I am subjected to this from my very own maid, I cannot say.

Some days I feel as if there were something welling up from under the harbor—as if a wave were swelling from deep underneath, and will soon crash down upon us.

Rose shut the journal gently, smoothing its cover and her linen skirt with one sweep of her arm. "Well, now. I suppose that is enough for our first day together, don't you?"

Kate sat stunned at the abrupt shift—as if Rose had dangled a life preserver in front of Kate's flailing, drowning form—the element for her research that might land her a final chance in the department—then blithely walked away.

She laid a hand on the old lady's arm. She was willing to beg. "Rose, don't stop there. Please. This sort of find is invaluable. I'd love us to read on. I'd love to know more. This could be really, really important." *Not just to the advancement of historical scholarship,* she wanted to add, *but to my survival in the department. The only place I really belong. If I belong anywhere.*

"Of course, dear. However, as you and I are only getting to know one another, let us proceed accordingly, with properly small steps, shall we?" Rose leveled her gaze, the old woman's eyes so pale, so nearly translucent, Kate had the odd sensation of seeing straight through them, even as Rose was seeing out.

Kate made herself nod. "Of course. It's your journal, Rose. And I'm grateful for the chance to look at it. I would so, so love to come back again." She risked adding, "Soon."

"I believe I would like that as well, Katherine. Do give me a way to contact you, won't you? And I'll be in touch."

Scanning the phone number that Kate jotted down, Rose Pinckney raised a julep tumbler as if in a toast. "Trust, my dear, is earned over time. Wouldn't you agree?"

And with that, Mrs. Lila Rose Manigault Pinckney saw her to the door.

Kate emerged onto Meeting Street, blinking against the sun. At the street's end, where it ran headlong into a swath of crushed shell and live oaks and, beyond that, the sea, sat the sprawling white inn where Percival Botts was staying.

Botts, who had yet to answer her calls.

Taking two steps at a time, Kate leapt up to the porch of the inn and rang for the innkeeper, who answered the door with a broad smile and the smell of vanilla about her.

"I'm sorry to bother you," Kate said. "I was scheduled to meet with one of the guests of your inn, but he failed to show up for our meeting. A Mr. Percival Botts. I just wanted to be sure he was all right."

The innkeeper bobbed her head. "Well, how sweet of you to check on Mr. Botts. The attorney you're meaning, right? As a matter of fact, dear, he seemed fit as a fiddle—for a man of his age, I mean—when he checked out yesterday afternoon. Bless his heart, I had to charge him for the room, since it was a last-minute issue that called him away. I do so hate to do that, but I couldn't very well rent the room. He did understand. So kind of you to check."

Yesterday afternoon. Which would have been right after he'd left Penina Moise. Right after, no doubt, seeing Kate there.

What was it he so wanted to avoid being asked about her father or about her mother or about their connections with—and their fears of—Charleston's past?

What was Botts wanting to hide?

Not caring what direction she walked but needing to think, Kate found herself at the City Market, with its stalls of T-shirts and sweetgrass baskets and porcelain magnolia mugs.

Replaying in her mind what she'd just heard, she collapsed onto a bench, around her the chatter and swirl of the market—the Gullah and Spanish and Mandarin Chinese, the rumble of horseshoes on pavement and the shuffle of tourists through the merchandise stalls—like the low churning of the sea a few blocks away.

Her gaze swinging out to the water, Kate thought of Tom's name on the list of Russell household possessions, his beginning to craft bayonets not long after the list had been penned. And Sarah Grace, her pages of notes and underlinings, all of them determined to prove that Tom

Russell, blacksmith and weapon maker, somehow survived that summer—the turmoil and violence that was coming.

Kate heard Rose's voice forming Emily's words again—Emily, who in that spring of 1822 must have sensed deep down what she would have never spoken aloud:

Some days I feel as if there were something welling up from under the harbor—as if a wave were swelling from deep underneath, and will soon crash down upon us.

Chapter 19

1822

The four men huddled under the trees froze.

Nothing moved. Nothing except for Morris Brown's Bible, one page lifting in a soft sea breeze.

"It's not death," Morris Brown said again, "we should fear."

Their eyes on the patroller, whose gun was still leveled on Tom, Mingo and Ned raised their shovels and gently began sifting the sandy soil onto the coffin's lid.

"When Shadrach, Meshach, and Abednego stepped into the fire, who was it they feared? Was it the approval of the king? Tell me now. Or was it the Lord?"

Mingo Harth looked up at the preacher. Shoveled again.

Dismounting, the patroller seated himself under a live oak and rested his gun on his knee, its mouth still pointing toward Tom.

"And when Daniel got dropped into that den for failing to obey the law of the land, was it the jaws of the lions he feared? Was it? Or was it the roar of the justice of Almighty God?"

The preacher's words came faster now, gathering force like the pull of a tide.

The patroller's chin sank back into the fleshy rolls of his neck.

"Here's who we have to fear: the one who said, 'I stand against those who cheat the worker of his wages, oppress the poor widow and the orphan child.'"

On the sermon rolled, wave upon wave, cresting and ebbing and cresting again.

Tom took his turn with the shovel, the burn and strain of his arms and back a welcome relief from the standing-still fear of wondering what the patroller might think to inspect.

The patroller's face was dropping now, parallel with the ground. The clay and the sand rumbled and shushed on the pine lid of the coffin.

"Here's who we have to fear: the one that tramples the wicked, the one makes ashes of the folks caring only for their own pockets."

One shovelful after the other refilled the hole. Crunch and toss and rumble. Rhythmic and steady. Crunch and toss and rumble.

"Help us, Almighty God. Give us hope."

Crunch and toss and rumble.

"Give us courage."

Crunch and toss and rumble.

"Teach us to look for the day when *your* will is done. When *your* kingdom comes."

At this, Ned tossed his next shovelful high in the air, shell and rock pummeling the new grave like distant thunder, a storm coming.

The patroller woke up with a start and a curse. Stretched. "Finished?" he yawned.

Morris Brown raised his head. "It is finished."

The patroller herding them from behind, the four men trudged back to the buggy and dropped the shovels into its bed.

Mingo Harth tipped his head toward Morris Brown. "You prayed for mercy. And we thank you for that, Reverend. You and your merciful God." He spat this last phrase.

Ned raised a restraining arm to Mingo's chest. "Enough for now, Mingo."

Mingo ignored him. "But here's what I got to offer back, Preacher. A curse. For every drop of blood shed by every slave ever lived in this city. A curse. And not just today. But generation to generation. From the fathers all handed down. A *curse*, Reverend, that's what I got to call down."

The patroller still a few yards away, twirling his pistol as he waited for them to check the harness traces, Morris Brown turned to the other three men. Looked Mingo Harth in the eye. And nodded.

"I cannot disagree with you. How could I when I look at the pain of this world?" Morris Brown's gaze swept over the three of them and rested finally on Tom. "I simply believe the curse will not have the last word."

The patroller whirled his horse then, reining the creature in only inches from Tom. "You know, blacksmith, there's something I don't like about the kind of slave who don't live at the quarters where he belongs. You live in the Neck, boy, am I right?"

Muscles twitching, Tom forced his gaze to stay on the ground. He nodded. But then—he could not stop himself this time—he raised his eyes to meet the patroller's.

Gripping his gun by its barrel, the patroller circled the firearm once over his head and brought its butt down on Tom's skull with a thundering crack.

Chapter 20

2015

The clang of iron on asphalt echoed up the street. She'd barely set foot on the sidewalk of East Bay when she heard her name—or a form of it.

"Katie, Katie, Kate!" On the first row of the passing carriage, a little boy had bounced to his feet, waving with both hands.

"Gabe!"

Laying a hand on his father's arm to rein in the horse, Gabe bounced on the seat. "Want to join us, Kate? We're near up to the end, so no charge." He turned to his father. "Right?"

Daniel nodded as Gabe leapt down from his seat, grabbed her hand, and tugged.

Kate shook her head. "It sounds great, but honestly, I've got so much more research to finish today and more appointments to set up. And I left all my notes spread out in the Special Collections archives. I wish I could."

Gabe gestured with his head toward the buggy, where his father stood waiting in the driver's seat. "Didn't you say you'd got some research-finding questions to ask me and Daddy? And didn't my daddy say you'd better get to Mother E soon if you want to understand squat about Charleston?"

Lifting a hand to Daniel's wave, Kate read the sign on the carriage's back for the first time:

GULLAH BUGGY
"THE ONLY THING NEW IN THE WORLD IS THE HISTORY YOU DON'T KNOW."
—HARRY S. TRUMAN

Her gaze swung back to Gabe. "Are you really passing by that church with the sculpture as part of the tour? And the two of you narrating . . . I was about to pass up my best source, wasn't I?"

"She'd love to," the boy answered for Kate and hauled her to the first row beside him.

From the rows behind, a man with a Brooklyn accent muttered, "Is that what it takes to get to ride free—be a friend of the kid's?"

The man's wife elbowed him hard in the side. "You got more money than you know how to spend, and the girl looks exhausted. How about you show some compassion for once?"

Kate collapsed onto the bench, her backpack at her feet. "You know what? Thanks. I'm whipped from reading two-hundred-year-old handwriting all day." She shot a glance sideways at Daniel, whose face streamed with sweat. "Which," she added more quietly, "doesn't sound very exhausting now that I say it out loud."

"Welcome"—Gabe swept an arm back to the carriage full of tourists—"to Gullah Buggy."

Daniel's head ticked back as the carriage rolled forward. "Gabe here brings with him both superior social skills *and* connections with people in high places."

"My daddy was just telling these folks about how we run this business together, me and him," Gabe said.

"How's this strike you for a job title? Supervisor of Song Quality, Harness Readiness, and All Right-Hand Turns."

Gabe considered, a finger to his chin. "I like it."

As Daniel launched back into his stories, Gabe cuddled into Kate's side. Awkward at first, she patted his back. "Nice to see you again," she whispered.

As Daniel spoke, both hands helping make his points, Beecher ignored the bounce of the reins on his back. Kate checked Daniel's neck for the leather cord attached to the medallion—but he wasn't wearing it today. That question could wait.

Hardly pausing to look forward as he told his benches of guests about the town, Daniel guided Beecher onto Church Street. "Dead ahead would be St. Philip's Episcopal Church, its present structure completed in 1838, in whose graveyard are buried a number of notables, including the infamous senator John C. Calhoun, who made a political name for himself spinning slavery not just as an economic necessity but also as a God-ordained good. And who, by the way, abhorred Charleston and its hedonistic, too-tolerant ways."

Interspersed with his stories, Daniel sang, a deep bass rolling from him.

"These were songs the people worked to," Daniel said. "The songs they wept to."

> *Steal away, steal away, steal away to Jesus*
> *Steal away, steal away home,*
> *I ain't got long to stay here.*
> *My Lord, he calls me, he calls me by the thunder . . .*

He seemed to know stories about every building in Charleston. "If you listen real close, you can still hear the sounds of those days." He cupped a hand to his ear. "Come on now. Listen."

All the people on the buggy cupped their hands to their ears.

"Because there was music down by the water in Charleston: the beat of waves slapping onto the seawall—the wall lower back then. The rhythms of the street vendors' Gullah. The snap of ships' sails coming unfurled. The chuckle and clink of kopecks and ducats and rupees, pennies and francs, all changing hands."

"I'm starting to hear it," the woman from Brooklyn said, her accent taut against the sway and roll of the driver's voice.

"And you can hear, too"—he nodded—"the music of languages: Scots brogue with Sephardic Hebrew with French creole. People from all over the world. In the taverns. In the market. On the wharves."

"Hold on. Mixing? *Here?*"

"Before, that is, a slave revolt planned in 1822 made all that mixing suddenly seem like a security threat."

Kate sat forward then, knocking Gabe out of an almost doze.

"Damn city government," groused the man from New York, "getting in the way of free enterprise. Like always."

His wife threw another elbow at him. "Shut up, Harry, for God's sakes, and listen."

As they passed the Old Slave Mart Museum on Chalmers, already closed for the day, Gabe swung his legs back and forth from where he perched on the edge of the buggy's first row. "Something about the dusk-end of a day always sends me to pensive."

Kate chuckled.

"What? Didn't I use the word right enough?"

She tousled his hair. "Sends me to pensive, too."

Gabe squeezed her hand. "Whenever you're feeling the sad coming on, I got your back."

She squeezed his. "And I got yours."

Arms never still as he talked, Daniel told of Fort Wagner on Morris Island and its beachhead defenses. About the Fifty-Fourth Massachusetts Volunteer Infantry Regiment featured in the film *Glory*.

Gabe closed his eyes, lulled by Beecher's rattle and clop.

"Let me ask y'all," Daniel said, "to think on whatever sorrows you got. The old slave spirituals were written to code the longing for freedom, to help carry the sad." Gabe leaned close to his father as Daniel's voice swelled up low and soft as the dusk:

> *Deep river, my home is over Jordan.*
> *Deep river, Lord, I want to cross over . . .*

"That young man," said the woman with the New York accent, "has a voice made for the stage. I've not heard a first-class baritone like that in years."

"How many first-class baritones do you hear in Queens?" the woman's husband wanted to know.

She pinned him with a glare. "I get out, Harold, more than you know."

Daniel sang on without missing a note:

> *The trumpet sounds within my soul:*
> *I ain't got long to stay here.*

"I'm sorry," Kate whispered, "about your momma."

"Me too." Gabe sighed, his body giving a small shudder. "Real sorrowful sorry."

Daniel pulled Beecher to a stop on Calhoun Street in front of a steepled white brick edifice, a sweep of steps climbing to the second story and above that a soaring arch of stained glass.

Daniel raised an arm. "Ladies and gentlemen, you see here before you a church that hope built. And rebuilt."

Cameras clicked, the whole buggy of passengers straining for a good and then a better shot.

The moon full above the steeple, the church's white-painted exterior glowed, its neighbors on Calhoun dark. The tip of its steeple glinting and its form staunch and towering in the moonlight, it stood like a soldier refusing to retreat when the rest of a battalion had run into the night.

Kate sat bolt upright. "Oh my God, this is exactly where I needed to come next for research. This is where Denmark Vesey taught a class, and—"

But Daniel had already launched into the church's founding, his voice projected for the back row to hear. "Come back for a morning Gullah Buggy tour on a Monday, and I'll give the whole history of Emanuel African Methodist Episcopal Church. For now, I'll just say that in recent history, a number of key political, cultural, and Civil Rights leaders have spoken from this pulpit: Booker T. Washington, for example, and Martin Luther King Jr. Coretta Scott King led a march in support of striking hospital workers that began right here at this church. It was formed out of a general frustration by slaves and free blacks alike having to worship under the leadership of whites only. A man named Morris Brown founded this church, and a good three-fourths of Charleston's black population came with him. But in its earliest days, a number of the key strategists of a slave revolt in 1822 were members of this church."

Kate was sitting so far forward on the driver's bench she nearly toppled off.

"Which was fitting, given the church's fierce independence from the very beginning. The first African Methodist Episcopal congregation in the South, it's now widely referred to as Mother Emanuel. *Emanuel* for 'God with us.'"

"And *Mother*," Harold quipped, "for first."

Harold's wife rolled her eyes.

"Dan," Kate asked—and she was willing to beg—"is there any way we could have a look inside?"

The others murmured agreement behind her.

Daniel checked his watch. "Maybe just a few minutes. It so happens Gabe and I have connections here." He dropped to the ground, running a hand under the harness traces as the passengers stepped off the carriage.

~

The sanctuary's vaulted ceiling covered a vast nave of flame-red carpet and pews polished to gleaming—so bright, in fact, the late-day sunlight streaming through the stained glass reflected off the wood in blues and greens and violets. Kate lagged behind the group and breathed in the silence, the light.

She stroked the top of a pew, the silk of its decades of varnish and human touch: the faithfulness that had come this way. And the courage.

Gabe, clearly at home here, cavorted away toward the altar.

Kate stood at the rear of the nave. A few yards away, as some of the tourist group gathered to see what was happening, a man with a TV camera on one shoulder listed sideways under its weight, and a blond reporter was thrusting a microphone into the face of a man in a dark suit, a clerical collar at his neck, with a receding hairline and glasses. Appearing startled at first by the foam globe shoved at his chin, he seemed determined now to reflect patience.

It was that studied, steady patience that Kate recognized even before the man's features: the clergyman by the fountain.

"In the wake of the incident," the reporter was saying, "involving the death of Walter Scott just six miles north of here—"

"Incident," the clergyman corrected her, "is too weak a word. Far, *far* too weak."

"I beg your pardon?" The reporter glanced back toward the camera, as if unsure whether to encourage him to continue.

"When we see the video, we see the truth: Mr. Scott was shot from behind. Fell to the ground. Died with his face in the dust." His voice slowed here, enunciating each word as he faced the camera directly. "Was gunned down like game."

"Like . . . ?" she echoed.

"*Game,*" he returned calmly. "An officer of the law shot an unarmed black man in the back—not once but several times—as the man ran away. Then, without checking to see if he was alive, without attempting to resuscitate him, without calling for medics, the officer handcuffed Mr. Scott." The clergyman faced her again. "Gunned down. Like game."

Kate cringed and had to look away from the intensity in the clergyman's eyes.

The reporter took a moment, apparently to gather her courage. "To which you are responding how, Reverend—or should I say Senator?"

"Either is fine. I might not have believed it myself had I not been able to watch, along with the rest of the country, the online video of the shooting. Which is why I and several others are presenting a bipartisan bill to the august body of our state legislature advocating the use of body cameras for our police—a protection for our proud and great law enforcement and for citizens alike."

"And you don't find, Reverend," the reporter asked, blue eyes shifting back to the camera, "your role here as shepherd of a flock in conflict with a role as lawmaker?"

"In my tradition, we have always felt the work of a congregation should never stop at its walls, but be integrated into the life of its community—a beacon. Though this church in which we stand is of historic significance, it is not a museum, but continues to be a place that works in the minds and hearts of people toward change." He smiled down at her. "And now, if you'll forgive me—"

"Do you see yourself, then, as a kind of cultural agitator?"

He gazed back at her a moment before answering. "Sometimes one has to make some noise." He nodded to the front of the sanctuary. "This church was founded on struggle. We understand here that sometimes you have to be willing to die like Denmark Vesey in that struggle."

Kate drew a sharp breath. To hear that name she'd been scanning two-hundred-year-old documents for all day suddenly mentioned here in this place made the former slave seem flesh and blood somehow—as alive as anyone here.

The pastor nodded to the reporter. "Thank you for coming. And now, as it is Wednesday evening—"

"Senator . . . Reverend, if I could just ask one more thing. There are, from time to time when these incidents happen—"

"These *incidents*?"

"When these . . . *tragedies* happen," she revised, "there are from time to time some calls for the Confederate flag that flies on our state capitol grounds to be taken down. Would you call now for its removal?"

A long pause. "Given my other positions, I think you can surmise how beneficial I believe that would be for the good of *all* citizens of our excellent state—for our unity. I regret to say, however, that the issue is so entrenched here, I'll never see it come down in my lifetime. Now, forgive me, but it is a busy time, and I have guests to welcome." In response to the reporter's attempt to ask one more question, he held out his hand. "Know that you are warmly welcomed here. And please do feel free to stay for the study."

The reporter turned back to the camera. "That was Clementa Pinckney of the Emanuel African Methodist Episcopal Church characterizing the incident this past April 4 in North Charleston, as an"—she paused here and seemed almost to concede the next word— "unarmed"—and then, swallowing, rushed through the rest—"man gunned down like game. This is Brooke Butler, reporting from Calhoun Street. Back to you, Alston."

The clergyman, walking now down the aisle toward Kate, shook hands with an even taller man who'd stood at the edge of the listening crowd. The taller man now fell into step with Clementa Pinckney.

"Welcome to Emanuel." The clergyman extended his hand to Kate, warmth exuding from him.

"Oh. Thanks. Our driver brought us here to your . . . place. He said he knew someone here." She flushed. "And, to be honest, I asked if we could come in."

"Glad you did. You are welcome here. Forgive me if I step away now. It's Wednesday night, and we hold a Bible study downstairs. I hope it goes without saying that you all are invited to join us."

Kate hesitated.

The smile on one side of his mouth tipped his glasses slightly askew. "And also most welcome to just look around." Nodding, he strode toward the door.

The taller man wore a dark suit, expensively cut. He was gazing past Kate to the stained glass. But as his gaze dropped to her, he reached for a pew as if to steady himself.

Kate realized with a start that she knew him—in a way: the man who'd been arguing with Botts outside Cypress & Fire. He'd charged off without taking notice of her or of anything else.

Daniel was jogging toward them from where the group had pooled near the central pulpit. "Thanks, Pastor Clem!" he called. "I knew you wouldn't mind if I brought a tour in."

The clergyman waved from the door and disappeared.

But the other man blinked, his eyes darting to Daniel, then back to Kate. "Son," he said, his voice gone thin, unsteady.

Daniel enveloped him in a hug. "Dad, you okay?"

His father? The man arguing with Percival Botts outside Dan's shop was his father?

Daniel didn't wait for a response. "Kate, that right there was the Reverend Clementa Pinckney, pastor of this historic church and senator for the great state of South Carolina, which means I got friends in high places—and, Lord knows, I'm likely to need them. And *this* is the Honorable Elijah Russell, family-court judge and proud father of yours truly, and prouder-still grandfather of Gabriel Ray."

She held out her hand. "Nice to meet you, Judge Russell. Wait . . . *Russell*." She turned from Daniel to his father and back again. "Your last name . . . is *Russell*?"

They nodded together, both watching her face.

"So the name Ray . . .".

"Is Gabe's middle name. After my daddy here, the judge Elijah Ray Russell. And also Ray Charles, but we don't generally mention that second personage in my daddy's presence."

"I realize Russell's not the most uncommon name in the world. But the connection—here in Charleston. And this church. I don't suppose there's any crazy chance . . ."

They both looked back at her, not helping her—waiting for her to go on.

"That your family is descended from the early nineteenth-century blacksmith Tom Russell?"

Gabe, who'd raced up the aisle and slid under his father's arm, stood looking from one to the other of the adults, suddenly quiet. "How'd she divinate that, you reckon?"

Daniel's lips gathered at one side. "Like to know myself. How *did*—?"

"How'd a white chick like me come to know about Tom Russell, weapon maker of the Denmark Vesey revolt?"

He chuckled, shrugging. "*Yankee* was what I was thinking, but have it your way, white chick. Seriously, is the name Russell part of your research?"

"Like, *central* to it. And I've never known anyone—outside my adviser and the handful of scholars who write on this stuff—who's ever even heard of Tom Russell. So there *is* a relation for certain between him and your family?"

Daniel held up his hand. "Actually, no."

"No?"

"That's to say we don't really know. Some debate in the family. Especially just lately." He tried to exchange glances with his father, but Elijah was staring at Kate. "Lots of debate as to whether it's a biological relation back to Tom Russell or whether it was some ancestor's way of honoring him after Emancipation by taking the name."

"So it's not been traced officially?"

Daniel leaned forward. "Never mattered too much one way or the other, we figured. Until"—again, the glance toward his father—"lately."

Kate shook her head. "This is amazing. You've no idea what a find this is."

"A find?"

"To my research."

"Look, Kate . . ."

"Sorry. Did that make it sound all about me?"

"Pretty much."

"What I meant was, even if there's not biological descent, the connection of oral tradition is amazing. That your family generations ago would have honored his memory."

Daniel nodded carefully. "For some folks, the question of biological descent is the *only* question." Again, his gaze shot to his father. "But that's not been verified. Yet."

Judge Russell had sunk slowly down into a pew. "And your name would be, young lady?"

"Oh. Sorry. Guess we didn't finish the introductions—me and my interrupting. I'm Kate Drayton. The thing is, I've done some reading on the whole Vesey revolt. I'd love to ask you guys some questions. And, Judge, I think our paths crossed earlier."

He eased against the pew's back. "Our paths?"

"Outside your son's shop. You were just leaving. And looking perturbed—after talking with Percival Botts, the attorney. He has that effect on people." She held out her hand. "Good to meet you."

The judge stared at her hand before taking it. "Yes," he got out at last.

"Dad," Daniel broke in, "you didn't tell me about talking with Botts. The lawyer, right? What was that all about?" Daniel winked at Kate. "Settling old scores?"

Judge Russell pushed himself back to his feet. Just a moment ago, the pleasantness of his face had made him seem not too imposing, but now, his eyes dark and impenetrable, he looked his height, maybe four or five inches over six feet.

The judge's gaze had drifted away. "Yes," he said. "Exactly."

"Dad." Daniel positioned himself in front of his father's face like he might wake him from some sort of stupor. "What's gotten into you?"

But the judge addressed Kate. "So. You would be Heyward Drayton's daughter?"

"Wait. You knew my father?"

A long pause. "When we were both young. We were at the College of Charleston together."

"You and my father were friends?"

"Did I imply friendship?"

"Dad, what's up? Why the combative tone?"

The judge's head swung toward his son, then back to Kate. "Young lady, I regret to say that your father and I were never friends."

"Oh. Then . . ." Something fierce in his eye made her stop.

"I have no wish to be rude, Kate. But now is not the time to say more on this subject."

"I understand. It's just that my father—"

"Now," he repeated, more sternly this time, "is not the time."

At one side of the sanctuary, the tourists from the buggy tour had congregated around a particularly striking stained glass window.

"Ready?" Daniel called to the tour group, the bulk of them now turning toward the altar with a kind of awed distance, as if trying to picture Martin Luther King Jr. there. "I got to get this buggy off the street before the tourism commission has my hide for having a horse-drawn conveyance out past time." Turning back, he wrapped his father in a bear hug. "I'll give you a call tomorrow."

The judge nodded absently, and he dipped from his considerable height to land a kiss on Gabe's cheek. But his eyes, stormy and dark, returned to Kate.

Rattled, Kate returned his stare. But she could not read what she saw there.

"I was wondering," she ventured, "if I could set up an appointment with you as well, Judge. I have so many questions about what you know of your family."

She took a step back from the expression on his face, which she could not read. "Questions, I mean, in relation to Tom Russell. But I understand if you're too busy."

He was silent a moment. "Your questions are important ones. I'd be happy"—his face said he was anything but—"to make time."

Why had she put the judge on the spot when he'd obviously disliked her father so much—and probably couldn't help but distrust his daughter? She promised herself she'd hold off on calling too soon.

Daniel thumped his father on the shoulder. "Dad, you look awful. Get some rest. Big guy, you ready?" Backing away, he flung up one arm in a wave. "You reckon you better help down there with the study? What's it on tonight? Do you know?"

Judge Russell straightened but balanced himself on the back of the pew, his voice still thin and uneven. "On the sins of the fathers," he said.

And looked straight at Kate.

~

"I think I upset your father somehow," Kate said as she and Daniel ran to catch up with the group, Gabe waving to them from the side exit. "And I was so engrossed with the inside of the church, I nearly forgot the sculpture. The black marble children."

Dan nodded. "I hadn't forgotten. Follow me. We'll take the group down a floor."

Once there, just outside the ground-floor exit, Kate studied the black marble faces, veined pink marble behind them like a Charleston sunrise over the harbor. "Innocence," she said. "You were right. And their faces are so . . . wise. And beautiful. And so sad. Like they are watching tragedy unfold."

Calling to his tourist group, all gathered around the Vesey memorial sculpture, Dan motioned toward the buggy. "Ask me anything you like about them once we're on the drive back. The city makes all the carriage tours stick to a timetable, and I'm running late."

He leapt onto the driver's seat. "And, Kate, my dad's thing about old scores to settle: he didn't mean that."

Kate scrambled up after Gabe, the others taking their seats on the benches behind. "My father's attorney is the kind you want to settle old scores with. I have some to settle myself, if I could track him down, since he went weaseling back out of town and won't answer a call or e-mail or . . . but that's a whole other story."

Gathering the reins, Daniel turned to give Gabe a high five. "You ready to roll?"

Kate swung up beside the child. He tilted his head back and smiled. "Glad you came, Katie-Kate," he whispered.

As Beecher leaned against the weight of the carriage, Harold called from the back, "I saw a plaque inside about the preacher Morris Brown—the one you mentioned before. So he knew about this revolt being planned?"

Daniel spoke over his shoulder. "Hard to say for certain. The leaders of the Vesey revolt wanted to protect him, like I said—keep him ignorant of the plans. He had a reputation for being a man of remarkable courage—one who could preach down the gates of hell."

He gave a tug to one rein, and Beecher changed lanes. "If you'll look to your left as we make our next turn in a minute, we'll pass what was called Potter's Field during Morris Brown's time—where they buried people too poor to afford anything else. And people not counted as people. Two hundred years ago, city leaders were scared of this place. Starting to figure out that for all the death here, there was rebellion and whole heaps of trouble alive. Growing strong."

Kate listened. Or tried. But it was hard to shake that look in Judge Russell's eyes. Some sort of barely restrained anger—was that it? But maybe not only anger . . .

She glanced back once at the church, its bright heft rising against the dark.

Its Gothic arches were striking. Substantial. This church's architecture, minus the pointed steeple, looked very much like what her mother had posed on in her cutoff shorts, perched there on a pediment, her legs dangling far above the ground.

Just like, in fact.

Kate scooted to the edge of her seat and waited for a break in the commentary. "Daniel," she asked, "odd question—sorry—but was there ever a time Emanuel was without its steeple?"

He tilted his head at her. "The white chick scores a point. Hurricane Hugo in '89—took the thing clear off."

Kate sat back heavily against the bench. "Any idea when it was rebuilt?"

"Yep, 1990. That May, I think."

So Sarah Grace had not only been here in 1991 to view the memorial sculpture as part of the Spoleto exhibit. But nearly two years before that, she'd apparently crawled from one of those upper arched windows onto the empty pediment and been photographed in her cutoff shorts at this church, Denmark Vesey's.

And put one of those pictures, with a kind of farewell note on its back, into an envelope meant for someone who knew more about her, apparently, than her own daughter.

Chapter 21

1822

Making his way down from the Neck and passing Morris Brown's church, Tom paused as its front door cracked open. His head still ached from the blow the patroller had landed on him with the butt of his gun the night of the funeral.

Or not funeral, Tom corrected himself, *burial*.

From the door of the church, Brown himself was emerging, shoulders a little hunched—which was unusual for this man—his brows drawn together in worry.

Seeing Tom, he stopped. For a moment neither of them moved or said a word.

With only shreds of daylight clinging to the tops of the palmettos and myrtles and oaks, Spanish moss hanging like cobwebs from this forgotten corner of town, whispers seemed to stir with the breeze.

Morris Brown broke their silence first. "Tom."

Tom shook his head, his way of saying they shouldn't speak.

Morris Brown lowered his voice and spoke quickly. "Let me say only this. I am here if I can assist you in any way. And I know others who are willing to help. Inside this congregation"—he paused—"and *outside* it. Should there be a need."

Checking behind him to see if anyone was following him, Tom only nodded. And walked on—faster this time. Heart pounding.

The City Market was already beginning to rouse. He breathed in curry and citrus and cloves brought here on ships that had only to raise their square sails and skim away to be free.

Pelicans and gulls flapped and squawked on the seawall. Russian kopecks and French specie and Dutch rix-dollars passed from palm to palm, a steady jangle that kept time with harness rings rattling. Some of the merchants were free blacks from the Sea Islands who'd steered their boats into harbor before dawn, their Gullah lilting above the rumble and clang. Turkey buzzards kept their morning appointments with merchants who staggered, groggy and cross, to the brick bays and the flimsier wood stalls with their pyramids of coconuts, their pineapple towers, their mountains of oysters, their bananas beginning to rot.

Rot. In the days before he'd signed on to Vesey's wild scheme of a plan, Tom had often pictured himself rotting inside.

Silent beside the dawn hubbub of the market, the mansions that lined the harbor slept on, indigo dreams fleeced in cotton and rice. Buzzards dove for their plunder of discarded fish. Vendors waved brooms at the big birds. The Gullah women selling their sweetgrass baskets on the corners shouted at them. But the buzzards provided the public service of removing the refuse left at the close of each day. Tom hardly looked where he walked, toppling stacks of papayas, catching them before they hit the ground, handing them back to glowering merchants.

"Qué bella, qué bella!" one vendor called to her neighbor, nodding in Tom's direction. She held out two peaches to him.

Tom shook his head and pulled out one empty pocket from his trousers.

Waving away the mere suggestion of money, she maneuvered her hips in two swoops around her table, which was heavy with fruit. Taking first one of his hands and then the other, unfurling first one palm and then the other, she positioned a ripe peach gently on each palm. She smiled up at him, her earrings bobbing.

Tom pressed the peaches back into her hands and walked on.

"Molds. For fishing-net weights, supposed to be," a voice whispered behind him as he paused at a stack of crates bulging with pineapples. "Now for bullets."

Tom did not turn. He knew the voice.

"One of our men slipped it from the farm where he works. Nobody missing it yet. What you make, we hide strategically all over town. Ned dropped off a barrel of rice, mold deep inside, at your shop before dawn. Behind the ash heap in your alley."

"*What!*" Tom spun on the man they called Gullah Jack. Then turned back away. "Too risky. What would that look like if the wrong person goes to open the barrel?"

"We're needing ammunition down Battery way. Got nothing so far down to the tip."

Tom did not stay to hear more. Hurrying, without calling attention to himself by actually sprinting, Tom reached his shop on East Bay and dragged the barrel through the door on the side alley.

He labored all day over his forge, mostly on hoes and shovels. Rebolting the side entrance and keeping one eye on the front door, Tom crafted one bayonet head after the next—always with a hoe propped at the edge of the forge as cover. The newly cast bullets he stashed in a box of hand-cut nails under a set of fleur-de-lis gates.

Just as dusk neared but before the curfew bells, Tom dropped the box of nails—and bullets—into a large cotton sack full of hammers and handsaws he could claim he was delivering and strode south, meeting nobody's eye, toward the Battery.

In the shadows of the last lot on Meeting Street, its outbuildings surrounded by brambles and weeds and a circle of young oaks, Tom Russell looked right and looked left.

No one.

Taking three steps from the base of the largest of the live oaks, he dropped to his knees. With a trowel he'd slipped into the bag, he dug a shallow hole and dropped the box of nails and bullets into it. Hastily covered it with a thin layer of crushed shell and dirt.

Looked right. Looked left again.

Heart pumping, he slipped back through the shadows and the warren of outbuildings back to a clearing, and from there to East Bay.

A few blocks north on East Bay, the water's edge just steps away, sailors leaned against a tavern, its stucco clinging thin and wearied to its walls and its walls no longer perpendicular to the street, as if they had taken in a few flagons too many themselves.

The tavern's sign swung on its wrought iron bracket—which Tom Russell had crafted.

Spilling out from its door were sailors of all skin colors, speaking every language Tom could imagine and more, sweat mixing with drinks and drinks passed all around.

A red-haired sailor with an Irish accent lifted his pint to Tom. "You're a man looking in need of a drink."

Tom shook his head but took a place leaning against the stucco as he and the sailor looked out over the harbor.

"It's not making much sense to me, that much I'll say, the way things would be working down here. For example, it's not legal exactly, I'm told, for a man such as yourself"—the sailor's eyes fell to the badge at Tom's neck—"to be drinking alongside the whites. Yet I'm reading in your newspapers those who'd write in to complain of it happening, which tells me it does. And I see it with me own eyes. Sometimes, a white man complains. Sometimes, nobody does." He paused for Tom to comment, but Tom, stiffening, kept his eyes on the harbor and said nothing. "'Tis inconsistent, I'd say."

The sailor was gauging Tom's face. Abruptly, Tom turned his head away toward the harbor's mouth.

But something in the line of his mouth or some spark of defiance the sailor must have caught in his eye—or just the fact that Tom had come here to the tavern and did not march away from this conversation—must have told the sailor that he could go on.

"Or here's another I've heard since me ship sailed in from Boston last night: a man who's a slave can purchase a lottery ticket and, just saying for instance he won, could be purchasing his own freedom."

The sailor was speaking as if he knew something of Vesey. As if he were hoping Tom would acknowledge some sort of code.

Tom had heard rumors through Gullah Jack that a handful of whites—three or four at the most—had been trusted with the plans for the revolt. Everyone knew that sailors heard the news of a port faster than anyone. Maybe this sailor was speaking only in general terms and knew nothing specific.

Still, this conversation was dangerous. It could be a trap, set by the likes of James Hamilton.

Heart pounding, not meeting his eye, Tom took one step away. And checked to be sure no one was close enough to be listening.

But if the sailor was aware of Tom's unease, he took little notice. Pitching back his head, he pointed into the sky. "Looks different here, that it does, than below the equator, you know—the constellations. Not dark enough yet to be making out, but there's one star that's brightest."

Tom shook his head. Better to appear not to know what he meant. "Always lived in the city. Never needed to be watching the stars."

The sailor lowered his voice and plucked out a folded paper from his pocket. "There'd be a store in Boston, there is, where I just bought these fine pants, a couple named Hayden that owns it, and they'd be making a point of sticking these pamphlets in all of the pockets, especially of seafaring men like meself. 'Tis their way, I s'pose, to get their point spread round."

Tom did not have to give the pamphlet more than a glance to see that it was abolitionist propaganda—the kind that could get a slave beaten here or even a free man arrested. *"Put. That. Away."*

"'Tis no one close enough to be hearing me whisper, lad." But with the shrug of one shoulder, the sailor stuffed it back in his pocket. "They say there's people can escape by the North Star." He shook his head. "Not that it makes any difference if you live this far to the south."

Tom's hands gripped the brick behind him, but he said nothing.

"It's one thing, they say, trying a run from a border kind of a state where a skiff across a river at night could be all that'd be needed. But down here this far into the South, 'tis not a bonny pig's sense in trying, I'm thinking." The sailor let his head topple toward Tom. "Or is there?"

Laughter, raucous and loud, from inside filled the silence for the next moment.

Not a bonny pig's sense in trying.

But we are! Tom wanted to shout. *We are.*

Instead, he turned to the sailor.

Something in his face must have said more than he'd meant it to, because the Irishman's eyes grew wide.

"Jesus, Mary, and Joseph," he breathed. "God help you, lad." The sailor lifted his pint high in a toast. And he tossed back the rest of its contents.

A few yards away, a man stepped from behind the corner of the tavern.

Tom froze, eyes straight ahead on the harbor. Teeth clenched, he waited for the man to speak.

Could he possibly have heard anything?

The man walked past them slowly, his simple gray coat and dark, round-brimmed hat hardly more than a shadow here at the daylight's end. He turned, his face toward Tom. The man stroked his beard.

An occasional customer at the blacksmith's shop, the man was a Quaker. One of the handful left.

People said they spoke out against slavery—the reason they'd left the Low Country in droves. But this one was still here, which could mean he was more sympathetic to Southern law.

Tom had been careful to say nothing that could incriminate him. But he'd stood there too long and too close and listened. That alone could be viewed as sedition.

The man walked on without speaking.

The sailor turned to Tom. "It's not trouble I've gotten you in now, have I?"

But the curfew bells clanged into the dusk.

Tom's only answer was breaking into a run.

Chapter 22

2015

The light just beginning to edge through the crack in her motel curtains, Kate reached for the photo on her bedside table and studied the face in it. Even in this little light, she could see her mother's head thrown back, her long, tanned legs dangling from what must have been the just-emptied pediment of Emanuel AME's steeple. Just as Gabe had noticed that first day on the seawall, her young face stretched into a smile that seemed too big or too forced—for display only—as if to announce to the world, *See? I'm smiling.*

Kate reached for the light and sat up in bed, papers and photos and a sterling hairbrush tumbling from the paisley bedspread where she'd fallen asleep studying them. She googled the date that Hugo hit Charleston: September 21–22, 1989. Kate calculated: the fall of her mother's senior year at the College of Charleston. By June of the next spring, Sarah Grace would have married Heyward Drayton—and as far as Kate knew, the kind of defiance and laughter that showed on her mother's face in this photo had ended with her marriage vows. So this photo must have been taken sometime between the fall of 1989 and the spring of 1990.

And the note on the back: *I beg you to hold close what only the three of us know—and I wish to God it weren't even three.* When had Sarah Grace written that? And to whom?

On a whim, Kate reached for her phone on the bedside table and scrolled through her recent calls to the number she'd found at the bottom of the *Places with a Past* brochure. A half dozen rings and still nothing. Kate dropped the phone to her lap to tap "End."

"Hello," said a man's voice suddenly.

Kate popped the phone back to her ear. "Yes! Hello. Yes, my name is Katherine Drayton, and, forgive me, this may sound very odd, but I found this number in—"

Click.

The line went dead.

Kate stared at the phone. Had the man thought she was a telemarketer and hung up, annoyed? Or had there been something about her name that had spooked him?

Screwing up her courage, she called back—better to risk being a nuisance than never know. But this time the line rang with no answer.

Easing herself out of bed without knocking more of her mother's memorabilia and Kate's own research notes to the floor, she peered through the parted curtains. The motel's parking lot lay glittering with glass, its asphalt erupting. It reminded her of the wood-veneered frame, broken on two sides, which had at one time held a picture of her parents together. Most of her growing-up years, though, it hung empty against a bare wall.

Maybe, she'd thought as a kid, her mother had left the broken frame empty so Kate could imagine something cheery to fill it—a deliriously happy family, perhaps, gathering hermit crabs in a tidal pool at the beach.

Or maybe Sarah Grace's rage and defiance had lasted only long enough to rip the picture out of the frame, but not the frame from the wall.

Showering quickly, Kate dressed, and a glance in the cracked mirror showed the glint of the silver herons still in her ears. She must have slept in them.

She shrugged at her own image. Time someone wore them, since they may have sat in that box unused ever since her father had given them to her mother.

At the edge of the mirror, where she'd wedged it between glass and cheap plastic frame, was the postcard of the Wayside Inn in Wadesboro. She'd yet to find anything even remotely resembling a clue about that. Maybe it was, in fact, only the place where she and her mother had stayed the first night after leaving Charleston and, for Sarah Grace, represented that step.

Frowning, Kate wedged the postcard back into the frame.

An e-mail appeared in her in-box. From Julian Ammons. Only one line:

Have you found the Avery Center quite helpful?

Cringing, Kate googled to see what exactly this was—apparently something obvious for any *real* scholar—before replying. Up came links for the website of the Avery Research Center for African American History and Culture, located on Bull Street and operated by the College of Charleston. The museum specialized, Kate read, on the African diaspora, with an emphasis on Charleston and the Carolina Low Country.

Just walking distance away. Very nearly under her nose.

Kate typed back a few lines of her own:

Actually headed there today, as it happens. Will apprise you of any developments.
Thank you for checking on me!

It wasn't a lie, exactly. Not since she would now spend the day there.

Gathering some notes and her laptop into her backpack, Kate knocked a manila envelope onto the floor from the bed. One of several from the last of her mother's boxes, this one was marked in red ink *Car*

Deeds—SAVE. Since no car of Sarah Grace's had survived the wreck of her Ford Taurus, Kate had not opened the envelope. But now, for some reason she could not have named, she tore open its seal.

Inside were letters, dozens of them, with the return address of the law firm of Rutledge, Wragg, Roper & Botts.

Kate fanned them out on the bed and opened one toward the bottom. Here was a typed letter from the firm signed by Percival Botts. And another. Several of them.

Plucking letters from random years, she found the same in each: a letter from Botts—the only difference that the attorney's tone became more familiar—affectionate, even, as the dates wore on, and he signed his name *Percy* in later years. Kate opened several more letters.

Let me help you with your secrets, Botts wrote Sarah Grace in one.

A strange tone to take with the wife of a client.

Kate tore open several others from the succeeding months. But Botts's tone turned more formal again. With no more mention of secrets.

Botts. Whom she'd called every day since he'd disappeared from the inn. She left messages every time that they would meet soon, if she had to track down his home somewhere near Beaufort—she'd found out that much already—and show up on his doorstep some evening in the near future.

What had Botts meant, trying to help Sarah Grace with her secrets? What secrets? And why would her husband's attorney care?

Kate picked up the photo of her mother with long, tanned legs dangling from the church steeple's pediment.

"What was going on?" she demanded of the young woman in the photo.

She hurled a stack of the letters across the room and shot another text to Botts:

Just found some intriguing letters

from you that my mother saved.

She paused to consider. Was it time yet to play hardball? Probably.

I admit it startled me that a client's
attorney can have such a close personal
relationship with his client's wife.

Did that imply enough of a threat?

The American Bar Association must have
instituted new guidelines—I'll be sure
to check. Looking forward to meeting with you
very soon.

So there.

Snatching up her backpack and plastic motel key card, Kate would have stalked out of the room then—except for the photocopied page at her feet.

It must have fallen from between several of Botts's letters. She knelt to examine it.

There, staring back at her from the copy of an old photograph, was the sepia-toned image of a man, broad shouldered and dark skinned, propped back against the railings of some sort of ship. His hat in one hand, the man had gray hair, but the compromised quality of the image—a probably three-decade-old copy of an antique photograph—made it hard to determine just how old he might be. Across a thin span of water sat a shoreline of elegant mansions.

Flinging open the motel curtains and holding the photocopy up to the light, Kate squinted at the blurred skyline. The line of mansions with their soaring piazzas and Greek Revival columns only yards from the water had to be only one place: Charleston, the view people called Battery Row—seen from the harbor.

Peering more closely at two words someone had penned on the original photo in the right bottom corner, Kate's hand went to her throat.

The ink was faded, but she could still make them out, barely. In evenly sized block letters, Kate read: *MY TOM.*

In any other context, the name Tom, common for a nineteenth-century American man of any race, would mean little. But the fact that Sarah Grace had saved this along with the rest of her research on Tom Russell must have meant something—or at least, she'd suspected some sort of connection and was trying to prove it.

Sure enough, on the back of the photocopied page—in Sarah Grace's handwriting—were the initials *T. R.*

Could this possibly be Tom Russell?

But in the remote chance that it was, the fact that someone had taken an early photograph and not a daguerreotype of him had to date the image sometime after the Civil War, didn't it? And a dark-skinned man propped leisurely against a ship's rail seemed to suggest that, too. Which meant that if Sarah Grace had been right and this "My Tom" was in fact Tom Russell, he had survived not only the summer of 1822 but also the war and Emancipation.

Perching back on the bed, fingers flying over her laptop, Kate called up websites on the development of early photography. A daguerreotype would have had a more silver, mirrorlike background, the images in the foreground appearing almost to float, like the slave images she'd shown in her catastrophic classroom presentation. This had to be an early photograph, then, although she couldn't make out enough about the different stages of progress to date the image any more closely than the 1860s to the 1890s. She'd have to find a visual archivist here who could help pinpoint a date.

Still, even assuming the photo dated from just after the war, and even assuming it was Tom Russell—which went against every historical record of the aftermath of the Vesey revolt—why had it mattered so blasted much to Sarah Grace?

And what connection with their family troubles had Kate's father made in warning her away from this history?

A history that can only hurt you.

Baffled, Kate shot an e-mail to Dr. Ammons with the subject line "Grateful for your thoughts" and only two lines of message:

> Found a piece of evidence suggesting Tom
> Russell may have survived the summer of 1822—
> and been living in Charleston after the War.

The War, she thought wryly. She was beginning to sound like a Charlestonian: *the War* meant only one thing here.

Conflicted over how to describe her source—since cardboard boxes of Valentine's Day doilies and Christmas lights and old photocopies sounded less credible than this probably was—Kate left it at that. And hit "Send."

~

After several hours at the South Carolina Historical Society, Kate rose from the desk where she'd fanned out her notes and stretched. Then she clicked on her e-mail again—she'd made herself quit checking every few minutes after the first hour.

Still nothing from Julian Ammons.

She leaned again on the front desk and smiled at the librarian. "It's kind of you to let me know when Dr. Sutpen comes in."

"Oh. Right." The young man looked up from the stack of folders he'd been labeling. "Forgot about that." With his head, he gestured across the room to where a man was reaching for a stack of books with threadbare bindings. The elbows and knees of his seersucker suit appeared little better, but he held himself with a regal air.

Wanting to bound across the room, Kate made herself walk slowly, casually.

"Dr. Sutpen." The librarian sighed as if he'd tired of saying what he was about to have to repeat. "We cannot allow pipe smoking here."

"Mah pipe is not lit," Dr. Sutpen pointed out. "Why, what sort of barbaric behavior would that be with precious documents present?"

"Or even your walking about with your pipe clenched between your teeth, sir."

With a white goatee and a string necktie, Dr. Sutpen looked like a Low Country Colonel Sanders. Huffing, Sutpen pivoted on the heel of one loafer. "Soon they'll be outlawin' the mere possession of a tobacco receptacle."

Sarah Grace's imitation of him had been perfect.

Kate thrust out her right hand and pretended not to see his frown at being waylaid. "Dr. Sutpen, my name is Kate Drayton, and I'm looking for information on a number of things, including information on my mother, whom I believe was a student of yours. I wonder—"

"Jumpin' Jehoshaphat, I cannot remember students I had last semester, much less decades ago. Now if you'll excuse—"

"Sarah Grace Ravenel."

He pivoted back slowly and examined Kate. "Well now. There is a name I do seem to recall."

Kate's heart leapt. "I wonder what you could tell me about her. Anything at all."

Annoyance flickered over his face. "An odd thing to ask, young lady."

"Maybe you recall a bit about her research—for her senior thesis with you? About the Denmark Vesey rebellion." Kate took a chance here. "She had some theories about the weapon maker Tom Russell. That perhaps he survived?"

"Unfounded in fact, and I told her just that," Sutpen railed. "Sheer wishful thinking. An absolute shame for a young woman that gifted to be wasting her life pining and plodding after a theory doomed from the start."

"But—"

He bent toward Kate and glowered. "*Doomed*. In fact, now that I recall, she'd never have graduated on time, not after missing that spring semester, had I not been willing to guide her through independent studies one summer, then passed off on her senior thesis, insufficiently supported though her thesis was." He shuddered. "Good Lord."

Kate's head snapped up. "Missing that spring semester? Which year was that?"

He eyed her with disdain. "You'll forgive me if I don't track the lives of every student who has passed through the History Department at College of Charleston."

"Of course. I just . . . that's the first I've heard of that. I don't suppose," she ventured, "you'd have any idea why she might have taken a semester off and then made it up later?"

Had she left to conduct her own research, determined to prove her theories, however connected they'd been to her actual life? Had she run off with Heyward Drayton—surely not to the Wayside Inn in Wadesboro—and then come back to marry him?

Something sparked in his eyes—some sort of memory. He shifted uncomfortably and avoided Kate's eye. Then picked up his pipe again from the table and chewed on its stem. "I'm afraid I cannot assist you." He turned to go.

"Wait. Please. It's just that I know so little about her."

"I was her thesis adviser. Not her counselor or confidante."

"Of course. I don't suppose you'd know where I could find a copy of her thesis?"

"There is no such copy!" Sutpen exploded, turning back. "I signed my name to the damn thing only because Sarah Grace Ravenel was so hell-bent to graduate and bury herself in some society marriage. I saw the thesis shredded myself."

Kate hurried after him, so close that Sutpen glared a warning. "Bury herself? So you knew the young man she was going to marry?"

He waved this away. "I absolutely did not. He was a"—he shuddered again—"business major, not in the liberal arts. I merely knew of him—and was struck with the peculiar fervor with which your mother pursued him. Nothing like the crowd she'd run with her first years."

"No?" Kate asked, fearing her saying more might remind him he was admitting more than he liked to think that he knew.

"Free spirit, that's what she was at first. Eager to learn. Eager to experience life. Unafraid to cross boundaries. She cared little for how people talked." He gestured with his pipe. "But all that changed, more's the pity. All that changed."

"For how people talked?" Kate leaned forward again—too far and too fast. Sutpen glared. "Sorry. But I'm wondering what exactly people might have been saying. Or what might have changed."

He snorted in disgust. "Your mother had a good mind, yet threw it away. Colossal waste. For the record, I never believed her capable of an atrocity."

"Atrocity?"

He chomped on the pipe. "And then to chain herself to old-money Charleston."

"Dr. Sutpen, what did you mean by *atrocity*?"

Glowering at her use of the word as if she'd laid a trap for him, he showed no sign of supplying more.

So Kate took a risk. "Are you referring to her crossing boundaries, possibly back in the late '80s in the Deep South, possibly racial divides or—?"

"If it only had been that!" He snorted, and his accent deepened. "Ah do not employ words willy-nilly, let me assure you. Ah would remind you that Ah did not believe she was capable of it."

"Capable of . . . ? The thing is, I know so little. You seem to have known at least some of her personal life and—"

That was the wrong thing to say.

"Ah *neveh* involve myself in the personal lives of my students," he blustered.

"Of course not. I only meant—"

"That is all Ah recall. And that is all Ah will say. Ah'll ask you not to accost me again, young lady." Gathering his papers, Sutpen stormed from the room. "Utterly unfounded in fact!" he pronounced from the door before banging through it.

Kate stared at the door he'd slammed.

Atrocity? What could he possibly mean?

Suddenly, Kate was seeing the note her father had written in red ink across the portrait she'd sketched for him:

I assume you and your mother do not wish to expose yourselves to yet more public scorn . . .

And Sarah Grace's response:

He means that for me, Katie. Not you.

Even at the time, it had seemed that more than a lost spelling bee had been on his mind when he wrote the note, its scathing tone unmistakable. Had Heyward assumed Sarah Grace was guilty of this atrocity that Sutpen referred to?

She was still staring openmouthed at the door Sutpen had slammed when her cell—which she should have silenced before coming in— trilled loudly.

Springing to her seat and pawing in her backpack, Kate caught Dr. Ammons's name on the screen. Snatching the phone with one hand and dashing past the front desk, she burst through the door to the outside steps and answered before he hung up.

"Dr. Ammons. Thank you for calling."

"Not possible, I'm afraid."

And that was his opening line.

"Not possible? I'm afraid I don't—"

"That any of the key leaders of the Vesey revolt would have survived. What is this source you've uncovered, if I may ask?"

Kate hedged. "My source is hard to describe adequately." This latest interaction with Sutpen had made her more desperate than ever to finish her mother's search—and understand what had driven it.

"Hard to describe, Ms. Drayton?"

Secretive was not something a graduate student could be. She tried again. "It's a photograph, not a daguerreotype. With identification that would lead me to think it's Tom Russell. The backdrop is definitely Charleston."

A beat of disbelief that Kate could hear even across the thousand miles.

"I assume it's misidentified, then. There are several superb visual archivists there in Charleston. You've had it examined for a fairly pinpointed time period?"

How could she explain it was only a copy of a faded picture with the block letters *MY TOM* and the scribbled initials *T. R.*, which meant only that her mother, who'd barely finished her college senior thesis—and only because her professor had signed off on it grudgingly—persisted in believing that it was Russell.

"I'll be doing that soon, yes." *And,* she nearly added, *trying to connect it somehow with my family's falling apart.*

This, though, didn't need saying aloud.

Atrocity . . .

A history that can only hurt you . . .

Yet more public scorn . . .

"Ms. Drayton, I will await with interest your delving into this matter."

"Yes, I . . . um . . . look forward to being in touch."

"One final thing, I assume you've begun searching for records there at the Avery Center—one of my favorite venues for research, by the way—of names in the group who came to the newly freed Charleston with Daniel Payne?"

"I . . . was hoping to begin that today," she assured him. And yanked the pen out of her jeans pocket to write on the back of her hand *Daniel Payne*—a name she'd not even heard before.

"Again, I'm afraid Tom Russell's survival past 1822 is simply not possible, but if you're determined to pursue finding out who this man of color is in a post–Civil War photo of Charleston, it occurs to me you might explore the group that came down from the North with Payne to teach literacy to the former slaves."

And before she could think what to ask without betraying the depth of her ignorance, he had signed off with an "I do wish you well, Ms. Drayton."

And her phone's screen went black.

Downing the Diet Coke she'd been craving as she paced the College of Charleston campus—acres of live oaks forming a canopy of green over winding paths where cyclists spun by her—Kate dragged herself toward the Avery Research Center on Bull Street. It seemed unlikely she'd find anything related to her mother's life or search, but it was one avenue she'd not tried yet.

On the way, her phone dinged with an incoming text—from a number she didn't recognize.

Kate, it's Scudder Lambeth, and before
you hit Delete—I know it's tempting—

He'd recognized her need for walls—to keep him at a safe distance:
well, a point for him on that.

Just hear me out pls. Miz Rose—standing right here—gave
me your # if I promised to delete the minute I sent this msg
re- something I overheard that might help u. I know u were
trying to meet w/ P Botts.
You said it was important. I believe you.

The text ended there.
You said it was important. I believe you.
Something oddly innocent—almost childlike in the trust of that
line. Something kind of thoughtful about it, too.
Still . . .
Now another text slid onto her screen.

Press N for NO MORE CONTACT EVER AGAIN FROM YOU,
INCLUDING THIS INFO. Press Y for YES PLS CONTINUE
WITH MORE INFO BUT NO OBLIGATIONS (that's 0, our
commitment to you) ATTACHED.

He was inventive—she'd give him that. And the bottom line was
that Botts had yet to respond. She'd already been laying plans to find
his residential address—which wasn't listed online, but she'd find it
somehow—drive up to his sweet coastal town where he'd semiretired,
and jump out of the shrubbery at him.
Short on alternatives, she tapped "Y."
Immediately, another text arrived:

If you haven't gotten Botts to talk w/ u yet—hard to catch for me, too—I met him today to finish our talk from the inn. Overheard him say he'd be at Magnolia Plantation for a fund-raising thing Tu night. May not be helpful but thought I'd pass along. No need to respond. Rest easy: am deleting all trace of your # right . . . now.

"So," she said out loud. "It's Tuesday night then."
She kept her response to him short:

Thx. Helpful.

More than that might sound like an invitation to talk—and to know more about her life than he already did, which was already more than she'd planned.

She dropped the phone in her backpack. She would remind herself later to delete his number from her recent calls. Just in case she was tempted later to thank him again. And then he might respond.

Better to keep a safe distance where no one got hurt and no one got left sitting alone at the side of an empty road.

Head aching, she bent alongside the Avery Research Center archivist as they sifted through file after file that might contain something on the African Methodist Episcopal workers—at least one of them born in Charleston, one source had said—who'd sailed down from the North after the Civil War to assist former slaves in beginning their lives in freedom.

A needle in a haystack, that's what she was looking for, trying to find Tom Russell's name anywhere in these mentions—and worse, a needle she didn't even know the purpose of. She might have turned up some interesting clues, but none of them had connected so far. She was no closer to weaving together what role a blacksmith two hundred years ago played in the unraveling of her family than she had been when she'd first come down.

Returning the last stack of folders to the front desk of the Avery Research Center's Phillis Wheatley Literary and Social Club Reading Room, Kate scanned a final page as she walked: no mention anywhere of a Tom Russell. Or a Tom at all.

Nothing.

Red-eyed and defeated, she was about to close the file, the archivist looking sympathetically at her.

That final yellowed page, handwritten and nearly illegible, listed a handful of names, including Daniel Payne. And at the top, it said:

Our co-laborers who left their homes in the North to serve the cause of the former slave.

Holding her breath, Kate scanned the names.

But again, no Tom.

At the far bottom, though, in an ink that was more brown than black and a script that was more flowing than the first, someone had added just seven words:

And also Dinah, a native of Charleston.

Chapter 23

1822

Dinah heard the city marshal approach from behind, could even feel his breath near the back of her neck. But she walked on.

Until he snarled, "I'll tell you that much, you wandering round here in this kind of rain. It don't look good. Ain't nobody out here don't have to be. And you listening to what ain't a world of your business." Grabbing Dinah's arm, he spun her around, then leered at her protruding belly. "Well, now. Looks like you right up on foaling time, ain't you?"

Dinah jerked away just as another unearthly howl came from the windows of the workhouse. She rotated back toward the sound.

Tears streamed down her cheeks, mixing with rivulets of sweat and the falling rain. It was hot today for only the end of May, even with the passing storm, and the heat, combined with her condition, had already made her dizzy and faint.

But now this. She'd been walking home the long way from the milliner's and the stationer's on King Street she'd visited for Emily Pinckney. Maybe she'd meant to walk down this street, just to be sure, or maybe she'd been so absorbed by her own thoughts she'd not looked up to see where she was until the shrieks and moans had made that perfectly clear.

The city marshal ran the fingers of his right hand over the pistol at his side. "You listen to me now. You stand here listening to that like you's sympathetic, like you'd be on the side of a bloody traitor to this city, and that kind of sympathy, I tell you what, will get you a ticket yourself inside them walls to feel the end of a cowhide strip. You understand me good?"

Dinah kept her eyes on the workhouse walls. But she held her breath to slow the flow of tears. "Who is it?" she asked when she could speak.

"His name's none of your damn business. But I'll tell you this: twelve hours ago, he wasn't talking none. But now, *now* that he's been *encouraged* to talk"—he leered meaningfully at her—"I'm guessing we're real close to a full confession."

Dinah's hand dropped to her belly. "A confession?"

Pitching back his head, the patroller sent a gob of tobacco sailing over her shoulder. "Now, 'less you cotton to getting tossed in the hole inside there or keeping company on the bloody end of the whip, I suggest you move along. And look a little less sorry the devil in there's getting all the hell he deserves."

Dinah did move along, trembling, her steps aimed now for East Bay. If the shop were empty, the forge cold, she would know. She would know who it was inside the workhouse.

From a block away, no smoke billowed from the chimney.

Her knees went soft. Her head spun.

Dinah leaned heavily against brick, then made her feet move forward. One more block.

She had to see. She had to know.

The windows reflected the perfect blue above in their undulating panes. The sky was such a liar, reflecting all the beauty of this place and none of its pain.

Dinah made herself lean into the glass and cup her hand against the sun to see to the back of the shop.

She collapsed onto the sidewalk.

Someone came running.

Ned Bennett. Hauling her up by the elbow. "You lose your balance? Can't be having that baby right here on the street. Easy now. You hold on now. You hold on."

Tears coursed down both cheeks again. "I heard the screams. At the workhouse."

Ned nodded grimly. "It's bad. It's real bad. But don't you think for a minute it's over."

"No. I mean, I thought . . . I thought it was Tom."

Both their eyes went to the window. In the back of the shop, Tom Russell was bent over his forge, its coals dark and cold, but the dark of his back muscles like thunderclouds churning.

Looking up just then, he spotted Dinah. Ran to the glass. Laid his palm against the window.

She raised hers to the glass to meet his on the other side. And they stood like that, Ned Bennett holding her steady, as she wept tears of relief.

Dinah tried to enter quietly, slipping through the back door next to the kitchen house without the hinges creaking. Emily might scold her for taking so long with the errands. But that was the least of her worries right now.

As she crept silently past, the door of Jackson Pinckney's study flew open. "So," he said.

Dinah did not meet his eye. Tried to walk on.

"In here," he commanded.

Eyes still looking down and away, she stepped to the threshold.

"In. *Here.*"

She took one more step. But she crossed her arms over her chest, her whole body tense with loathing.

Jackson Pinckney swept up a black leather case from his desk. "I wanted, Dinah, for you to be the first to see my new purchase." He held the box beneath her face.

She kept looking down and away.

"Finest dueling pistols money can buy. Imported from Prussia." Picking up one of the guns from its silk enclosure, he stroked its barrel. "I like to keep them both loaded. Because, you know, one never can tell what the future may hold. To quote the Bard of Avon, whom you would not have read, 'The fault, dear Brutus, is not in our stars, but in ourselves.' I'm not pleased, Dinah, as you well know, with your recent behavior. Don't think I'm such a fool as not to have known if someone who didn't belong to me went sneaking back to the quarters behind my own house."

Dinah averted her face as he circled.

"And I am not pleased with what appears, if the Prioleaus' servant Peter was not merely hallucinating when he reported it all, to be some sort of nefarious plot in this city. William Paul is being thoroughly questioned even now in the workhouse—has been all night."

Dinah swallowed but kept her face rigid. She'd not known William Paul was involved. But that wasn't surprising. Each person who was informed of the plot was supposed to know only the name of the one person who'd approached with that whispered news—to protect everyone involved. *Thousands,* Dinah had overheard in the market.

How much did William Paul know? And if they were torturing him, how much could he keep to himself?

Jackson Pinckney ran a hand down her front from her neck to her thigh, his hands small and fumbling and sickeningly soft from a life of no work. Revulsion shot through her.

He lowered his mouth to her ear. "A man need not merely stand still for the knife to be thrust in his back, don't you agree? That a man should not put up with betrayal?"

Dinah kept herself rigid and focused on a spot on the doorframe. She pictured Tom's face, the curl of his lashes above the soft of his eyes. Such soft eyes for a man who was so strong. She made herself see his eyes.

"The city council can, and will, discover the root of whatever it was this William Paul whispered in Peter Prioleau's ear—whatever bloody plan that scared the faithful Peter so badly. When faced with betrayal, a man can take action. Don't you agree?" He circled again. "And I am not pleased, Dinah, with your being with child."

Dinah's whole body shook, but she kept her gaze steely. "And you standing there like you'd got no hand in it!"

The words were out before she could clamp her jaw closed, her voice the slash of a blade.

And now it was done.

His whole arm landed the slap to her cheek, her head snapping back with the force. "I believe a trip to the workhouse might curb your tongue."

Dinah righted her head slowly to level a gaze back at him. But she said nothing.

"You may know that my daughter has fixed on the baby's father. A certain blacksmith we all know, owned by my old friend Mrs. Nathaniel Russell. My daughter is certain of this. So again I would ask you: Ought a man merely stand still while the knife of betrayal is thrust in his back?"

A trip to the workhouse was already assured. She had little to lose—and could not hold back the words anymore if she'd wanted. "You know good as I do who the father . . ."

She stopped there, unwilling even to form the words *might be*.

Jackson Pinckney lifted one of her hands, blistered and calloused from lye and from long days of work. Then he rested his right arm on her chest so that the pistol's muzzle pointed at the bottom of her jaw. "Since Emily is your mistress, the rest of us would assume that she knows the truth." His arm tightened across her front. "The fault, dear Dinah, is not in our stars, but in ourselves."

In one sudden wrench from his grasp, Dinah pulled herself free, sending Jackson Pinckney off balance—and the heavy pistol crashing to the floor and firing straight up.

Jackson Pinckney glared from Dinah to the hole in the doorframe.

"Father!" Emily called from the floor above, running footsteps already on the front stairs. "Is everything all right?"

Pinckney's whole body had gone stiff with fury, his morning coat looking as if it hung upon a wax figure. "Get the hell out of my sight," he hissed, backhanding her cheek. Pulling a coin from his pocket, he yanked up her hand and pressed it into her palm. "You'll need this to pay the workhouse for their trouble. I'll send a message right now that a servant of mine is on her way there."

Chapter 24

2015

Kate leaned with Rose over the photocopied image of "My Tom" at Battery Row and the photocopy she'd made herself of the notation at the bottom of the postwar AME workers list: *And also Dinah, a native of Charleston.* Stifling a yawn, she flopped back against the settee cushions. "Sorry, Rose. It's not the subject matter or the company. I just had trouble sleeping last night for wondering about what might have happened. To Tom. And to Dinah. If these are the Tom and the Dinah you and I know. I mean, not *know* exactly but . . ."

Rose glanced up from the pages. "You can't be faulted for lack of trying—I will give you that." Smoothing her skirts, she added, "I hope you were not annoyed with me for giving that sweet and consistently honest contractor of mine Mr. Lambeth your number, sugar."

"You know, Rose, you add *sugar* to your speech more often when you want something."

Rose gave a flip of her delicate hand. "Why, I don't want a blessed thing."

"That makes two of us then. Remember, I don't want any attachments in Charleston."

Rose raised her chin. "Don't you think that's just a wee bit over-confident—to assume Mr. Lambeth's interest in you? It might very well be he is simply a thoughtful young man. I understand there are one or two of them still left." Sniffing, she lifted her left wrist with its filigreed watch. "I've only a few more moments before my next commitment. Shall we resume reading from the journal?"

"Please."

Smoothing her linen skirt, Rose began where she'd left off.

My lady's maid has continued lately in her peculiar distraction. Perhaps it is only her condition and the spring heat well upon us. But then today, things became so much the worse.

Today I'd only just returned from the bookseller's shop on King when a most horrid clatter sent me racing downstairs, where I found Father standing alone in his study with a pistol, of all things, under one arm.

Dinah stood but a few yards away and seemed . . . I know not what she seemed. Upset by the noise to be sure. I could not help but think that she'd only just come from out of his study.

"To the workhouse. Now!" Father shouted at Dinah. Then, slamming the door so hard it knocked the miniature in the brass frame straight off the wall, he marched out the front door.

I flew after him. How could I not? Dinah's silence has annoyed me, to be sure, its swings toward anger and even defiance. But the workhouse is a sentence I would never wish on a servant of ours. I tried to stop Father. Let me say only that I was given to understand my efforts were not valued. And that I was to desist. For a moment, in fact, I was certain my father would strike his own daughter.

Do I have any choice now but silence?

I am crushed. I fear what this will mean not only for my lady's maid, but for the child Dinah carries.

For several moments, neither Rose nor Kate spoke, only looked at each other.

"Heavens," Rose said at last.

"I know."

"This might be a good time to voice what I've been thinking, Katherine: that I am thankful to get to read this journal with someone—and in particular, with you."

Kate surprised even herself by reaching to squeeze the older woman's hand. "It's an honor to read it with you, Rose."

Rose's mouth lifted on one end in a sad smile. "Not a pleasure, however. Not reading these sorts of scenes."

"No. Not a pleasure." Kate rubbed her temple with two fingers, then pointed to the bottom of the page, dog-eared at the corner. "We're getting close to where the journal's final pages and back cover have been torn away. And, Rose, look at this quote she ends this entry with—in the margin, what little there is. And it's in an ink that has more brown in it and more thickness than the original entry—like she wrote it later with another nib and a different ink. Emily's handwriting, though. What do you make of this?"

Kate read it aloud:

> *"Nought so of love this looser dame did skill,*
> *But as a cole to kindle fleshly flame,*
> *Giving the bridle to her wanton will,*
> *And treading under foote her honest name."*
> *—Edmund Spenser*

And there was another quote squeezed in the margin at the end of another entry:

> *"Iris all hues, roses, and jessamine*
> *Reared high their flourished heads between, and wrought*
> *Mosaic; underfoot the violet,*
> *Crocus, and hyacinth, with rich inlay*
> *Broidered the ground, more coloured than with stone*

Of costliest emblem."
—*John Milton,* Paradise Lost

Rose ran a frail finger above the script, then sighed. "Frankly, my dear, I haven't a clue."

The two studied the journal.

"Rose, you can tell me the truth: When I first told you that I was searching for some sort of connection between my mother's interest in this person Tom Russell—the whole Vesey revolt—and my own family, did you think I was nuts? You didn't say much, you know."

Rose shook her head delicately. "*Nuts* would be a relative term in the South, first of all. But also, no, I did not."

"So there's nothing else you can tell me—nothing else you recall about either of my parents?"

"Only . . ." Rose's lips moved slightly, as if she were trying on words. "Only that your momma was a dear girl. Despite . . ."

Kate waited. But Rose was staring out toward the water. Kate scooted forward in her seat. "Despite . . . what?"

Rose's gaze swung back. "What's that?"

Kate was feeling desperate: so close to another piece of the puzzle—and yet if she pushed too hard, Rose might withdraw. Kate tried to pitch her voice with a patience she did not feel. "You were saying my mother was a dear girl *despite* something."

Rose's nearly translucent blue eyes widened. "Did I? Heavens. As if it weren't bad enough losing one's balance with age. Now I appear to be losing my filters."

"Rose, you can tell me. All I'm looking for is the truth about my mother—not a plaster saint. I knew better than anyone that she lived with some sort of sadness or regret I couldn't understand. The past haunted her, made it so hard for her to let go and live in the present, and I never knew why. But nothing you could tell me would change that I loved her."

Rose's gaze swung out toward the sea, as if the grand span of ocean and sky might grant her permission to share whatever it was she knew. She sighed, her eyes still on the water. "Your mother as a young woman was quite lovely—and you look a great deal like her, as I have said. But it was more than her looks. Sarah Grace had something you didn't."

Kate held her breath, afraid to say anything that might make Rose stop speaking.

"A certain endearing . . . helplessness. Especially with men. She was smart as a whip but learned to cover her brains with those big brown doe eyes of hers. She was always laughing, always making everyone around her feel strong and clever and brave. Men adored her, you know."

Incredulous, Kate was afraid to break Rose's reverie, but the words tumbled out. "Always *laughing*?" It hardly seemed possible that could be the same person who'd raised her.

Rose nodded. "Oh yes. Always. In fact, when I met her, during the time she was engaged to your father and invited, of course, into . . ." She paused to phrase it delicately. "A different world than that to which she'd been accustomed, to all the balls and soirées and fund-raising dinners"— she waved a dismissive hand—"she was almost . . ." She faltered there. "But then who am I to judge another's journey?"

Kate dropped her voice so that it was nothing but a soft nudge— nothing that would startle the older woman into stopping. "Almost what, Rose?"

"How shall I say it nicely? Almost . . . doggedly happy. As if she'd determined she would appear fancy-free at all costs."

"No matter how she actually felt?" Kate suggested quietly.

Rose nodded.

"She had . . ." Kate searched for the word Rose might use. "Admirers? Before my father?"

"Oh yes. And after." Rose jerked straighter in her seat at that, as if she'd said more than she intended. Her eyes swung to Kate's.

Kate swallowed. "People said things about her? About her relationships with men?"

Rose stood suddenly, as if in protest. "People are imbeciles, generally speaking. And repeat whatever comes to them, unexamined. Sarah Grace," she added hotly, "was never unfaithful to your father. And Heyward behaved, as was his wont, like a damned fool."

Kate sat slack-jawed at this vehement defense of her mother that seemed to imply there'd been plenty said in opposition. "Rose, I talked with someone at the College of Charleston who insisted that he, for one, didn't believe my mother capable of *the atrocity*—which implied some people did. Do you have *any* idea what he could have been talking about?"

"No. Decidedly not," Rose said in a tone far less decided.

Rose brushed invisible crumbs from her linen skirts with gusto. "That, my dear, is all I have to say on the subject—and it was doubtless already more than I ought. Do let's switch topics, shall we?"

Kate took a moment to recover. Briskly, Rose marched about the piazza, stacking teacups and saucers onto a wicker side table. Her ramrod-straight posture and her back toward Kate said she was done with that portion of their conversation and there was no going back.

Reaching for her wallet inside her backpack, Kate fished between dollar bills. "I haven't shown you this yet, I don't think. This tiny key. And this scrap of a name, Palmetto 8, left in my mother's things. I don't suppose you have any idea what it could be."

Rose examined the key in her wrinkled hand. "I wish I did, Katherine. I do wish that I did." She lifted the watch at her wrist. "Oh my. My contractor, Mr. Lambeth, is coming to begin sanding the floors in the room adjacent. Which I assured him would be convenient, since I will be running an errand."

Disappointed, Kate glanced up from the journal. "That's right. You said you had another commitment. I don't suppose . . ."

"It's Thursday," Rose said—as if that were sufficient.

With a wistful glance down at the journals and letters splayed there, Kate packed up her notes and moved reluctantly toward the stairs.

"On Thursday, one banks. Fridays being the day weekly wage earners come hording in." From her rolltop desk, Rose drew several papers, including what appeared to be bank statements and a letter with an embossed letterhead. In one corner of the stationery was a gold palm tree.

Or, given the state tree here, Kate reminded herself, it was more likely a palmetto.

Plucking the Palmetto 8 scrap attached to the tiny key from her wallet, Kate squinted at the number eight, nearly flat on one side. Unless . . . Could the eight be an uppercase *B* instead?

Palmetto B.

As in Palmetto Bank?

Kate spun back toward the letter gripped in Rose's hand. "Actually, Rose, I wonder if I might walk with you." She held up the key with its scrap. "What if this was part of the words *Palmetto Bank*? And what if the key went to—"

"A safe-deposit box." Rose snapped her fingers. "Lord, I feel like a complete, sugarcoated fool. Come on now, Katherine. Let's see if your pretty little twenty-five-year-old legs can walk as fast as mine do."

Rose ignored the crosswalks and glided diagonally across the street. She paused as a middle-aged tourist wobbled ahead of them on the sidewalk, the effort of running making her short denim skirt ride too high on her doughy, undercooked legs.

Rose's lids dropped to half-mast. "Has the use of a mirror gone out of fashion entirely?"

Kate hurried to catch up as they reached Broad Street, and Rose, purse clutched tightly, marched toward the towering doors on the corner.

Just before the bank's entrance, Kate nodded to the sign etched in gold overhead. *"Palmetto Bank,"* she read aloud. Then pulled the key with its Palmetto B scrap from her wallet again. She hauled on the heavy door. "Shall we give it a try?"

A soft ripple of whispers followed them in, like the far reach of a wave shifting shells on the shore.

"Does *everyone* here know you?" Kate whispered.

"That would be likely, yes. And there will be the usual nonsensical fawning remarks on my age: *That hair! Still thick in her eighties! How handsome she must have been in her day* . . . as if the days one could claim as one's own ended with the first varicose vein."

Across the full length of the bank, Rose carried herself, shoulders back, to the manager's desk, where a man in a glossy gray suit stood, his wide-set eyes lifting to the two women.

"Yes? I'm a bit busy at the moment."

"I am Mrs. Lila Rose Manigault Pinckney."

A pause.

Then the manager bolted up from his seat. "Well, now. My mistake. I'm still a bit new. And not enough coffee this morning." He nudged her. "Or too much Captain Morgan last night."

Rose skewered him with a look.

But he tittered on: "Mrs. Pinckney, let me just say it's an honor. And how can Palmetto Bank assist you two beautiful ladies today?"

"As I've no immediate plans to consolidate my accounts from other institutions into this bank, you needn't overplay the toady. So you are new in this position, Mr. . . ." Rose glanced at the gold tag pinned to the too-glossy suit. "Vonnit." One silver eyebrow arched. "Mr. Grich Vonnit."

He pitched toward her like they were intimate friends. "An old nickname." He nudged her again.

"An ill-advised one." Rose half lowered her eyelids. "Actually, I remember you now, vaguely, as one of the young Turks who went to prep school with my second cousin's son."

The manager puffed out his chest. "How can I help you, Mrs. Pinckney?"

"*May* I. How *may* you help. I've come with a question about the ownership of one of your safe-deposit boxes."

"Oh, now, Mrs. Pinckney, ma'am, all that information would be confidential—after all, they're *safe*-deposit boxes, right?" He grinned.

She did not.

"I should have added, Mr. Vonnit, that during the time I served on the board of your school, it seems there was a certain C-minus student giving some trouble, a pimple-faced prankster who wore mirrors on his sneakers and stood up close to the girls when they wore skirts."

Grich Vonnit's eyes rounded, and his unfortunate skin blushed.

"I recommended against expulsion at the time, though I did wonder if the student's poor judgment might not come back to haunt him in later life. It is *such* a shame, don't you think, when the mistakes of our youth follow us into the present?"

He cleared his throat. "I appreciate your not mentioning that. To anyone here."

"And I appreciate your cooperation with my request." She surveyed him coolly. "If you would be so good as to tell us whether or not you have a safe-deposit box here in the name of Sarah Grace Drayton, we would be most obliged."

Clacking away at his keyboard, Grich Vonnit scanned his computer screen. "I'm afraid there's nothing, ladies." The manager started to rise.

But Rose placed a frail hand on his shoulder—which sat him back down.

"Try Sarah Grace Ravenel," Kate suggested. And then it hit her. "Try that together with the name Katherine Drayton."

A sulk seeping into his professional smile, the manager settled back over the keyboard and clacked away. "Aha!" Vonnit threw both arms of the shiny gray suit up over his head.

Rose's eyelids dropped back to half-mast. "Have we made a touch-down, Mr. Vonnit?"

Kate's hand shook as she rubbed the key between two fingers. "A safe-deposit box."

"Your wish, ladies, is my command." Then he stopped, turning to Kate. "But unless you're Sarah Grace Ravenel in the flesh, I can't let you back to the box. Palmetto Bank policy."

Rose pulled herself to full height. "I can see, naturally, the need for policy—for the general public. In this case, however, my young friend here, who holds, as you see, the key to the box, is the daughter of the recently deceased Sarah Grace Ravenel."

He chewed on a bottom lip. "You got a death certificate on you?"

Rose patted his arm. "No doubt, young man, you can imagine the impracticality of that."

"Palmetto Bank policy says I can only let the owner back to the box."

"Given that my young friend here is holding the key, and given that her mother is recently deceased and she is the only living heir, and given that I do so hope to be able to keep to myself the unfortunate circumstances from the past by which I remember your name, Mr. Vonnit, I would imagine you might want to escort us now to the box." Lila Rose Pinckney smiled at the young man.

Head down, he thrust his hands into his pockets. Sighing, he motioned for them to follow.

Kate tipped her head close to Rose's as they walked. "You know what people whisper about you, Rose, don't you?"

"Enlighten me, sugar."

"How Mrs. Lila Rose Manigault Pinckney *always* gets her way."

Rose smoothed the pleats of her peach linen skirt. "And why would it be otherwise?"

∼

Kate's legs and arms had gone numb as she followed Grich Vonnit back to the locked room with the boxes.

"This particular box," he pronounced, "was paid for in advance for the entire calendar year. Paid up again last week."

Kate shook her head. "A payment was made *last week*?"

"That's what our records say. And our records are never wrong."

"That can't be. My mother died several weeks ago."

Kate and Rose exchanged glances.

Vonnit shrugged. "Somebody paid for it. And has been paying for it the past twenty-five years. Our largest size."

"This whole thing makes no sense," Kate whispered to Rose. "She wasn't a jewels or bank bonds kind of person."

Rose patted her arm. "That is God's honest truth. Yes. I remember that well."

"You do?"

"In those months she was engaged to your father, she arrived at the St. Cecilia Ball with nothing around her neck—not one strand of diamonds or pearls. Despite, I understood, all Heyward's offers to provide them." She smiled with fondness. "For all Sarah Grace's diminutive sweetness, I always suspected a streak of the renegade. Bless her."

What was it that Dr. Sutpen had said about Sarah Grace? *She cared little for how people talked?*

Vonnit tapped his shoe on the floor with barely restrained impatience, but both women ignored him.

"She died with nothing in assets. With," Kate added under her breath, "one notable exception. Which was missing from her things I gathered up from our house after she died."

Rose placed a forefinger on her chin. "Yes, that great block of a diamond—the engagement ring Heyward gave her. My Lord, I recall how it looked on her tiny finger: like a kind of glittering membership card she was supposed to flash to be let in the door. Maybe that was Heyward's hope in giving it to her." Rose stopped, her eyes cutting to

Kate's. "Once again, I have said more than I'd set out to do. I appear to be slipping in my post-younger years."

Kate squeezed her hand. "I suspect you had it just about right. Thank you."

The safe-deposit box was up ahead, and Grich Vonnit gave an obsequious sweep of an arm, indicating that Kate should try the key.

"I typically take my leave at this point," Vonnit was saying, "and allow the customer time to review a drawer's contents in privacy."

"Rose, would you stay with me? It sounds crazy, but I'm kind of nervous." As an aside, she added, "Mr. Vonnit, you're welcome to stay."

A little too eagerly, Vonnit gushed, "It would be my pleasure."

Rose slipped her arm around Kate's waist. "Whatever you need. And listen to me, Katie."

Kate blinked at the name—that only her mother had used.

She gripped Kate's hand in hers tightly. "Whatever's in there or not, that's not going to change what you know of your momma. The kind of sweetness she had. You hear?"

Weakly, Kate nodded.

Atrocity, Sutpen had said. *I never believed her capable of an atrocity.*

Vonnit's thumbs smoothed the insides of his lapels. The bank manager helped Kate slide the long, deep box to the table nearby. Inserting the key, Kate inhaled, then turned it clockwise.

The three of them stood there unspeaking. Gaping.

At seashells.

A long, deep drawer full of seashells. All shapes and sizes. And Kate knew all their names.

What's this one called, Mommy? she'd demanded, landing with a splat in the surf and scooping up a handful of shells.

Kneeling beside her, Sarah Grace had dumped the pink plastic pail they'd been using to hoard that morning's haul of shells. One by one, she'd held up each treasure: a Scotch bonnet and a banded tulip, a gray lightning whelk and a pink channeled whelk, a silver moon snail's shell and a keyhole sand dollar, a white angel wing and a black striated ponderous ark shell, red sunset clams, a brown horse conch shell, a mushroom coral, and iridescent oyster shells.

Her chest tight, Kate scooped up two handfuls now. "Sarah Grace's idea of riches. Not money. Not things you can buy. But this. Things you have to find for yourself. Things of beauty." Eyes filling, she ran a finger over a large conch.

Rose's arm had not left her waist, and it pulled her in now. Kate leaned into her and closed her eyes against the tears welling again.

"Rose, this is so like my momma. A treasure in shells. And more unanswered questions."

Grich Vonnit cleared his throat. "Perhaps you two ladies would like to confirm that the entire contents would be to Ms. Drayton's satisfaction? And sign here?"

Ignoring him, Kate turned the box on its side. Let the shells spill to the table.

Beneath was a small blue velvet box, identical to the one Kate had found in her mother's possessions—the one that contained the earrings instead of the rings. Lifting the box, her eyes went to Rose. Her voice shook: "The one thing, maybe, she had of value."

"Lands." Rose brushed the velvet with one finger.

Kate held it a moment unopened.

Slowly, she lifted the velvet lid.

The slot for the rings was empty.

Kate stared at where they should have been.

And fluttering to the table from inside the box was a slip of yellowed notebook paper torn from a larger piece. Numbly, Kate reached for it.

Sarah Grace had penned a note—her handwriting shakier than usual.

My precious Kate,

If you're looking here for my rings, then you know at least part of my story. I am so deeply sorry for the pain this empty box and what you may be learning of me have surely caused you. Remember that everything I had in life was yours, paltry as that was.

If only for the peace of your own heart, I hope you can come to terms as best you are able with all my unforgivable failures to act: the done—and all I left undone.

But how I have loved you, my daughter.

Tears spilling onto her cheeks, Kate stared at the note. And the empty box.

What you may be learning of me.

All my unforgivable failures to act.

Gripped by a spasm of sorrow for Sarah Grace—so shut off, even from her own daughter—and missing her mother so much it nearly doubled her over, Kate troweled her hands into the shells and let them sift through her fingers. She closed her eyes against what she saw there on the bank table before her.

Saw. But could not understand.

Chapter 25

1822

Tom ducked out the side door of his forge and let the wind off the harbor clear his head for a moment. He'd worked all through the early morning in a frenzy, a set of farm tools propped at the forge as his cover for the order he was supposedly filling—but he jumped each time the front door flew open. Now the coffin that sat along the far wall near the alley was filled, its lid concealing just-crafted pikes and hatchets and spears.

Sweating, although the day wasn't yet hot, Tom stood behind his oak counter and faced the front door. Eyes on the door and hands shaking, feeling their way, Tom fumbled under the counter as he lifted bullets one by one out of the mold and dropped them in a barrel filled with rice.

A clamor just outside his shop door. A man's shout.

Tom crammed the rest of the bullets still in their mold into the barrel of rice.

Now a child's cry of pain.

Tom stepped to the paned windows of his shop. Three top hats towered just outside. A vicious thump sounded on his door.

He gave a quick backward glance to be sure the coffin was covered— and across it he tossed several of the cloths he used when painting wrought iron black so that it appeared to be a kind of workbench piled with stained rags. The barrel of rice with its buried bullets sat where he'd left it. *Of course that's where it is—like bullets would somehow move themselves out of hiding at the mere presence of a white man.* Still, Tom's hand shook as he opened the door.

But the thump must not have been a demand for him to open. The three white men stood there glaring at something a few feet away, James Hamilton's walking stick apparently having fallen against the door. Colonel Drayton was tapping the end loop of his riding crop against his chin, as if contemplating the scene. But Jackson Pinckney's mouth twisted into contempt.

Ned Bennett stood, bending over a child. "What'd you call the buckruh, child?"

Tapping the brim of his top hat lower over his eyes, Pinckney stepped closer. "What vile thing was it he said?"

The flat of Ned Bennett's hand landed on the mulatto boy's cheek. "Don't you *ever* call a white man that again!"

The boy cowered, his eyes bright circles of fear. "Didn't say nothing but what I heard."

"What was it he said, boy?" Hamilton demanded.

Ned shook his head, doleful, and his tone took on the extra measure of calm and servility he reserved for crises—which could only mean, Tom realized, that Ned was worried. "It don't bear repeating—I swear it don't. Could hardly say it out loud. He won't never say it again, though. You can be sure of that." Ned cocked back his hand again.

Hamilton's gloved hand lifted his walking stick. "I insist you tell us."

Ned shook his head, sorrowful still. "Heavy head. What he called you. What he calls all the buckruh, he say."

The boy's face changed from fear to surprise, and he jerked his head left and then right like he was shaking it no, but Ned's hand closed on the boy's shoulder.

Pinckney bristled. "Explain yourself, boy."

Ned sighed. "Said white men must have bigger, heavier heads, too big for they own bodies, he say, maybe because they got so many more brains to be holding up there." Ned bowed his head. "Don't reckon the child meant any much harm."

Hardly able to breathe, Tom marveled at the attitude, all this bowing and scraping and flattery and distraction, that Ned could throw on like a cloak, not once betraying his disdain for his own words. Not so much as a blink.

Colonel Drayton straightened. "Good God. There's no call to take the child's head off his shoulders for that." He studied Ned's face. "You are Ned Bennett. The governor's Ned."

"Yes, sir. That's who I be. And proud of it, too."

"You were the one who voluntarily appeared at the workhouse today. To testify to those of us on the council Mayor Hamilton called. To clear your good name."

Tom's heart lurched in his chest. Had Ned sold them all out to save his own skin?

And here Tom stood, only one breath away from discovery, three city leaders tensed and waiting.

"Yes, sir, I did, sure enough. Heard around town my name'd got mixed up in these ugly rumors, somebody's idea of a terrible joke. Couldn't sleep, not for two seconds straight, thinking somebody might think there was some real kind of danger to Charleston. Couldn't stand thinking Governor Bennett might waste any worry. Sorry thing when rumors get spread."

The mayor tapped his walking stick on the palm of his opposite hand. "Indeed. So it would seem that Peter Prioleau's testimony of some sort of murderous plot would be only the ravings of an unsound mind."

Ned Bennett's head dropped lower still. "If you'll forgive me saying, Mayor Hamilton, sir, Peter Prioleau's mind never was much hinged onto sound. Alltime be the victim of nightmares he'd wake up to thinking was real."

"Nightmares," said Jackson Pinckney—with less conviction than he might've been trying to muster. He spat to one side.

Their top hats tipping together as they conferred, the three white men walked on. Only Jackson Pinckney glanced back once, eyes narrowed, as if not quite sure what he'd just witnessed.

Ned Bennett stood where he was a moment, the boy fleeing up the other side of the street.

"So. Tom Russell," Ned said after a moment.

Shakily, Tom stepped from the doorway and waited until the top hats had disappeared around the next corner. "You want to tell me what that was about?"

"A performance," Ned murmured. "And a damn fine one, wouldn't you say? One of the best audiences I had today."

"Pinckney wasn't convinced."

"Maybe not. But Drayton and Hamilton, they both were. And Hamilton's made hisself the head of the council he's gathered to see if there's any fire behind the smoke of that traitor"—Ned spat the name—"Peter Prioleau."

Tom dropped his voice even lower than Ned's. "Prioleau's a house slave. Vesey said he wasn't trusting house slaves."

"It was William Paul"—Ned shook his head in disgust—"trusted Prioleau with the plans. Prioleau went straight and squealed. William Paul been at the workhouse all day." Ned cut his eyes now at Tom. "Torture got a way of making even a brave man talk."

Tom made himself ask, "All of us named?"

Ned shook his head. "Not by Paul. My name got listed by Prioleau, what I heard—and me in Governor Bennett's house. I don't got to tell you how much the mayor'd like to pin something like this on the governor—for him being too soft on his slaves, Hamilton thinks, and look what kind of chaos gets whipped up. So I took myself there to chat with the council. Scared the pants off Hamilton, me showing up, smiling and wanting to clear my good name."

"Hamilton won't let this thing lie. If Prioleau—"

"Prioleau's a fool." Ned's whisper cut into the quiet. "They got no evidence but his word. And they got their own egos to argue everything's fine—all of us black folk just real happy in chains." Ned turned back to Tom. "All us, we'll just keep on"—he glanced over his shoulder—"what we been doing."

In the late afternoon, as Tom was crouched at the back of the shop, frantically painting an iron grille to distract himself from the waves of *what-ifs* pounding in, the front door eased open. Tom's eyes swung over the breadth of the forge for a possible bayonet or bullet or knife showing, but all was well covered. He rose.

A small, bearded man in dark pants and a dark shirt stepped softly inside as if he did not wish to disturb the silence. Tom stayed back from the counter and let his right hand drop to the ball-peen hammer lying across the anvil. Here stood the man from the tavern—a Quaker, yes, but also a white man. A white man who'd stayed behind when nearly all the slavery-loathing Friends had left. And who may have heard more than was safe.

"Shovel," the man said. "If thee would craft one more shovel, I would be grateful."

Warily, Tom nodded. Stepped closer to the counter. "When is it you need it by?"

The man looked toward the window. "Sooner, perhaps, than I'd thought. It may be that I have to leave town very suddenly—a death in the family that my good wife and I fear is imminent. And may occur sooner than planned—that is, than we expected." He turned back and met Tom's eye. "And I wish to be prepared. Perhaps thee can understand our concern for the possible hurry."

The Quaker made no attempt to discuss the length of the handle or size of the scoop or payment.

Tom stared at him. For a moment, neither man moved.

Rumors had raged last Sunday at Morris Brown's church, warning that city leaders were trying to lure house slaves to spy on those who might know something of a planned insurrection. So why wouldn't the same city leaders try to use this left-behind Quaker?

Tom's mouth opened for a question he'd no idea how to word.

Shouts on East Bay sent both of them to the front window. A horse was galloping full tilt up the street from the peninsula's southern tip, its rider's top hat blowing off his head, the rider never slowing to retrieve it—or even seeming to notice. The rider's face came into focus as he approached.

"Well, hell," said a white man just outside the front window. "If that ain't the mayor. Wonder what's got him stirred up."

Gripping the windowsill, Tom kept his face blank.

Trying but failing to meet Tom's eye, the Quaker slipped through the front door without saying more.

For the dregs of the afternoon, Tom lived in the silence that deafens: the tension of hearing nothing, knowing nothing. For hours he swung his hammer up into its arc and brought it crashing down on his anvil—his only relief that he had something to do with his hands. Pouring sweat, refusing to let himself rest, Tom crashed his hammer down.

Despite William Paul's so stupidly spreading the word to a house slave against Vesey's order, despite Peter Prioleau's squealing, despite the torture and interrogations of William Paul, despite three servants in the governor's own household being named as part of the revolt, the city lay quiet now in the late afternoon.

Maybe Ned Bennett's gift for the theatrical, his volunteering himself—eagerly, humbly—to the council for questioning, maybe that had saved them.

Maybe the plans for their own version of storming the Bastille—when the captives would walk free—could go on as planned.

But Tom did not feel like celebrating as he ducked from alley to alley, the streets too still on this Friday evening. In place of the usual bustle of businesses bringing their affairs to a close and carriages venturing out in the evening's relief from the heat, East Bay sat eerily silent. Not peaceful in its stillness, but as if something sinister hung over Charleston, the city holding its breath, waiting.

It was well before the curfew bell, but still his instincts told him to hide. To run. That something in the course of the day had gone terribly, terribly wrong.

At the last lot on Meeting Street, he slipped into the shadows of the oaks and palmettos. His burial of the latest batch of bullets he'd hidden well, the locations already shielded by brambles and weeds, then sand and shell swept with palmetto fronds over the freshly dug holes so that no part of the lot appeared disturbed. It was the least safe of the locations—most of the weapons they'd made were concealed at Bulkley's Farm, and they would capture many more by raiding the city arsenal and gun shops once the revolt was in motion.

But this little stash was vital, Tom thought—and Gullah Jack had agreed: a small store of ammunition hidden here at the peninsula's tip. If, by some remote chance, the bullets were discovered before the revolt, they might appear to be only the fishing-net weights their molds intended for them to be. And even if someone suspected they might have been intended for bullets, nothing about them would lead to Tom Russell or anyone else.

To be sure of that, Tom buried the bullet mold now and covered it quickly before a phaeton rattled past, its driver not even glancing to the circle of oaks where Tom hid.

Just then Dinah appeared on the second-story piazza of the Pinckneys' Meeting Street home. Holding an evening gown, she shook it out with gusto—her eyes on the shadows across and down the street where Tom hid.

He emerged for only a moment, just long enough to be sure she saw him, and nodded at her. It was enough. That would comfort her spirit.

But a cry and running footsteps stopped him in his tracks.

Instead of diving back into the shadows, Tom stepped into the street.

"George!" he called. "What is it?"

George Wilson hurtled against him as if he were running with his eyes closed. Then, shoving himself away from Tom's chest, George stumbled headlong across the Battery toward the seawall.

Then up onto the seawall itself.

"You!" called a white man. "You, boy! Seawall's only for whites!"

But the man needn't have bothered. Because George Wilson had already thrown himself off the wall's far end and into the harbor, where the water at high tide would be well over his head.

By the time Tom Russell got there, George had disappeared. Tom dove under, grasping, feeling. Emerged for air. Dove down again, powerful arms against the currents.

Nothing.

Until one hand brushed the sleeve of a shirt. A man's arm.

Tom kicked hard. Grasped the body from behind, one of his arms across George Wilson's small chest. Tom kicked, gasping for air, hauling the man to the seawall, then up over it.

Convulsing, George Wilson coughed up brown water, then lay still, curled on his side.

Dripping and spent, Tom bent over him.

"Sorry you did," George whispered.

Tom bent lower still. "What'd you say?"

"Be sorry you saved me when you find out."

"Find out what?"

"That I told. Told it all."

Heart exploding inside his chest, Tom froze where he bent.

Moaning, George shook his head. "God help me. God help us all."

Forcing himself not to run as every instinct told him to do, Tom let George's limp form slide to the ground.

Straightening, he walked away. Slowly. Deliberately. Pulse racing.

So they knew.

Tom could see Dinah leaning heavily against the balustrade, her middle protruding so far now she'd turned sideways to be able to lean out over the railing. One hand dropped protectively to her belly. The other hand covered her mouth.

She would have heard at the church the whispered warnings that spies could be infiltrating every meeting, every conversation.

She must have seen just now George Wilson, trusted house slave, try to take his own life.

She must have guessed.

Mingo Harth appeared at the ragged hem of the crowd, a straw hat pulled low over his face, but with the same swagger that always marked his walk.

Mingo worked his way closer to Tom. Tom edged away, but Mingo would not be shaken, wandering up East Bay after him.

A half block from his shop, Tom jerked his head back but did not slow down. "Won't have you seen anywhere near me or my shop."

Mingo kept strolling slowly forward but didn't turn his head toward Tom as he passed. Hardly moving his lips and keeping his eyes far ahead up the street, Mingo said, "New orders. All plans moved. June 16, this Sunday, we fight. Middlenight, we begin. Messengers already left for the outlying farms."

June 16. Midnight. Two days from now.

Tom knelt to retie a shoelace that was not untied, its thin leather strips stiff and shaking in his hands. "Tell Vesey," he said, head down, "George Wilson's gone and reported it all. On top of Prioleau . . ."

Mingo Harth stopped here, a good three paces past where Tom knelt over his shoe. Mingo peered in the window of the shop where he'd halted. "On top of Prioleau," he choked out, "they'll believe Wilson."

Tom shifted to attend to the laces of the other shoe. *"Tell Vesey."*

Mingo Harth had already vanished into the mouth of the alley that ran alongside Tom's shop.

A white woman in a simple gray cotton dress and a plain close-fitting bonnet was hurrying past, pausing a few feet from Tom as she dropped the handbag she clutched and bent to retrieve it. "By North Adger's Wharf," she whispered—so low he wasn't entirely sure what he'd heard. "Two lanterns. Tomorrow night just after dark. If thee are in need of help."

Tom stared at the woman.

"My husband," she said. "I believe thee know my husband. He has come to thy shop, yes? For a shovel most recently."

She fumbled with the handbag, its contents spilling across the brick. "How clumsy of me," she said. "Would thee be so good as to hand me the comb that's bounced to thy feet? My husband and I must travel to Flat Rock to bury our dead, a dear friend, tomorrow, just after dark, and the grief has made me clumsy, I fear."

Tom bent for the hair comb she'd dropped, carved whalebone, two words etched crudely at its top: *STEAL AWAY.*

"I thank thee." She smiled at him. "It's a favorite song of mine that's carved into the comb."

"I'm sorry," Tom said, watching her face and scanning the street, "for your grief."

The woman stood. Met his eye. "We do not grieve as those without"—she paused before the last word—"hope."

From several blocks north, near the workhouse, two riders approached, their horses in a fast trot.

James Hamilton, still hatless, was one, looking paler than ever, even well into summer.

And the other was Jackson Pinckney.

"I must go," said the woman.

Tom would have slipped into the alley alongside his shop if Mingo hadn't just gone that way. None of them could afford to be seen with the others now.

Not ever again.

But this was no time for looking frightened. Tom straightened. Flexed back the full breadth of his shoulders. Turned toward the door of his shop.

"It would seem," Jackson Pinckney was saying—louder than needed, "that Shakespeare was right."

"My *God*, Pinckney! What the hell has Shakespeare got to do with the Armageddon we're facing here?"

"Only this," said Pinckney, still louder—and Tom knew for certain he meant him to hear. Maybe because he'd connected Dinah with Tom. Or maybe because he'd already heard Tom's name linked with the rebellion.

Tom turned and met Pinckney's scowl.

"That our informant George Wilson," hissed Pinckney, his face purple with rage, "has revealed for us what we should have known for some time: that 'hell is empty, and all the devils are here.'"

Chapter 26

2015

Kate glanced up from her notes spread over the counter of Cypress & Fire, glad for the refuge of this place. After her experience at the bank yesterday, she needed time just to think. To reread her mother's note. To try to cobble together the bits of truth she'd gathered so far from the past—both the recent and the far past—and see if they fit into anything other than a still-bigger puzzle with yet more pieces missing.

She bent down closer over the copied picture of "My Tom." The image was too blurred and faded to determine much about the age of the man, except that he was decidedly older.

Spinning the planes of his Rubik's Cube, Gabe caught the eye of his father, who was affixing gold and turquoise glazed tiles to the fluted edges of a large mirror. Setting his cube aside, Gabe sheepishly drew his homework closer. To Kate he whispered, "I told you this would be a good quiet place to get some work done. And sort out the sad."

"Thanks, big guy. The archives were seeming kind of lonely today."

The boy raised his hand to hers for a fist bump. "What friends do. Alltime." He bent his head over his book.

Surreptitiously, checking to see that both father and son were engrossed in their work, Kate held up the image of "My Tom." Gabe's curls flopped over the forehead he'd bunched in concentration. Daniel's back was turned as he focused on the tiles. Trying to determine family resemblance from a photocopy of an indistinct image two hundred years old was pretty futile.

And Daniel caught her at it. Turning before she'd set the page down, he shook his head, chuckling. "I'll give you this: You don't give up easy, do you?"

"Stubbornness is one of my few virtues."

"I keep saying if I knew more about the family connection back to Tom Russell—or not—I'd tell you. Like to know myself."

Sighing, she set the page down. "Sorry." Her eyes resting on the leather cord at his neck, its medallion hidden by his T-shirt, she opened her mouth to ask to see it.

His eyes following hers, Daniel's hand went to the cord, pulled the disc gently out to rest on top of his shirt, then dropped to run along the grain of a cypress board, as if he were feeling its movement. "Gave this to my wife."

Gabe's head drooped. "Me and Daddy, we're both of us missing her extra today."

"That makes for a hard day." Kate gave him a side hug. "I'm so sorry."

She restrained herself from lunging over the counter to inspect the disc. This was more than a historical artifact; it was also a memory of someone cherished—and lost. She of all people ought to know how that felt.

But still she had to force herself not to stare. From this distance, maybe even up close, the disc was too timeworn to make out any possible numbers or words.

Daniel continued sanding the cypress board.

Gabe followed Kate's gaze to the disc.

"Sorry." She looked quickly away. Daniel would offer for her to see it when he was ready.

But Gabe intervened. "Looks like a big dirty penny. You're wondering about it."

"Is it . . . ?" she murmured to Gabe. "The real thing? An urban slave badge?"

He nodded vigorously. "So now you'd be wondering how come my daddy would want to go and give a thing like that to my momma, a thing some *slave* somebody wore?" Gabe's eyes swung to his father, who glanced up and nodded for him to go on. "Pride. To remember who's come before—all the somebodies, name and no name."

Daniel tossed a match into the metal can in the fireplace, the newspaper inside it flaming, its lid, in the instant before he placed it over the can, reflecting a perilous, pulsing red. "To remember," he agreed.

Knowing she couldn't be the first one to break the silence that followed, Kate waited for one of them to speak as the three of them watched the fire, and let her gaze shift back to the disc at Daniel's neck. But the quiet stretched on.

Behind them, the front door suddenly clattered open.

A small black leather case clutched in one hand, Rose Pinckney paused at the threshold of Cypress & Fire. "I see what you mean about the shop's age. I'd guess there are as many inches of paint here on this door as there are of wood." She stepped through into the gallery. "I'm glad you called to let me know where you'd be, Katherine, since I had to delay our meeting. Because I have something I think you'd like to see. And Mr. Russell here is just the man I need to put it to rights."

Before anyone else could speak, Rose ran a hand over a chess table of cypress and inlaid ceramic. She called back toward the kiln, "You do yourself—and all of Charleston—proud with this work, Daniel Russell."

Dan raised one hand in greeting. Sweat pouring down his face, he wiped his eyes with the upper sleeve of his shirt. "Good to see you again. Be with you in just a minute."

"Katherine, dear, I wanted you to see this, too: a family heirloom you may recall from the"—she lowered her voice and glanced back toward the kiln—"journals."

Kate laughed. "Rose, the Russells won't tie you up and force you to donate Emily's journal to the Southern Historical Collection at Chapel Hill." She gestured toward Gabe. "I think you've met Dan's excellent son before, right? This is Gabriel Ray. The middle name for Ray Charles and for—"

"His grandfather the Honorable Elijah Ray Russell, family court judge." She lifted her chin. "I've told you, Katherine: I know Charleston."

Rose studied the child. "Well," she said at last. "Such beautiful curls." She reached a hand, tentatively, toward the wild, swirling bounce of them. "Splendid."

Dan approached now, wiping his hands on a towel. From her feet, Rose lifted the black case, its outer leather cracked and peeling, and placed it on the stone counter.

Unsnapping the tarnished brass clasps, she opened the case to reveal a silk lining, torn in only one place, and deep in its cushioning, two matching guns.

"Prussian, I'm told," Rose said. "Late eighteenth-century or early nineteenth. This from a dinner guest back when my husband had these on display in the parlor—before I relegated them to the attic. My dear departed husband's temper needed no firearms near it, loaded or not."

"Rose." Kate laid a hand on her arm. "The pistol in Emily's journal. Have you looked these up to find out more about them?"

"That, my dear, is why I have a research partner."

Kate slid her laptop down the counter and called up images of handheld firearms from that period made in Prussia. "Look!" She turned the screen so the others could see. "These look remarkably similar. Dueling pistols."

Daniel nodded. "Breech-loading. Ready-primed cartridges." All their eyes turned to him. "So I liked guns as a kid. And read about them." He plucked two items from the case and held them out to Gabe. "Ingenious, really, paper tubes with their tin bases and the piston-fired needles that punctured them."

"It was my great-grandfather's—seven greats, I believe—prize firearm," Rose offered. She looked at Kate. "Jackson Pinckney's."

Gabe's eyes wide, he ran a finger in a circle around the muzzle.

Kate reached to touch one of the barrels but drew back, feeling as if she'd stopped short of stroking a viper. "So this might have been the one he used . . ."

Rose's fingers slid to the trigger. A distinct click. A spring-loaded bayonet about five inches long snapped into place.

Kate gasped.

Rose touched the tip of the knife and flinched. "It usually jams. I suppose it's been bent over the years." She looked at Daniel. "If you're willing to take on another project from me, Mr. Russell, it could stand restoration to its original state."

"Not original," Daniel corrected. "The bayonet switch was added after the original got cast."

"Yes," Rose agreed. "Of course. You're right."

His finger ran the length of the blade. "Somebody needed the defense of bullet *and* blade."

Seeming to address no one at all, Rose said, "My grandfather used to hold this gun and muse over whether a firearm still ought to require a real man to handle a ramrod and mallet." Slowly, delicately, she snapped the bayonet closed with one finger.

Gabe shook his head, eyes round and earnest. "Miz Rose, why'd your seven-greats granddaddy want a big knife on his gun anyhow?"

Daniel bent toward the kiln door.

Rose faced the child. "That, Mr. Gabriel Ray, is an excellent question. Which reminds me to say that I understand you are a particular friend of Katherine here."

"Only I call her Kate," Gabe said a bit territorially.

"Ah, the informal. A lovely name, nevertheless. Mr. Gabriel Ray, as a particular friend of *Kate's*, I wonder if you'd like to come with her sometime to visit me at my house. Assuming your father says it's all right."

Beaming, Gabe hesitated.

"And if I know when you're coming with Katherine—*Kate*—I might just have a whole platter of Penina Moise house biscuits, steaming hot, ready for you."

From behind the kiln, where he was sanding the cypress board, Dan lifted a hand. "So long as he brings his daddy back one."

From the door, Gabe and Kate watched Rose Pinckney go.

Behind them, the ring of a hammer, steady and strong.

"I like things that sound alltime the same," said the boy. "A beat you can count on. Like hammers. And waves. And heartbeats. Only . . . only you can't always count on the heartbeats, can you?" His head fell against her side.

"Not always so much the heartbeats," she agreed, eyes filling like his. Because sometimes there was nothing to say but the truth.

Daniel joined them at the door, his eyes on where Gabe was pointing: to their three shadows racked to monstrously tall. Gabe laughed and raised both arms overhead, reveling in his own bigness. The shadow of a palmetto stabbed at the bare of the boy's feet.

Gabe looked down at his hands, which were filthy from cleaning out watery ash from the metal can, then up at Daniel. Then he focused in on his daddy's jaw, the crop of dark stubble over the chin. Lifting a hand to stroke his own jaw like he was deep in thought, the boy rubbed sooty fingers over the lower half of his face.

Daniel laughed. Not much more than a chipped piece of a chuckle, really, like it rumbled up from somewhere deep down inside and rusted to stiff but somehow still lurched its way up and out. Then Kate was laughing, too.

Daniel put a hand to Gabe's jaw. "You're past needing a shave."

"Hadn't you ever seen a man with a beard before?"

"What I see's a boy looks like he's been crawling up chimneys."

The pout was losing its hold on the boy. "I reckon I'd be about as good at that as anything else." Gabe turned to inspect himself in one of the gallery's raku mirrors.

Chuckling, Daniel stepped up beside him. Gabe's curls and his face had gone as dark as his father's, both of them with their poet's eyes, round underneath the broad foreheads, and jaws square as a box: as alike as two etchings by the same hand.

Leaving the gallery in the hands of a kindly middle-aged woman in a voluminous purple skirt, they invited Kate to walk with them as far as the harbor to see it at dusk. Daniel and Gabe sat on the seawall laughing together, the two of them backdropped by the harbor turning carnival colors like a party about to begin.

Settling down beside them and promising herself to stay only a minute, Kate wanted this moment to stretch on, herself not a part of the two but included somehow. The waves rolled in steady and faithful, their swell and their splash, their rumble and roll a song from djembes drumming inside the earth.

"A kind of music you can count on not stopping," she said to Gabe. "Not ever."

Kate turned toward the child, the trust in his face nearly knocking her flat.

Behind them came a stumbling shuffle of footsteps unsure of themselves. As she glanced over her shoulder, three young white men with nearly identical sun-streaked hair, sunburned cheeks, and foam sunglasses straps looping behind their heads were heeling hard to the left as they wove their way down the seawall. Kate turned back to Gabe.

"It's a shame's all I'm sayin'," one of the young men slurred, stopping a few feet away. He tried gesturing with his head toward Kate and Gabe and Daniel but upset his own balance.

A second man steadied him. *"Shhh!"* he warned, louder than the first. "Wha', you think they can't hear you?"

"It's all I'm sayin'," the first argued. He held a finger in the face of the second. "An' don' shush me again."

Gripping the edge of the wall, Daniel straightened his back. "Tourists," he muttered.

The third young man, his red plastic cup tipped precariously sideways, was staring down at his deck shoes, where brown liquid from the cup was pooling on their tops—though he seemed mystified as to why.

Looking up, he blinked as if he were trying to clear his vision. "Gen'l'men, le's not argue." He lowered his voice—but not low enough that he couldn't be heard. "We agree—basi'ally: it's not fair to the children, all this racial"—he swished his hand in a circle—"mixin'." And he flopped an arm toward Gabe as if to give evidence of this wisdom.

Kate reached to cover Gabe's ears, but, gently, Daniel stopped her hands.

Rising to face the young men, he crossed his arms over his chest.

"It's not racis'," the first one defended himself, "jus' to observe something."

Dan stood even straighter, eyes leveled on them, but said nothing.

"Wha' the hell, man?" the second one said. "You don' have to get all upse'. We weren't bein' racis'." He turned to the first for confirmation. "Righ'?"

Daniel cocked his head. "Let me get this straight: So you're asking your buddy here with his three sheets to the wind if you're being racist by 'observing' that racial mixing is bad for kids?"

The second one raised both hands, palms out. "Whoa, whoa, whoa, dude. You people can be so touchy."

Kate rose then and turned. Folded her arms to match Daniel's. "Who exactly would be 'you people'?"

Gabe rose and folded his arms in the same manner.

Scowling, the first young man backed down the stone stairs of the seawall. "Jus' sayin'."

The second scurried to follow the first.

The third, though, hoisted himself up to sit, just barely balanced—the harbor shallows lapping below—on the rounded metal rail just a few inches from where Daniel stood. "I jus' need to make one final poin'."

Daniel raised both eyebrows and waited for him to go on.

"Jus' tha' . . ." With his right forefinger, the young man cheerfully poked Daniel in the chest on each word to punctuate his point: "We. Are. No'. Racis'." His left hand raised the red plastic cup high, the crowning moment of his argument—which unbalanced him from his perch. He tumbled backward into the harbor below.

Kate, Daniel, and Gabe leaned over the railing to see his head pop up, water spewing out his mouth. Flailing, he staggered to his feet in the shallows.

"Wai'!" he called. "Thi's very impor'an' to know." Earnestly, he held up the foam strap of the sunglasses he'd scooped from the water. "They float!"

His eyes gone steely, Daniel dropped himself off the seawall and offered a hand to Gabe, who leapt down by himself.

"Gabe . . . ," Kate began, falling into step beside the child, "forget everything you just heard."

"C'mon, Kate. He's heard ignorance before. Not often here. But he's heard it before. Better to face it head-on than pretend not to hear."

"I guess growing up in the South . . ."

Stopping in his tracks, Daniel shook his head. "Don't kid yourself. It's not just here. Wasn't it your town, Cambridge, Massachusetts, where a black man got harassed for supposedly breaking into a house—and he turned out to be not just the home owner but also some celebrity professor at Harvard?"

Suddenly cold even in the evening heat, Kate crossed her arms over her chest. "Yeah. But still."

"Those men back there?" Gabe bumped against her, his eyes on the ground. "They thought you and my daddy were a couple and I was your kid."

She tipped his chin up to her. "Which would've been fine, since your daddy is awesome—except for the little detail of our being just friends. But listen now: anybody in their right mind would be proud as hell—and I mean the real actual place—to have you as their kid. You know that, right?"

He nodded slowly. Then turned to his dad. "I'm thinking maybe Kate here might like to see the badge. She kept staring at it before. Maybe now's a good time."

For a moment, Daniel did not move. "You're right," he said at last.

Kate held up her hand in protest. "It was your wife's gift. And not after"—she jerked her head back toward the harbor—"those idiots. I can see it another day that's not . . ."

But Daniel slipped the copper disc on its cord from his neck.

Chapter 27

1822

The circle of young oaks blocked the light of a waning sunset. Tom crouched in the shadows and waited.

He hadn't much time. Only enough to dig near the hidden bullets for the single knife he'd buried there. Knock the sand from it. Slip it inside his shirt. And pray for some movement, some sign on the piazza across the street.

He should have left already. The city was on high alert. Hardly a soul on the streets except for droves of patrollers on horseback. Inspecting the wharves. Manning the city arsenal. Guarding every road that led through the Neck into the city.

Word of the revolt had blown through Charleston like hurricane winds.

He might already have waited too late—his own chance to get out maybe already gone.

But he would not leave without Dinah. No matter what it might cost.

The circle of oaks blocked whatever breeze might have cooled him. Tom wiped sweat from his face with the back of his arm.

Light at the second-story bedroom. A single candle.

A figure slipping out onto the piazza. Skirts of coarse blue muslin: it had to be her.

Tom rose. Stepped soundlessly to the edge of the circle of oaks.

For her, he'd risk being seen.

Another figure joined the first on the piazza. A swish of satin and lace. A voice—not hers—asked: "Is it any less beastly hot out here, Dinah?"

A pause. Then Dinah's voice, her face toward where Tom stood—as if she knew he would be there: "I'm glad the night's come."

"For the cool, yes," said the other voice.

"And the dark. Glad for the dark."

Another pause. Then the voice said: "Dinah, let me suggest that you think carefully how you phrase what you think—especially during these harrowing days."

"The Lord throws his shadow over the earth. And it is good."

"Oh. Yes. If that's what you meant, then yes." The first skirt swirled back to the threshold. The voice came more strained: "You continue to limp."

"Workhouse has a way of crippling."

Tom closed his eyes at the words. He had not known. Dinah, his Dinah, at that place. The whip against the bare of her back. Pieces of her flesh stripped away.

Bile rose into his throat.

A pause. Then Emily Pinckney's voice came, pinched: "The smell . . . are your wounds . . . worse?"

Silence.

"I assume that means yes. Perhaps Prue can wash them better tonight. I will insist that she does. And I want you to know . . . I want you to know the place you were sent, I think it's barbaric." The next words came out in a rush. "I wish I could have stopped it."

Silence again. A heavy quiet that carried with it an accusation unsaid: *Of course you could have done something.*

As if defending herself from what wasn't said, the Pinckney girl demanded, "What could I have said that would have stopped him?" Then, more bitterly, she added: "Men do as they wish."

Cicadas chirped from the garden. Somewhere up near the harbor, a buggy rolled past.

"Do come back inside, Dinah. If there's violence in the streets during the night"—the voice faltered here, as if frightened by the words it had just formed—"we'll be safe inside. Or so the city leaders would have us believe."

The blue muslin skirt did not move at first. Tom could make out the outline of her face, a glint of her large almond eyes.

Dinah's voice drifted, expressionless, almost monotone, from the piazza. "Miss Emily, I believe I left your hairbrush in the garden."

"In the garden? What an odd place to leave a brush. I don't—"

"Washing it out good this afternoon. Let me get it for you right quick."

Tom ducked beneath the magnolia and waited. When Dinah reached the garden's gate, he emerged. Daylight still clung in shreds to the tops of live oaks, and he knew even these few seconds standing like this with her could mean his being seen. But for the chance of bringing her with him, no risk was too great.

Dinah pressed her hand to his through the wrought iron gate—one he had crafted himself.

She rested her other hand on the swell at her belly.

"Come with me," he whispered, his voice coming hoarse. "You got to come."

Her hand pressed harder into his. "Can't hardly walk as it is. Slow you down to a crawl."

"Workhouse," he said, hardly more than a moan. "I'll kill the man. Kill Jackson Pinckney with my own hands."

Dinah touched one finger to his lips. "You got to go now, *right now*, if you want to slip through the Neck. King Street passage likely already blocked."

"I'll swim around the outside wall of the Lines if I got to. I'm not leaving you here."

"Listen." She held the flat of his palm to her cheek and shook her head. "You got to listen to me. I wouldn't make it past even the Lines, not after all this. Then what? We both dead." Now she pressed his palm to her lips. "You got to go on without me."

"No." He choked on a sob, his tears running over her hand as she reached to brush them away from his cheek.

"We got"—with one finger, she turned his face back to her—"no choice."

He gripped her hand in his. Hesitated. Pressed his lips hard together. Then yanked a roll of bills from his pocket. "What I saved up toward buying us free someday. Once the baby come, you use this. Find a way. Folks say there's people in Boston—other towns, too—that can help if you get yourself there. If you can't get out, don't care who I got to go through, I'm coming back for you and our baby."

Not *the* baby this time but *our*, and the word echoed between them. Wrenching. A question. And also a stake thrust in the ground—a proclamation.

Revulsion churned in Tom's middle. And fear. But right now he would only think about her.

He held her free hand to his lips. "You count on that."

Eyes streaming, Dinah nodded. "Won't take somebody long to mention your name with the leaders." But she pulled his hand to her cheek. "Scared I won't see you ever again." She let out a soft cry. "And scared that I will."

He knew what she meant: the gallows that were waiting for him, for any of them that were caught.

With one yank of the leather cord, Tom's copper badge fell loose into his hand. He felt his bare neck—with no tag hanging there.

Slipping the tag into her hand, he pressed his lips to hers. Felt the wet from her eyes and his, and tasted their salt.

"For you, I would risk the wide world," he said.

Chapter 28

2015

They paused at the gazebo on the Battery, and Kate cupped her hands together.

Carefully, Gabe passed the badge to her. She felt its edges: rounded but not entirely smooth, as if they'd been cut by hand, and thin. Its copper alloy warm from Daniel's skin, its leather cord strung through a hole at the top of the circle.

Kate gaped down at her palm and the copper disc in it.

"We're trusting you, Kate," Daniel said, nodding toward Gabe. "With pretty much our family's prize possession."

She tried to hand it back. "Dan, I don't want you to feel—"

"What I feel is glad for you to take a look. Just keep hold of it good. I've got a delivery of a nightstand to make here in town. Son, you come on home in a half hour, you hear?"

Waiting until Daniel was out of earshot, Kate tried to hand the badge back to Gabe. "I'm afraid your dad felt pressured, you know? Sometimes I get curious and can't let something alone. Listen, maybe you should take this right back . . ." Her voice trailed off, though, as her fingers hovered just above the worn etching, its letters not quite legible.

"Right now?"

Kate swallowed. "Just as soon as you and I do a quick rubbing so we can read it." The disc clasped in one fist, she swung her backpack to one shoulder and grabbed his hand.

Together they trotted the several blocks north and ducked in Penina Moise, where Kate ordered each of them a Fanta Orange from the blond waitress and set the disc gingerly on the table. "Hand me a napkin there, would you?"

She spread the napkin over the front of the disc, drew a pen from her pocket, tilted the pen at an angle, and ran it back and forth across the disc's surface. Pausing, she pushed the disc toward him. "Wanna give it a try? Here. Hold it like this."

Carefully, he ran the pen at nearly a horizontal angle across the covered disc.

Words began to emerge.

First *Charleston.*

Then a number, *422.*

Then *Blacksmith.*

And *1822.*

Kate sank back in her seat. "It could actually be Tom Russell's. I can't believe it."

Gabe sprawled back in his chair. "I could've told you. Had it memorized since I was seagrass size."

"Wait. You knew what it said all along?"

"Handed down in the family, the words held close more even than the thing of it."

"Sounds to me like an argument your family *has* to be descended from Tom Russell the blacksmith."

Gabe held up one finger, just as Kate had seen Daniel do on the Gullah Buggy tours. "Got to allow for the possibility, though, that somebody just took the name Russell out of honor and proudness. There were plenty of the people of color, my daddy says, took whatever last name they wanted after the War. This could've got passed down like the name—out of the honoring."

"Your dad's right. And real historians never jump to conclusions." Kate laid a five on the table next to the bill. "Let's just say I'm not known for my patience. Or my careful, methodical approach to anything. But it's one more step toward finding out, right?"

Gabe's attention dropped to her backpack, where a couple of sheets of paper peeked out the top. He squinted at them.

"You can pull those out, big guy. They're pictures I've been taking with my phone of a very old diary I'm reading through with Miz Rose. I print them out so I can study them later and mark them up with my pens and highlighters. I think this diary may have some things to teach us, maybe even about Tom Russell and the Vesey revolt." *Maybe even,* she thought, though this was probably too much for even a desperate woman to hope, *shed light on what drove Sarah Grace's research.* "Miz Rose's family has lived here forever."

"Like mine?"

Kate hesitated. "Like yours. Only we don't know if any of your ancestors had time to sit down and write in a journal at the end of the day."

Gabe thought about this. "Guessing mine didn't."

Kate winced.

But he'd already plucked several pages from her backpack. "Pretty handwriting."

"It is. But it would be a lot prettier if there were more of it."

"What's that mean?"

"Just that this diary looks like somebody tore it in half—at least the back cover and probably a good many pages have been ripped away. And nobody knows where the end part would be. If it's even survived at all."

Gabe's brow crumpled as he deciphered the handwriting letter by letter and word by word. "But how come she ends these days here with a treasure map *X*?"

Kate shook her head. "No, see, she's just marking with an *X* how she's ending those entries, with a quote from a famous writer or thinker. Like, here. This one's from John Milton, a seventeenth-century poet: 'Iris all hues, roses, and jessamine / Reared high their flourished heads between, and wrought / Mosaic; underfoot the violet, / Crocus, and hyacinth.' Nice, right? Though who knows why Emily's quoting it here. Maybe just favorite lines from what she's reading. And here's Edmund Spenser. He was the sixteenth-century poet who wrote *The Faerie Queene* for Elizabeth I of England. And here's the Reformation theologian Martin Luther: 'Faith must trample under foot all reason, sense, and understanding.'"

"Who's the hippo?"

"What?"

He pointed to the top of one entry that sat like the others to the right of an *X*.

Kate laughed. "That's Augustine *of* Hippo. It's a place. He lived . . . a long time ago. Listen to this one: 'We make a ladder of our vices, if we trample those same vices underfoot.'"

"Mm-hmm," Gabe said. But his head stayed bowed over the pages. He fanned them on the table, his eyes jumping from one to the next.

"It's especially intriguing that this young woman, Emily, would include that particular quote about trampling vices—getting used to them, maybe. In fact, it's part of my theory that young slaveholding women in the early nineteenth-century South weren't at all blind to the atrocities of the 'peculiar institution,' as people called it. Its brutality was all around them. In fact, there were more antislavery societies in the South than in the North before 1830. But given that these women had everything to lose by trying to buck a system they had little say in and had lots to gain from, they seemed to become increasingly hardened as they grew older to the brutali—"

"But why feet?" Gabe interrupted.

"Feet?"

With one finger, he pointed to the last several days of entries in June 1822.

Kate shook her head. "I'm not seeing the pattern you're seeing, Mr. Rubik's Cuber. Unpuzzle me." Digging into her bag, she offered him a yellow highlighter.

Gabe skimmed neon yellow over the surface of several pages.

Taking the pages one by one from him, Kate read aloud what he'd marked:

We trample those same vices underfoot.

Treading underfoot her honest name.

Underfoot the violet.

Faith must trample under foot.

She lifted her eyes to meet his. "*Underfoot.* It shows up in the margins at the end of the last several days of entries."

He nodded, pulling his Rubik's Cube from his pocket and spinning its faces.

"Gabe, what if you were right and the *X*s were actually a kind of treasure map?"

He bounced once on the seat. "For pirate gold?"

"Don't go raising the Jolly Roger on me just yet. What if this Emily decided to tear off the diary's final however many entries and bury that part for some reason—maybe because it contained thoughts she didn't want anyone to read anytime soon? But she wanted to remind herself where it was. Or even tip off some future descendant who might figure it out."

"Underfoot," Gabe said earnestly.

"Underfoot. Exactly."

He lifted his Fanta to her. "Can I help, *please*, Kate, with the treasure hunt since I found the feet? Where do we start?"

Kate scanned the printouts with Emily's florid scrawl, the yellow lines leaping out at her now. "Underfoot," she mused. "I think we start by asking your dad's permission for you to turn pirate with me."

"And then?"

"And then, assuming I'm right in thinking the mention of jessamine and violets and roses is a clue for where we need to start looking, we make sure we have our shovels handy."

"And then?"

"*Before* then, we ask Miz Rose's permission to tear up her garden— with very little evidence that we'll find what we're looking for there."

∽

The next afternoon, dirt caked up her bare legs to her knees, Kate straightened her back, brushed dirt from Gabe's face and her own—and tried to avoid the skepticism implied by the arched silver eyebrow a few feet away.

"Rose, you said these roses here were antiques and had been in this spot for as long as you knew. We were careful not to hurt them. But is there any way of knowing how this garden was laid out two hundred years ago?" Kate shook her head. "Even hearing myself say that out loud, it sounds ridiculous."

From her knees, she flopped back to sit on the ground. "I was just so convinced that somehow that diary would be underfoot in the garden and that the diary would give us answers not only about Tom and Dinah and their world but also about what my mother was trying to find—and why. I'm so sorry if I've led us on a treasure hunt with no treasure."

Gabe pulled her head close. "Okay if it still was fun?"

Kate laughed. "That's always okay." She pressed her cheek to his. "Rose? What is it? You have the oddest expression on your face."

Studying them, Rose did not answer for a moment. Then she turned away and sniffed. "My facial expression, sugar, was merely one of an investor in an expedition that has not, as yet, yielded results. I suppose I'll be called upon to provide the two of you more Penina Moise biscuits in order to fund future outings?"

Not waiting for an answer, she thrust her hands into the pockets of her linen skirt. Plucking a lollipop from the right side, she seemed to feign surprise at what she'd found there.

Nonchalantly—a little too much so, Kate thought—Rose offered the candy to Gabe. "My banker provides these, and I'd quite forgotten I'd kept it." She shot a glance at Kate. "Lord knows he ought to provide something besides resistance to simple requests."

Kate cleared her throat. "Speaking of requests."

Gabe, crunching into the lollipop, stopped chewing a moment to listen.

"Yes?"

"I have a big one. You know I've been trying to talk with my late father's attorney—and yours. And that Mr. Botts has managed so far to return none of my calls or e-mails and has stonewalled me at every turn. I've been wondering what would happen if I cornered him in a public setting—where he couldn't run away. And here's where the rude part comes in." Her words came faster. "He's supposed to be at some fund-raising event out at Magnolia Plantation this Tuesday—for the opera or symphony, something. I've thought about just showing up, sneaking my way in somehow."

Rose finished the thought for her. "But you thought it might be even better to come as my guest, if I could secure you an invitation."

"Rose, could you?"

Rose considered. "I'm invited, of course, to the Magnolia event."

"Of course." Kate hid a smile.

"But I'd actually not planned on going. One's social obligations can overwhelm."

"Not a problem, Rose, honest. I'll find a way in."

"Let us not dispose of the last remnants of good manners and breeding just yet." She adjusted the linen pleats of her skirt. "I am willing to go and take you as my guest, Katherine. You may recall that Percival stood me up as well that day in Penina Moise. I'd like to know just what's behind such behavior."

She turned to Gabe with her palm up. "Do let me throw that away for you, Gabriel Ray. I have always loathed the aspect of lollipop sticks lying about that some careless child tossed."

"Rose?" Kate touched the older woman's arm. "Thank you. Botts knows something about what happened to my parents. There has to be a way to get him to talk." Rose squeezed her hand as Kate bent toward Gabe. "C'mon, big guy. It's getting dark, and your dad'll be wanting you back at the shop."

Together, they looped past Battery Park and headed toward East Bay, reaching Cypress & Fire just as the harbor was going dark. High heels clattered past, and gas lanterns flickered.

Standing there as night fell, Kate wondered, if—*if*—Tom Russell had tried to escape the manhunt that swept Charleston once Vesey's plot had been exposed, just where might he have run to escape?

Maybe she'd been out working too long in the Low Country sun this afternoon and read too much history this morning, her mind paranoid and jumpy now, running to secret plots and violence—prone to seeing things that weren't there.

But in the dance of streetlights and shadows, she could imagine a lone figure running away up the alley, his life depending now on the speed and the silence of every step.

Chapter 29

1822

Dodging from alley to alley and shadow to shadow, Tom slipped through the night.

Approaching horses allowed him to move without his footsteps echoing in the streets. Still, he could not be seen.

Behind crates, he huddled. At the corners of carriage houses. Along garden walls.

Block upon block of the city he ran—north toward the Neck. But he would have to get through it quickly somehow.

Dodging and darting, he neared the north end of King Street. And could see that the break in the Lines was already blocked. He was trapped in the city.

STEAL AWAY had been etched on the Quaker woman's comb.

Two lanterns, she'd said. *Just after dark. If thee are in need of help.*

It might be a trap. But he had no options left.

~

Near North Adger's Wharf, Tom slipped behind a warehouse to wait.

It finally took shape in the dark: an old buggy, lanterns swaying from a singletree that creaked behind the plod of a broken-down horse.

Two lanterns. Two lanterns and two people, the white woman in the plain dress who'd dropped her handbag yesterday on the street, along with a bearded white man with a plain, poorly fitting gray coat—the man who'd been at the tavern and come by the shop.

Here they sat on the driver's seat of the old buggy. And in its flatbed, a coffin.

Leaping to the ground, the man raised a forefinger to his lips, stood listening, then waved at Tom to hurry. Sliding the flimsy lid of a pine coffin to one side, the man hobbled around the wagon, checking its axles, adjusting its harness.

"I am sorry, friend," whispered the woman, not turning her head, "thee will have to ride in such stench. The good Morris Brown who sent us said thee would know this secret conveyance. Thy friends cannot step onto the streets."

Moving slowly to avoid sound, Tom lowered himself into the box and very nearly fell back, the reek of death and decay enough to knock a man flat.

The full moon threw enough light into the box to suggest the forms of three chickens. Headless.

"May the death of these three creatures assist thy life, friend," said the woman. "And may God dull thy sense of smell."

Wedged into the narrow coffin so that his head was hooked at nearly a right angle from his neck and his bent knees touched the top of the casket, Tom lay still, suffocating in air gone thick and putrid.

The wagon rattled through the night with the creaks and groans of leather and wood straining across deep-rutted sand roads. They must be approaching the Lines and the King Street pass-through.

Over the whine and groan of leather on wood and wood on earth, Tom heard a shout. Then hoofbeats approached.

And stopped beside the buggy.

Tom Russell lay there still as death itself in the coffin.

"Thee must not let me despair, husband," the woman was saying loudly. "'Where, O death, is thy victory? Where, O grave, is thy sting?'"

The rider alongside the buggy shifted in his saddle, his horse pawing at the crushed shell of the street. "You got to pardon me, folks. Got a duty to check all conveyances leaving the city. Had some disturbance tonight."

It was again the woman who spoke. "Of course. We've every wish of being good citizens, even at this grievous time. Thee must search as thee see fit."

The saddle creaked again. "You all understand now I wouldn't ordinarily stop folks in this here kind of circumstance as you. It's just my damn orders is all."

"We've no wish to slow thee down, sir, in thy duties."

A thud. The patroller leaping onto the bed of the buggy.

"We're bound to North Carolina," said the woman. "To Flat Rock. Our ancestral home." Her voice collapsed into a sob. "A slow journey with an old horse. Thee must forgive us, sir, for the dead has been such for some time now. And has begun, I fear—"

A scrape of the coffin's pine lid.

A shaft of moonlight.

"Jesus Christ!" More thuds on the bed of the buggy. A creak of the axles as the patroller leapt off.

"—to emit a most powerful stench," the woman finished.

Horseshoes on the crushed shell. A scramble. "Y'all done satisfied the laws of Charleston," the patroller said. "You folks are free to proceed."

Hoofbeats receded into the distance.

"And thee," said the woman, "have satisfied the laws of God."

The wagon lurched forward again. Rolled into the night.

∼

It may have been only an hour; it may have been more, but finally the buggy jolted to a halt.

Footsteps over the shell. Then both the woman and man were lifting the lid. Helping Tom out.

"Thee must forgive us," said the man, his voice sad and strained, "for leaving thee here. We've gotten word they're checking every inch of every conveyance up Ashley River Road. Thee would be found for certain."

Half crippled from being wedged so long in the box, Tom stumbled out and collapsed onto the road but made himself stand. "Thank you," he managed. "Thank you."

The man hurled the three chickens far into the palmettos that lined the road.

"God be with thee," said the woman as she scrambled alongside him up onto the seat. Reins slapped on the flank of the old horse. "Courage to thee, friend. And hope."

The full moon rode high now, black clouds sometimes billowing over it—but moving quickly away.

Tom ducked into a thicket of brambles so dense he had to slither under its tangle, thorns piercing a grid on his arms and back.

Heart crashing into his ribs, he thrashed a place for himself at its center. His skin gone clammy and cold even here in this heat, he waited for dark.

Mosquitoes swarmed his eyes, his mouth, his ears.

Up ahead, a burying ground. Tom skirted its edge, the ground here turning soft, kinder on his bare feet.

Drayton Hall. The brick mansion—which he could see only silhouetted against the moon—hulked up ahead. But its details he knew well—even after two decades. He'd been born here. Then sold along with his momma into the city. And his momma, alone, sold back.

Its quarters on the bluff line nearby were one-room hovels. Here lived the people who, with the thousand years of rice-growing knowledge they'd brought from West Africa, had made the fields yield gold in every sense—gold-husked rice that had made generations of the planters rich.

Tom paused at the far edge of the burying ground—this one for Drayton Hall's slaves, a cemetery separate from the whites. He looked back once more toward the quarters. The people there, including his momma, if she was still alive, would help him without a thought for themselves. But he knew too well what it would cost anyone who was caught.

Tom ran now, past the burying ground and toward the rice fields, their trenches controlling the freshwater flow—and helping him drown his scent.

Mist wrapped itself around the outbuildings of Drayton Hall and the live oaks that shaded them there. Mist nestled into dips in the contours of the fields and banded the pine and palmetto trunks.

Tom's feet met the sides of the full trenches, his footprints swallowed in silt.

He left the rice fields, diving past the dark curtain of live oak and pine. Skirting the edge of the blackwater swamp, he hurled mud and now blood from the shredded soles of his feet, his pants and most of his shirt splashed as dark as his skin.

On three sides of him now lay the swamp, vast and throbbing with sound. Cypress trees, their bases swollen wide, waded deep in the water. With their roots buckled up like bent knees, the trees looked to be bathing with the shredded remains of discarded silk stockings: Spanish moss slung over the branches and vines.

Above the castanet rattle of cicadas and the deep-throated call of the bullfrogs, Tom could hear his own heart.

The wind was gaining more power, black clouds wrestling each other lower and lower.

From now on, what lay behind was the woman he loved, the woman he would do anything for—anything, even now. Anything.

What lay behind, too, were steel balls on fire and barbed rope that furrowed the flesh.

And gallows.

Chapter 30

2015

"I've been reading about the swamps," Kate said as she and Rose careened up Ashley River Road Tuesday evening. A pink scarf flapping back from her neck and all her silver Mercedes's windows down, Rose drove more like Jay Gatsby than the little old lady she technically was. The walled gardens and stacked piazzas of Charleston had given way to cypress and dark water glimmering through tangled palmettos and silver tendrils of moss.

"And I've been reading how the swamps made Charleston a kind of fortress that was easier than perhaps any other city to keep slaves from escaping." Kate pictured her mother's notes. "Do you think Tom Russell possibly could have made it outside the city—maybe even gotten away?"

"Through blackwater? That would be quite the feat."

"Blackwater?"

"The cypress trees stain the swamp water to what looks for all the world like ink. Although during Emily Pinckney's time, much of the swampland had been drained for rice fields. The land alone is worth seeing at Magnolia—as is true also of its neighbors Drayton Hall and Middleton Place." Rose banked into the next turn with screeching tires, a smile of pleasure sliding across her face as she accelerated out of it, foot all the way to the floor.

"We're in a hurry, I take it," Kate ventured.

Rose turned her head, her hands turning with her, the Mercedes swerving right. "Punctuality is a virtue too lightly valued these days."

Clutching the passenger door's handle, Kate kept herself mostly upright, though white-knuckled. "So, Rose. About my talking with Botts. Do you think he knows where my mother's rings are? And why?"

Rose pursed her lips. "Percy's a conundrum—I'll grant you that."

"But you must trust him if he's your attorney."

"Technically, dear, he was my late husband's attorney. I've just never gotten round to giving him the hatchet."

Kate stared out the window into the tangle of palmettos and vines. "Could he be capable of outright theft?"

Rose swung into another curve, her right foot stomping on the gas to rocket the car out of the turn. "I believe the creeds, dear."

Kate peeled herself off the passenger door. "The creeds?"

"Of the Episcopal Church. Which assures me we are all quite capable of most anything."

Across a well-tended lawn, Kate maneuvered beside Rose among the well-heeled and pressed guests. Sterling platters of clam-stuffed mushrooms and bacon-wrapped shrimp floated on servers' hands. Rose glanced down once, but only once, at Kate's little black dress—a small thundercloud among the pastel linens and Lilly Pulitzer prints and seersucker suits.

Kate wished she'd at least stopped to iron the dress's duffel bag wrinkles.

"Your scarf," Rose pronounced, "adds a nice feminine touch, dear. To balance, you know, the I-know-more-than-you message that black always sends."

Magnolia Plantation consisted of a picturesque house—"Though built," one of the other guests grieved to Kate, "well after The War"—with a wide skirt of a wraparound porch raised a full story above the ground and hundreds of acres of azaleas and magnolias.

The sun warm on her face, the gardens rolling out to a river and, beyond it, the swamps, Kate listened to the friends of Lila Rose Manigault Pinckney—all four names aired out and in use for this sort of event, it appeared—recounting the history of the place. But Kate's attention kept swinging across the crowd to search for Percival Botts.

A tray of pesto shrimp on toast points was passing close by. Rose turned this away with the flat blade of an imperial hand but accepted a second flute of champagne.

The string quartet just shifting from Brahms to Carolina beach music, Rose motioned for Kate to follow as she swept across the lawn to greet another cluster of guests.

"So," Kate observed, "it would appear that you know every last person here."

"My family, as you well know, has lived in the Low Country for as many generations as I have fingers. Perhaps toes, as well."

A gaggle of older women passed and reclustered close behind Kate and Rose.

"Heyward's daughter," one of them said, forgetting to lower her voice. "My Law'."

"They say the Ravenel girl had the most inappropriate friends. Before Heyward took her away from all that."

"I once heard the most scurrilous gossip about her—nothing to do with the unfortunate choice of friends. And nothing I would ever dream of repeating."

A beat of silence.

"Well, now you've gone and made our imaginations run perfectly wild, Adelaide."

"Not wild enough to come up with this. But I'm not one to gossip."

"This one certainly has her mother's good looks, bless her heart. Let us just hope she doesn't share the poor girl's more . . . unfortunate characteristics."

Dumbstruck, Kate turned toward the women. Swinging back the weight of her hair, she opened her mouth to respond—viciously.

But Rose lifted her champagne flute in a toast. "It is precisely our *unfortunate characteristics* that make any of us interesting—wouldn't you say, ladies? Those of us, I might add, who *are* interesting."

Maneuvering Kate away from the gaggle, Rose led her through the gardens and down to the river.

"Rose, what did they mean, those women back there? All their catty insinuations."

Rose flicked this away like an insect. "For some people old age means growing stiff in the joints; others grow stiff in the head—as if the brain calcified on what people were thinking six decades ago."

"'The most scurrilous gossip.' What did that mean? Do you know?"

Rose hesitated.

"Rose, you know more than you're telling me."

"Actually, Katherine, I do not. And if I did, it's not really my story to tell, now is it?" She waved an arm across the acres of azaleas beneath a canopy of oaks. "Do let's admire this before returning to the party so that you can accost Mr. Percival Botts. We might allow him to arrive unaware that you're here so you can pounce, don't you think?"

"Rose," Kate tried again. "What Dr. Sutpen said about an atrocity that—"

With a raised eyebrow, Rose made it clear they had switched topics for the time being. "I assume, Katherine, that you read a bit about the history of this place before coming. You probably know that Magnolia Plantation was owned by a John Grimké-Drayton."

"I . . ." Her mind back on the older women, Kate was struggling to switch subjects. "Read that today, yes."

"And you noted the Grimké and Drayton family connection?"

"I had no idea my father's family might be tied with the Grimkés. I was blown away."

"Again, dear, all the old names are connected somehow, a vast and complex cousinage, much like an intricate tapestry—or, depending on your perspective, like the bramble of the thorns that grew over Sleeping Beauty's kingdom and kept out all visitors." Rose said this cheerfully, as if she were equally willing to accept either view.

"It's huge to me, Rose—that connection."

"Related—cousins of some level, I suppose—to both Judge Grimké and the daughters, Sarah and Angelina, of hell-raising fame, as well as the Drayton line. John Grimké-Drayton never wished to own slaves himself, but when his older brother died in a hunting accident, he inherited this plantation and all 'property' attached to it. Nearly broke the man's heart to inherit the slaves. And why didn't he just release them, most people ask."

Kate accepted a piece of warm goat cheese with walnuts on toast points from a passing tray. "By that time in the Deep South, or soon after, at least, emancipating them would've been next to impossible, as in an act of the state legislature. Still, if he really believed it was the right thing to do, you'd like to think he'd have found a way."

Rose nodded absently and gazed over the marshland. "That's right, yes. If it's the right thing to do, one finds a way."

"What are you thinking about, Rose?"

"Hmm?"

"Something specific's on your mind."

"Yes. But that's for another day." Musing a moment, Rose suddenly plucked a small oval frame from her handbag. "I thought you might like to see this." The frame held a miniature sketch of a man in a silk vest, its gray the same color as his hair. Kate leaned in to inspect it.

Above the vest was a face whose skin sagged sallow and loose from its cheekbones, sinking into dry, colorless pleats, the whites of the eyes gone yellow around the dulled hazel, like too many gin slings had stained them forever. The top of the man's spine had bent to a shepherd's crook.

"You and I, Kate, know him well. For a man just shy of fifty, he'd aged powerfully fast."

"Jackson Pinckney!"

"None other, my dear. When I found this yesterday packed away with a bundle of sterling cutlery I suspect no one has used for years, I knew you'd want to see it."

Kate studied his hands. "Like hooks. Made of old wood left out on the shore."

"You know, family legend had it that, when sober, old Jack Pinckney could hold forth on how slavery was economic suicide in the long term. He wrote treatises on it—remind me to show you those. Not on slavery as a moral outrage—clearly, he lost no sleep on that—but how the average planter would do better to hire Irishmen cheaply and rid himself of 'this millstone on the neck of the South.' Deep in his bourbon, however, he was convinced that *he* was the real slave to that way of life. Pitiful, really."

"I think I'd manage to hold up dry-eyed."

Slipping the frame back into her purse, Rose lifted her flute of champagne.

Kate motioned toward the river. "I've read about the intricacies of their rice growing—the trunks and gates and trenches, and how they had to protect the rice from salt water that might seep in during a freshet. But I'm still searching for clues as to whether somehow Tom Russell might have made it out of here."

They aimed their steps back toward the main lawn.

"Meanwhile," Kate said, "let's see if anyone else has made it out here." Increasing her speed to a racing walk, Rose right beside her, Kate rounded the edge of the main house.

And there he stood: neck jutting forward, his tiny head encircled by seersucker and pastels like a gargoyle surrounded by flowers.

Kate made herself speak as she approached. "Well. Mr. Botts. I was planning on contacting you. *Again* today. Honestly, I keep trying to imagine why you won't respond to my calls and e-mails. Unless you have something to hide."

Champagne flutes stilled.

Botts paled.

"The manager at Palmetto Bank found a record that last winter someone—perhaps my mother, perhaps someone else—removed a ring she'd stored in her safe-deposit box. I thought maybe you and I could schedule a chat about that—at long last."

"Do you mind"—Botts kept his voice low but barely restrained, like a dog snarling at the end of a leash—"if we do this elsewhere?"

"You mean instead of in front of a crowd?" Kate's eyes swung over the faces. "Actually, I think these are the perfect people to join us in discussing Low Country family issues."

The gray of his eyes narrowed. "You are making a fool of yourself in public, Katherine. And making these people unspeakably uncomfortable."

A woman in a kelly green and pink sundress raised her champagne. "Now don't you all mind us. Pretend we're not here, hanging on every last word."

Botts straightened to his full height and seemed to expand at the neck. *Like a cobra,* Kate thought.

His head did come down in a flash, his hiss directly in her ear. "Listen to me well, Katherine. I *did* remove the object in question. Trust me when I say that is *none* of your concern."

With that, he stalked away.

"Do *not* turn your back on me again, Botts," Kate called after him.

Shoulders hunched forward, he kept walking.

Before she could stop to think, before she remembered just where she was, Kate yanked a platter from a passing waiter and hurled it, a giant sterling Frisbee, toward Botts's retreating back. As it spun, the long lines of Sperrys and sandals and white buck oxfords sprang back from the scattershot spray of goat cheese and toast points and bacon unfurling from shrimp.

The sterling hit Botts between the shoulder blades. Then clattered down to the lawn.

Silence. All the guests had gone still.

Only Botts moved, his small head swinging slowly around.

Kate followed the stares of the onlookers down the lawn to the grounded circle of silver. Vaguely, she saw that Rose had quietly raised her champagne.

But the rest did not move, waiting, perhaps, for Kate to make some gesture of penance for making a scene in public—and, worse, in posh, old-money public.

But she was too angry for gestures or penance.

Shoulders squared, she ignored the gawking crowd as she marched to meet Botts. She didn't care who might be listening. "Look. I need answers from you. You look horrified. Good. Your stealing the only thing my mother owned of value is despicable. And your trying to convince her for years to trust you? *Pathetic.*"

Botts's throat spasmed. "My trying to convince Sarah Grace to trust me?"

"Your letters. To her."

Hands visibly shaking now, Botts nodded. "I will contact you with a time for us to talk. Again."

"I need a date. As in tomorrow. And a time."

Small eyes boring hard into hers, Botts finally nodded. "As I happen to be back in town for a few days: tomorrow."

"How can I trust you to show up?"

Kate tucked her hair back behind her ears, and Botts's eyes went to the heron earrings. He stared at them.

"Where did you get those?" he demanded. And before she could answer, he turned, muttering, "My God, she never let go. She never did let go."

Kate chased after him, the high heels of her sandals sinking into the lawn. "Sarah Grace? Let go of what?"

He rounded on her. "If she'd meant you to know, don't you think she'd have told you in all those years? Why do you have to disturb her memory with these hammering questions, questions, questions?" He threw up an arm in exasperation. "We will meet tomorrow at noon. At my firm's office on Broad. You can be assured I will be there."

"No." Kate planted her feet. "Someplace that's neutral territory. The porch of the inn on Meeting. Where we met last time."

Botts's head ticked back. "Where you ambushed me, you mean." He stalked forward, but over his shoulder, he snapped, "Tomorrow then. Noon. At the inn."

Suddenly aware of the weight of the crowd's stares, its stunned and mortified silence, Kate turned and knelt by the grounded platter as Rose came to stand over her.

"Katherine, dear, there are people here to take care of the mess."

Kate shook her head. "Rose, I was your guest. And I behaved like a lunatic."

Rose patted her shoulder. "Good manners can be so very predictable."

Stumbling back to her feet, Kate handed the silver platter to a server, who winked at her.

"A streak of the renegade," Rose mused. "So like your momma—in her earlier years."

Kate turned. "If that's true, then what happened to her? I can see where maybe she still had that streak, but what she became was more broken than fiery."

Rose patted her hand. "That's what's brought you here, yes? To find out why for yourself."

Sighing, Kate turned her back to the other guests, who were beginning to murmur again and still glancing her way. Botts had already stalked toward the valet stand and was motioning for the valet to hurry. "Rose, forgive me. You've already been so kind. But I need to leave." She grimaced. "Before the gracious hosts of this lovely affair ask me to leave. And honestly, I'm too embarrassed to stay. But I don't want you to have to leave early."

Rose considered. "I'm perfectly willing to make an early departure, now that we have made our presence felt, you know." She smiled meaningfully.

"Or"—a thought was occurring to Kate, but she wasn't sure it was a good one—"I wonder, if I could find a ride back to town, how would that be? You'd probably like to have a conversation with some civilized, nonviolent folks at some point tonight. And you'll want to distance yourself from me."

Rose patted her cheek. "No chance of your losing the fiery, my dear. You come find me if you can't come up with a ride, hear? At my age, my mark in society has been made and no longer requires time spent with buttressing at these sorts of events. Although the champagne tonight is particularly good." Marching away, she called back over her shoulder, "And for the record, I *neveh* distance myself from a good telling off."

~

Kate had forgotten to delete Scudder Lambeth's number from her phone. There it was, under "Recent Calls." She blurted into the phone as soon as he answered. "Scudder, this is Kate Drayton, and before you hang up—I know it's tempting—"

He laughed. "Actually, I'm way too curious to find out what's got you talking so fast."

"I'm no good at the whole damsel-in-distress role—"

"Why does that not surprise me?"

"But I could really, really use a ride back into town. I'm out at Magnolia. And you're probably busy, which is totally fine, and I understand—"

"Whoa now. I'm just finishing work for the day—on Miz Rose's floors, as a matter of fact. I'd be happy to come out there. But did something happen to Miz Rose?"

Kate shut one of her eyes as if she might make the scene go away, then gave him the gist in one long, rambling sentence.

He let out a whistle. "Sorry I couldn't have seen that. Was it a good, solid throw, though? I'd like to think you have a good arm."

❧

Plunking down—in spite of her little black dress—by the side of the sand driveway, Kate waited. And tried not to relive all the times she'd waited for her father like this on the side of a road, no headlights ahead in the distance.

Scudder's truck, with *Restoration Inc.* on its doors, arrived in a cloud of sand dust. "I'm honored" was the first thing he said as he swung down to greet her. "Didn't think you'd have called me to help."

Kate felt her throat tighten with panic. "I don't want you to think that I . . . mean anything by it."

"It's just a ride, Kate. From a friend. Not a declaration of undying devotion. I swear I won't get any ideas." He plucked at the front of his T-shirt, which was filmed in sawdust. "Exhibit for the defense number one: I didn't even change out of filthy work clothes before coming."

Her shoulders relaxed as she climbed up into his truck. "Honestly, after my little display of temper back there, I'm not sure there's anybody else in Charleston who'd give me a ride."

"Gabe would've. If he could drive."

Kate brightened. "You're right. Gabe would've. That's two."

Scudder snapped his fingers. "I take that back. He and Dan are doing something at Mother E tonight. Guess you're back down to one."

Scudder's pickup rolled past curtains of mist hanging on the banks of the Ashley. Cypresses bent to dip the silver moss of their hair in water the color of ink.

Blackwater swamp.

"Okay." He shot her a look. "At the risk of sounding like I'm taking advantage of being your one and only ride back, as we've established, let me just ask: You want to see anything else while you're out here?"

"Actually . . ."

"Name it."

"Listen, you've been gracious already just to come out—but could we pass by Drayton Hall? I think it's close, and I was reading today about the slave burying ground."

"Next property over. You got it."

They walked through the Drayton Hall burying ground without speaking. Before them was nothing but uneven land, some plots marked by plain, unmarked stones half sunk into the earth or by upended bottles.

Kate broke the silence at last as she knelt over some pottery shards piled on one mound. "If only there were a way of knowing for sure who was buried here. How they died. What they were like." She made her way to the far end. "Most of them have no names at all. Maybe none of them do."

Scudder knelt a few yards away. "Kate. You'll want to see this."

"What is it?"

"A name—if we can make it out. And a date."

She knelt beside him on the spongy earth and ran her fingers over the stone that someone had etched into by hand with something sharp, its ragged letters and numbers weathered nearly smooth and covered in moss.

Kate bent closer. "The name's hard to make out, and there's no birth year, just a *d* and a period. The death year's almost not visible anymore. Looks like eighteen . . ." She and Scudder dug at the base of the stone with their bare hands.

And read out the year at the same time. "Twenty-two."

They exchanged looks over the stone.

Kate ran her fingers over its moss-covered letters. Then her hand flew to her mouth. "Oh God. I think I know what this says."

Chapter 31

1822

A storm was rolling above him now, the rain hammering hard at the far edge of the swamp and approaching.

Tom ran until he was sure his lungs had caught fire. City-soft feet split open, shed layers of flesh. Flailing at the edge of the water, he was cheating the bloodhounds. For now.

His feet snagged on roots submerged just under the cypress-stained black of the water, his arms beating back whetted points of palmetto. Then he lurched sideways, one leg sunk to its knee in some swamp creature's watery refuge.

Thunder rolled on top of what was already a roar in his ears, his breath and his blood coming too fast.

He slipped again, this time thrown to his back in the mud, his head slamming onto the knee of a cypress. For a moment he lay where he fell, unmoving but for the heave of his chest.

He lay flogged by exhaustion, the thunder approaching, a hammer hitting its anvil and, with it, the lightning, sparks from the forge.

Pale fire shattered the sky into shards of black glass. Saplings bowed near to double in the buffeting wind, rain falling in silvery sheets. Magnolia blooms trembled, withered petals glowing white.

A crash of lightning now, straight overhead.

Over the thunder and over the rain and over the roar in his ears, there was another sound, too.

It might only have been a marsh owl.

It might only have been in his mind.

Or it might have been bloodhounds baying into the dark.

∼

As the storm's fury stilled, only drizzle remained, like an apology after a tantrum.

Tom's thoughts filled with Dinah—with the hell he had left her to. With the baby she would deliver. *Ours,* he tried to believe. But it was no good. He had seen what he'd seen: her head thrown back in terror, her soundless scream.

He longed for her now, and for a life he had not ever known: to hold the woman he loved all through one single night. To protect what was theirs.

Tom's whole body ached—with wounds and strains but mostly with wanting her.

A blue heron stood not ten feet away, the water halfway up its long legs. Its neck arched back in a *C*, its crested head not moving, wings folded and quiet—a promise of power, waiting and still.

Tom saw the gator surface just then, its eyes appearing first above ripples of black, followed by high-vaulted nostrils and a long, sinister snout.

He saw it too late.

The gator's jaws opened, a great yawning chasm. And snapped down.

But the heron was quicker, lifting off from the water. The gator's jaws clamping on air, he sank back into blackwater.

The swamp sat silent again, as smooth and still as an ebony floor, as if a man could walk on top of it. This place of mist and darkness and death would be his home now, until he found a way out.

Or until they found him.

Whichever came first.

～

Above the swamp, the moon was nothing but the white of a thumbnail, only just emerging again from behind a dark, thin skin of clouds. There were no stars, as if some lamplighter, lazy or drunk, had neglected to light them.

They would have determined by now that he'd been a part of the plot. Even if no one had named him yet—and that was unlikely—his disappearance from the shop on East Bay signaled his guilt. Old Widow Russell would be staving about with the brown leather book where she recorded profits and losses. She would be livid about what his running had cost her.

Tom was dizzy with hunger, his last meal more than a full day ago—had it been only one day since the world had crashed in?—before he'd saved the life of the traitor George Wilson.

In the distance, a marsh owl.

And then something else. Tom was certain this time: bloodhounds.

And they were closer. The dogs would be fresh and just fed, while he was raw and spent and bloodied.

None of this—his eyes swollen to slits, his grated feet, the baying of hounds, a rifle lowered and cocked—had been part of the plan. Yet his running had also been coming for years, laid up in him like the coals in his forge blown into fire by the bellows.

The baying grew louder behind him. Coming faster.

His mosquito-swarmed eyes fast swelling shut, cypress trunks blurred into a line.

But he could still hear.

All too well he could hear.

Tom splashed headlong into the water, one hand grasping for a fallen cypress, its trunk mummified in moss and resurrection fern. As he eased deeper, the ooze of the blackwater's bottom fell away from under his feet so that he could no longer stand. He clung to moss, his nails prying into the wood, sodden and soft, which broke away like an old sponge.

Feet churning for something solid, he threw one arm over the top of the log. And there he hung, face pressed hard against rot and water-logged wood and ferns that thrived on death.

The hounds, bellowing, had reached the far edge of the swamp, where they circled and whined, maddened to frantic at the scent that disappeared into blackwater.

They tore back and forth, barking and baffled. Then, led by the largest, they bore right. Tom, sinking still lower into the water, heard their howls growing close.

He clung to his log, his face hidden from the shore by the downed tree. Blood pounded in his ears. Deafening.

The dogs circled the swamp, its mist thickening as the day leaned toward dusk. Night settled over the Low Country, tucking its edges first beneath the live oaks, then spreading out to blanket the swamp, the land holding fast to the last glimmers of day like a child fighting sleep.

From the water where he clung to his log, Tom heard every curse of the slave catcher, every whine of the dogs. So close. They were so close.

He could not afford to breathe. Could not so much as shift a finger on the log where he clung.

If the dogs picked out his scent or the gunman heard his intake of breath, there would be no running, no fight that wasn't met with a shot to the head. And if they took him alive, it would be for the pleasure of hauling him back into the city, executing him in front of a rapt and breathless crowd.

The bloodhounds circled, sorting one scent from the jumble of swamp-fox lairs and marsh-owl nests and egret eggs. They seemed to have lost the trail. The dogs' whining faded at the far end of the swamp.

For a moment, Tom's fingers relaxed, just barely, there on the log.

For a moment, he drew a breath.

Then a tail thrashed through the water behind him—something else that had not lost his scent.

The gator.

For a moment the creature stayed there, suspended in water, tunneled eyes unblinking, examining Tom, its square snout submerged but for the nostrils.

His arms clamped on the rot of a log. Swamp algae and roots and vines were wrapped around his ankles, his calves, his knees. Tom forced his body still, terror sending his fingers deep into the log's bark as if it were butter.

As the swamp inked darker with night, he inched himself down the log, away from the reptile.

But the gator's snout rose out of the water. His mouth opened, teeth gleaming.

Tom threw himself backward and under the water, the gator's jaws snapping above him.

Then finding his arm.

Tom's head fell back in agony, his mouth open in a scream that was soundless. The gator's jaw sank into his forearm, each tooth impaling past skin into meat.

Using the full force of the strength he'd gathered swinging hammers over his head hundreds of times every day, he fisted the gator between the eyes with his right hand.

The creature, stunned, loosened its hold. Drew back. But only a foot or so.

Slowly, making no sudden moves, Tom eased away. Found his footing. Left arm limp and losing blood fast by his side, he reached with

his right for a nearby vine to stop himself from falling, the pain excru-
ciating. Staggering, he backed more steps away, eyes still on the gator.

Its snout floated there at the surface, the creature not yet retreating.
Just stalled for a moment in its attack.

Tom stumbled onto dry ground, the bloodhounds baying not far
away. Still searching for his scent.

And here he stood with a row of speared wounds in his arm, gushing blood.

Pain crashed through him, fuzzing his vision. Tom pressed on the
wound with his opposite hand. Limping and staying low, he retraced
his steps.

Desperate, he was making his way in the only direction he could
think to—a path his feet had known from childhood.

Back in the direction he'd sworn he would not go.

But the blood was still flooding from under the hand he held to his
mangled arm, his head already dizzy, feeling unloosed from his neck.
He stumbled once. And then again.

At the edge of the rice fields of Drayton stretching ahead in shimmering grids of gold, Tom swayed forward and back, barely righting
himself. Only a matter of time now before he collapsed.

He heard the workers approach before he could see them. They were
singing, not in the flooded rice fields now that it was dark but for the
moon, but in the patches behind their own cabins, the bit of earth
where they grew their own food to add to what scraps they were handed.
Some of them bent over a fire and a common pot, some of them bent
over their gardens, and some bent over nursing babies, but their song
rose from the quarters:

> *Deep river, my home is over Jordan.*

Deep river, Lord, I want to cross over . . .

Closing his eyes, even as he forced one foot in front of the other, he let the mournful current of the tune wash over him.

Hoes smacked into the mud, and mothers rocked in time with the song.

He staggered forward through an irrigation ditch.

Then a sharp cry.

He had been seen.

His legs gave way, the pain in his arm and the loss of blood taking him down as he crashed backward through a wooden barrier that held in the freshwater pushed there by the ocean's tides. Landing on splintering boards, he rolled himself with effort onto his uninjured side and lay still.

Now came her voice, its scream muffled by age and her own hand over her mouth.

"Tom!" She dropped down beside him. Cradled his head. Her cry then was something ruptured and raw. *"My baby, my son!"*

Chapter 32

Kate grabbed Scudder's hand and positioned his fingers on the stone's letters. "Tell me what you think that says."

He traced the letters a moment. Then murmured, "Mary."

Swallowing, Kate sank back from her knees to sit on the grass. "That's what I thought, too. In the archives, I found a Mary who was the mother of Tom the blacksmith, the one who made weapons for the Vesey revolt. The name Mary wasn't as common among slaves in the American South as you might think—as opposed to, say, Tom or Jim or Lucy or Phillis. Sometime before 1820, this particular Mary was sold away from the Russell house out to Drayton Hall—where she'd been purchased from originally. Sent back to the fields, I guess. For"—she made quotes with her fingers—"'insubordination.'"

Scudder looked back at the stone. "So all we know of the Mary here is first, she was respected or loved or something enough by the people here to be the only one with her name on a marker."

"And second, she died somehow in 1822. The year of the revolt."

Scudder's gaze swung out over the swamp. "I have to tell you I had my doubts about your theory that Tom Russell might've tried to make it out here to escape. But what if he knew something of the terrain out here because he'd lived here as a kid?"

Kate nodded, her eyes on the name. "And what if he knew for certain that *she* was out here?"

❦

They climbed back into the truck, the gray silk of evening blurring the live oaks and the Spanish moss into shadows. Scudder flashed on his headlights against the falling dusk as the truck wheels crunched over the crushed shell of the road.

For a time, neither spoke.

"It's hard to shake the feeling of that place," Kate said at last. "The sorrow. The beauty, too. Thank you, by the way."

His head ticked toward her, then back. "Hard to shake the feeling, you're right. Which is probably the way it should be."

"Those were Draytons who owned that place. And thought they owned those people in that burying ground."

Scudder glanced toward her once but said nothing.

Which was right, Kate thought. Not to try to make it feel better.

"So," he said at last. "You're needing to know about the swamps, sounds like. I'm no expert, but I've been out here a lot. And read a good bit about them."

"Which makes you my current primary source for swamp study."

"Yeah, that'll knock their socks off in the bibliography: contractor for Restoration Inc., page one."

She laughed. "I'll find some stuffy, old scholarly source later to document whatever you show me in person. I'm just grateful to be outdoors for a change."

"All right then." Hardly taking a breath, he described in vivid detail the creatures who lived there: the yellow-bellied slider and the brown water snake, the redbreast sunfish and the striped bass, the spotted sucker and blackbanded darter, the white-tailed deer and the great blue heron. "All of whom," he concluded, "live among the cypresses and the tupelo gum trees and call it home. But as far as your question about whether Tom Russell could have made it past the blackwater, maybe. Although it's hard to imagine."

"That," she said when he'd finished, "is a far better lecture than I've ever managed to give."

"False modesty again."

"Not this time. Trust me—I have witnesses." Tugging at the skirt of her little black dress, she shifted toward him, then quickly away.

No attachments, she reminded herself. *None.*

"So, Scudder Lambeth. Dan said you moved back to town not long ago from the West Coast. Was it a shot at the dream of starting your own business, the restoration work, that brought you back here?"

"Hardly." His voice, hard and sharp, startled her. "It's a long story."

"How long?"

"Longer than you want to hear."

"I doubt that."

His eyes left the road to look her full in the face before swinging back. "How 'bout longer than the miles we've got left to the pull-off where we'll see how much you can make out in a blackwater swamp at dusk." He gave her a crooked grin. "How 'bout we start with you?"

Kate drew a circle in the condensation on the passenger-side window, gave it eyes and a crooked smile. "Bunking out with a mountain of musty books in a one-star motel in the Deep South wasn't exactly plan A for me."

Another silence.

"So, Kate Drayton, how 'bout we trade longer versions one of these days?" Across the cab, his left hand on the wheel, he offered his right. "Deal?"

She shook it, his hand rough and calloused, and pulled hers quickly away.

In the distance, a long, low roll of thunder.

"Kate, this might be a bad idea, me bringing this up, but maybe I should be honest with you about something."

A shard of lightning split the sky now, and they both jumped. A spattering on the windshield followed, slow at first, then harder. Something in his tone, too, made her brace for what was coming.

"Look, it's not your fault, but some folks in town—nobody I'm close to, and probably nobody who's actually met you—think your showing up all cozy with Rose Pinckney, and your being a Drayton, is part of some bigger plan to influence her decisions."

"Her *decisions*? What decisions?"

"It's the timing of things, you got to realize. Rose Pinckney is rewriting her will—which everyone South of Broad knows—except probably you. She's got loads of charities she supports here: foundations, museums, you name it. And, conveniently, no heirs, so far as anyone knows."

Incredulous, Kate stared at him.

"And here you come. Part of the old blood—way back at least. Probably even a third cousin once removed, if anybody sketched out the tree. Here you are suddenly, Miz Rose's shadow."

"*Unbelievable.* So you're implying I've been conniving to get into the will?"

"Nope. Hear me now: it's not what I think. Just how it could look."

Glaring out the window, then back at him, she crossed her arms. "My God, the Low Country and its rumors!"

The windshield wipers beat time as she glared through sheets of rain.

His shirtsleeves rolled up to his elbows, the muscles of his lower arms flexed, he was gripping the wheel so hard the veins on the backs of his hands bulged. "Shouldn't have brought it up. I'm sorry. Guess I thought you should know at least what everyone else does—about Miz Rose rewriting her will and deciding where the money will go. But no one who knows you would think—"

Kate held up her hand to stop him. "That I'm a con woman with a whole lot of nerve and really good timing? Although that sure is what it looks like to plenty of people."

The truck's headlights showing a still frame of cypress and Spanish moss above an ebony gloss of water, Scudder shut off the engine. "This is a favorite pull-off of mine. Best angle of the swamp."

"I ought to be getting back."

"Kate, look. I upset you. Understandably. It was stupid of me."

"I just . . . suddenly, I'm just tired." She sighed. "I feel like I spend every day trying to get answers to my family's questions and secrets and rumors and how that fits with the past. And meanwhile—great—I'm creating more Low Country rumors." She crossed her arms over her chest. "I'm just discouraged. I'd like to go back now. If you don't mind."

"You sure?"

"I'm sure."

He rammed the key back into the ignition and turned.

A click.

And only that.

Again, he turned the key. Again only a click.

Muttering under his breath, he made his way to the front of the truck, then wrenched open the hood.

Kate joined him. "What is it?"

"Starter's gone bad is my guess."

Her face must have said what she was thinking.

"Must look pretty suspicious. The old broken-starter ploy, right? Only notice how old this Chevy is and how many miles I've put on her."

More than three hundred thousand on the odometer, Kate saw.

He closed the hood, pulled out his cell, and dialed. "Dan," he said into the phone. "Sorry for the hassle. Wonder if you could come pick us up on Ashley River Road out toward Drayton Hall, near the Audubon Swamp Garden. Problem with the truck. Yeah, you did tell me so."

He gave specific directions. "Thanks. What? Oh. *Us* would be just me and a friend. Of yours, too." He lowered his voice and turned his back to the truck. "No, I didn't arrange the breakdown, idiot. And if you weren't laughing so hard, you could already be headed this way."

Slipping the phone into his jeans pocket, he leaned through the passenger-side window to punch the truck's radio on—it was tuned to an R&B station—then scrambled up onto the hood. "Worst of the storm's passed, and it'll be a while 'til help comes." He extended a hand. "View's better from here."

Kicking her sandals into the cab, Kate navigated the climb onto the hood in her little black dress.

Scudder settled himself against the windshield. "I approached it all wrong before. For some reason, it just seemed like you deserved to know what people were saying so you could fight back if Botts or anyone else got nasty."

"Botts," Kate repeated. "So he's part of the chorus that thinks I'd try to con Rose?"

"Best I can tell, he's just been poking around, asking questions, trying to see what you're doing—but that's enough to make people talk. Truth is it bothered me, what I overheard. Not because I believed it. Bothered me because from what I was seeing of you and hearing through Dan and Gabe, you're somebody who's smart and determined and kind. Didn't seem fair."

Kate looked back at him. The arms she'd folded across her chest relaxed. "You left out one of my strongest traits: a good arm. And not just for a girl."

He laughed. Glanced shyly away. "But if I added anything else to that list, like saying that you were nice looking or something like that . . ." He shrugged, his eyes still fixed out ahead. "You'd think it was only part of the whole evil plan: trapping you out here against your will."

"In the middle of a blackwater swamp." Kate nodded. "You're totally right. Tonight, I would not believe you."

No attachments, she reminded herself. *None.*

Not even if a guy seems trustworthy at first. Lots of people seem trustworthy at first. But nobody comes through in the end.

His fingers drumming along to the beat of the music on the hood, he pitched his face up toward the sky. He looked absolutely at peace as he was—a little pensive, maybe, but quiet and calm and listening to the sounds of the swamp.

Leaning toward him, she tipped back her head at the same angle. And listened.

Ahead in the truck lights, a great blue heron spread its wings and lifted up from the water. In the distance, a marsh owl called.

Chapter 33

1822

Tom lay on his back in the rice trench, the mottled sky and its moon above him spinning and spinning like a kaleidoscope in a restless child's hands. He shut his eyes.

It must have been the loss of blood from his arm. He tried sitting up. Tried lifting his head. The mottled blue overhead spun faster.

"Stay low now!" a man's voice whispered. Panicked. "Your mam coming back. Went for some food. Stay low."

Tom was sure he was dreaming then, swept back to childhood. Delirious from the loss of blood. From hunger.

A face swam into focus, its skin darker under the cheekbones where it was hollowed. And darker under the eyes. Only the eyes were young still, as soft and as deep as he remembered. The brown of the eyes blurred, though, above him, and he realized she was crying.

"My baby," she said. "My son."

Tom reached for the face before the world went blank.

～

When he opened his eyes again, she was lifting his head. Pouring water a few drops at a time into his mouth.

"Get some water into you. Some food. Then see can you walk." She cradled his head on her lap, her palms resting on either side of his face. Whatever blessing she gave, whatever prayer, Tom felt strength flow from her small, weary form into his.

From behind her, she pulled a small ceramic plate piled with rice and peas and corn and ham mixed together, the scent of it wafting around him. "Hoppin' John. This still your favorite, Son?"

He saw the decades of grief hammered into her eyes. She ladled the food into his mouth.

He tried to push himself up to sitting. But fell back. His left arm she'd bandaged with wide strips of blue calico—the bottom hem of her skirt. The strips were red through, but she'd stanched the bleeding.

His tongue was nearly too swollen to speak. "You can't let yourself get seen . . ."

She held his face in both hands. "Now you listen to me. You hang on to hope. Don't matter what trouble come roaring in. No buckruh, no gun, no kind of cruel can take that away."

She gripped his face tighter now, the fingers of her left hand jutting crooked from the middle knuckles as if they'd been broken and healed back at an angle, the palms calloused and blistered, but something fierce—powerful even—in the clasp of her hands. "We got to see can you walk."

What Tom knew for certain was this: the baying of bloodhounds was coming closer again.

Her body bent over his own, defiance—strength, even—somehow in the grip of her arms, palsied and wasted. She bowed her face to his, her words coming steady and strong.

"Though I walk through the valley of the shadow of death"— shouting now—"I fear no evil."

The quake and rumble of hoofbeats.

"*No* evil," she said again, as if the quake of the earth as the horses approached had shaken an echo from her. "I fear no evil."

The hoofbeats stilled beside them, the ground quieting. A horse pawed the sand.

"Well, hell," said a voice. And the speaker spit, the juice landing on one of Tom's legs. "Looky here what we got."

On the bank of the rice ditch, two bloodhounds lunged and spun and barked, their paws churning a crater of mud.

A voice from the bank called: "Well, this here'd be a real shame, you getting protected by an old hag. Her not knowing you was a man with a price on his head. A real hell of a shame."

The world over Tom's head unsteady, its colors and forms sloshing as if he were underwater, he kissed his momma's hand and attempted to rise. But fell back, legs buckling, the world above and beside and below him nothing but water.

Tom felt his mam throw her body over his as a shield.

Heard the swell of her voice.

"Fear no evil. *No* evil. For thou art with me."

Then a gunshot.

Her arms going limp around him.

And now the water around him was going red. His mam slumped, unmoving, onto his chest. Ripples and ripples of red.

Tom's cry of anguish rose over the tops of the cypress trees and was carried away by the wind.

In the swamp, a great blue heron lifted its head, its long, slender neck stretching up to its full height. Listening. The cry that the wind bore troubled the waters, stirred the dangling moss.

The heron unfolded its wings.

Chapter 34

2015

Kate sat up straighter on the hood of the truck. "Something about this place. I keep thinking about the headstone back in the burying ground. I keep picturing what it would have been like if Tom—or any slave— tried to escape through here."

Scudder lay against the windshield with his arms behind his head. "I know what you mean."

She pointed down through the glass to a dog-eared book wedged between windshield and dash. "You know, you can tell a lot about a person's character by the paperback classics he carts around in his pickup."

Scudder's eyes followed hers to the book. "So what exactly does *The Sound and the Fury* tell you about me?"

"Well, let's see. That you have an interest in Southern lit."

He held up a finger. "That's one."

"That you perhaps believe, as William Faulkner did, that"—she lowered her voice to her best Mississippi male drawl—"'the past is never dead. It's not even past.'"

Grinning, Scudder held up a second finger. "Two."

"And that, contrary to your athletic physique"—she gestured in game show–assistant style, as if displaying a new car—"and participation in a number of socially acceptably rough, high-contact sports, you were a closet nerd in high school."

Reluctantly, he held up a third finger. "No one else knew. Except Dan. I hid my books under my cleats. He hid his sculptures behind his free weights."

"Tell me the truth: How many times have you read it?"

"Not saying."

"Remember, you're talking to a woman who reads two-hundred-year-old journals for a wild time."

"Here's all I'm saying: I've read Morrison's *Beloved* more."

Kate studied the blackwater swamp up ahead lit by the truck's headlights. "About a fugitive slave."

He sat up and stared with her into the cypress trees. "You thinking about Tom Russell?"

She nodded. "And the present-day Russells. The journal from Rose Pinckney's family that she and I have been working our way through makes me convinced on the one hand that if Dinah, the woman Tom Russell loved, even lived long enough to bring her baby into the world, its father is just as likely to have been the white owner who lived on the same property."

She pulled her knees to her chest, not caring anymore about the condition of the little black dress. "And for Dinah and Tom to have had other children, he would've had to survive the city's reaction to the revolt, and nothing I've found even hints at that—except my mother's research." Kate rested her chin on her knees. "And none of that gets me any closer to understanding why the research was so important to her."

Scudder rubbed the back of his neck with one hand. "Kate, since you're friends with Gabe and Dan—and me—how much do you know about genetic genealogical research?"

"You're serious?"

"Dead serious."

She gave a wry smile. "My time at Harvard has taught me one should always cover for complete ignorance with phrases like, *My ion-mobility spectrometry skills aren't as current as I'd like*, or, *My Serbo-Croatian might be a bit rusty*. But just between us, it might be the case that I know absolutely nothing about genetic genealogical research."

He traced a *Y* on the truck hood. "Descent through the male line is apparently where the better matching would be on the STRs—short tandem repeats, the markers on the *Y* chromosome. Apparently, ninety-five percent of it doesn't change one generation to the next, father to son. That's why it's so good at tracking who's descended from whom. Although it's possible to track a matrilineal descent—through the mother's line."

She nodded, forehead buckled in concentration. "STRs," she repeated.

"And even though they prefer buccal swabs—a scraping inside the cheek—they can get DNA samples from, like, baseball caps, licked envelopes, stamps. Hair, too, as long as there's follicle or root . . . I'm boring you."

"No. This isn't my bored face. This is my *can't believe I'm having a conversation about buccal swabs on the hood of a pickup in a swamp in the Deep South but I'm intrigued* face."

He grinned. "Okay, so, this might not be my go-to conversation on a first date. Not that this is," he hastened to add. "And not that I'd have chosen this particular venue, with a broken-down truck."

"Oh, I don't know." She stretched her arms overhead and gazed up at the sky. "The view's awfully nice."

Silence for a moment from his side of the hood. And when Kate rolled her head toward him, he was looking at her.

Suddenly self-conscious, she lowered her arms and sat up. "You were explaining about how they collect DNA samples."

"So I have an . . . acquaintance who's gotten interested lately in genetic research."

"Rose Pinckney."

He looked startled. "What makes you guess that?"

"She dropped some results she'd gotten in the mail one time when I was there and volunteered that she was having genetic testing done. But are you trying to tell me her tests have something to do with the Russells?"

He looked away. "The situation is not what she thinks. There are things she doesn't know that aren't mine to tell her. I'm just the guy who's restoring her molding and floors. And even what I think I know, I'm not sure I've got right."

"And you don't trust me enough yet to tell me. Is that it?"

He swung his face to meet hers. "I do trust you. But all I'm free to say is maybe Miz Rose should slow down with the tests."

Something moved in the water close to the truck, a swish through the inky black.

Kate swallowed. "Gator?"

"Probably."

From all sides, the deep-throated echo of bullfrogs.

"So, Kate." He was nudging the conversation to something new. "Will the Ivy League be pulling you back soon?"

The truck's headlights caught the outline of a large cat creeping across the log.

Kate wrapped both arms around her knees. "Truth is I'm on academic probation. Don't know if I'll be going back."

Scudder stared with her out into the swamp. "You'd give up the history."

"The history I love. Guess I'll always keep that. Somehow. Just wouldn't get to have the letters after my name that would say"—she paused—"that I'm smart enough, finally. Like I'm not as easy to ignore as my father seemed to believe."

It was more than she'd meant to say. And not something she'd have admitted she knew about her own life, her choice of grad school and the stamp of approval—at long last—it would place at the end of her name: PhD.

"Kate, you know you don't have to finish out a life sentence you set up just to try and get your father's attention, right? Unless it's something *you* want."

She let out her breath. "I wish I could tell you which it is."

A marsh owl called again over the croon and slide of the radio, a bouncing blues-shuffle rhythm.

Scudder kept his face aimed out over the swamp. "Hard not to spend up the life we've got now railing at what we wish hadn't been."

Kate put her hand on his shoulder—her gesture as involuntary as the small shudder that went through him. She could feel the muscle under the white cotton of his shirt.

He lifted his head. Face inches from hers.

Behind them in the truck cab, the radio hemmed up the rough edges of quiet with the lilt of a new melody line.

With this ring, a tenor crooned, *I promise I'll always love you, always love you . . .*

"Those are the Tams," Scudder said, leveraging himself to his feet there on the hood. "Carolina beach music. Not to be confused with California and the Beach Boys. We used to dance to this stuff at oyster roasts. On the sand." He extended his hand. "Care to?"

Kate looked at his hand. Felt the music throbbing beneath them.

She knew beach music and the South Carolina state dance that went with it, the shag, a kind of slow jitterbug. Sarah Grace had taught her when Kate was small, the two of them holding hands and twirling, as Kate's bright-slippered feet—Winnie the Pooh's head bobbing there on the toes—shuffled out the patterns in time with her momma's, sometimes to this very song: *With this ring, I promise . . .*

Sarah Grace showed her how to loop their linked hands overhead and then down as they pulled away.

I'll always love you, always love you . . .

But sometimes in the midst of their giggles and spins, her momma's face would take on a faraway look, the pivot and slide of her steps becoming clumsy and slow. And then she would no longer be dancing at all but staring at a blank space on their kitchen wall that might have become some sandy place at the shore, her feet dancing in surf and the music blasting from a cassette player close by and her laughter and her dance partner's lifting with the squawk of the seagulls.

At these times, Sarah Grace would turn from whatever scene she'd been seeing and kiss the top of Kate's head with a ferocity that sometimes hurt.

I'd better start dinner now, Katie, she'd whisper. And the dance would be done.

Nearly submerged now by a wave of grief at the memory, Kate took Scudder's hand and let herself be hauled to her feet. "And if we misstep," she managed, "we're gator meat."

"Pretty much. I'd be careful if I were you." Bare feet moving in four-four time across the truck's hood, he held out both his hands.

Kate let herself be spun into the music, pulled with both hands toward him, then back, forward, and back again. Scudder lifted their arms overhead, feet still in a step-ball-change shuffle, then a slow pretzeled spin of arms tangled and untangled. And below the sloped metal span of their dance floor, blackwater.

At the end of the song, they stayed where they'd ended the last spin, both facing away from the swamp, Kate's arms crossed over her front, both hands holding his as he stood behind her. Scudder's head bent, his cheek touching hers.

"This place," she whispered. "It's so full of beauty but also of . . ."

"Pain," he said. "I know."

Slowly, she arched back her neck to brush her lips against the rough of his jaw.

He spun her gently so they were facing each other. Then circled her waist with both arms and pressed her to him, his mouth finding hers, blackwater throbbing around them.

Chapter 35

1822

Emily crouched in lace imported last fall from Belgium, here in the dirt behind a crumbling brick wall. To her right crouched Nina and Dinah beside her, the moon over the marsh grainy and fogged, like they were watching it all through a silk screen.

He'd had it coming, of course, the prisoner. Emily knew all about why.

You didn't go lathering up hundreds, maybe thousands of slaves for revolt like this Denmark Vesey had done and expect the old families of Charleston to hail you as their hero. She knew that city leaders were hauling in score upon score of slaves, plus the free black leader and four white men for questioning, and she knew that some of the blacks had been tortured for answers—though no man would have said this directly in the presence of the more delicate sex. Through her father and his friend Colonel Drayton, a member of the council Mayor Hamilton had gathered, she knew the interrogations that the council was calling a trial were being conducted behind closed doors—with no evidence but a handful of frightened informants.

She understood why the white people of Charleston, outnumbered by slaves and free blacks, lay awake every night terrified now. She understood Vesey had to be hanged, and fast.

Then why did she feel as if she were the one in line for the noose? Why did she want to leap from behind the brick wall and shout for the whole thing to stop? Emily's hand went to her throat, which was throbbing.

A huddle of men, including Emily's father, had shown up today to be sure the job got done quickly and right—and in secret, just the silver-gray side of daybreak. Emily and Nina and Dinah had been together on the second-story piazza, Dinah brushing Emily's hair, when they'd overheard her father and Colonel Drayton speaking on the piazza below.

"The other executions can be fully public. But not this one," Drayton had said. "The last thing we need is creating a martyr of Vesey. The whole thing will be done before dawn. On Blake's lands outside the city. And no one else must know."

The three girls had exchanged glances. Emily tried to recall now if they'd spoken or if only those glances had sealed their agreement they'd go.

～

The top hats of the men stretched them a foot or so taller, the hats blurred into their collars in the near dark. They'd come this morning with the purpose of killing, and that purpose, ancient as clubs and sharp stone, gave a hunch to their shoulders.

The noose swayed now in a slow, sluggish breeze.

Maybe it was the presence of Nina to her right, cheeks chalky white and eyes stricken. Or maybe it was the presence of Dinah to her left, the same age as Emily, the same long, slender neck and much the same build, except for the rounded bulge at her middle. A baby. Whose father was . . . who?

Emily fought back the nausea that swirled over her.

This summer, that's when the trouble had started.

Until this summer, the world had been well ordered and good. There'd been no discontent among slaves, no fear among whites until that monster Vesey. Had there?

Emily wiped a hand over her brow, glowing with perspiration.

The *Mercury* and other papers and the mayor and all his closed-door council might be trumpeting how happy and contented, how safe and secure they'd all been *before*.

But it was a lie.

The truth of this broke over Emily Pinckney with a crash that rocked her back as if she'd been smacked.

Dinah was watching her face. Dinah, the closest friend of her childhood, who was bearing a baby that was probably Emily's half sister or brother.

Emily pressed a hand to her mouth and cursed herself for the foolhardiness of coming. And now it was too late to leave. She focused on the horizon and tried to make her mind blank.

A breeze off the marsh jostled a line of palmettos and set them to rattling fronds like flimsy wood sabers. By noon there would be little breeze, and a Low Country sun would be searing the city again—like every day of summer in Charleston. The sun would soon be chinning up over the edge of the marsh, and the temperature with it.

Dear God, it was hot, already so hot. Emily thought she would faint.

The men at the base of the oak squirmed like they couldn't get enough air, and they tugged at their necks, at those fine silk cravats that must've been cinching up tight. They stared at the prisoner there under the live oak, its branches dipping and reaching in long, graceful black lines, the tree far wider than it was tall.

But against the ragged edge of the marsh, the prisoner was still just a dark smudge, the black silhouettes of palmettos framing the group of men, nothing but scribbles of charcoal all down both sides.

All of a sudden, the figure clanked one stride toward the cluster of men, and the men jumped like they'd been attacked. Their hands shot to inner coat pockets, and they groped for the pistols they'd loaded before leaving home.

Emily reached for the other girls' hands, and they held on to each other.

Even chained, the prisoner possessed some sort of strange power that made a whole clump of rich white men with pistols skittish as overdressed rabbits.

They look scared, Emily thought of the white men in charge. *Guilty and scared.* The former slave with chains on his wrists and his ankles stood with his head up and eyes steady.

Dying, she thought, *with such courage.*

The men huddled there by the oak shifted from one foot to the other, tugged more at their necks, like maybe the whispers had wended their way past their mansions that even manacled, even here moments from death, Vesey was a fair match for the pistols and rope.

Now Emily's father touched a hand to his morning coat's inner pocket, which held his pistol. "Where the devil is Belknap?"

Dinah was watching the scene and watching Emily's father, with eyes that told Emily volumes. Emily had seen it before, that rage in Dinah. But now those eyes above the rounded bulge of her middle made it all too horrifically clear.

"I told you, Pinckney. He was just leaving the workhouse. This unpleasantness will all be finished in moments."

Jackson Pinckney looked out past the rope toward the shifting ghost-shadows of marsh grass. "It's nearly light. And, no, it won't all be finished. Not even in my own lifetime."

"That much," Emily murmured, making no sound the men could hear, "would be true." Pinckney's gaze jerked from one of his collaborators to the next like he was hoping someone would argue with him, assure him he was dead wrong.

But no one so much as lifted his eyes from the ground.

Then, like they'd got the stiff pulled out of their spines, they hunkered down over their pistols, and their gazes swung over to Vesey.

The man in the chains met their looks with one of his own that was clearly a challenge, a look that all but announced that he, Vesey, was the only man present who wasn't afraid.

Beside Emily, there behind the brick wall, Dinah spoke for the first time. "Thought I knew," she whispered, "how it ended." And she molded her palms, shaking a little, over the baby inside her like she was feeling it stir.

Emily Pinckney did not ask what her maid meant by the whisper. She did not want to know. She herself half expected a rescue, a band of armed rebels galloping up in a cloud of white dust.

For a moment, nobody moved. Then the armed huddle at the live oak drew in shoulder to shoulder. They mopped sweat from under their top hats.

A scrabble of boot heels and hooves marched out from an alley nearby. Another white man joined the group by the live oak, his hand grasping a cracked leather lead. A bay colt side hopped behind, and it was a bundle of nerves, flank all aquiver, ears twitching forward and back.

One of the top hats stepped forward. "Good Lord, Belknap, what the hell's kept you?"

"Calm yourself, Hamilton."

Belknap was hauling back on the lead. "Couldn't be helped. The bastard they call Gullah Jack tried to sneak through the Neck just a few minutes ago—on his way to a rescue of this one." His head jerked toward Vesey, who remained motionless. "Reckon he thought he couldn't be caught, like he'd got powers or something. Surprised as hell we took him down."

Hamilton waved this away. "More delay and we may as well hang him in broad daylight from St. Philip's steeple."

Her leg cramping, Emily shifted her weight, bumping against the wall and knocking a loose brick to the ground. All three of the girls froze.

Hamilton spun then toward the brick wall. He stood, listening, watching.

He stalked toward the ruined brick wall two paces. Then a third.

Emily dug her nails into Dinah's arm and with her free hand covered her mouth again.

It occurred to her now—far too late—that if they were caught, she and Nina would be roundly scolded. Jackson Pinckney would rant and curse. But Dinah, so heavy with child, would be beaten senseless again. Or hanged with the rest.

The girls held to each other—and held their breath.

But Hamilton turned then. Marched himself back toward the prisoner.

There were the marsh and the pink fingers of sunrise and the welcoming reach of the long-armed live oak—Low Country beauty so deep and so wide that it hurt, a real physical pain that wrenched clear through the chest. And then that rope, the dark vertical slash to one side of the oak—like the canvas of the little scene had been torn.

In the brightening gray, the rope swayed. Then stilled. Nothing but a vertical line and a gaping *O* at its end.

Like a howl, Emily thought. *A howl about to begin.*

Hamilton reached to help steady the horse. "You'll also be disposing of the body? We can't have a martyr's grave on our hands. I won't have the thing where it can be found."

"Potter's Field," Belknap returned, "is where it's got to be done. Not far from here, and no marked graves. Plenty of unknowns dropped in the dirt. Reckon he'll be safe enough there."

Hamilton shook his head, and he furrowed the flat plain of his forehead. "His soul, I trust, will be anything *but* safe."

Vesey looked toward the sky as they slipped the noose, scraggled hemp twisted into a spiral, over his head. He was still staring up at the sky, as if he were watching for billowing curtains to part on some opening act. He climbed onto the back of the colt.

Emily's heart hammered out time while the seconds ticked by.

The rumors about Vesey and his band of lieutenants had spread all over town, seeped into the slave quarters of her very own home. She'd heard their whispers, swelling and growing, a rising tide.

Divine justice would punish the slaveholders, the whispers said, *just like those sloppily printed abolitionist pamphlets had been shrieking for years.*

God's own hand would reach down through the sky to save the rebels of this revolt.

And Vesey himself, a man who could not be killed.

Not on that tree.

Not today.

Not ever.

Chapter 36

2015

Gabe could make out far down the road the big, still form of a truck just off the shoulder. His daddy's headlights stabbed at the dark and made it back up.

They pulled to the side of the road, and Gabe's daddy, Dan, arms over his chest, and him chuckling, took the scene's measure. "Mm-hmm."

Gabe scrambled out and took the same stance, arms over chest, beside him. "Mm-hmm," he said, too.

Because there in the headlights were Uncle Scudder and Kate, standing up there like they were protecting each other on the hood of the truck. And no marsh foxes skulking around, no cougars or gators or a single good reason Gabe could make out.

They slid down, all embarrassed.

Uncle Scudder started explaining to Kate something, talking real fast, like folks do when they got to cover for something. "Dan keeps this bad boy of a redneck truck for the delivery end of the artisan biz."

The men, including Gabe, secured the winch. He and the three grown-ups squeezed into the long vinyl front seat of the truck, which took up nearly a whole lane of the road, hardly straining as it towed the smaller pickup behind.

Gabe's daddy had that look he got when he was pushing down hard on a grin that didn't want to be staying boxed up. "How exactly again did you two end up picking that particular spot for a dance?"

"Stopped for the view," Scudder said. "Truck wouldn't start back up. Had to pass the time. Somehow."

"Believe I mentioned that truck of yours needing some work."

Gabe leaned forward. "Believe he did, Uncle Scuds. Heard for my ownself."

"Whose side are you on, big guy? Wasn't like I stranded Kate out there on purpose."

Earnestly, Gabe leaned his head close to Kate's. "Uncle Scudder didn't do it on purpose, I swear. He'd not risk his truck just to strand you in a swamp."

Everyone laughed, Uncle Scudder going red to his hairline.

"Thank you," Kate said. "That's helpful to know."

The truck eased into the next curve, the headlights silhouetting the wide skirts of cypresses wading in water. Its engine growled into the silence. Gabe's daddy looked to be letting the engine noise give him time to size out what he'd say—and what he'd keep tied in the mouth. When he finally talked, it came out careful. "Kate, you've got lots on your mind."

Gabe could tell that himself.

She nodded. "Maybe it's just the difference between reading about events, even seeing physical evidence of what happened, like your slave badge—but then sometimes you stand in a certain place, and the past, the reality of it, just smacks you in the head." She patted Gabe's leg. "I'm not doing a very good job putting it into words."

Kate could be peculiar that way, her carting that big stack of books and the computer she kept slid in that backpack of hers, but her sometimes not knowing what a lap child knows about life—how it's struck through with good and with hurt. How the good and the hurt of last year and all the years past didn't go away ever, not really: they're just what you got to build on top of.

Daniel looked at Kate, and Gabe could tell he was ready to trust her. "You asked about our last name. Said you thought it was amazing we were connected with Emanuel Church and maybe descended from Tom Russell. Sounded like you wanted to know more about our family, Gabe's and Scudder's and mine."

Crammed tight in the seat, Kate had to lean forward to look at them all at once. "Hold on. Gabe's and yours . . . and *Scudder's*?"

"A little history—*recent* history—might help. Scudder grew up at my house. My *two* boys, the judge always said."

Scudder looked straight ahead. "My home life wasn't the best. Dan's momma could always tell when my daddy'd come home in a bad way and been swinging at me."

Gabe lowered his voice. "It's how come Uncle Scudder's got the scar on his cheek like all the bad guys in books. Only it turns out it's a chick magnet, that scar."

Daniel nodded like this was serious stuff. "Must pull on the female heartstrings or something—damned if I know. Don't fall for it, Kate."

"Ignore them." Scudder turned his half grin on Kate. "Dan's momma'd make biscuits—little pieces of ham all through them—and gravy to die for. The more beat up I turned up on their doorstep, the more biscuits she'd make—piled up to my chin some mornings. Best things you ever put in your mouth."

Kate let herself study the scar, and she touched a finger to the tip that ended close to his mouth. "I'm so sorry."

Gabe's head swung toward his daddy. "Chick magnet," he whispered.

Laughing again, they slid back into silence, thick as the hot summer night. Gabe could feel things there in the quiet he didn't know how to name. But he knew they made him miss his own momma.

"That's sad," Kate said after a time. "About your growing-up years."

Scudder shook his head. "The Russells taught me how to be family. My old man taught me"—he and Daniel exchanged glances—"how not to give up. Comes in handy when you're writing songs and nobody's buying. Or when you're restoring old wood and parts of the floorboards have rotted clear through."

The road rolled under them, the hot night air beating into the cab—and its quiet.

Kate was still leaning forward. And Gabe could tell from the wide of her eyes she had something urgent to say. But "Floorboards" was all that came out right at first.

They all stared at her funny, but it was Scudder who asked the question: "Are we supposed to know what you're thinking?"

"Rose Pinckney's ancestor's journal. The missing part of it. I assumed *underfoot*—when Gabe figured that out—referred to a hiding spot in her garden somewhere because of all the quotes about flowers. But what if *underfoot* meant under the floorboards? Scudder, is there a way we could pry some up in what used to be Emily's bedroom?"

Gabe plopped his chin onto his fists, both elbows propped on his knees. "Rose Pinckney. She the buckruh—"

His daddy shook his head. "Leave the Gullah for now."

"She's the lady who keeps real good candy in her house. Right there for the eating."

"You didn't go asking her, did you?"

Gabe raised both hands in protest, palms out. "Not a lick of an ask. It was her doing the asking. Her handing me a lollipop and asking wouldn't I take it please. Her being your customer, I figured you'd say it was fine."

His daddy's jaw squared. He punched the accelerator too hard, and all four of them jerked backward, then up. "Let me guess: By any chance, did she take the stick from you when you were finished—not tell you to throw it away, but took it from you?"

Gabe was saucer-eyed. "How'd you divinate that?"

"I think," Scudder offered, "we know now that Miz Rose thinks she has her DNA sample for the modern-day Russell line. Despite the Russells telling her no."

Kate's mouth was hanging wide open by now. And it wasn't her best expression for looks, really, Gabe thought—like a bass just snagged on a hook.

"Wait." Kate looked from one to the other of them. "*That's* what her genetic genealogy test was supposed to explore? Her ancestors' connections with the modern-day Russells? Not the modern-day Pinckneys?"

Gabe's daddy frowned. "As I understand it, it was whether or not her ancestors who owned slaves back in Tom Russell's day were biologically related somehow to our family that calls itself Russell but may or may not be descended from him."

The truck took a turn wide, with the pickup trailing behind swinging out so far it nearly took out a guardrail. But Gabe's daddy didn't seem to care.

Kate addressed Daniel, his face all shadowed shut in the dark of the truck but the lines of his shoulders big and wide as ever. "Dan, you know I've been trying to find more evidence for research my mother did on Tom Russell—about what happened to him in the end. And what happened to the woman he loved, Dinah. Is there any verbal history in your family that Tom Russell survived the hangings?"

"Only old family stories that say somebody left Charleston somehow in the midst of the chaos—after the revolt got informed on. Only later came back. After the war. *If* there's any connection to him."

"But if they were hunting Tom Russell, and probably caught him, and if the father of Dinah's baby was not Tom Russell but Jackson Pinckney, like I'm afraid it could be"—she twisted her hair into a knot as she concentrated—"and like Rose Pinckney must think it is, then how did the family go on?"

"We," Daniel said, and Gabe watched him grip the wheel hard, "would like to know the same thing."

Kate bit her lip like she was thinking so hard it might hurt. And she spoke slow. "So Rose wants to know if she's related through Jackson Pinckney and Dinah to"—she looked from Gabe to his daddy and back—"you two and the judge. And you all didn't want to be part of her testing, so she pulled the clever lollipop caper. Meanwhile, all the present-day Russells would love to know if you're related all the way back to Tom in more than just name."

She rubbed the side of her head with two fingers. "And then there's my momma. Knee deep in the whole thing—and my father calling it 'a history that can only hurt you.' And I've still no idea why."

Even there in the dark, Gabe could see how the moss dripped long and moved side to side, like a circle of ghosts watching them close, and there was his daddy, nodding to Kate.

Gabe never heard the adults agree to it exactly, but something must have been said, because the truck was suddenly shooting not down the ramp into town but out over the water on the Ravenel Bridge, and Gabe knew what that meant.

Sure enough, with their coconut shrimp and beer and Coke, they sat on the beach at the Isle of Palms and talked and talked, Gabe wondering why his daddy didn't say it was way past bedtime but happy it had got so forgotten.

Kate put her knees to her chest and her chin on her knees, just like Gabe, and the two of them sat watching the waves.

"I used to come here with my momma," she said. "Used to make me feel safe, being here. Collecting seashells. Or just sitting." She tilted her head to one side. "What about you?"

Gabe's eyes were heavy, and he leaned against her, but his daddy couldn't see him too sleepy, or they'd have to go home. "Mother E," he whispered. "It was her favorite place. Still feel close to my momma there."

Gabe felt his eyes sliding down, and that was okay, the froth of the waves at the tips of his toes and the moon over the sea oats. The last thing he heard before sleep was Kate's voice, low and easy and soft as the waves: "Summertime, and the livin' is easy. Fish are jumpin', and the cotton is high . . ."

Chapter 37

1822

Belknap rolled the sleeves of his shirt, focusing there on the cuffs, and did not look up at the prisoner. "Denmark Vesey, you're gonna stand the hell up when I give you the sign. I'm assuming you done said your prayers."

Hamilton tried placing one hand on the colt's jittering muzzle, but the colt jerked away. He snapped the lead so hard the bay's eyes rolled back to white, and then Hamilton answered for Vesey: "As God will have no mercy on his soul, we needn't pretend to have any."

Vesey rose slowly to a standing position on the back of the horse, his gaze sweeping over the circle of men at the foot of the oak.

Nobody moved. Not the three girls hidden behind the brick wall. Not any of the circle of men. Not Vesey or the colt or even so much as a gull over the marsh.

Emily wanted to scream. Or to rush at the men to stop. Or to run away.

Frozen with horror, she stayed where she was. Completely and utterly silent.

Then Hamilton raised a riding crop high and brought it down, slicing the flank of the colt, who reared.

Vesey's bare feet thrashed for a hold on the colt's back—and then slipped, stopping just short of the ground. His eyes fixed on the sky.

The rope was pulled taut, and it swung now—without help from the breeze off the marsh. Vesey's own body spoiled the clean, straight line of the rope, his head flopped at a right angle to where the skin kept its hold on his neck.

His eyes stayed open and staring.

His arms and legs jerked and twitched, and twitched and jerked, then fell limp, like a stringed puppet left there to dangle by a bored child.

The eyes bulging out now from the black swell of face. The body still swinging.

Emily Pinckney curled to one side and heaved.

Above her, as she tasted the sourness of a stomach turned on itself, she heard the screech and the flap of turkey buzzards already beginning to circle and dip, come for the banquet of barely dead flesh.

Bent like this, eyes squeezed tightly shut, Emily Pinckney could still see the scene—like the image had been burned into her eyelids: the sharp angle of neck, the feet twitching, just missing the ground, and the eyes that stayed open and staring.

No, her father had said, *it won't all be finished.*

Chapter 38

Dropped off at her motel just after midnight, and walked to the door by Daniel and Scudder both—Gabe curled up and sweetly snoring in the second row of the truck's access cab—Kate flopped down, exhausted, and fell asleep fully clothed on top of the paisley bedspread, which was still covered in research notes. By dawn, she'd risen and, still in last night's little black dress and heels with sand still clinging to them, snuck into the back of St. Mary's and limped forward to receive the host.

The splash of waves she'd heard for hours last night and the priest's rhythmic tenor at Mass flowed together now in her head: *Kyrie eleison, Christe eleison.*

~

After a shower but still bleary-eyed, she'd come to Meeting Street to see if Rose Pinckney might be curious enough about Kate's latest theory to allow the floorboards in Emily's room to be crowbarred up one by one. Even now, Kate could hear Scudder prying up another board, old nails giving way with a clatter in the next room.

Pausing in leaving her voice mail, Kate gulped down the last dregs of her coffee, then said into the phone, "Sorry this message is so long and possibly only vaguely coherent, but maybe I should end with the quote 'The only thing new in the world is the history you don't know.' Dr. Ammons, you—and Harry Truman—were right. I feel like I've only just begun to understand their story, all the people behind the revolt. And the stories behind the story."

From the next room came the complaint of old wood being roused from a long rest in one place.

Then Rose Pinckney's protest followed: "If Katherine is wrong in her guess, I shall not be happy with the state of these boards."

And Scudder's voice, low, unperturbed, answered: "I got to admit I thought it was crazy, too, Miz Rose, 'til I got to thinking about the part of the floor where the nails change from hand cut to molded. And places the width of the boards doesn't match exactly—like some got replaced at some point."

Kate returned to finishing her message. "I mentioned I have a number of new research leads. And there is this journal owned privately, and the part of it that's been missing, we think we might be close to tracking down if"—more banging from the next room, more groaning of wood, more of Rose's protests—"all goes well. Oh, and if you do come down here for your own research at Morris Island, we could use a historian here—a *real* one. I'll e-mail you soon."

Kate touched a hand to her eyes, puffy and circled from a night with so little sleep. She staggered back into Emily Pinckney's former bedroom and had stationed herself between Scudder and Rose when another floorboard popped loose, revealing nothing.

Then another. And still another.

Kate dropped herself onto the floor. "I'm so sorry. I was so sure."

Another floorboard. Still nothing. The next one was stuck, pulling loose with a groan.

"It's okay, Scudder. Must have been just wishful thinking on my part. I have to leave in a few minutes anyhow to meet with Botts, so don't feel like you need to tear up any more of your lovely wor—"

But then she saw something underneath the board: a flash of yellowed paper.

Kate and Rose gasped at the same time.

Scudder bent for a single letter, addressed in broad, looping script to Miss Angelina Grimké. Kate dove for a stack of handwritten pages beside the letter—the pages cut in nineteenth-century fashion on one side but ragged on the other, as if they had been hurriedly wrenched out of a book. Across the middle, they'd been tied with a frayed and faded pink ribbon.

Squealing like schoolgirls, she and Rose threw their arms around each other as Scudder stood grinning.

"And here I thought we were wrecking my work for nothing," he said.

Grabbing him around the neck, Kate pulled his head to her and planted a kiss at the corner of one eye. *"Thank you."*

Rose arched a silver eyebrow. "We had better aim in my day."

"Treasure found, Rose!" Kate spun around, the bundled pages clutched to her chest. "Can you believe it? Where should we start reading?"

Rose slipped the crumbling letter from its envelope, bits of its brittle edges floating like snow to the floor. "It's from our Emily, all right. 'To my dear Nina.' And it's dated August 9, year of our Lord eighteen hundred and twenty-two."

"Just after the last of the thirty-five hangings. But look at this envelope, Rose. There's no postage."

"So our Emily wrote it but never mailed it." Rose checked her filigreed watch. "Given that we haven't an abundance of time at the moment, to say the least, before you need to leave, let us save the letter to read together later and begin by skimming the journal."

"Rose, I can't stand for us not to dig in. Now that we finally might have some answers."

"As if I would let you be late to your meeting with Botts, given what you've been through to corner that man. This journal has been waiting for nearly two hundred years to be found. It can wait a bit longer to be thoroughly read."

She motioned Kate to the piazza. "Scudder, sugar, you too. I made you tear up your own work on this treasure hunt. You may as well enjoy the spoils." Scudder took a seat at Rose's left and watched with interest but without speaking.

Gently, Rose untied the ribbon from the stack of pages Kate held. "You do the honor, my dear. Keep them in order, but skim through for now to see what we have here—and what they contain that might have induced her to mutilate her own diary. I've a meeting of the symphony board this afternoon, but we can study them more thoroughly this evening."

Donning the white gloves Rose had saved from her young womanhood and offered up for their research—their fingertips were now covered in dust and ink—Kate lifted and turned the delicate pages. "Oh my God, Rose, look at this." Rose bent her head close to Kate's. "Emily describes witnessing the hanging of Denmark Vesey."

Kate's left hand went to her chest. "And she refers to more hangings. But she goes dark on details. And she refers to Dinah's being unwell since the workhouse. And to Dinah's condition impeding her pace and the baby's being due any day, but . . ." Kate shook her head. "Look at how her penmanship that was always tidy and regular becomes wild and erratic. It's like she was finding it hard to record any of it by this time."

"For good reason," Rose mused.

"And look at this: pages and pages about a Spaniard that she and Nina saw at the Planter's Hotel." She and Rose and Scudder exchanged looks. "What do you suppose the point of that was?"

"We shall read with exceptional care this evening, Katherine, and begin unraveling the mystery at last." Rose checked her watch again and placed a hand on Kate's arm, the old woman's veins like ribbons of blue on lantern-paper skin. "Your time is nearly out, dear. Before you go, you say she witnessed Denmark Vesey's hanging?"

Kate flipped back to July 2. "She and Dinah and Nina seem to have been there—though she doesn't name them. But that's who it must be. The entry for that day is short—and light on detail. And the penmanship is awful, really hard to make out. But . . ." Kate's heart thudded as she skimmed the next line. "Rose, listen to this." She read aloud.

Have made a decision today. God help us, we cannot go on in this way. Unlike N-, I am not a woman of great courage. But I am faced now with a choice, and I have made my decision—one that would earn me the scorn of my neighbors and the fury of my father. I think, however, that for the first time in my life, I am more concerned with the judgment of Almighty God, who will surely not stand by and watch things as they are here.

In my small way, I will act.

Scudder raked a hand through his hair. "What's she referring to—do you know yet?"

Exchanging glances, the two women shook their heads. Rose patted the pages in Kate's hand. "But we know now that we will."

Kate's phone alarm trilled—five minutes until noon. "Oh my God, Rose. Of all times to have to leave. We'll pick up here tonight, right? Read more if you have to, but no spoilers, okay?" Kissing Rose hurriedly on the cheek, she spun to kiss Scudder on the line of his jaw.

"Her aim does need some work," he said to Rose as Kate catapulted herself down the winding staircase and across Meeting Street toward the inn.

~

She was elated with their finding under the floorboards today. And nothing Botts could say could spoil that.

Kate took the stairs to the porch two at a time. This time Percival Botts would have to begin answering questions—including what had happened to her mother's rings.

She'd reached the first bend in the wraparound porch when someone raised his voice—Botts, it sounded like—from its opposite side.

"It's not your decision to reveal what she wanted no one to know!"

Guests of the inn, lounging on the porch with their wine and their sweet iced tea, looked up.

Charging from the porch's far end came a tall man—strikingly tall—with dark skin and a dark suit jacket over one arm. But even with his face turned away, Kate could see by the set of the jaw that he was angry. He reached the stairs in only a handful of strides.

"Judge Russell!" Kate called as he passed.

He paused, his eyes going wide at the sight of her. "Kate."

"Are you all right?"

A pause. "I am not, I may as well tell you." Something in his face, usually calm and wise, frightened her—something barely contained.

"Judge, I'm here to see my late father's attorney. I think you know him."

The judge's color deepened, scarlet flushing over the brown. "Let me suggest, Kate, that you do not attempt to see Botts right now."

"But . . . I have an appointment with him. And I've waited too long already."

"I can *assure* you that *now* is not the time." Striding past her, he muttered something she could not hear.

Dazed, Kate watched him storm away up Meeting Street.

~

Kate found Botts facing the harbor, his back to her, bony shoulders rolled forward as if he were being attacked from the front.

From one hand dangled a scarf. Delicate and filmy, like the spray of a wave woven somehow into silk.

Intending to begin with asking about the judge, Kate stopped in her tracks. "My scarf. I left it at Magnolia."

Botts's voice was hardly more than the rasp of rusted iron. "I am returning what is rightfully yours."

Drawing beside him, she was surprised at how small and insubstantial this villain from her childhood nightmares seemed today. She asked her question more quietly than she'd planned: "Does that also apply to my mother's engagement and wedding rings?"

His shoulders rounded so far forward his small head appeared to be contracting into a shell, his eyebrows crimping together over the points of his eyes. He thrust her scarf at her. "Those rings are not rightfully yours."

"So you stole them."

Botts glowered at her. "I took them from the safe-deposit box of which Sarah Grace made me a cosignatory years ago."

Kate stared at him. "I don't believe you."

"Who do you think was paying the fees on the box? And how else would the bank have given me access to its contents?"

"So you did take the rings."

"Only as a temporary measure—to keep them from you."

"To keep them from *me*? Her daughter?"

"Sarah Grace entrusted me with seeing that in the event"—he swallowed—"of her untimely death, the rings would be delivered to their rightful owner."

Kate scoffed. "Your client Heyward Drayton, is that it? But since he predeceased her . . ."

Botts shook his head. "Because I have yet to make good on this particular obligation and"—he paused here, his eyes darting out to the harbor—"personal promise, I cannot discuss the terms or the parties involved. I can only say that you must believe me that it pained Sarah

Grace not to leave you the rings. Yet she believed this inclination of hers to leave them elsewhere was the right and the honorable thing to do."

Incredulous, Kate studied his face. "*Honorable.* The word you just chose for my mother. That would be a first."

Botts winced, the lines of his face deepened to trenches. He jerked toward Kate. "And *you.* Dropping her scarf in the mud. As if her memory were nothing."

"*Her* scarf. You knew when I dropped it out at Magnolia that it was hers. That's why you took it after I dropped it." Kate stared at him. "Oh my God. You were in love with her, weren't you?"

The misery lined into his face deepened now, and she knew she'd guessed right.

"That's why all your letters to her—above and beyond the call of legal duty. Your offers to help her with her secrets." Kate's tone softened. "Offers she never accepted."

"Sarah Grace," Botts groaned. "I wanted to help *you.*"

"You were nervous I would find all those letters of yours. Which I did—only I never saw past what I thought they were—your representing my father and your feeling drawn to my mother and sorry for her like everyone else. But your feelings went deeper than that, didn't they?"

Botts's words were hardly audible now, as if misery and regret were crushing him. "There were things Sarah Grace asked me to do for her. Secrets of hers I'd fight to the death in order to keep."

Chapter 39

1822

Dinah made no secret of what she wore on her arm.

The cook, Prue, threw her own shawl over the maid's shoulders. "Girl, have you lost your mind? One look at that and Mr. Pinckney come down on you like hell on a hot day."

But even Prue shrank back when Dinah turned with the full force of her eyes, dark and round and blazing. *"Let him."*

Dinah's willowy limbs and neck had become skeletal, all sharp angles and lines, the only real curve now at her middle. She threw back her shoulders to make clear the state of her mind—and because her back had not fully healed yet, the cloth of her dress sticking to scabs and still-open sores.

Emily Pinckney crossed the foyer and hesitated. Dinah saw her glance at the armband but look away. "Dinah, I am not going anywhere near the . . . unpleasantness today. And I am hoping today will be the last of this turmoil in our city."

"There *will* be more hangings. No question on that."

Prue's eyes grew wide at Dinah's retort—nothing careful or respectful about her tone, not even an attempt at it.

Emily hovered there on that grand sweep of the entryway stairs. "I think," she murmured, eyes darting toward her father's study near the base of the stairs, "that you had better come up with me now. It's time I changed to go out. And I need to talk with you."

Jackson Pinckney's voice boomed from his study as he emerged into the foyer, his black leather account book open in one hand. "One bayonet addition to each of two dueling pistols. Paid in full in June of this year." He slammed the book shut. "Though I wish to God I'd waited to pay the blacksmith." He rounded on Dinah. "As it turns out, I need not have paid a criminal with funds he would use to further his treacherous schemes."

He glanced toward his daughter. "I believe it would be helpful for Dinah to witness today's and all future executions in this city." With one swift gesture, he ripped the black band from Dinah's arm. "Let me remind you that in this city, we do not mourn criminals."

Dinah did not speak as she walked with Emily Pinckney back from the day's hangings. Despite her exhaustion, despite the shredded flesh of her back, despite the weight of her condition, her strides were long, rage and disgust fueling her steps. Then, without warning, she stopped. Gazed out at the ships, the harbor, the ocean beyond.

Eyes on her face, Emily stopped as well.

Dinah hummed, the notes strung tight with pain. She sang only the first part of one line, low and hoarse: "Ain't got long . . ."

"To stay here," Emily Pinckney finished for her. "The last line of 'Steal Away.'"

Dinah did not blink as she met her eye. "Couldn't have said you knew that."

"I see more—and understand more—than you might think."

Dinah waited. It sounded very much like a threat. A warning, at least.

"I know . . ." Emily Pinckney faltered here. "I know you are planning to run. I don't know how you're planning to try it."

Dinah was surprised to find she felt no fear, not even with this revelation. It changed nothing.

Regardless, she would try to escape just as she'd planned—just as soon as she'd delivered this weight. She'd surely have been caught even without Emily Pinckney already being suspicious. But it did not matter. If the first attempt failed, she would try again. And again. Until she found her way free or they killed her for trying.

Bracing herself for the full smack of an accusation, Dinah turned from the harbor to find Emily's face red-eyed and wet and contorted with God only knew what—spasms of something ferocious and sorrowful both.

"If you want me to help you somehow," Emily choked out, "just tell me."

A wind blew over the harbor. Dinah's face—the high cheekbones and the eyes, dark and alive—lifted to meet it.

The offer of help might be a test—not an offer of help at all.

But something in Emily's face looked more like the girl she'd once been, headstrong and determined and a little defiant, playing in the garden with Nina Grimké and Dinah—only her eyes now were bloodshot and flooding.

"I would like to help," Emily murmured.

Dinah drew a breath so deep that her front hurt with the bulge of weight, and her back with her wounds. *You could have helped sooner,* she wanted to scream. *You could have tried to see the world outside all your satin and lace, your big house and balls. You might have stopped him. You chose to be silent. You chose to be blind.*

But Dinah did not speak, those words too ready to come if she opened her mouth. The words past any use now.

Instead, with effort, Dinah nodded.

Chapter 40

2015

Still trying to process Botts's ferocious refusal to tell her more of what he was hiding, Kate stood at the harbor's edge, a stray afternoon breeze sweeping across the water.

But if Botts would not talk—out of loyalty, Kate had thought, to her father, but maybe as much to her mother—then maybe Judge Russell would. Maybe his feud with the attorney could shed light on what Botts might be hiding and what made him think Sarah Grace's rings were his to hoard. It was time to pull in more legal help anyway, now that Botts was persisting in stonewalling her.

The midday late-summer sun was rolling a hot gold over the harbor, the waves swelling and splashing below the seawall. Kate checked her watch: still hours until she and Rose would be meeting again to pore over the newly found portion of journal, since Rose had commitments until evening.

Kate googled the judge's work number. No point in bothering Daniel for his father's contact information if it was right there online. Up came not only the phone number but also the address of his office on Broad Street—like most of the historic district, just a short walk away.

What could it hurt, after all, to show up in person?

He'd reacted almost violently to her father's name: *Young lady, I regret to say that your father and I were never friends.* But Rose Pinckney came from the same social circles as Kate's father, and even she had confessed Heyward Drayton was no easy person to please.

Based on the judge's son and grandson, who both spoke glowingly of the man, surely he was not as intimidating as he'd seemed at Emanuel. And his animosity toward Botts, a common enemy, made Kate wonder if Judge Russell might not be more in the line of a friend.

At worst, he'd be out of the office or booked with clients—or annoyed with her, but that was okay.

Kate speed-walked the blocks to his office on Broad with her shoulders squared, and she swung back her hair as she flung open the door. But there, her confidence left her.

Judge Russell himself was just turning from having picked up a memo from the receptionist, and at the door's opening, he glanced back. Seeing Kate, he froze.

"Judge Russell, I just had a couple of questions I thought you might be able to help with. I apologize for not calling to make an appointment ahead."

He met her gaze, then looked out through the front windows onto Broad and opened his mouth to speak. But then fell silent.

Even the receptionist swung her head back to stare at him now. "Judge?"

Kate was regretting her decision to come. "You know, I could come back another time."

He shook his head. "Actually, Kate, I am the one who owes you an apology."

"I'm sorry . . . what?"

"For hanging up on you when you called my home number."

～

Too dazed to think straight, Kate stumbled into a leather seat in the conference room at the back of the law office. She waited with her mouth hanging open as Judge Russell instructed the receptionist to hold all calls—and, yes, he assured her, he knew he was due in court.

Seating himself opposite Kate, he spread his hands. "I only have a moment, but this is important."

Kate tried to settle herself into the chair but still found herself perched at its edge. "That was *your* number I kept calling?"

"May I ask how you happened to have gotten the number?"

"I found it in my mother's handwriting, scribbled at the bottom of an art exhibit booklet, along with a name I couldn't make out with the ink blurred." But it certainly wasn't Elijah, she wanted to add.

He waited for her to go on, his face a mask.

"The name above it started with a *C* and maybe an *l* or an *h* after that."

"Chloe," he said decisively.

"Chloe?"

"My wife. Late wife."

He volunteered nothing else.

Kate felt her way carefully. "This would have been in 1991, about a year after my parents were married. I think you said you knew my father—though didn't have a very favorable opinion of him—from your College of Charleston days. Am I right in thinking, then, that your wife, Chloe, knew my mother?"

"Yes," he said.

Kate waited.

"Yes, they were friends."

"That would explain her jotting down the phone number, then. Amazing that you still have the same number."

He shook his head. "Given that it was after your parents' marriage, I confess I'm surprised Sarah Grace would have had it."

"But if my mother and Chloe were friends . . ."

Again, he looked away. "I'm not sure that after your parents' marriage I would have characterized them as friends anymore."

A grandfather clock at one side of the room ticked into the silence.

"Judge Russell, did you know my mother?"

He nodded. But kept his face turned away.

"Given that your wife was, at least at one time, a close friend of my mother's, is there anything you can tell me that would explain her to me? Like maybe whatever it is that Botts wants to protect—some sort of secret she had."

Swallowing again, he met her eye. Then glanced at his watch. "I have to be in court in just a few moments. And this is a longer conversation, I'm afraid. Let me make this commitment to you, Kate, in the meantime. I will tell you the truth to any question you ask—when it's time."

"*When it's time?* Judge Russell, with all due respect, I've waited my whole life to understand what happened between my parents and why my mother ran away from her life here when she loved the Low Country and why she never stopped researching it."

Elijah Russell rose slowly. "Forgive me, Kate. The court will not wait. But I will meet with you soon. I am committed to that." He held out his hand.

"The Wayside Inn," Kate blurted out. "In Wadesboro, North Carolina. Would Chloe, if she were still living, have known anything about why my mother would have saved a postcard from there?" Already she was cursing herself: Of all the questions she desperately needed to ask, why that one?

The judge held out a hand to balance himself on the conference table as if he'd gone unsteady. But his voice was level and slow—like a man who was telling the truth. "I can tell you this much for now. Neither Chloe nor I have been to that place. But, yes, I suspect I know why your mother kept that postcard."

For a moment, he squeezed his eyes shut as if trying not to see what his memory had just shown him. Then, he shook her hand quickly. "I will be in touch." With that, he was gone.

∼

Dazed, Kate made her way back toward the harbor and tried to sort out what she'd heard as she walked. Nothing about what Elijah Russell had said made any sense. And yet he—and his wife, Chloe—had somehow known things about her mother's life that no one else so far had. Except possibly Botts, who refused to talk.

At least the judge had promised to meet. And Kate would make sure that happened. Soon.

The sun sparkling a hot silver on the water, she dug in her backpack for sunglasses. There, fallen out of its folder, was the photocopy of the old photograph of "My Tom," a blurred Battery Row behind him.

A tourist ship was trolling back into the harbor, its passengers pointing and gawking from its deck.

"That's it," Kate muttered aloud as she dug for her phone. "Maybe a little nautical outing would help."

She dialed Cypress & Fire. "Dan, it's Kate. I know this isn't exactly advance planning, but if Gabe's walked in yet from school, could I take him with me on a little excursion? I need to do some research by looking at the city from out on the harbor, and I could use my head research assistant, the guy who's better than anyone at seeing patterns and variations in patterns. Any chance he could meet me at the fountain?"

She nearly added that she'd just seen his father, the judge, and that his parents had known her mother. But all that could wait until there was time. And maybe until she understood why Elijah Russell had looked so sorrowful as he'd said her mother's name.

∼

At the fountain, Gabe barreled toward her, his arms out. Behind him, a figure in jeans.

"Scudder!" She tried not to look as pleased as she felt. He'd already edged past more of her walls than she'd intended.

He ducked his head. "Tell me the truth if I'm intruding."

"It was my idea, honest," Gabe said. "My daddy has to finish a piece and ship it today, and Miz Rose kicked my uncle Scudder out from his work there when she left for her meeting." He lowered his voice. "But if he's in the way of our research, all you got to do is explain and he'll leave."

"Please tell your uncle that as long as he doesn't get in the way of my head research assistant helping me figure this out, we'd be honored if he would stay."

～

The pier teemed with tourists, open maps fluttering in their hands like the spread of bright-colored wings. Many were boarding a harbor cruise boat. Scuffing up the gangplank, they milled onto its deck, the ship's brass and wood all polished to glowing. As Kate and Gabe and Scudder raced up the pier, a sailor in full costume was just pulling a scarlet rope over the gangplank's lower entrance.

Probably no more than sixteen, the sailor's face was pitted and red as a plowed field of bad clay. "Y'all got you a ticket?" Then, remembering his costume, he plucked at the hat a full size too big for his head and shifted into a stilted stage brogue. "Aye, and me captain's given his orders, me pretty wench. We're all booked up, that we'd be."

"Pretty *wench*? Look, we really need to get on. For research reasons."

"No stowaways, lassie, or it's into the brig ye go."

"Now listen here!—"

Scudder stepped forward, one hand out to shake the sailor's hand, the other holding several bills. "I'm so sorry we're late. Here's cash for the tickets and a small thank-you gift to you, my good man."

The sailor narrowed his eyes at Kate.

Scudder leaned toward the sailor's ear. "I understand she's a good hand in hoisting the sails in a beam sea."

The sailor saluted. "Mizzenmast set. You've barely arrived before we launch." With an about-face on one heel, he unclipped the scarlet cord.

Gabe threw back his head to examine the boat. "All I see is a bunch of decks and—"

Scudder thanked the scowling teenager and hurried the boy ahead.

"Blimey awesome of you to help a wench in distress," Kate said.

Gabe cavorted up the gangplank and motioned them to follow him faster. The boat rolling on the wake of a passing cruise ship, Scudder followed him to the stern's rail.

Kate joined them. "I saw this ship on my first morning here."

Scudder gestured toward the open ocean. "Circles past an island or two. Owner tries to add a little historical touch with a crew of high school theater students who get to practice their craft."

Several teenagers dressed as sailors skittered over the deck, looking earnestly busy with ropes they made a great show of pulling.

Scudder turned his face into the wind. "There's nothing like seeing it from the sea. As a kid, I used to think Charleston's steeples poked holes in the sky."

"I can see why." Kate pulled the photocopy from her backpack, but the boat, still maneuvering past a cruise ship and a tanker, wasn't close enough to the Battery yet.

"Gabe, your dad and I used to come out here on the harbor a lot," Scudder said. "Whatever rowboat or half-sinking dinghy we could beg, borrow, or steal. Holy City."

"Holy City," Kate echoed. "I'd forgotten about that name."

"Just what some people call it. Charleston was a refuge, back in the earliest days. Dan and Gabe here tell the stories best."

The boy took a step forward, lifting one hand as if he were holding Beecher's reins.

"Here's how it was, folks. There were Catholics running from Ireland. Huguenots running from France. Baptists running from Maine. And Jews running from a whole world that would not leave them alone. So the Catholics and the Huguenots and the Baptists and the Jews all raised their synagogues and their steeples"—he swept an arm toward the city—"to punctuate a skyline."

Kate applauded. "Just the kind of commentary every harbor cruise needs."

As they churned through the harbor, the steeples behind them turned into a phalanx of soldiers, their spears rising above them, stabbing the sky.

Kate rested her elbows on the railing. "Funny how much I've read about this place for months—pages and pages of history. And no idea how little I knew until I came for myself. So. The Holy City."

Gabe placed his elbows beside hers.

Scudder placed his elbows beside Gabe's. "Dan likes to point out there was some irony in the name Holy City from the beginning. Charleston had a reputation as a place of tolerance. And a fair shake of hedonism." His eyes dropped to Gabe.

"I know what it means," Gabe whispered.

"Figured. I don't need to tell you, Kate, it was a major port for entering slaves. The workhouse. Brothels. Steeples. All here together. Holy City. God help her."

Glowing in the gold slant of the sun, the mansions along East Battery stood graceful as ever, their white balustrades winging out, light and loosely tied to earth, over magnolias and palms.

Kate held up the crumpled photocopy. "Okay, Head Research Assistant. Here's where I need your help. You and your dad probably know the buildings of the historic district as well as anyone here."

"Or better," Gabe suggested.

Kate chuckled. "Or better. Of course. So I've been trying to make out which houses are in the background behind this man, Tom, in the picture. The thing is, if we could date it somehow, at least eliminate that the photo was taken before or after a certain date, we might be able to know if this could even remotely be Tom Russell in his old age."

Gabe and Scudder both studied the photo.

"A visual archivist here in town was generous with her time, but the quality is too poor in this photocopy to date it very closely purely on the development of photographic technique. We're sure it's post–Civil War. And if it is soon after the war, it could be Tom Russell in his late sixties, perhaps. But the later the photo in the nineteenth century, the less likely it could be the same Tom."

Scudder nodded. "And you said out at the Isle of Palms that your mom was convinced for some reason this was Tom Russell."

"She was sure of it. And for some reason, it mattered to her—personally. But every early American historian on the planet specializing in the Low Country would argue he was already dead. This photo was with one of the Wayside Inn in the middle of nowhere, North Carolina. And if you can figure out the connection between them, you're way smarter than I am."

Scudder's eyes widened.

But Gabe lifted the page to his face, just inches away. Kate could see him going down the row of houses, his head nodding as he moved on to the next.

"I've looked up the construction date of each house," Kate continued, "and as best I can make out, what's behind him would have been built mostly in the 1840s, '50s maybe—"

Gabe looked up suddenly. "Drayton."

Scudder tilted his head. "Kate's last name?"

Gabe jabbed at the background of the photo. "This house. It's called the Drayton house."

Kate followed where he was pointing. "Right. The one over his right shoulder—with the Victorian embellishments that were added after it got shelled in the war?"

Gabe shook his head. "Daddy does a tour down the Battery, too. The house that was there got shelled to bits—not much left of it standing. Drayton—some later Drayton after the war, you'd have to ask Daddy—built a new house on the same lot."

Kate bent toward him. "Gabe, that's exactly the kind of information I needed, since I'd gotten it wrong before. So"—she bit her lip—"when was this one built? Because the picture clearly would have been taken some time after that."

"Mid-1880s, I think." Gabe gave a bob to his head for emphasis.

"Oh no. No, no, no, that's not good. You think or you know?"

He cocked his head. "I know. Just try on the fit of the *I think* sometimes so I don't sound so much like a smart-ass—*aleck*." He grinned impishly.

Kate leaned dejectedly onto the rail, her chin on her elbows. "That would put Tom Russell, even if he were young—like twenty or twenty-two or so during the revolt—in his eighties at least." She held up the picture again. "Hard to say for sure. This guy's no spring chicken. But he couldn't be in his eighties."

Scudder and Gabe bent down again. Both shook their heads.

"You want me to lie to make you feel better," Scudder asked, "or agree with what you don't want to hear?"

Kate sighed. "Guess I'll be back to tracking down my mother's connection with the Wayside Inn. Another dead end."

She tried to put on a brave face and threw her arm around Gabe. But the truth of it was, she was devastated to have had her latest theory—and her mother's—dashed all to bits.

So the current histories were right after all, were they? So Tom Russell had been hanged with the rest, and there was an end to it.

Then why did she feel like there was still more she did not understand about this? And why had Sarah Grace, who must surely have seen what Gabe did—the mid-1880s Drayton house behind the old man in the picture—insist on labeling the photograph with Tom Russell's initials?

Kate smiled back at Gabe, who was pulling on her to come hear the music. And she tried to look interested in what he and Scudder were saying—but her mind kept drifting back to the scene of Battery Row.

From inside the boat's dining room, a brass ensemble launched into another tune. The trumpet and trombone players swung their instruments to the beat.

"Under the boardwalk," the Drifters cover band crooned, "down by the sea, on a blanket with my baby is where I'll be . . ."

Scudder tipped his head toward her. "If you and Gabe weren't researching, I'd ask if you're willing to take another shot at a dance."

Her breath caught in her throat. "If I weren't otherwise occupied, I might accept."

Gabe looked from one to the other of them and rolled his eyes.

"Beach music," said Scudder, "makes me remember how things seemed like they'd turn out, Gabe—back when your dad and I were stupid and young and hopeful—in high school. Whatever troubles we'd had, whatever ugly past the South had, it let go its hold, like the future had flung open its doors."

Some sort of protection had dropped from his face, leaving nothing but the deep sadness of his eyes.

The sax gave way to a keyboard, this time joined by guitars and drums. Kate recognized a cover of the Black Eyed Peas' "Where Is the Love?" Kind of an edgy thing, she thought, to play on a harbor cruise for tourists out to forget the world's troubles—but why not?

"I like the way Charleston's skyline is compact," Scudder was saying. "Distinct. Not sprawling like LA."

"LA?" Kate asked.

"Lived there for a while. Wrote some music for a couple of B movies. A soap opera." He chuckled. "A laundry detergent commercial."

"What happened? I mean . . . if it's okay to ask."

"Friends are allowed to ask questions. I made a living. But I never made much of a life there. I missed the Low Country. Missed being where I was needed." He rested an arm playfully on Gabe's head. "It was Chloe, Dan's mom, who suggested I might want to think about coming back. I didn't have to think long."

Gabe tugged on Scudder's sleeve. "Show her the picture of Gram at the beach."

Scudder pulled his wallet from the back pocket of his jeans. "This picture's old—but it's our favorite—Gabe's and mine—of his gram."

In the photo, four people ran on the beach toward the camera, their heads thrown back, laughing. Elijah Russell ran at the far left, beside him a maybe ten-year-old Scudder, sunburned and lifting his hand in a high five to a young Daniel, brown curls blown back from a round, open face. At the far right was a woman with close-cropped hair and high cheekbones. She was darker complexioned than either her husband or her son, a petite, remarkably pretty woman with brown eyes that smiled, beaming, directly at the camera.

"She looks like the very picture of warmth." Kate held a finger above Daniel's face without touching the picture. "And he looks so much like his father. The forehead. The build. Everything."

"Yeah." Scudder studied the picture over her shoulder. "Which is pretty crazy, considering."

"Considering what?"

Scudder hesitated. "I thought you knew."

"It's no kind of secret," Gabe put in. "My daddy was adopted."

Kate blinked at the child. "Adopted?"

"Proud of it, too," he added. "Means you got picked special."

Kate laid a hand on his shoulder. "You're right. Of course. It is special." Her face swung toward Scudder. "But all Rose Pinckney's obsession with the DNA tests . . . her finagling to get a DNA sample from Gabe with the candy."

Scudder nodded. "You may have seen me trying to talk Miz Rose out of the thing. I know you saw me trying to talk sense into Botts that one day at the inn on the porch, when you showed up to see him. It's not like the judge or Dan or Gabe, any of us, wanted anything to do with her money. What's genetics matter, anyway? I'm as part of the Russells as if I'd been born into it. Dan was Chloe and Elijah's son. Pure and simple. But, yeah, he was adopted. Toddler, I think, at the time."

Kate studied the faces. "You see that sometimes with adoptions: a child that's not biologically related ending up looking an awful lot like a parent. And Daniel at this age looks so much like you do now, big guy. Those curls. The eyes."

Scudder bent closer to the photo. "It was this picture—along with what Chloe said—that made me come back."

"How so?"

"Here was Gabe, pretty much the age I was when the Russells took me in time after time. And here was Dan raising Gabe by himself—with Elijah and Chloe to help, but still." He shrugged. "I can sell songs from a distance. And I can pick up contractor work anywhere. But I couldn't help make a family for my best friend's kid from the opposite coast." He opened his wallet to slip the picture back in.

Kate pulled his hand to her but didn't force it open where it had curled over the picture. "Scudder," she asked, gently turning over his hand so that it was palm up, "could I see the picture again?"

Watching her face, he opened his fingers.

"Daniel's curls," she said.

Scudder nodded grimly. "Stuck out from under his football helmet. Drove the ladies mad."

352

"The shape of the eyes, too."

Kate ran a finger above the face, then thrust the picture back at him. "It's a crazy thought, but . . ."

Her mind was racing, pieces of a great puzzle seeming to fly in front of her eyes, some falling into place. A few pieces fitting, connecting for perhaps the first time.

On her phone, she googled the Wayside Inn, the article on its closing that she'd skimmed before. And this time, a handful of words popped out:

. . . suspicious activity, drug deals, abandoned children, and sordid assignations . . .

"Oh my God," she said. Kate's pulse was racing even as the boat's speed slowed to a drift as they neared the wharf.

Distracted, Kate stepped away to try to think as Gabe pulled on Scudder.

"Daddy lets me walk by myself up to Mother E sometimes on a Wednesday, and he comes to pick me up later."

"I know he does. You wanting to walk there now? Want us to walk with you?"

"Rather walk by myself, if it's all the same." Gabe leaned in. "Kind of need to be alone for a while to sort out the sad. Don't mean to hurt your feelings."

"No feelings hurt, big guy. Listen, if you want to go now, you'll be there long before dark. But use my phone to ask permission from your dad just in case, huh?"

∾

As they disembarked, Gabe hugged Kate around the waist, waved to them both, and jogged away.

Scudder held up his phone, to which Daniel had just texted back. "It's a Wednesday night. Plenty of daylight to walk the few blocks. Lots of church ladies to fawn over him—have him eating peach cobbler with cream by the time we get there. We'll pick him up in a bit."

Kate nodded, only half listening.

"Kate, you okay? You seem real far away."

"I'm just . . . I think I need to go talk with Judge Russell again. Like, tonight."

When they reached Cypress & Fire, Daniel was just completing a sculpture. He waved to them as they entered and was washing his hands when he focused on Kate. "You okay?"

She blinked at him. "Yeah. I think so."

He exchanged glances with Scudder. "You two want to walk with me up to Emanuel? Nice night for a walk, and we got plenty of time before Gabe's done being fussed over."

On Church Street, Scudder pointed up at the steeple of St. Philip's Church. "I've always loved that steeple at night, those circular windows, like portholes. As a kid, I thought St. Philip's was a lighthouse somebody built a few blocks too far inland."

But Kate hardly heard. She looked up and down the elegant street, the Dock Street Theatre there in the old Planter's Hotel, its wrought iron balustrades like yard upon yard of gray lace. Not hard to picture it as it must've been in Emily's day—and Tom Russell's: the street teeming with beaver top hats and silk skirts and goblets of red Planter's Punch that sloshed in and out of the hotel.

They strolled along, Kate wanting to speak, wanting to put order and words to the patchwork of her thoughts—but not ready yet.

The sky overhead was losing the last of its navy blue, the two-century-old buildings looking down on both sides, their Corinthian columns and carved cornices looking stately and proud. But not aloof, somehow, tonight.

It was as if, Kate thought, somehow this street, in all its storied strength, had seen sorrow before and was braced for it again.

She stopped in midstride. What an odd thing to think.

She shook her head.

Daniel had stopped, too, and was scrolling down his phone. "Something's happened somewhere on Calhoun, somewhere near the library. Or . . . Mother Emanuel."

Scudder stepped closer to read the text on the phone along with him. "What is it? Car wreck?"

Dan shook his head. "Looks like some sort of . . . nobody knows yet but . . ." His eyes rounded with horror, and his voice broke. "Gunfire was heard."

The three of them broke into a run.

Chapter 41

1822

The prisoners, two dozen or so in all, were paraded down Meeting Street in carts, including the prisoner most recently caught: the blacksmith, captured in a blackwater swamp.

"Weapon maker, as it turns out," Jackson Pinckney said to his daughter, lifting one of the dueling pistols from the inside pocket of his morning coat, "of the heinous plot. Apparently I picked a smithy who did indeed know how to attach a bayonet spring. And knew what it might be used for."

Tom Russell and the other men, all shackled, their chains clanking against the wood boards of their carts, were being rolled north down the street toward the Lines, the sky over the harbor a cloudless blue, the midday summer sun searing.

Emily walked by her father but did not take his arm for support, despite her head's beginning to swim. By contrast, her maid, Dinah, moved taller than ever, chin high above her long dancer's neck. If Dinah had heard Jackson Pinckney, she gave no sign of it. Emily stole glances at her, but Dinah's face was a mask, her steps behind Emily graceful and sure, despite her belly's protrusion.

"Not yet," Jackson Pinckney went on, answering questions Emily had not asked. "Wherever the devils stockpiled the weapons for their bloody purposes, we've not yet found them. But it will not be long. Mayor Hamilton will see to that. No stone of this city will go unturned. We did, however, intercept more than a score of canoes loaded with rebels from the coastal islands. They will be dealt with accordingly."

The crowd at the Lines swelled, pressed in, tense and ill-tempered in the heat.

"I suspect Hamilton did not anticipate a crowd of this number," Pinckney observed.

"I wish, Father"—Emily kept her voice low, her head turned away from her maid—"that you'd not forced Dinah to come. She's approaching her time. I see no possibility that her being here could be other than horrific."

Pinckney let his eyes swing back to Dinah. Let them rest there. "Perhaps the horror of the day will be just what she needs."

Emily ignored this. Tried locking her knees to keep her legs from buckling.

The crowd jostled. People began shouting at one another above the general jeers. A child shrieked. Fists flew. A horse shied back from the vortex of panic, the screams. And then he reared, front hoofs beating over the heads of the crowd—and landing in it.

The militia beat the crowd back. At the feet of the horse that had reared lay a dark-skinned body, unmoving.

"Dear God in heaven." Emily, suddenly faint, gripped Dinah for support. But Dinah seemed to see none of this, her eyes glazed, her back straight as the gallows as she walked ahead.

The captain of the guard spit sideways, his horse shying. "Bloody mob. Keep up this damn chaos and we'll see something of value hurt next." He spun his rifle to his lap.

When the militia calmed the crowd enough to proceed and the dead man was carted away by his friends, the prisoners were prodded with the muzzles of guns to mount the low gallows.

A long line of crude structures, planks nailed hastily together, had been erected for today's purpose.

One by one, twenty-two men stepped up onto makeshift stools—in some cases shipping crates, the flimsiest sort that a single kick might destroy.

One by one, each bent his head for the noose.

At the front end of the line, Tom Russell was scanning the crowd. His eyes found Dinah and stayed there as the rope passed over his head.

Chin high, Dinah moved toward him.

Emily wavered. But then, feeling the stares of the crowd, feeling their censure—*Why is that Pinckney girl tagging along after her maid? Why are they moving so close to a dangerous man?*—she laid a hand on Dinah's back and followed.

Only feet from the prisoner, they stopped. Dinah lifted an arm toward Tom.

A horseman pushed forward. Brandished a battered musket.

But if Dinah saw him, she did not move, her arm suspended, tears beginning to spill onto her cheeks.

The blacksmith's gaze stayed on Dinah when the first signal shot was fired.

The crowd hushed. Tom's lips moved, but no sound came out. Emily's fingernails dug into Dinah's arm, a cry rising in her throat. Jackson Pinckney, adjusting the silk cravat at his neck, scanned the long line of ropes and of men attached at the neck.

As if, Emily thought suddenly, *he were surveying his rice along the Ashley and watching his golden fields bow to the sickle. He is that calm.*

Now a second shot. The footing was kicked out from under twenty-two men. The gallows groaned as twenty-two bodies dropped.

But not far enough to snap a neck or render a man unconscious.

Vesey's longer drop from the skittish colt must've severed some sort of vital cord, Emily realized, the revolt leader's death nearly instant.

Here, though, twenty-two men, wrists bound behind them, were choking slowly to death—in agony. As the crowd jeered and laid bets.

Dinah threw herself to the ground beneath Tom's dangling feet. His face swelled and contorted, eyes bulging.

Emily clamped a hand over her own mouth, only a small, desperate whine escaping her. Here writhed a man that she knew, the man Dinah loved, and he was dying before them, one tortured breath at a time.

The whole crowd had gone mad. Horses were spooking, guns were shot in the air, and everyone was shoving—both forward to see the chaos firsthand and back from the horror. A full ten minutes churned by, and only one condemned man had stopped breathing.

Now two more.

Emily sank to the ground beside Dinah, the crowd roiling around them.

Tom's cries for mercy came in shreds of sounds, gasps.

A horse with no rider galloped toward them, his eyes rolled back to white, stirrups flying.

Flailing to her feet to keep from being trampled, Emily gathered her skirts, her new yellow silk. And saw her skirts had gone red. Gone bright, brilliant red. And wet.

For a moment she thought she'd been injured and too panicked and sickened to feel it. But then she saw Dinah beside her—bloodier still.

A sound came from Dinah then. Not so much a scream as a stifled, dying thing: a moan. Around where she'd collapsed on the ground at Tom's feet, the crushed shell puddled in water and blood. The coarse blue of her skirt had gone nearly black and was soaked.

Dinah's time had arrived, the baby she carried choosing this day, this moment, this place, surrounded by suffering, to make its entrance into the world.

James Hamilton pushed forward from where he'd joined her father and put out a hand to restrain Emily. "Don't involve yourself in this mess, Miss Pinckney. You'll sully your hands."

Emily shoved past him and dropped to Dinah's side, water and blood everywhere. She took Dinah's hand.

It's going to be all right, Emily wanted to say. But the strangling cries of the dying men and the taunts of the crowd and Dinah's moans and her own tears, none of them would let the words be spoken aloud.

Time slowed, as if the pendulum swing of the twenty-two bodies had reset some celestial clock and turned moments to hours.

Down the line of the choking forms, another mounted guard rode. Here and there, he answered a scream for mercy by aiming his rifle, its silver frizzen and sight polished to gleaming, at a man's head.

But then did not shoot.

"Hate to cut short your last minutes on earth," he sneered.

One by one, the writhing bodies hung still.

Except Tom.

Jackson Pinckney pulled his dueling pistol from his morning coat pocket. Triggered its bayonet spring. Then he raised his hand to the guard, who was just reaching the end of the line.

Pinckney nodded toward Tom Russell, the last one convulsing there on his rope. "This one I'll take care of myself."

Chapter 42

Gabe had meandered up East Bay. At number 321, he'd paused to squint up at the three-story clapboard house where the Grimké sisters had lived. You had to wonder what it was like to live way back then.

Which was why, he'd thought with a rush of pride, his momma had loved the Gullah Buggy idea: to help people take a peek into what it was like.

Gabe had turned left on Calhoun and walked to Mother Emanuel, where he passed the Vesey memorial kids in black marble and tipped his head to them, just like his momma had done every time she walked past Mother Emanuel's ground-floor entrance. Above where he stood, a big arch pointed up like it was making bold. He'd always liked that about this building, the way nothing about it was too soft, too weak, nothing about it bent over like the back of an old woman, and it had none of the fancy filigree prissiness of some other churches built a long time ago when people thought carving curlicues and swirlimigigs got the attention of God.

Gabe kicked at the linoleum as he made his way down the hall. A couple of the older church ladies, gentle and strong and alltime smelling like cobbler and kindness, called to him, but he ducked out of sight. It was the reverend he wanted right now. And nobody else.

Pulling his Rubik's Cube from his pocket, Gabe stumped along the hall and kicked at a baseboard.

Voices from the next room.

The colors shifting under his fingers, helping steady him up, Gabe paused outside the door.

"Others, like seed sown among thorns . . ."

The Bible study was still going.

If he stepped in right now, the folks in the circle would pat his head and ask if his daddy or his granddaddy knew where he was and shouldn't he be nearing bed and was he hungry, because he was sure looking thin. Or they'd make him sit down, and someone would put an arm around him and tell him how his momma had loved this one of the parables, how she loved coming here to this place—*such a* fine *woman*—and ask how he was doing and how that hardworking daddy of his was bearing up now and if there was any way, any way at all, they could help.

He could not sit still and listen to all that tonight. Through the crack in the door where its hinges held on to the wall, Gabe could make out Tywanza Sanders there in the room—he was young, college maybe, or just out—smiling at Gabe right now through the crack. But he wouldn't be calling Gabe out. Instead, he winked friendly at him, then looked back respectful at the woman leading the study. Gabe's momma had loved that about Mother Emanuel, how it brought people up, women and men, trained and ordained for the ministry.

And there was a young girl—Gabe couldn't make out her face good, but he knew who she was—her feet swinging loose from the folding chair and her grandmother holding her hand.

And there was a white boy—or undergrown man—in the circle of chairs. Shoulders hunched forward. Dark circles under the eyes. Dirty-blond hair cut in a bowl.

One of the church ladies reached now and patted the boy-man on the shoulder. Not interrupting the study, just a *we're glad you're here, hon* kind of pat.

Gabe would just sit here behind the door with his cube and wait. Catch Pastor Clem when it was done.

Slumped in the hall near the door, Gabe's head rested against the wall. He'd assembled all the white squares on one side of the cube. But the reds were a mess. He spun the rows. Red. Red. Red. His fingers flew.

From the next room, that smooth-rolling current of the voice leading the study: "They hear the word, but the worries of this life . . ." Gabe let the voice buoy him up and along for a while as the lesson flowed to its close. Through the crack at the door's hinges, he could see the circle of heads bow for prayer.

He let the cube rest on his lap. Let his eyes shut. Let the silence settle around him.

A bang ripped through the quiet. Gabe shot up straight from his slump. A crack of thunder, maybe, right overhead. Must be. Lightning smacking the steeple, ripping clear to the ground.

A shout then: *"He has a gun!"*

A flood of screams. Like they'd washed up over his head. Like he couldn't breathe for the screams.

His heart seizing up in his chest, Gabe peered through the door's crack and saw a figure—a man, an older man—diving in front of Pastor Clem. The kindly, elderly minister Daniel Simmons. Gabe saw it as if it were all in a blurred and grainy slow motion: the old reverend launching himself like a rocket over the body of the younger pastor to shield him. Convulsing. And falling. The body behind him, the man he'd tried to protect, falling, too.

Tywanza's voice rose over the screams: "Don't do this. You don't have to do this."

A child's muffled cry.

The voice, the one Gabe didn't know, came back: "I have to. I have to do this."

Pressed behind the door, the cube clutched in one hand so tightly its corner pierced into his palm, heart slamming the sides of his chest, Gabe peered through the crack between the hinges.

Something on the floor like a sack. Barely moving.

The words from inside the room came muddy and garbled and monotone. "My mission. Somebody has to."

Tywanza spoke again: "You don't have to do this. You don't. Not this. You don't."

More screams.

There stood the boy-man with the dirty-blond hair, skinny back to the door. "Raped our women."

The arms were bent, holding something in front of him Gabe couldn't see.

"Taking over the country. I have to."

One arm jerked up.

The flash of black metal. The mouth of a handgun aimed at sweet Mrs. Jackson.

Tywanza Sanders launched himself to cover the woman, his aunt.

"Ty!" His momma's scream. Agony spiraling out from the sound. "Ty!"

Ty's body taking the bullets that sprayed from the gun.

Nightmare, Gabe thought through a haze. This wasn't real but just a nightmare beyond all believing.

Or maybe he was asleep and waking up to his daddy watching a war movie, and the heroes turned out to be Ty and all the folks in this room, the kind of soldiers they made movies about giving their lives for somebody else and saving a city, a country, the civilized world.

Then a hammer and hammer and hammer of bullets that went on and on. Red on the accordion pleats of the movable wall. Red on the ceiling, spatters and spatters and spatters of red. Red in bright, growing clouds on the floor.

Gabe doubled over, but his feet would not move. Like the stones from the shop counter had gotten stacked on both his feet.

Gabe's vision had gone dark and rippled, like a curtain you could see through just barely—folds and folds of a fisherman's net—dropping slow from one side of his head across. But he could make out bodies there on the floor. And a young girl's feet, one shoe missing, sticking out from under the momma, who lay facedown in the spill of her son's blood.

Explosions. More of them.

Shot after shot.

Chunks of flesh blasted on chairs.

The chairs gone red and running.

The gun turning now. Mouth to the door. Black metal still hurling out death. Then it stopped. And the boy-man bent.

"Let you live so you can tell what you saw," he said to someone there on the floor.

Stopping once to look back, he dropped the hand that held the black metal down to his side but still clutched it hard, like a child hanging on to the hand of a daddy who just might let go.

Another shot.

Gabe collapsed, legs buckling, the Rubik's Cube tumbling down to the floor.

Red side up.

Everywhere, red. Red above and below and behind. Red flowing.

And then there was no color at all.

Darkness. Just darkness.

Chapter 43

1822

Pandemonium reigned, the shouts of the crowd deafening, the militia firing into the air, the captain of the guard sitting his horse in a cloud of dust and gunpowder.

In the blur of the moment, buzzards already swooping, Emily saw her father approach, pistol raised.

Tom's eyes were lit like his whole soul had caught fire—like the rage and the sorrow would burn him up from the inside.

Jackson Pinckney raised his hand to aim at Tom's face.

The pistol fired at the same moment Dinah screamed.

Emily buried her head in her own skirts, the wet red mass of them.

"Water," someone behind her was saying, "be one thing. Blood's a whole other. This here's more than just water bust loose. This colored girl here's needing a doctor."

In a fog of gunpowder clouding twenty-two bodies swinging from ropes, Dinah was giving birth.

The body of the blacksmith convulsed once more, the muscled arms twitching. Then grew still.

Dinah's teeth clenched through the last tearing and push and gushing of blood of the baby's arrival. Another scream—of more than just pain. A scream powered by rage.

A mounted guard galloped into the crowd, drawing back his arm and cutting down one body after the other with a slash of his sword. Each crumpled onto crushed shell as the crowd watched. Tom Russell's body fell in a heap next to Dinah.

Emily drew a handkerchief from the sash of her dress and pressed it to the blooming hole in Tom Russell's forehead. Blood soaked into the monogrammed silk, the *ERP* going dark first, then the whole ivory square turning scarlet.

"Awful," said someone behind her.

Numbly, Emily nodded as she wiped her face, eyes and nose running, with the bare skin of her left arm and drew the handkerchief back from Tom's head. "Yes. All of it. Awful."

"I meant your pretty little silk there. Got to be throwed out now. Burned, what I'd do."

Emily did not lift her head to see the speaker's face but wiped the wet of her face again with her arm. With her free hand, Emily reached for the still form of the infant, lying limp and lifeless in the tangled mass of his mother's skirts.

"Don't touch it," said a passing white woman, face dirty, erupting in sores. She bent over the body. "Thing's dead. Just as well, seein's when it got foaled."

Eyes still shut, Dinah rolled to her side.

"Well, I'll be," said the white woman. "Look at them little black fists start to move."

Emily gasped. "Dinah, *look*!" she cried. *"Look!"* Blood had soaked through her petticoats and onto her legs, and she did not care. Frantically, she pulled the child from inside Dinah's skirts and laid him against her chest.

Wearily, Dinah opened her eyes.

"Look!"

Dinah raised an unsteady hand to grasp five small dark fingers against her own lighter hand. *"Ours,"* she breathed.

The baby bawled.

Dinah, weeping and rocking the child close against her breast, held his tiny hand tight in her own. "Black," she said over and over again. "Thank you, Jesus. His hands are black."

Chapter 44

2015

Far up ahead, sirens shattered the night.

Murmurs rose from passersby on the sidewalk as Dan and Scudder and Kate hurtled past, ignoring the oncoming cars and plunging into the street.

"A shooting."

"What? Here? Couldn't be here. Those sirens?"

"Where, damn it?"

"Some church, they're saying."

More sirens. Wailing. Shrieking.

Even the couples strolling to a nice dinner stopped, high heels poised in midstep. Heads dipping to cell phones. Cars failing to go on green. Failing to stop on red. Block upon city block listening. Straining.

"What happened?"

"Who? Where?"

"No. Dear God, please no."

Kate did not know she'd lost her shoes until she stopped, doubled over to try to breathe, and saw her feet bare.

She ran on, flesh slapping the cobbles and bricks, tears coursing together with sweat down her cheeks, down her neck, down her chest.

Crowds milling. Cell phones to ears.

"On Calhoun."

"God. Oh God."

"Anyone hurt? How many?"

"No. God."

"No."

A middle-aged white woman on her cell phone dropped to her knees in the middle of crossing the street, the wine bottle she'd carried crashing. Both hands folded into each other. As if the prayers she needed to make could not wait until she reached the other side.

Kate ran on, Daniel a block ahead of her now, Scudder just yards behind him.

Kate willed her bare feet to move faster, pressed her lips hard together against the stone and slivers of shell that cut through her skin. Faster. She had to run faster.

Now there was the church up ahead, its white steeple glowing against a dark sky. Red and blue lights flashing into the darkness. Sirens shrieking. A crowd gathering. Trembling. Holding hands. Reaching for someone to touch. Someone to walk through these moments beside.

Medics charged out the lower doors of the church with a stretcher, a man on it. A grown man. An old man. Not Gabe. The man still alive. Was he still alive? Thrashing suddenly in pain.

The crowd silent. Only breezes of whispers. Choked sobs.

"More inside. Dead."

"In the basement. Bible study. Basement. Dead."

"So many."

"Everyone in the church. Dear God, everyone, not everyone dead."

"So many. So many dead."

Kate saw Daniel barrel toward the lower doors, where the medics had just emerged with another stretcher.

Leaping over the yellow tape, he was nearly to the doors, Scudder a few seconds behind him, Kate after that. A medic reaching for one of the stretchers was saying, "Hollow-tip bullets. Seen it one time before. Enters the body, comes apart there, and rips it to hell."

Officer Mulligan, his round Irish face twisted now and without color, was blocking Dan's path at the church door. "Oh God, I can't, Dan. I'm so sorry. Can't let anyone in."

Daniel lunged to knock Mulligan out of the way, but rather than raise an arm to him, Mulligan raised a hand to his own face. Swatted tears from his own cheeks. "It's orders," he said, voice splintering. "Jesus, it's bad. It's so bad." He straightened, as if reminded of all his training. But his shoulders, even squared to attention, still shook, his chin clenched hard against words he could not cry out.

"Sean. *Please.* I have to get in. My son is in there. Listen to me: *my son is in there!*"

Mulligan shook his head, tears coursing over his cheeks.

Daniel leaned his head in, "Sean. You and me, we been friends for years. You got to let me through before I break through myself."

"Hale!" Mulligan shouted. "Get your butt over here to this door."

Daniel surged a step forward, looking betrayed.

But Mulligan lowered his voice. "Dan, I'm going inside. Where would your boy be? I'll find him. I swear I'll find him for you. Even with all the—" Choking on his own words, he stopped there. "I'll find him for you. I swear."

Dan shook his head miserably. "Inside. With Pastor Clem."

Mulligan's face went more ashen still. "Pinckney." He laid a hand on Daniel's shoulder. "Dear Jesus."

Kate could not breathe. "We let him go," she murmured, the words fractured. "He was . . . and Sarah Grace never . . . oh God, Dan."

Daniel's whole body shook under the cop's hand. "Sean. If you know, *tell me.* That's who Gabe went looking for. Where's Clem?"

Taser in hand, Nick Hale was ramming his way through the crowd. Reaching the door, his square form blocked off the opening. "Back," he barked. "Everyone *back*."

With a nod to Daniel, Mulligan ducked inside the church.

Daniel did not step back. He met Hale's eye. "I got a son in that basement."

Hesitating, Hale rounded on Scudder and Kate. "Everybody but families, get *back*."

Daniel nodded over his shoulder. "Those two stay here with me."

"Everybody but family, damn it!"

"That's right," Daniel said. "Those two. With me."

They stood dizzied by the cyclone of red and blue and white light, the shriek of sirens, the squeal of tires. A dark Honda screeched up to the yellow tape, and Elijah Russell leapt out of the car. Barreling through the crowd, he found Daniel, and the men buried their faces in each other's necks and held on.

From the street, a tide of low notes was rising. Single cries of fear that crested and crashed and ebbed. And under that, a tune flowing forward. And words somewhere in the wash of it, sometimes drowned out by a sob.

"Through many dangers, toils, and snares . . ."

An officer emerged through the church doors, his arms covered in blood.

"I have already come . . ."

Now a stretcher. Carried slowly by medics whose faces had drawn into themselves, lips pressed into straight, quivering lines. The body they bore covered fully with a white sheet.

"'Tis grace has brought me safe thus far . . ."

Another stretcher. Another body whose face was covered. Blood leaking through the sheet.

A woman covered in blood gripped the side of the stretcher, reaching up for its end, pulling the sheet, and cradling the head of a young man.

"Son." She wept, her arms around him, her words, her whole body suffering: "My hero, my son, my sweet child."

Someone's cry echoing now from the walls of the church. *"No. Please, God, no. Not . . ."*

Behind the woman the song was rising. Broken and off-key and splintered by sobs.

"And grace will lead me home."

Another stretcher. Another body not moving.

"A child," somebody called from the edge of the crowd. "There was a child in that Bible study tonight. I know for a fact . . ."

Daniel and Elijah linked arms, Scudder on one side and Kate on the other, the four of them leaning in hard.

Kate stared at the blood soaking the sheet of the stretcher that had just passed and felt her knees begin to give way. The swirl of the red and blue lights. The scream of the sirens. The hymn rising up from the street. Daniel's face, his whole body rigid. For Daniel's sake and for Elijah's and for little Gabe's, Kate spread her feet, stiffened her arms, willed herself not to collapse.

Whenever you're feeling the sad coming on, I got your back.

And now Sean Mulligan's face behind a medic. Mulligan moving this way. Mulligan, tears streaming down both of his cheeks, his hands not swatting them away now, not bothering anymore.

Mulligan weeping.

Mulligan carrying something. Someone.

A boy.

Daniel leapt forward. Hale raised an arm to hold him behind the yellow police tape, but then pulled the arm back, waving Dan on. Roughly, Hale drew the back of his hand over the hard square of his face, wet and pinched with what he had seen—and even more he had not.

A boy lay limp, lifeless in Mulligan's arms. Head dropped back. Eyes closed.

Gabe. Unmoving.

Another siren's wail filled the dark now. Another ambulance screeched to the corner of Calhoun and careened toward them.

In the blue-and-red scrabble of light, EMTs raced toward the little body of Gabe.

And then silence.

While the sirens howled on.

Daniel reached for his boy, the name on his lips a shattering moan. *"Gabe."*

Scudder fell to his knees, tears tumbling over his rough jaw.

Sodden black curls fell back from the child's face, his lashes long and lush, his skin the same cinnamon-stick color as his daddy's. A beautiful child.

A child who was not breathing at all.

"He's . . . ," Mulligan managed, choking.

Gabe opened his eyes. Reached one hand out for his daddy, who clasped the boy in both arms, Daniel's own back braced over him like a shield.

"Okay," Mulligan finished. "He's okay. Found him passed out behind the door of the room where . . ." He swallowed hard, tears coursing. "Jesus, the hell inside that room."

Gabe was trying to lift his head now, Daniel gripping him close, Elijah holding Gabe's leg like he might never let go.

"They did," the boy murmured. "Just like he said."

Daniel pressed his cheek hard alongside his son's. "Who did, big guy? *Who?"*

A medic staggered out through the door, his hands and his pants covered in blood. Another stretcher behind him. Another face covered.

Gabe's head fell back again, black curls on his daddy's arm, the blood draining again from the boy's face, his lips only just forming a handful of sounds before his eyes closed again: "They welcomed a stranger right in."

Chapter 45

1822

Clutching a black valise, the gentleman stepped to the threshold of the Planter's Hotel. As Emily watched, he lifted his face to the sky, only moments ago a deep, dazzling cerulean, now turning a deep navy as storm clouds gathered in the west.

She did not stare at the man at the threshold. But she could tell by watching the faces of passersby what they saw in looking at him.

Immaculately groomed, he wore a morning coat that cut away at the waist, and his black hair was oiled into curls that fell over his forehead. A bandage covered his neck and one side of his face. His right hand, too, was thickly bandaged to the wrist. Small boned for a man, there was something almost feminine about him, about the way he swung the valise, bent toward it as if to peer inside, then changed his mind and swung it again, all in one elegant movement.

"Spaniard, that one is," said the proprietor of the Planter's Hotel, following the gaze of a guest just checking in. "Don't speak the language none. Touchy about having to have a private room way to the back of the place. Got hisself injured somehow—on the boat over, I reckon. Can't hardly talk with the wound he got, and his hand's bandaged so bad couldn't hardly write his own name. Nothing but scribble. And you know them foreign names."

The guest brushed dust from the beaver skin of his top hat. "An unfortunate injury. Poor man."

The proprietor smirked. "Not too awful poor. Didn't say a thing, not a whit, at the price for the best room. You know them Europe types. Got money to burn."

"Hmm," said the guest, unimpressed. He turned to examine the Spaniard for himself. "If you ask me, he needs a better tailor."

The proprietor looked blankly back.

"And," the guest continued, "I've never much trusted the swarthier denizens of Europe. Some of the Spaniards, you know, are infidels."

The proprietor blinked.

"My good man," said the guest, *"infidels."*

"Oh. Well, then."

"And I'd wager this man is one. Do you really want his sort staying in a respectable establishment?"

The proprietor considered a moment, watching the Spaniard wave away the boy who scurried to try to help him with his valise. A rip at the top of the valise near the handle spoiled the look of the thing—and would let in the rain on a day like today if those clouds kept gaining ground.

As if reading his mind, the guest sniffed. "One would think that a gentleman with that kind of money would have his bag repaired."

"Funny you saw that, too. Saw it first thing myself and tried to take it off his hands to send out and get fixed. Fellow wouldn't hear of it. Acted like I'd offered to saw off his arm. Don't much matter, though. He's leaving today. On the *Heron*—fancier clipper than most is—headed up Boston way." The proprietor shrugged. "And I tell you what, his money worked good here as any."

The guest sniffed a last time. "If financial reward is your only criterion for whom you allow to stay in your hotel, then so be it. You might want to notice, however, that young lady near the front entrance keeps glancing the Spaniard's way. No doubt she's as uneasy in the man's presence as I. Infidels can have that effect, you know. When one chooses to welcome them in one's door."

But the proprietor only squinted up at the sky, the clouds digging in over Charleston, pressing down, the sun gone slinking away. "Hell if there ain't some kind of storm comin'."

Chapter 46

2015

Thunder rolled off in the distance, and Kate touched Gabe's cheek, his face a mannequin's lifeless stare since the shooting. As she leaned against Beecher, the big horse shifting in his harness traces, Gabe looked up once from his seat on the driver's bench—then lowered his head again. He'd not spoken a word since his release from the hospital two days ago.

From his daddy's arms the night of the shooting, the medics had whisked him to Roper St. Francis to be checked over. Physically sound, they'd pronounced him. But suffering badly from trauma.

I was only outside the church, and only there after it happened, Kate thought, *and still my nightmares wake me up in the night, screaming and sweating and gasping for air. And I lie there for hours, unable to sleep. What must it be like to have been there when the horror erupted?*

They'd come here today to Calhoun Street to see what people from not just all over Charleston but all over the world had done and said and sent in response to a blind, festering hate. Kate turned to take in the towering banks of flowers and letters and signs and wreaths that mounted Emanuel's base, and her eyes filled all over again. Coffee in one hand, Scudder swung himself up onto the buggy to sit beside Gabe, Daniel on the child's opposite side. Gabe let Scudder take his hand but said nothing.

Judge Russell, standing a few feet away, raised the newspaper he'd held tucked under one arm. Unfolding it to its front page, he read, voice catching, to the cluster gathered around on the sidewalk outside Mother Emanuel. "Here is what the *New York Times* had to say yesterday about the bond hearing Friday: 'One by one, they looked to the screen in a corner of the courtroom on Friday, into the expressionless face of the young man charged with making them motherless, snuffing out the life of a promising son, taking away a loving wife for good, bringing a grandmother's life to a horrific end. And they answered him with . . .'"

The judge paused, blinking hard.

"'Forgiveness.'"

Elijah Russell read on from the *Times*, behind him bank upon bank of flowers and balloons and American flags piled on the sidewalk up to the wall of the church: "'It was as if the Bible study had never ended as one after another, victims' family members offered lessons in forgiveness, testaments to a faith that is not compromised by violence or grief.'"

Sliding from his seat, Gabe walked slowly down the banks of flowers and bent to run a finger across the petal of a pink rose. His small hand shook.

Kate, setting down the spray of lilies—Sarah Grace's favorite—she'd brought, stood close to the child and felt him lean into her. She leaned back against him and felt something ragged and raw inside sweep to still for the time being.

He scanned the flood of flowers and signs and balloons.

"Lots," he said, barely audible. Only that. But he let Kate hug his shoulders.

She walked with him to the block's end and paused to read aloud to him notes from all over the world tucked among the flowers. Someone had propped up a poster board with the names and pictures of the nine victims.

MRS. CYNTHIA GRAHAM HURD
MRS. SUSIE JACKSON
MRS. ETHEL LANCE
REV. DEPAYNE VONTRESE MIDDLETON
HON. REV. CLEMENTA PINCKNEY
MR. TYWANZA SANDERS
REV. DR. DANIEL SIMMONS, SR.
REV. SHARONDA COLEMAN-SINGLETON
MRS. MYRA SINGLETON THOMPSON

Kate touched the corner of the first photograph, the librarian's black bob framing a smile that was easy and warm as always. "See you tomorrow," Kate whispered.

Not listed were the three survivors who'd been in that room, but they were victims, too, Kate knew, having to live with those moments of horror forever: Felicia Sanders, Tywanza's mother and the grandmother of the young girl she'd shielded under her own body, both of them pretending to be dead; her granddaughter; and Polly Sheppard, the woman the shooter had purposely left alive—to tell the world what happened, he'd said.

And the world heard what happened, all right. But it was a story like nothing the shooter could have ever imagined.

Because he knew about the history of this place—that's why he'd picked it—but he did not understand it. He did not understand its long journey, unbroken through a vortex of hate. He did not understand its people's refusing to return violence for violence.

Kate ran a finger down the edge of the librarian's picture.

That shooter did not calculate on a love and a strength that could live on after gallows and floggings and flames and a barrage of hollow-tip bullets.

He did not understand.

At the top of the board were these words in purple:

THOUGH I WALK THROUGH THE VALLEY OF THE SHADOW OF DEATH . . .

And at the bottom was written:

I WILL FEAR NO EVIL.

Kate stood beside Gabe as he brushed his finger over each picture, each name. He wiped his eyes with the inside of his wrist.

In a tumble of roses, a wooden rectangle framed the image of a smiling older woman with a younger one, words hand printed across the top: *I'll miss you, Granny, and I'll continue to make you proud.* A massive easel with the words *CHARLESTON UNITED* sat propped against a cardboard support, both the easel and the cardboard crammed solid with signatures in red and black and blue and green: a Jackson Pollock, with the dribbles and swirls turning to letters as the viewer approached.

"Gabe, you able to get any sleep last night?"

He shook his head.

Kate knelt by a large spray of yellow lilies and put both hands on his shoulders, the sweet, weighty scent of the flowers filling the hot summer evening.

The pictures of the nine gazed out at the river of people passing by, kneeling, arms around one another. At the base of the board of photos, Kate pulled several photocopied pages from her backpack and propped the pages below the portraits of the nine.

Daniel leaned forward to read the names there. *"Peter Poyas. Ned Bennett. Rolla Bennett. Batteau Bennett. Denmark Vesey. Jesse Blackwood. Gullah Jack. Mingo Harth. Lot Forrester. Joe Jore. Julius Forrest. Tom Russell . . ."* He looked up. "The names of the thirty-five men executed over the course of more than a month of hangings during the summer of 1822. Many of them members of this very church."

Kate nodded.

None of them spoke for some time, the street hushed, full of shifting shadows and silence. The banks of flowers hemming Emanuel had grown again even in the past hour, their height up past the mourners' waists now. People coming and coming, stopping to hug. Black arms, white arms twining around each other. Knees to the sidewalk. Tears falling unchecked onto the flowers and the American flags, onto the front page of the *Post and Courier* propped there. Its headline read,

Hate Won't Win

And onto the poster board with a quote that Tywanza Sanders had posted on Instagram only moments before the Bible study began—and before he stepped in front of a bullet to block it from his aunt:

"A life is not important except in the impact it has on other lives."

—Jackie Robinson

Kate turned back toward the church, its steeple bright, startling even in the waning sun. Up there was where her mother had sat for the picture so long ago, Sarah Grace wanting maybe to claim, at least for the snap of a shutter, some sort of connection. Maybe, too, to draw peace and strength from this place—the sorrow that it had survived, the courage that could not be hanged or beaten or burned.

"Or shot down," Kate added aloud, tears welling all over again. And the judge, watching her, nodded. As if somehow he knew what she meant. Or maybe she'd been thinking aloud.

Still unspeaking, Gabe moved back to her side.

"Gabe," Kate began, "about what happened here." But she found she had no words to make everything better or paint the world as a place of kindness and goodness and warmth.

383

Instead, they both squeezed shut their eyes and did not reach for the crutch of words.

Kate's tears splattered on the child's hand. Fiercely, she kissed the top of his curls. "And just so you know, we're all right here when you need us. Right here." She lifted his hand and pressed it hard to her face. "You lean on me if the sad's coming for you, you hear?"

Pacem, Kate heard her mother's voice say and saw Sarah Grace's face lifting as it did only during Mass, when the crush of life would loosen its grip for a time, in the moments when the peace the priests spoke of was something she could believe—until the next onslaught of regret.

Runnels of tears coursed down Kate's cheeks. *Pacem,* she heard. Just that.

No assurance things would be fine.

No guarantees.

Just a word, set there in the midst of a storm, like a rock you could rest on.

Holding hard to the small hand in hers, Kate knelt near the lilies, which smelled of sweetness and death and compassion. And cried.

Gabe held his daddy's hand as they stepped off the shuttle that had brought them to the foot of the Ravenel Bridge, which spanned the Cooper River from Charleston to Mount Pleasant, Scudder and Kate and Elijah Russell one step behind. From her silver Mercedes, double-parked, stepped Rose Pinckney, lifting a cupped hand to them. They slowed to let her catch up.

"I wasn't sure," Kate called to her, "that you'd come after all. It being so hot still, even this late."

Rose arched one eyebrow. "The truly great thing about aging is how much credit one gets simply for showing up and not drooling onto one's chin."

"You have to admit, Rose, there aren't a lot of white heads in this crowd."

The arched eyebrow again.

"Or silver," Kate corrected herself.

"The most important votes, dear, that one ever places—"

"Are with one's feet," Daniel finished for her.

He and Rose exchanged a small nod.

Police cruisers sat at the bridge's base, blue lights flashing. Gabe's head swung from the view up ahead, a solid river of walkers, to thousands more in the opposite direction.

"Lots," he murmured.

Exchanging glances with Kate, Daniel laid a hand on his son's back. "That's right, big guy. *Lots.*"

Scudder spun through his Twitter feed on his phone. "They're saying they were expecting about three thousand for tonight."

From behind them came a voice: "We were just discussing the number."

Officer Mulligan was climbing out of his squad car, Hale already in the midst of the crowd. "Up above fifteen, maybe twenty-five thousand by now, we think." He fell into step beside them.

Watching Gabe's face, Kate read aloud the signs others held as they passed on foot and on bikes, some with strollers. Blinking big eyes up at her, Gabe nodded for her to go on, as if her reading those words out loud, if only for those few moments, kept a constant replay of horror at bay: *"Bridge to peace. We stand united. Forgiveness is key to unity. #IAmAME. Hate will not win. #CharlestonStrong."* Kate paused.

Without speaking, Gabe pointed to a sign a walker had raised high overhead.

"Need me to read that aloud, too?" Kate linked an arm through his. *"Love never fails."*

At the apex of the bridge, the two rivers of people met, cheering, boats blaring beneath.

Rose blinked at the racket, startling a couple of times when a driver pounded a horn directly beside her. She half lowered her lids at these drivers. But she did not correct them aloud.

Nine moments of silence followed, the Low Country breeze across the Ravenel Bridge sultry.

"This little light of mine," a woman began singing, her voice bluesy and gravelly and perfect, "I'm gonna let it shine."

Kate had heard Bruce Springsteen sing this once in concert, with trumpets and keyboards and sax and guitar. But here, nothing but one raw, hurting human voice, the woman's song rose over the river and soared.

The crowd joined in, black arms over white shoulders, white arms through black, hands keeping a two-beat time.

"This little light of mine, I'm gonna let it shine . . . Every day. Every day. Every day."

Even Rose, stiff at the too-chummy bump of the crowd, allowed her hand to be raised overhead by the black cyclist in Lycra shorts and neon-yellow Under Armour standing next to her. Just once, Rose glanced sideways, wide-eyed, at Kate, as if to say, *Well, would you look at me now.*

Gabe did not sing with them but pressed close in. His eyes ran up and down the arc of the bridge on both sides as the sun set, turning the Cooper River a rosy gray. His eyes darted as if scanning logarithms. He was calculating, estimating their number, those thousands on thousands of heads. He did not smile, but Kate felt him press into her side.

"Lots," she whispered.

Without asking if he was tired, Scudder bent double, and Gabe crawled up on his back, laid a curly head on his shoulder. Daniel walked alongside. Rose Pinckney, hesitating a moment, fell into step. And when Daniel Russell offered his arm, she took it.

~

Elijah Russell walked beside Kate as they descended the bridge, neither of them speaking at first.

"I wonder, Kate," he said at last, "if now might be the time. If you're ready. There's a story I'd like to tell you."

Kate listened to the tread of the thousands of walkers over the span of the bridge, let the drumming of their feet fill the silence awhile, the lights of their cell phones and flashlights pushing against the dark.

"You knew my mother well, I think." Now that she heard herself say it, there was no question mark in her voice.

His eyes closed, then opened again. "That's right."

"You knew her very well."

He turned to face her. "Sarah Grace was an unusual young woman. I remember she loved things in pairs that made no sense together at all."

"Diet Cokes in glass bottles, never in cans," Kate offered, "with big old vats of fried okra."

He nodded. "At eighteen, Sarah Grace wasn't much bigger around than the oar of a boat and could eat a feed bucket of fried okra all by herself without looking up."

Kate felt herself smile. "She loved the English poets, their quiet, their reverence for nature. But for music, she loved Motown. And she loved it loud."

"Cranked up to a tremor of the earth's crust."

They both laughed then. Looked at each other. Then looked away.

"Sarah Grace," he said, looking down at the Cooper River beneath them.

"She had someone take a photo of her at Emanuel. Not long after Hugo."

He hesitated. Then nodded. "I wasn't the one who took it. But I can guess what she might have been thinking about at the time."

The judge did not hurry to fill in the gap he'd left yawning wide open.

"You should first know, Kate—at least, I owe it to others to say first—how much I loved my wife. Chloe and I were married for

387

twenty-seven years. I adored her, and Lord only knows why, she loved and put up with me. I was faithful to her every day, in thought and in deed."

Her eyes on the crowd still flowing down from the bridge, Kate nodded for him to go on.

"But when I was eighteen, I loved your momma. As much as eighteen can love. Understand now, I'm not making light of love at eighteen—not the intensity of it. But the true intimacy—how wide and how long and how deep. There's a beauty, and there's a strength, you know, that grows only in a long walk together in the same direction."

Afraid of what he might say next—and afraid he might stop speaking—Kate watched his face.

"I say that not to diminish the excellent woman your momma was. But she and I never had that, the long walk. Forgive me: I felt I owed it to my Chloe to start out with that."

Kate reached for a strand of the Spanish moss that had blown onto the bridge railing and studied it between her fingers. "I guess it's time I ask what happened. That spring of Sarah Grace's freshman year that she disappeared." She turned her face back to him. "Somehow, I think that involved you."

"I'll need to take you back a little further in time," he said. "So the weaving of family and family and Charleston itself begins to make a little more sense."

To Kate, the quiet tread of the crowd was becoming a roar in her head.

They were nearing the base of the bridge, the night heavy with the scent of salt water and sea grass and pluff mud and crepe myrtle all rising to meet them. Kate's hand went to her stomach, already wrung tight, and now with the churn of these smells, too heady, too thick, twisted in on itself.

She turned toward the judge. "I'm ready," she said, "to hear the rest."

Chapter 47

1822

Evening only thickened the smell of brine and fish and mildewing wood, the air gone acrid.

Emily Pinckney stopped and sniffed the air. She would not let herself think about the smell of death and rot she could make out these days—she would not let herself think. There was smoke in the air, too. Something burning. She raised her face to the sky.

Angelina brushed a hand across her own cheek. "Ash. Little bits of it falling all morning." Her eyes blazed. "They burned it, you know. The church."

No answer, Emily's attention elsewhere.

"I don't understand, Em. Why did you send the message to my house to meet you here at the wharves, of all places?"

By way of answer, Emily linked her arm through her friend's and pointed to a clipper docked at North Adger's Wharf, passengers boarding. But she did not explain.

Emily's stomach had not been steady since Vesey's hanging and all that followed: the ropes and gallows and strangulations and the pistol shot through the head—and the blood. Dinah's blood. And Tom's.

Emily's monogrammed handkerchief, stiff and dry now and nearly black, sat on her dressing table. As her father never came in her room and she would not be seeking him out, no one would try to force her to throw it away.

The last hangings were over, thirty-five dead in all, and the last set to be killed, the ones after Tom, left swinging stiff on their ropes as a warning to others. For days now, turkey buzzards had torn at their bodies, and the stench carried on the night breeze. But city leaders thought it a good lesson.

Heat and fear still roiled the city, as if a lid had been clamped over a boiling pot. Today, the ash hung in the air, on top of the sweet, salty scent of the mud. The smells of the fish and the rot, putrefied and thick, wafted through, too, and churned inside her. She kept a flat palm on her waist as she asked, "What did you say was burning?"

"You didn't hear? About the church?"

Emily frowned. "There's too much to hear these days. I've tried to stop. Hearing, I mean. Any news of any kind. What church?"

"That church in the Neck—Vesey's church. They've burned it; a mob did. To the ground."

Emily met her friend's eye. "Where the Bennett slaves were members, too." She folded her arms over her stomach to try to still the nausea. "And Dinah."

As Emily focused on the line of passengers walking up the ramp, her stomach churned harder. Faster.

Nina faced her. "How is Dinah today? And the baby?"

Emily hardened her face, then shrugged. "It's Sunday. She'll have the day, nobody looking for her."

Nina's brows drew together.

"No one expecting her to do much," Emily clarified. "So she can rest."

"And the baby?"

Emily met her friend's eye. "Tom's fine."

Nina's hand went to her mouth. "I didn't know she'd already named him. Hard even to hear that: *Tom's fine.*" She bit her lip. "Poor little innocent Tom."

Silence from Emily.

Nina drew her mouth to one side. "Was there a reason we needed to walk here to the wharves in such a hurry? Or," she added bitterly, "are we just bored with no public hangings to gawk at today?"

Emily swatted angrily at the tear that escaped down her cheek. Now another. "It's barbaric. No matter what they've done."

"The hangings? Or the system that caused the revolt in the first place?"

"*Hush*, Nina. Someone will hear you."

"Good! It's time we spoke up, time we quit being so proper and nice—and so afraid. I tell you, if we don't—"

Emily spun toward her. *"Hush!"*

Nina stepped back, startled at the ferocity of it.

"I may not be you, Angelina—I will never be you—and may never do another brave or rebellious thing in my life. But today of all days, do not tell me what I ought to do."

Eyes wide, Nina searched Emily's face. Took her friend's hands in her own. "You see the same things I do. I know you do. Even when you don't want to."

Emily kept her eyes on the wharf. A familiar figure, the young woman Penina Moise, hurried by with a sweetgrass basket of bread and pies for the shop she kept on East Bay. Penina paused as she recognized the two girls and looked as if she might like to talk. But one glance at their faces seemed to make her think better of that, and she ran on.

Gulls called to each other from above and beside and under the wharf. Bales of cotton swung overhead. Waves slapped the wharf pilings.

"The ship," Nina mused. "I wonder where she's headed."

"Boston." The answer slid from Emily Pinckney too quickly.

Angelina stared at her friend. "How did you come to know that?"

"Harbor schedule published in the *Courier*. Don't you read it?"

Nina frowned. "Why do you know today's harbor schedule?"

Emily crossed her arms over her chest like she was suddenly cold, the wind whipping whitecaps across the harbor. "We were scheduled to sail to Newport, you know—my father and I. In mid-June. We'd be there right now in Rhode Island if all this had not happened."

"But that's not why you know the harbor schedule, is it?"

Silence.

"Why are we here, Em? Why would you want to come out here today with the rotting fish and the buzzards and mud—and the smoke drifting all over the city?"

Emily rubbed her hands briskly up and down her upper arms. "Maybe it makes me feel less odd, less alone, when I see people coming and going to places other than this."

Together, the girls watched the passengers board the *Heron*. Crates of indigo and rice swung precariously over their heads, the ship's hull sinking steadily lower.

Sailors hauled on the ropes that secured the *Heron* to the wharf cleats.

Stevedores piled trunks and valises higher, their hands swinging and tossing in rhythm. Black hands.

Black, Dinah had cried. *Thank you, Jesus. His hands are black.*

Walking briskly, the Spanish-looking gentleman in the morning coat swung the black valise by his side—swung it forward and back like a swing. A bandage covered his neck and jaw and one side of his face. He looked neither to the right nor the left.

Except once. Just once. When he made eye contact with Emily.

And Emily, who never made eye contact with strange men, nodded to him. Then turned away quickly, eyes welling.

The Spanish-looking gentleman waved away the porters who attempted to take his bag from him. Black curls oiled into ringlets dropped over his eyes as he set down the valise a moment, dug with his good hand into his inside coat pocket, and pulled out a sheaf of bills.

In a cluster of passengers behind him, a white woman in billowing satin boarded the ship with a bawling infant. Red-faced herself and flustered, she patted the baby's back. And when that failed to help, she gave the child a quick shake. Which made it shriek louder.

"A little wine," observed Nina, "would help that child sleep. With my mother's bearing fourteen of her own, I've heard her say she tried . . ." But here Nina's voice slowed. Stalled. As if something were just occurring to her. "Every method there is. No matter how fraught with risk." She looked hard at her friend.

Emily Pinckney said nothing but kept her arms hugged over her chest.

The ship's captain, cheeks leathered to the color of an old saddle, passed in front of them and doffed his cap. Rum wafted from his clothing and beard as he leered at the two girls.

"Fair winds and following seas!" he said to them as he strode up the gangplank.

"Yes," Emily murmured. "Indeed."

The captain stormed fore and aft, dispatching curses and orders. "Have we all boarded, Mr. McIntyre? I'll not keep Boston waiting much longer."

"Aye, Captain. We're set to sail."

"See to the crew, McIntyre. You bloody mole of a man."

The five-story sails commenced in defiance, snapping their halyards into the wind. But then the sails smoothed, white squares checkered against the blue like a tablecloth tossed to the sky. Sails swelled. Waves rolled out from the bow of the ship, the sea parting.

Emily hummed several lines from a song the servants sang when they washed. And perhaps out in the fields. "Ain't got long," she whispered, "to stay here."

Nina stared at her friend. Then at the dark-haired, slender man on the deck with the valise, his face set not on the city like the other passengers as they waved good-bye, but on the open sea—as if by keeping it constantly in his sights, he could draw the ship faster toward the horizon.

Nina reached for Emily's arm and clutched it. "It can't be."

Emily felt as if she were speaking from the bottom of a deep well. "She would have gone regardless—with or without my help. And she wasn't afraid. I trembled all night, jumping at every sound. Told me she'd come back here someday when she was free and show Tom where his father had died." She shook her head. "And she wasn't afraid."

Nina gaped, taking this in. Then she spoke in a rush. "Let's leave Charleston. Let's go to my sister in Philadelphia. We can't stay here, Em, where—"

Emily pulled away. "I'm not you, Nina. I never will be. I did what I did. But I'm not you, with your boldness and studies and way with words." She passed a hand over her eyes. "I will never leave Charleston— it's all I know. All I love. But how I will stay in Charleston after what I have seen"—her voice broke—"I don't know."

Neither spoke for a long time.

Her knees giving out, Emily sank to the wharf's planks and clung to her friend's sleeve. But her eyes stayed on the Spaniard at the ship's bow, who was clutching the valise now to his chest, his face toward the sea, full of hope and of trust—and lifted up, like he was listening.

With no breath and no courage left, Emily's words did not sound above the squall of the gulls. But her lips made their shapes: *Forgive me*.

Angelina knelt by her, and the two girls huddled there on the wharf, silk skirts puddled on splintered boards smelling of fish, as the ship slipped silently out of Charleston Harbor.

Chapter 48

2015

Letting the others walk on ahead, Kate and Elijah Russell stopped at the end of the bridge, where they could still see the lights winking all down the Cooper River and into Charleston Harbor, still hear the boats honking beneath the bridge. Behind them, walkers tipped heads together for selfies, consulted watches to make dinner plans.

Elijah Russell spoke slowly. "Scudder mentioned to me he showed you this picture." He pulled out a copy, more creased than Scudder's, but the same picture of the four people running on a beach toward the camera.

"Daniel has his daddy's smile," she said—flatly. A statement. But also a question.

The judge nodded. "Daniel came to us from a foster home."

Together they studied the photo of the four laughing people there on the beach, as if the picture itself might speak up and explain.

"Allow me to back up, Kate, if I may. Your father, from one of the oldest and proudest ancestor-worshipping white families in Charleston, fell in love with your momma her last year at the College of Charleston." He sighed. "But before that she had other friends."

"Including Chloe. And you."

"First Chloe, actually. They became close right away that first fall. Then a group of us formed. Chloe was dating someone else in our group. I saw a lot of"—he met her eye—"Sarah Grace."

Kate nodded. Waited for him to go on.

"It was a generation ago in the Deep South. Even when your momma and I were seeing each other, I'm not sure a future together seemed like a real option to her or to me. We were eighteen, the whole pack of us friends, young and wild and not thinking of much but the day."

Kate waited. Trying to breathe.

"She just disappeared that first spring, our freshman year. Wouldn't answer anyone's letters while she was gone—and no way to call before cell phones. None of us even knew where she'd gone. Came back the next fall, but it put her a semester behind. Would have nothing to do with me or Chloe or anyone from the crowd of that first year."

He shook his head. "By that time, that second fall, I'd been spending a whole lot of time with Chloe. And I've wondered sometimes if word ever leaked back to your momma while she was gone. What I know for certain is what happened when she came back: passed us on campus like we'd never met. Seemed hell-bent to let everyone know how happy she was and carefree—like she'd made some sort of decision while she was gone to reinvent her whole life. And she was hell-bent to make friends with old money. Old family names."

"Including Heyward Drayton."

"Including Heyward. Like an orchid deciding it wanted to grow inside an ice castle."

"Only the castle didn't stand long."

"I don't imagine they were ever much happy. He might have been, in his own way, for a time. Not Sarah Grace. I'd taken up with my Chloe by then, but I watched Sarah Grace from a distance. And I think,

God forgive me, I think I was glad—still struggling to find a place for a smart, angry young man of color in Low Country Carolina—to see how unhappy she was in latching onto the safety of old white Charleston money."

"You were glad she was miserable?"

"Not in the end." His tone dropped still lower. "But you'd just as well know the kind of young man I was then. I was no saint, Kate. Lord knows, still am no saint. Some days I'm not a very good wretch."

He faced her again. "But I'm not the bitter young man I was then, selfish and smashing up people and things."

She met his eye. Saw something there so honest, so without guile or meanness, she wondered if maybe it was only the ones who thought they were furthest from being a saint who had some sort of shot at the role.

"They were married the spring she finished college—Heyward was one year ahead and already making good money by then. It was a couple of years maybe before your daddy somehow caught wind of those missing months from your momma's first year at the college. He'd been studying abroad when she was a wild thing of a freshman, when she and I ran together. Wasn't 'til all that time later that he heard the rumors."

Kate's throat swelled shut. "The rumors."

He paused. Looked her straight in the eye. "That she'd been pregnant that spring."

"And rumors that the child was . . . yours."

He nodded. "That his pretty, young wife, poor as a church mouse but with old Charleston blood running way back in her family line, in that name Ravenel, might've had a child out of wedlock with a black man as the daddy and delivered it . . ." He examined her face, as if to see whether she was ready for what had to come next. "All by herself."

Kate closed her eyes and pictured the postcard of the run-down motel paper-clipped to her own birth certificate—the closest her mother had come to being able to gather the proof of her bearing two children. "The Wayside Inn in Wadesboro, North Carolina." Opening her eyes, Kate met his. "Did she tell anyone?"

"I don't think a soul. Not sure the baby left in the room that day—"

"*Left?*" Kate echoed, barely able to speak.

He gave a small single nod. "Listen to me now, Kate—"

"She abandoned a baby in a motel room?"

"She ran away, yes. She was terrified and all alone, Kate. Didn't get but a few miles away when she stopped at a pay phone and called the police to go look for a baby left at the Wayside. Listen to me: she made sure he was safe."

Kate dropped her forehead to her hands. "She didn't at least take it to a hospital or a crisis pregnancy center or . . . anywhere? She left a newborn on a bed and just *drove away*?"

"And," the judge returned sternly, "spent the rest of her life paying for it." His tone softened. "Kate, she was eighteen and scared and poor—and with a daddy out in Goose Creek who'd have killed her, she thought—and probably was right. This is why she didn't want you to know the whole story. It was enough, she probably thought, that it ate away at her life—that it gave Heyward cause to call her a monster. She couldn't stand to have it hurt you. Or make you see her differently."

Kate rubbed her forehead, which was pounding. "So people knew?"

"There were a couple of articles in the North Carolina papers about a baby left in a motel room by a white teenage girl who paid cash for the room and snuck away in the night in an older sedan with South Carolina plates. And there were speculations back on campus about where your mother had disappeared for a semester and why. Some people tried to put it together. Far as I knew, nobody ever put it together for sure. And when your momma came back, all laughing and not a care in the world, using her family name for the first time to wedge open the door to the old-money crowd, people quit talking so much."

"But the rumors found their way back at some point. To my father."

The judge leaned forward and watched the boat that was passing beneath them. "The rumor alone was bad enough for a man like Heyward. But by that time, he and your momma had already learned they were different as tropics and Arctic blasts. There were storms. Any marriage not tended with care, Kate, can blow all apart. Then there was nothing but storms—with no rebuilding after. They had a toddler by then."

Head reeling, Kate gripped the bridge for support. "Which would have been . . . me."

"Which would have been you. They were living in Charleston. By the time you were getting on to two or three or so, Heyward had not only convinced himself your momma had been the girl from the Wayside Inn who'd left a baby after having a love affair with a black man—I'm not sure which was more awful to him—but convinced himself, too, she'd been for some time after whoring around. Forgive me: your daddy's words."

"Yes," she said. "His words. I remember."

"Heyward convinced himself not only that there was a child out there somewhere that was your momma's and some other man's but also that Sarah Grace had been stepping out with other men even since they'd been married—which was nothing but the fear in his own mind eating holes in itself. Sarah Grace and Heyward didn't just split—they exploded, him holding on to a cyclone of rage. You got to keep hate stirring around to keep it that full of storm. Heyward, he stirred it well."

"The rumors about the baby she'd left in the . . . that she'd had during college . . . you heard them, too?"

"They made their way to us, Chloe and me, after a while. It was Chloe who heard them first. It was Chloe who knew we had to find out—and me who wanted to hide, pretend there wasn't a problem. Pretend I'd not had a past that needed a present."

Kate waited.

"I never knew there'd been a baby born to her until then. Been in foster care by that time for maybe three years. Slow to walk. Slow to talk. Biracial. Hadn't been adopted. Records said—based just on the anonymous call from a pay phone—that the momma was a girl who'd run away scared but was never tracked down and the father was dead."

"But the father wasn't."

"No. He was not. Just in the dark that he was the father. And then the rumors found their way back to him, and him hoping the past would stay past. But the past never does, Kate."

She turned to face him. "So Daniel's real mother was . . ."

The judge's hand came up. "Daniel's *real* momma was Chloe, as sure as that woman breathed. That's how adoption works, Kate—a child gets born in your heart, and every ounce of your bone and your flesh and your soul become part of that child from then on."

Kate nodded. She could not speak.

"But he was no blood relation to her, if that's what you mean. Lord, Chloe loved that boy something ferocious. Wrapped him in love that never let go—not even now that she's gone. Still hadn't let go." His eyes filled. "In that woman's last week of life on this earth, hospice already called in, she got worried about me, made me plan a party with her she said we'd hold down in Waterfront Park. Made me write up a long list of food we would serve, music we'd play. You know what that woman's last words were? She asked would I like to dance."

Impulsively, Kate took his hand, the judge's skin surprisingly calloused, as if he'd hoed as many gardens as he had turned pages of legal briefs. Dropping his hand after a moment, Kate stepped out of her sandals, the crushed shell at the base of the bridge rough between her toes.

The two of them stood perfectly still as the walkers from the bridge strolled behind them. Stood as the breeze off the harbor cooled. As the shadows from the live oaks inched longer.

"So"—Kate formed the words slowly—"Sarah Grace's sadness, the way she always seemed so shattered inside . . ."

He nodded. "I contacted her once, just once, to let her know we were adopting Daniel. We met back behind the house she and your daddy had rented. I let her know Daniel would be safe now. And loved to the ends of the earth."

Kate couldn't form the question she needed to ask, but she knew by his face he'd heard it there in the silence that lay between them.

He shook his head. "I never heard from her directly again after that night. So we let her alone, Chloe and me. Chloe'd tried to make contact before, even after they married—which was perhaps why our number was written on the art-exhibit booklet. But your momma kept her distance."

"But that one time, you talked?"

"Years later, I heard how Heyward saw us that night, Sarah Grace and me talking at the back of the lot under the oaks. The both of us crying. Her knowing she'd have to see Dan now from a distance every time we passed her in town—Dan in Chloe's arms, Dan on my shoulders. She knew how hard it would be—your momma heart-gutted and grateful at the same time."

"My father saw you and her that night?"

"Part of his thinking he'd caught Sarah Grace in her whoring around. She was wearing"—his eyes dropped to the side of Kate's head—"the earrings you're wearing now. He'd seen her wear them a good deal—but Heyward'd never realized they'd come from me. Until that night. He guessed at where they'd come from, and she let him know he was right."

"From you." Kate's right hand went to an earring. "These came from *you*?"

He nodded.

She could feel the edges of the birds' metal wings, sharp and uneven, and pressed them into the pad of her thumb—the sting of hurt strangely welcome just now.

"There was a scene that night—her coming from talking with me, which he'd seen. Her having been crying. And wearing those—which, for Sarah Grace, was her hanging on to the baby she'd lost, but for Heyward, looked like her hanging on to me. The scene was a bad one. Went from shots of the harsh and hurtful to carpet bombing. That's when she took you and walked out."

The Spanish moss swayed again in a slow, sluggish breeze. "My mother's bouts of depression. Her drinking. Her hanging on to me sometimes like she was afraid for me to walk one room away."

"Your momma had a soft heart. Sometimes the people with the softest ones can't quit beating themselves for any hurt they've caused somebody else. Keep things churned up like that, there's no place forgiveness can take a deep root."

Pacem, Kate had heard her mother whisper after a Mass—like a question. A longing for what she could not quite reach.

"Judge Russell, you and my father—you didn't see each other again?"

"I went to him once. Tried to convince him that Sarah Grace had been young and scared and alone when she'd made some mistakes. That she'd always been faithful to him in their marriage. That Sarah Grace's claiming you and she wanted nothing to do with him ever again came just out of pride and maybe revenge. That he had no business washing his hands of his family like that."

He shook his head. "I was trying to do a good thing, Kate. But I was still young myself—and self-righteous by then—and brash. I was a black man in law school and a man he suspected had been with his wife. When I assured Heyward Drayton of God's forgiveness for his hard-hearted, bigoted, jackassed arrogance"—he shot Kate a smile, rueful and slow—"it did not go well."

"So your arguments with Percival Botts. That had to do with my parents?"

"With your mother's fervent insistence that Daniel's biological parentage not be revealed. That Dan not ever know her name—not one thing about her."

"So you and Botts?"

"Percy and I have crossed paths a few times in the legal arena, my being a judge and his being an attorney, but we'd managed to remain fairly civil—until your momma's death. When I heard the news, I thought I'd give it a few months of mourning and then see if Dan wanted to know about his birth momma. I knew it wouldn't change his feelings for the momma who raised him. But I didn't want him contacting you up in New England while your grief was still fresh—and you getting blindsided with too much at once. That was my thinking, at least—how to be kindest to her memory and both of you."

He paused to let her speak.

"Please, go on" was all she could manage.

"When I'd heard Heyward Drayton's daughter had shown up in town, the same week Botts came to me about something he had for Dan, that's when he and I disagreed about how the truth ought to be handled. Ole Botts, in his own kind of grief over the death of your momma—I see that now—couldn't let go of having made her a promise to never, ever tell about her first child. Then when the ring came to light—"

"The ring. I'd forgotten about it."

"Sarah Grace sent a letter to Botts some years ago letting him know where she'd stored her diamond engagement ring, the only significant asset she had, and that after her death, it was to go"—his voice dropped here, softened—"to her son. The ring's value, at least. But he wasn't to know where it came from. Drove down herself last winter and took it out of the bank—like she knew somehow she didn't have long."

He watched a pelican dive far out in the harbor. "After she passed, Botts started in, trying to figure out a way to deliver the *value* of the ring to Daniel while still keeping his promise to Sarah Grace. I'd let Botts know this was a foolish consistency. That it was time for light to shine in the darkness of too-long-kept secrets. Truth is, though, when you walked into Emanuel that evening"—he winced at the reminder of the church—"it turned out I didn't know quite how to get started myself with the full airing out of so many years of quiet and covering up. All I knew was it had to get done—somehow."

"So," Kate said as she traced the letters *SARAH GRACE* in the sand with one toe, "Daniel knows that there was another mother besides the one who raised him?"

"He's known there was some other good and giving woman behind his getting born—just not who it was."

Mind reeling, Kate traced a picture of two stick figures in the sand with her toe: a ponytailed girl on a bicycle with a taller boy running just behind her. "You know, as a kid I always envied the girls with an older . . ." She paused there to focus on forming the word. "Brother." Her eyes widened at the sound she'd just made, and a smile spilled slowly over her face—her eyes wide and surprised at the smile's coming. *"Brother."*

"I'm sorry you had to grow up without that, Kate."

Underneath the stick-figure children, Kate wrote the words *KATE* and *DAN* in block letters with her toe. "But here's the thing:

if I could have picked all the things I'd want in a brother, Dan Russell would be that guy." She looked up at the judge, both of them brushing at tears. "Thank you to you and Chloe for making him that."

"And he has a sister. Such a fine one. Sarah Grace may not have planned it this way." He waited until she met his eye. "But she gave Daniel and Gabriel Ray a great gift in you."

Together, they watched the river and the harbor beyond sink into black.

"My *nephew*," Kate exclaimed, suddenly laughing through her tears. "I've never said that before. My brother. My nephew. My *family*. Gabe was my very first friend in this town, you know. With my mother's curls and my mother's wide forehead and big eyes. I couldn't see what was right in front of my face." She tipped back her face to the sky, her hands clasped together behind her head.

Kate pictured the notes scrawled in the margin of her mother's history book:

But Tom Russell
SURVIVED

"Judge, did my mother know your family's verbal history—about possibly being descended from Tom Russell?"

"She was enthralled by it, yes."

Then the last portion of Emily's journal can be trusted, and Dinah's child was Tom Russell's, and if the Russells are descended from that little boy . . .

"In a way, then," Kate said aloud, "Tom Russell did survive the hangings, didn't he? In you. And Daniel. And Gabe. My mother may have hoped it was the blacksmith who somehow escaped, or maybe she guessed he had a child, but either way her theory turned out to be right: Tom Russell survived."

Judge Russell nodded.

In the sand, Kate drew a question mark with her toe. Then struck it through.

~

Daniel and the judge and Gabe and Scudder were in the shop later that day when Kate came in with red but smiling eyes. Daniel, whom the judge had told just a few hours before, greeted her with a hug that nearly crushed her.

"But Gabe doesn't know yet," he said in her ear. "Scudder took him out for ice cream while my dad and I talked so you could be here when he's told."

Gabe listened to a shortened version of the judge's story with ever-widening eyes, then flew at Kate so hard it nearly knocked her to the floor. He did not speak but buried his face in her neck, his arms locked around her shoulders.

And no one tried to make him let go.

Scudder sat quietly along one wall of the shop and looked from one to the other of them as their drama played out.

Finally, Daniel returned to his worktable, an iron wing spread across its width.

Kate strained to see what he was doing, but he waved her back. "Strictly top secret. Just something I wanted to do—because of what happened here."

"We are," said the judge, pausing to choose his word, "healing."

"We are mad as hell," Daniel returned hotly. "Homegrown terrorism, that's what it was."

His father paused. Then nodded. And nobody argued.

Daniel swung a hammer down onto the iron wing. Then looked up, his voice softening as his gaze settled on his son. "And yeah, we're healing, too." He set down his hammer. "Only for some of us, maybe forgiveness is more a journey than a moment in time. Me, I won't be getting there fast."

Kate found herself studying the far wall of the gallery, a new item hanging there between raku mirrors: a hand-drawn sketch of the Battery, the long-armed live oaks and the mansions and canons and carriage. Around the sketch was a carved cypress frame with ceramic-tile accents. "That can't be what I think it is. Is it?"

Daniel did not even glance toward the wall. "Yep. You left it here—which I think the good judge would tell us makes it legally this gallery's to sell on your behalf."

Elijah gave an amused nod.

"Your work's good, Kate. Wouldn't let it hang in Cypress & Fire if it weren't." One arm swept toward the others in the shop. "All these folks will testify to my being particular."

"You know that's right," said the judge.

"But it's just a sketch."

"Of Charleston. Which tourists can't get enough of. Sketch me more scenes, or better still, paint me some views of the city, the swamps, the Isle of Palms, and I'll have them sold by the end of the week, if you'll give your permission."

Kate dipped her chin to rest on the top of Gabe's head. "I was actually going to ask you today: If I stayed here in Charleston to write my dissertation, would you let me know if you need extra part-time help on the gallery floor? I could try and work on a good Low Country accent if that's required for your sales staff."

Gabe looked up at her, his eyes warm as ever but his mouth not quite managing a smile.

"Consider yourself"—Dan raised his head from his table, eyes as warm and earnest as Gabe's—"hired into the family business."

"You've seen for yourself," Scudder offered, "he and Gabe need more help than they've got here, especially with the tour company doing well, too."

"I'll be trying to find a part-time adjunct teaching position, too, but meanwhile—"

Dan twisted something on his iron bird's wing. "Meanwhile this place could use your help as much as you got time while you finish that degree. And, who knows, you could be a full-time working artist by then and using that diploma for shelf paper."

Kate grinned back at him. "I'll keep that in mind."

"I got to tell you: that day Gabe got ash all over his chin trying to look like me, and you and he had your heads together, laughing, I had the strangest feeling of your looking alike—the curls in your eyes, both of you, and the wide forehead and the mouth. And I thought I'd breathed way too much glaze back in the kiln, thinking my boy favored some Yankee white chick."

"The day you let me see the slave badge."

"Yeah, that was the one. Because I figured, however this kind of thing happens, we'd all got to be family somehow."

He gave a playful push to her head. "It may be too late for me to steal your toys in the sandbox or make fun of your braces, but don't be thinking you're too old for me to pick on." He shot a look at Scudder, who was watching from his wall. "Or chaperone your dates."

They all laughed.

Then suddenly, impulsively, Daniel hugged Kate's head to his chest. "I'm sorry I never got to know her. Sarah Grace."

"Me too," Kate whispered. "Me too."

In this grown man, his chiseled features softened now with emotion, his broad shoulders and tall, imposing frame curved forward as he bent to her, Kate could imagine the baby he must have been: the milk-chocolate skin and round cheeks, the long lashes and wide, trusting eyes. She imagined the wrenching loss: Sarah Grace seeing the baby, umbilical cord still attached, wrapped in the sheets of the one unbloodied bed, hearing him crying for her.

Sarah Grace desperate and despairing and scared.

And driving away.

The frightened teenager, barely able to walk, stopping to call from a pay phone so that someone would find the baby in time. So he would be safe.

But then never forgiving herself for leaving.

Kate lifted her face to the sea breeze as she tried to absorb what she knew now—what her mother had never quit thinking about, never quit hiding. How she'd never quit hoping she could create some sort of unbroken thread for her son from his present—through her, broken link that she was—back two hundred years.

Based on the Polaroid pictures and the descriptions of Sutpen and Rose and Judge Russell, Sarah Grace must have tried for a time to become someone new and different in those last college years—to paper over the past with old money and new friends. Maybe the birth of a second child and a failing marriage had brought it all back. Maybe the anesthetic of old money and new friends had worn off.

Kate conjured her mother's face, and it all made so much sense now: the nights she'd sat with her Scotch and her tears, she might've been wondering just who'd found him first, that baby left in the Wayside Inn. Had the police come right away? Or had a maid found him first, nearly choked by his own sobs? Had he been rushed to the hospital by some night manager disturbed by muffled cries from room number five, lumbering in with a metal ring full of keys—then finding a writhing form on the bed?

Elijah Russell was explaining more now, and Kate, her mind reeling, was trying to listen: Sarah Grace had tried to track the baby down in the foster care system. She'd lain awake nights wondering how he was growing and if he had enough food. Enough care. Enough love. What if he was one of those kids in the system passed hand to hand, never finding a real home?

And then when she'd heard from Chloe about the adoption, even then once she'd known he would be cherished, she must have wondered about the little boy's life—whether he was playing Little League baseball, whether he liked math or Legos or books. If he'd learned to tie his shoes yet.

And all that time there was Kate, sitting just inches away, wondering where her momma had slipped to and who it was she was missing so hard.

Sarah Grace's and Heyward's refusal to forgive her for what she'd done, how deadly that had been for them both.

Kate calculated the years: 1989, when Sarah Grace posed on the pediment of Emanuel, would have been a year or two after her mother came back from delivering Daniel and not long before she married Heyward. And the 1991 exhibit of the Vesey memorial in black marble that she'd come to at the church, that must've been soon after their marriage.

Both times, maybe it wasn't a connection with Elijah himself so much as the place, what it had stood for over the course of two hundred years. So it wasn't a hunt for a lost love that had drawn her back so much as something she'd sensed there: a courage or forgiveness or strength that she lacked.

Kate drew her fingers through Gabe's curls. Her nephew. *Hers.* And closed her eyes against the pain of Felicia Sanders, who'd lost her son Ty in the church, the young man who'd had his mother's name tattooed across his chest when she was battling cancer. A poet, he faced down rounds of hollow-tip bullets and found words of calm and reason to try and talk down the killer. Then died a hero trying to shield his aunt from the shots. All the families who'd had part of themselves ripped away that same night, mothers and sisters and fathers and husbands . . . all those bright years ahead that could never be given back. All that horror and outrage.

And yet . . . all that love that had been planted and had grown in that place of courage and beauty and pain—centuries of it, all that love that flowed in from all over the globe, all that love that pushed back, defiant, unbending, against all that hate.

Daniel lifted his head. "I wish she could have known." Gently, he laid a large, calloused hand on Kate's arm. "That it was okay. That love never let go."

His eyes filling and his voice hoarsening to just a splinter of sound, he used the name for her that Gabe had coined the day they'd driven Gullah Buggy to Emanuel Church, and he laid an arm around his son's shoulders. "I'm glad we get to be family, Katie-Kate."

Charleston sparkled today, hot and clear and bright colored—just as it had for the other funerals. Which struck Kate as cruel. The world *ought* to look bleak and broken this week. Instead, the pastels of its mansions and gardens glimmered and shone.

Even in the midst of the fog in her head, Kate was aware of the sound of the big black wooden wheels going round and round on the asphalt, the horse's hooves like hammers as the caisson hauling the casket rolled forward.

"Gabe wanted you to know," Dan offered as they walked down Meeting Street together, "the Gullah for times like this is *groan in the spirit*—for the nine that crossed over and everybody involved."

"Groan in the spirit," Kate murmured. "That fits exactly. Thank you, Gabe." He leaned toward her, and she marveled: her mother's forehead, her mother's impossibly long lashes—over brown eyes that filled as she looked into them.

He buried his face in her rib cage and did not move until it was time for the procession to start.

From the gardens on both sides, roses climbed up wrought iron and spilled into the street, their red flowing together as Kate's vision swam. Meeting Street was filling with red in her mind, rising up now to the horse's hocks, reaching to the harness traces, up to Kate's waist. She saw red flowing into a harbor lined with gallows, the water smelling of blood.

Kate shook her head to rid herself of the image. She rubbed her temples. Something brushed the backs of her hands. Her mother's silver herons dangling there. She must have slept in the earrings again last night. If she'd slept at all.

The silver herons must have symbolized for Sarah Grace the passion she'd known as a young woman, the longing for that. And they must have symbolized, too, a way of living in freedom that she'd always wanted to know but hadn't. All those years of searching for the connection between her life—and the baby she'd given up—and Tom Russell and the Vesey revolt had ended with her thinking she knew but perhaps didn't know for sure.

Or maybe, Kate thought, her eyes on the sidewalks where the mourners were spilling fifteen across, maybe she had been convinced. Even if she'd lacked some of the pieces to prove Dinah's story, and Tom's, somehow she'd sensed the truth: that the "failed" slave revolt won out in the end and the church that was burned and outlawed and attacked could not be crushed.

All along the route, crowds filled the sidewalks: block upon block of mourners in broad Sunday hats and baseball caps and dreads and bobs and blond highlights and pink tips and braids and weaves and buzz cuts—all heads bowed as Clem Pinckney's coffin passed on its caisson.

The College of Charleston's arena was overflowing, a swelling sea of black and white, men and women, clergy in clerical collars, surgeons with blue scrubs peeking out from under the suits they'd thrown on, big-ribboned, wide-brimmed straw hats and black pinstripes and black cotton patched at the knees and white linen and white polyester and black vintage lace. All the Low Country was here. Most of the South Carolina statehouse. And a good portion of Washington, DC.

Mordecai Greenberg, who'd shut down Penina Moise for the day, stepped from the column where he'd been waiting, flung open both arms, and wrapped them around first Rose and then Kate. "And did we ever think we would see this day come to Charleston? How could we know? And yet, 'man is born to sorrow.' This we do know."

Behind her, someone enunciated, "Katherine Drayton."

A head, brindled gray, rose from where it had been bowed over a dark argyle vest: Julian Ammons.

Before she could stop and remember New England reserve, Kate threw her arms around his neck—only vaguely aware of how he stiffened.

Hesitantly, he patted her shoulder.

She pulled back to look him in the eye. "Dr. Ammons."

"I had to come," he said simply. "I'd decided to postpone my research trip to Morris Island. However, the Thursday morning I opened the *Globe* and read the headline, I knew I had to come down."

Dr. Ammons stood beside Kate and Mordecai Greenberg and Rose Pinckney and the judge and Daniel Russell and Gabe and Scudder Lambeth as they sang, as they clapped for speaker after speaker after speaker, as the senior bishop of the AME Church, John Bryant, leaned over the lectern.

"Someone," he said, "should have told that young man . . . he wanted to start a race war. *But he came to the wrong place.*"

Thunderously, the crowd leapt to its feet.

And the crowd would leap to its feet again when the president of the United States stood behind the pulpit not long after that to deliver the eulogy, which he would end by singing a song more than two hundred years old and by pointing to what the nine victims shared.

"If we can find that grace," he told the crowd, "anything is possible. If we can tap that grace, everything can change."

Chapter 49

1822

The crowd stomped down the long gangplank and swarmed the jumbles of trunks and cases piled high. They groused and grumbled over the ship's arrival—a full three days later than someone with a first-class ticket ought to expect—and remarked on the stifling heat and shouted for someone to carry their bags.

But there in the midst of the swarm, Emily stood alone on the wharf.

To her left on a parallel pier, another crowd stood waiting for another ship. But these passengers did not stomp—did not budge at all. Their ankles shackled together, a long line of men were being deported—suspected of collaboration in the Vesey affair but not convicted to hang. They were the lucky ones. Who would likely die within the year on a sugar plantation in the Caribbean.

It had been ten days since the last set of hangings—the last, at least, until today's.

And three days since she and Nina had stood here together, watching the *Heron* be loaded. And the passengers board. The Spaniard and his valise.

Three days since Dinah had disappeared from Meeting Street. From Charleston altogether.

Ash from Morris Brown's church still fell sometimes from the sky when it rained. *Razed,* the mayor had announced triumphantly to the *Mercury* and the *Courier*—and to whomever would stand still long enough to listen. *Destroyed. Last of it we'll ever see. Done away with for good.*

But Emily had her doubts.

Tasting ash now in her mouth—though it couldn't be this many days later, could it?—she stumbled away from the wharf toward the tip of the city where Charleston sank into the sea: her own home, a witness. Along the way, workmen teetered on ladders above the wrought iron fences and gates of a number of her neighbors' homes. They were adding long, menacing spirals of iron with spikes spinning out: *chevaux-de-frise*, these were called. Iron hair. Protection against future slave insurrections, the Vesey revolt's architectural contribution to the city.

Her father had contemplated such an addition to their fencing.

"No," she had said, the first time she'd ever opposed her father. And the first time he'd ever been cowed.

Emily swept up her home's entryway stairs to her bedroom. Paused on her way at her dressing table to look in the glass. Let her fingers slide over the sterling sheen of her hairbrush.

Lifting the brush to her scalp, she pulled the pins from her tresses, letting the chestnut weight of it drop to her waist. These past ten days, for the first time in seventeen years, she'd brushed her own hair. And made clear to her father she would keep doing so.

No, she had informed him, she would not accept a new maid.

And, no, she had said, she could not imagine what had happened to Dinah after last Sunday when she'd disappeared.

"With her baby," Emily added, looking directly at him. "Such a beautiful baby."

He'd railed at her. He'd suspected treachery. Treason.

She passed through his tantrums like the moon through a storm.

He would place ads, she knew. But in local papers. Probably not in far-flung cities like Boston.

She thought of Dinah's face, serene and strong, as she'd slipped on the suit she'd secured from someone in the African church. So Emily heard the shouts of her father and walked on.

She let the brush drop with a clatter now from her hands to the dressing table, and she walked through to the second-story piazza. She'd left out paper and a quill this morning when she'd slipped out here to write a letter. Then found she'd no words she had the courage to put into ink.

But she would try again now.

First, though, she would remove the box from her sight. She opened its small cedar lid, just once. Took one last look at the monogrammed *ERP* of the silk handkerchief, gone black with Tom Russell's blood. Closing it quickly, Emily knelt and pried up the loose floorboards that ran the length of her bed.

In the hollow beneath the board lay a few private treasures dating back to her childhood: a tiny, hand-painted oil painting from her one trip to France, a dinner-guest list in the handwriting of her mother, the gloves Emily had worn on the night of the Bennetts' ball when John Aiken had handed her into the carriage, a nosegay of roses he'd sent her the next day.

Lifting her diary from her desk, she ripped its back cover and final pages from the rest. Tying the cover and final pages with a pink ribbon, she laid them carefully into the hollow.

Now she reached for the box with its bloody handkerchief. She could not throw the repulsive thing away. But also could not bring herself to bury it under the floor yet—as if somehow its presence on her dressing table stood in Dinah's place beside her. For the time being, it would stay there, the box in plain sight. The blood of a dead man inside.

Emily eased the plank back into place.

Perching at the edge of a chair, she lifted the quill. Perhaps now she could write.

Meeting Street lay unusually quiet, its late-afternoon lull when the heat smothered all movement. Charleston had grown weary of nooses and death. Today, it sat not only silent but scared. No longer a place where whites congratulated themselves, preening, proud of their benevolence and protection of inferior peoples. In this single summer, Charleston had become a city forever stripped of what it thought it had been.

Emily dipped the quill and began to write—rapidly, as if the speed of her fingers might outrun the breadth of her fear. And she spoke aloud each word as she formed it:

> *My dear Nina,*
> *I write this knowing I may well never mail it to you—I am frightened even to write it.*
>> *You saw my crime. You saw a ship sail away toward Boston with a Spaniard who was no Spaniard and a valise clutched for dear life.*
>> *You care little for the opinion of our city, and I envy you. I do care; I am no Joan of Arc—or half the brave soul you will become. And yet what else could I do?*

Here, Emily paused to glance back toward where she'd concealed the final diary pages beneath the plank. Then her glance swept to her dressing table. She dipped her quill again.

>> *You should know that I have kept something from the day of the largest hangings, the day Dinah's baby was born. You would be horrified to know what I kept.*
>> *And, Nina, you would be proud.*

Emily redipped her quill.

> *You are right to be willing to leave.*
>
> *You are right that you must leave Charleston—and I firmly believe you will do important things for what you believe.*
>
> *I will stay here, and do nothing important in the ways that you will—and to you, I must seem a coward, willing to be part of an evil system. It is true that I will overthrow nothing and make no brave public protests as you will. It is true I haven't the courage to break with my city.*
>
> *But know that in my own small way, I will continue to help where I can. If ever in your Northern home someday you should meet a fugitive slave from the Low Country, you might smile to yourself, suspecting you know an old friend from your girlhood who might have had a small, secret hand in helping with the escape.*
>
> *Know that someday, somehow, I wish to be of service, of some sort of tangible, material good, to Dinah and her son—or to her son's son, if it comes to that—if ever through the years I am able.*
>
> *I am, as always, your friend,*
> *Emily Rhett Pinckney*

Now Emily held the paper up for the sea breeze to dry the ink. To mail this letter would feel like a betrayal of her own father. But she'd had to write it; she knew that much. She'd had to watch the words flowing from her own hand. Her confession. Her shame. And to destroy it now would be a betrayal of her own eyes—what she'd finally seen.

Perhaps if her courage gave way and she did not mail the letter to Nina just now, she would do so in a few days. Or she would hide it somewhere for a time—perhaps with the tattered piece of the journal, its pages that recounted these past terrible days.

But for now, she folded it neatly. Sealed it. And tucked it into the cedar box on her dressing table, just beside the sterling brush.

Chapter 50

2015

Several weeks had gone by, tender and tearful and hard, when Kate joined Rose on the bench swing where she'd perched in Waterfront Park and laid a sterling brush in the older woman's lap. Rose's eyes still out ahead on the sea, her long, delicate fingers closed on its handle and traced the swirls of its sterling back.

"So Emily's brush came down in your family," Kate said. "It certainly took me long enough to make the connection."

The crowd in the park milled all around them, but Rose looked far past the noise.

Closing her eyes, she ran her frail fingers over the sterling as if she were reading Braille. "My wedding gift to your parents." She sighed. "I do not normally give items of this import for marriages I do not expect to last."

"Rose!"

"I had eyes, did I not? Not to mention a functioning set of ears. Your father, Kate, was a handsome man—with a fine pedigree, of course—but as brittle and controlling in his ways of approaching the world as your mother was a free spirit, with not an assertive bone in her body. It was like watching a Prussian soldier choose a butterfly for a pet." She shuddered. "I am gratified that Sarah Grace had the good sense to keep the brush. Perhaps it helped bring you home."

She squeezed Kate's hand, and Kate squeezed hers back. "I was just sitting here, thinking, sugar, about Emily and Dinah—as real to me now, heavens, as actual flesh and blood. More so, in fact, than some of the flesh and blood I know." Primly, Rose rolled her eyes. "You seem to have proved that our Dinah did in fact come back with Daniel Payne and the others right after the War to help the freed slaves and that she brought her son Tom with her, who would have been a grown man by that time."

"*Proved* might be a little strong still, Rose. But it's the start of a decent paper for a scholarly journal, for sure. And Dr. Ammons is willing to help us with the publication of Emily's journal, if you're still willing. It's a fascinating example of a Southern slaveholding woman who saw the system for what it was and didn't take the most admirable road of the Grimkés but also didn't pretend like so many others just not to see."

Rose met her eye. "So you'll be going back, then? To New England?"

Kate shook her head. "Didn't I make that part clear? I'm so sorry, Rose. No, I'm staying here. Since I finished my doctoral course work already, and since the department doesn't exactly relish my coming back as a teaching assistant"—she cleared her throat—"to say the least, I can research and write my dissertation from here and consult with Dr. Ammons via e-mail. I can probably pick up some part-time adjunct teaching while I write the dissertation—along with helping Dan out with the gallery." She flushed. "And the gallery's selling my art—*if* it sells."

Rose reached for her hand and squeezed it again—with startling force for a woman of her age. With her free hand, she lifted the sterling hairbrush from her lap. "That news, my dear, is your gift back to me."

"You're a part of what made a home for me here, Rose." She hugged the older woman's neck and pretended not to notice Rose dabbing moisture from her eyes. Kate shifted sideways in the swing to admire Waterfront Park, teeming with people.

Rose followed her gaze. "This is so very Charleston."

"What's that?"

"A time for every season, you know—a time to mourn and a time to dance. Only here in the Low Country, we sometimes do both at the same time."

Lights had been strung all through the live oaks and palmettos and crepe myrtles and from the pavilions that covered the bench swings, the harbor washed yellow and pink, and between the fountain nearest the pier and the pineapple fountain farther down the boardwalk.

It struck Kate again with almost physical force: the infernal beauty of this place steeped through with pain. When she'd first arrived back, she'd thought of Charleston as a city in amber, trapped in a two-hundred-year-old form. But it was alive, with a vibrantly beating heart—both vulnerable and resilient.

At a tent a few yards away, the staff of Penina Moise was roasting oysters for the crowd, Mordecai Greenberg himself not stirring the fire—his sideways nod to keeping kosher—but his leonine head swiveling right and then left as he greeted each person who passed.

Julian Ammons, pipe clenched in his mouth, was bending over the fire, inhaling the smell of roasting oysters, but he straightened now, a hand over his argyle vest. Seeing Kate, he walked to her. "So then. How are you?"

It had struck from behind, a spear of sorrow that took her breath.

And suddenly she was crying. For the Emanuel Nine—the nine victims—and the survivors, the families, the church, the city left maimed by the loss. For the workhouse and hangings. For the fire and fear and hate that had first brought that church to ashes. For the courage that had raised it back up. Crying, too, for her own everyday aching loss of her mother—the done and the undone: Sarah Grace, the open wound that had been her adult life, unable to forgive Heyward Drayton and, most of all, unable to forgive herself.

"I'm sorry," Kate managed after a moment, passing an arm over her eyes roughly. "I'm not sure where that came from."

Julian Ammons surveyed her for a moment. "We academics know more of obscure manuscripts than we do of the life in the office next door."

Kate nodded, grateful to let him talk, to keep her head down and regather herself.

"I was a teenager in Boston, in Roxbury—anything but upper crust—and worked hard to lose the accent I'd brought with me from childhood. I was a child in the South. Me, the angry black kid with the bad attitude who despised every last thing about Birmingham—Bombingham, we called it back then. Fire hoses. Attack dogs. Maniacs who could blow up four girls at church and get away without consequence. The azaleas in front of my grandmother's porch reached full bloom in April. She lived on the next block from the Sixteenth Street Baptist Church. Watered those shrubs with her tears—each one big as my office desk."

Kate looked up.

"It was the pines around her house, people said, that made them so lush. Acidity of the soil. Granny Ruth claimed, though, it was her tears and her singing to them." He shot a wry look sideways. "She never could get lyrics to stay put in their own song, though—Cole Porter and Jesus ending up in the same verse."

A hand slapped over his heart, Ammons crooned the next lines:

On a hill far away,
in the still of the night,
the emblem of suffering and shame . . .

Kate laughed—and surprised herself that she could.

424

Julian Ammons held up a finger. "Lesson number one from my grandmother's azaleas. A life worth living is one of compassion. And a life of compassion will include many tears."

On the bandstand nearby, Scudder Lambeth was playing along with the Satin Seagulls. He smiled over at them, but then his gaze swung to the street, and his fingers fumbled to quiet on the neck of his guitar. With a nod to his fellow musicians, he swung off the stage.

Kate twisted around on the bench swing. A buggy strung with black bunting was just pulling to the curb.

The boy up on the driver's bench beside his daddy was climbing aboard Scudder's shoulders, Elijah Russell alongside with a hand on one of the child's legs—like he needed to touch part of the boy's skin to be sure he was still there.

"I hear," said Rose quietly, "the child is improving at last."

"It's been a long several weeks. Nobody ought to see what he saw. But he's improving, yes. Want to come with me?"

"You run on, sugar. I'll pay my respects in a moment." Plucking a handkerchief from her handbag, she squared her shoulders toward the harbor before dashing at her cheeks with the silk—and Kate pretended again she didn't see Mrs. Lila Rose Manigault Pinckney cry.

Kate waited by the oysters and fire as Scudder swung Gabe to the ground and everyone else had had a hug—Mordecai Greenberg with his whole-body wrap and a long line of church ladies with their smothering kisses on Gabe's cheeks and forehead—even Julian Ammons with a stiff, pumping handshake.

Then, craning his neck, the boy reached out for Kate at the edge of the crowd and threw himself into her arms.

She hugged him hard around the chest—so hard she suddenly feared he'd stop breathing. He hugged her back, not letting go.

So much to say, all jammed there in her throat. "I'm so proud," she managed at last, "to be family with you."

Mordecai Greenberg raised both arms above his head, his head thrown back, that flat bush of beard parallel with the sky. "*Mishpachah.* To family!"

"To the past," said a deep voice beside Scudder. Julian Ammons had raised his glass, his pipe curled in one finger. "And what we learn from it. But also to the future. To hope."

Rose lifted her Chardonnay. "To a forgiveness that saved a city."

Judge Russell nodded, lifting his Coke. "And astounded the world."

Gabe listened, his eyes sweeping from one person to the next. "*Lots,*" he whispered.

~

Slipping out of the knot around Gabe to let others have their chance to hug him and ply him with another platter of shrimp with sausage and grits, Kate leaned into a live oak.

A wiry figure shambled up behind her, a yellow bow tie jutting out between the hunch of his shoulders.

"Botts."

"I am not at all sure I handled it well. Sarah Grace's request of me."

Kate kept her eyes on the harbor. "You knew about the Wayside Inn. About the son she had."

Botts gave a single nod—and even that appeared to cause him pain. "It was clumsily done, perhaps, my approach to keeping her secret. But my first loyalty was to her, you must understand. She trusted me."

Kate looked him in the eye without resentment for the first time she could remember. "My mother carried her own story around like a terrible burden. I can imagine it must have been heavy for you to cart around, too. Your affection for her. And your working for her former husband. I think I do understand, Botts. For the first time in my life."

Gratitude sprang into his eyes.

"It helps me understand my father a little better, too—all his treating me like I probably wasn't his child, his warning me against creating more public scorn, his fear of my digging too deep into the Low Country past. It doesn't make me like him now any more than I did. But it helps me understand why he felt lied to—betrayed, maybe, by the part of my mother's past he hadn't known—how he let himself become so tortured and bitter and mean. Maybe it's progress that I'm sadder for him now—all the hate he strangled himself with—than for myself, not having a dad."

She sized up Percival Botts—who, as it turned out, was more an awkward, lonely little man than a spider or gargoyle or cobra. "Guess I've learned a few things about forgiveness these past few weeks. So let me start by saying I'm sorry, Mr. Botts, for assuming you were the villain here."

Botts's tiny eyes closed, taking this in, then opened. Again, gratitude flickered there.

Rose was approaching, alongside Elijah Russell and Julian Ammons, the professor's plate mounded with shrimp and grits. "I was just telling these gentlemen, Percival—if we're not interrupting you and Katherine," said Rose, "that I will be setting up a trust fund."

She addressed Dr. Ammons. "The DNA tests I mentioned to you have concluded that the modern-day Russells do appear to be genetically linked to the dried blood on that grisly handkerchief that came down to me in a cedar box in my attic—which Kate and the judge and I are inclined to believe would be, according to Emily Pinckney's journal, the blood of Tom Russell. The judge here and his son had already spurned, albeit politely, my overtures at passing down a bit of inheritance—even if our families had been biologically related."

Kate leaned back. "So what's this about a trust fund?"

"As it's perfectly morbid, and no fun at all, to wait until one dies to watch others enjoy one's riches, the judge has agreed to help me set up a fund—"

"With the assistance," Botts interjected, "of her attorney."

"Of course." Rose surveyed her audience. "Scholarships for children of limited means. I've no delusion that several hundred years of cruelty can be made up for with one small gesture of one white woman of a certain age. But let me add this: I cannot go with a clear conscience to my heavenly reward—whose architecture I expect to look a good deal like Charleston—without the fund coming to pass."

Elijah Russell held out his arm to escort Rose toward a bench well removed from the band, which, she announced, was a good deal too loud.

"You, Judge," Rose was saying as she took his arm, "possess manners of the old school. Bully for you. And despite the lab's report that your family and mine may not be biologically connected in recent history, I hope I may consider you henceforth part of my people. A personage from the judicial branch in the family again might not be a bad thing. The last was during Prohibition, and a teetotaler. I do hope you're not the sort who makes others relinquish their bourbon."

The judge turned his head only once to grin back at Kate before he and Lila Rose Manigault Pinckney strolled out of earshot.

From the pocket of her sundress, Kate drew a faded receipt and a pen. In a few simple lines, she blocked in the palmettos, the pier, the lights shimmering over the harbor—and a boy scampering over the boardwalk now, his head thrown back. Not laughing exactly. Not yet. But there was release in his face and his running. The horror of the summer that was still too often reflected there on his face, a tumult that churned in his eyes, had calmed for the time being. For tonight, his brown eyes reflected the lights strung through the trees. For tonight, he could let his legs fly over the pier. For tonight, he could just be a boy.

And tonight that was all Kate needed to draw. A boy in a beautiful park. Her family. Her home.

"Someday," said Scudder, passing behind her, guitar in one hand, his eyes on the sketch, "you should really trust yourself to do something with that talent." Without looking back, he turned to walk toward the band.

But Kate caught his arm. "Maybe . . ."

He faced her, one eye crinkling at the corner. "I'll go with maybe if that's all I'm getting for now."

She laughed. "Maybe I should try trusting a really nice guy who's worked hard to be my friend."

"Maybe"—he bent his face to hers—"he'd be elated."

"Scudder!" someone called from the band.

Grinning, he pulled away. "I'll be back," he said. "If you'll have me." Several paces away, he turned again. "That is, if you're staying."

Kate smiled down at the lines of her sketch and stuffed the paper back into her pocket. "Why wouldn't I stay? I have family here."

The Satin Seagulls had begun to play around dusk—a peculiar but fitting mix of early nineteenth-century music Daniel had suggested, including old spirituals, as well as jazz and Carolina beach music, old sand-in-the-shoes hits, and the Black Eyed Peas' "Where Is the Love?" Just now, the band was setting down its instruments, Daniel stepping to the mike as the guest baritone, with Gabe pressed close by his side, eyes on his daddy's face.

Deep river, my home is over Jordan.

Dan's voice soared out over the boardwalk, over the harbor, over the long-armed live oaks and the hanging moss that seemed to tremble on the lowest, most sorrowful notes.

On the buggy behind Beecher, on top of a board placed over the benches, stood a structure covered in a black cloth. As Daniel reached the end of the song, Gabe tugged at the cloth, and it dropped away.

From a base of oyster shell cemented by tabby, a sculpture rose: a heron of cypress and iron lifting broad, powerful wings up onto the next current of the air. Over its head and neck and wings glowed ceramic shards, hundreds of them, glazed bluish white with copper edges, so that light sparked from the spread of its wings. Nine holes had been ripped through its body, but the heron's head and neck were arched steady and strong, the heron in flight. On its tabby base was a plaque bearing the names of the Emanuel Nine, followed by a single word:

Unfettered

Pouring from Waterfront Park and all up the boardwalk, a crowd circled Beecher and the buggy that bore the sculpture.

Kate saw Dr. Sutpen file by, admiring, his pipe bobbing from one side of his mouth as he exclaimed over the sculpture's virtues to anyone who would listen: "And if you look heah, y'all will notice the buhd's very holes give it its remahkable strength . . ."

The crowd kept coming. Kept stopping to study the list of nine names. Kept repeating the names to each other. Reminding each other just where they were when they heard what had happened one night in Charleston. And what had happened in the days after that.

When the band shifted back into rhythm and blues, the dancing commenced.

Kate was still gazing up at the heron. "Dan. It's perfect. Absolutely perfect."

Julian Ammons drew his pipe from his mouth: "Superbly done."

Smiling as Gabe raced past where Elijah Russell was spooning out roasted oysters, Kate leaned into a pier railing and marveled. At this place. At this strange turn of her life.

Rousing herself to lend a hand to the huddle of people wrestling a long board, Kate helped slide the oysters still in their shells across the long piece of plywood with a hole sawn into its middle. "Like this?"

Scudder laughed from where he sat perched, strumming his guitar softly along with the band. "You're getting the hang of it. For a foreigner."

She watched the sun's rays slant golden across the water from behind their backs to the west.

All around her, couples began the slow, shuffling steps of the shag as they spun and dipped. But Kate's eyes were fixed on the lights.

Lips pulled to a red bow of concentration, Mordecai Greenberg launched into the sliding steps with an older woman Kate recognized from the gallery staff of Cypress & Fire, but their progress was halting, with him turning every few beats to embrace another arrival at the park.

Julian Ammons, his pipe in his shirt pocket now, strolled down the line of steaming platters, his own plate mounded in shrimp and grits, baked clams, and roasted oysters. "I've been meaning," he was explaining to Mulligan, the officer's head cocked skeptically, "for some time to make more than my usual overly scheduled visit in my overly harried manner down to the Low Country. But now with my research regarding Fort Wagner, I'm able to call the remainder of the summer"—he lifted his plate—"scholarly duty."

"It's a very thorough approach to understanding this place you're taking, inside and out," Mulligan responded. "My hat's off to you, Professor."

Judge Russell, Officer Mulligan, and Julian Ammons stood close together now, their heads bent over a cell phone.

"Play it again," the judge said, shaking his head at the screen. "My Lord. It really did. Thought I'd see the Atlantic run dry before I'd see that flag coming down. One more time."

Two gray heads, a red shrub of hair between them, stayed bowed, the three bumping each other and nobody caring as the clip played again and again. And again.

Kate turned to take in the whole odd panoply of them, dancing and eating and laughing.

Something brushed her side.

And there was Scudder, hands thrust into his jeans, looking bashful. "You all right out here alone?"

"I was just thinking of the first time I stood there on the seawall and looked out over the harbor. I'd just met Gabe. And saw you there. And thought how looking at Charleston was like standing in the set of a movie studio where different actors from different period films keep wandering through—time all out of joint."

"That was just a few months and a whole world ago."

Scudder stood quiet beside her a long while, the two of them looking out over the water, where dusk was settling now—the colors of a blacksmith's fire at its heart, blue and yellow and red. And a ship set out to sea with its dinner-cruise load of sunburned tourists.

But as Kate squinted out at the ship, what she saw was a slender, dark-haired figure, a face with delicate features, the arms cradling an infant, her head swinging slowly to survey the city, then lifting up to the sky—eyes closing as if in relief.

"Dinah," Kate murmured. "Who made it safely away. And lived to come back with her son."

Gabe went cavorting by just then, a skewer of roasted shrimp and pineapple clutched in one hand.

"Tom Russell," Kate added. "Weapon maker. *Survived.*"

Scudder said nothing. Just nodded. And watched the harbor with her.

But the beat of the beach music conspired with the splash of the waves on the seawall, and soon they were swaying in time.

Taking her hand, he spun her away a few feet.

A cluster of others dancing around them, they linked hands, the music pulling them in and back out, then into a slow, shuffling spin. Daniel was there, and Rose, who allowed herself to be spun, her silver chignon perfectly sleek and in place. Mulligan and the platinum-haired waitress from Penina Moise. More and more, the crowd grew.

And Mordy Greenberg weaved his way in and out, spinning to hug a newcomer.

"A brother's job," Daniel said as he and Rose revolved sedately past, "is protecting a sister from bothersome men." Nodding toward Scudder, he winked back at Kate. "Just say the word, and he's gone."

Gabe appeared now, ducking into the ebb and flow of the dance.

"Would you, young man," Kate asked the boy, "care to dance?"

Bending so that his arm could swing over her head, she spun and he spun, and they missed not one beat.

The lights on the harbor shimmered there in the dark, the waves swelling and cresting, splashing the light into glitter just as they had for centuries now. And tomorrow, the sun would come up over long-armed live oaks and stocky palmettos and jasmine climbing over wrought iron, and it would find all of them dancing, still dancing, the past and its pain all around them, but hope rolling out ahead with the sea.

Acknowledgments

I hardly know where to begin in listing all those who've contributed to and supported this book in its formation and writing.

My agent, Elisabeth Weed of The Book Group, has earned my undying gratitude and admiration for her championing of this book and her many wise and insightful readings of it. Thank you, Ariel Lawhon, for connecting me with Elisabeth and for being a steady and selfless voice of perseverance. Thank you, too, to Dana Murphy at TBG, whose incisive comments helped sharpen this book.

Danielle Marshall at Lake Union Publishing has been in every way the editorial director I was most hoping for: warm, wise, consistently encouraging, brave, and straightforward. Her enthusiasm for this story and wisdom in how to make it stronger have made all the difference. Tiffany Yates Martin, you are an editorial genius who can make a silk purse from a sow's ear. Your humor and calm in the midst of technological mishap and your insight into the very heart of a story bring out the best in a writer. I am grateful to Jaime Wolf, too, for all his guidance—and for his kind words. The editorial and design teams at Lake Union—including Miriam Juskowicz, Sara Addicott, Kimberly Glyder, Janice Lee, and Katherine Richards—are an honor to work with and they make a writer look better and smarter than she deserves. Thank you for your endlessly hard work in fact-checking a thousand obscure details—and being a pleasure to work with.

This book is dedicated to the people of Mother Emanuel AME Church, and please let me add that each time I have been there, I have been touched and humbled by the welcome this community offers a stranger, including at a study in the downstairs fellowship hall just weeks after the tragic 2015 shooting in that very place. The arrival of yet another white stranger wanting to be part of a Mother Emanuel study could understandably have been viewed with suspicion or anger or resentment or fear. Instead, I was treated like a fellow pilgrim—part of the family. The Reverend Eric Manning, pastor of Mother Emanuel, Reverend Dr. Brenda Nelson, Maxine Smith, and Cathy Bennett have all been so gracious with their time in hearing about this book's evolution and offering their thoughts and support.

Also from the African Methodist Episcopal denomination, Senior Bishop John Bryant spoke eloquently not only at the Honorable Reverend Clementa Pinckney's funeral but also at the university where I teach part-time. I was and am so grateful for his warm and wise thoughts in reaction to my describing this book and its oddest of journeys. Longtime friends and mentors Ray Hammond and Gloria White-Hammond, AME ministers and medical doctors, guided my husband and me through premarital counseling and officiated our wedding. They continue to be among the individuals I most admire.

Thanks to Alphonso Brown of Gullah Tours (which offers a fascinating van tour and inspired this book's carriage-based Gullah Buggy), I was fortunate enough to get to see renowned Charleston blacksmith Philip Simmons's ironwork before his death a few years ago. Philip Simmons's grand grates and grilles all over Charleston helped serve as a model for how I described the work of the historical blacksmith Tom Russell, about whose work we know all too little.

Steve Hayden and Monica Philbin, my cousins and friends, were the inspiration for Daniel Russell's raku ceramics and iron sculptures. Hayden Arts in Meredith, New Hampshire, produces stunning, unique furniture and art, and if I have described the raku process imprecisely, it is solely my fault. Thank you for the detailed tour of your studio and workshop.

I would love to list whole pages of cherished friends, but since I would surely leave someone out and be horrified with myself, I will limit mentions here to friends who've contributed directly to this book and to friends who are professional writers who've shared their time, hard-won knowledge, and even their homes for writing retreats. For reading and commenting on a draft of the novel—what a gift of time!—thank you to Diane Jordan, Ariel Lawhon, Milton Brasher-Cunningham, Ruth D'Eridita, Suzanne Robertson, Elizabeth Rogers, Susanne Starr, Christine Doeg, Bonnie Grove, Joyce Searcy, and Walter Searcy. For supporting this novel in its earliest days, beginning in Boston and continuing when I lived in North Carolina and Texas, thank you to Ginger Brasher-Cunningham, Kay Brinkley, Elizabeth Cernoia, Anne Moore Armstrong, Kitty Freeman, Kelly Shushok, Christy Somerville, and Laura Singleton, who more than once over the years mailed historical books she'd found relevant to the novel. Benita Walker shared her amazing strength with me in a season when I'd put this novel aside. Blake Leyers, your editorial eye and developmental instincts on this book's earlier stages were invaluable. You are a gem. Paula Smith, a wordsmith in her own right as a gifted preacher, gave encouragement and wisdom at a particularly crucial point in this book's final stages.

I am thankful for writer friends (not previously mentioned) Lisa Patton, J. T. Ellison, Bren McClain, River Jordan, Patti Callahan Henry, Paige Crutcher, Dana Carpenter, Allisa Moreno, Marybeth Whalen, Tamera Alexander, Laura Benedict, Anne Bogel, the amazing Lake Union community of writers, and many others for understanding the crazy-making life that is writing books and for all the ways you toast the good news, rant over the bad, provide unfailing support, and freely share information.

A number of historians, librarians, and archivists in Charleston gave generously of their time and wisdom as I asked a boatload of obscure questions. Thank you to Georgette Mayo, processing archivist at Avery Research Center for African American History and Culture at the College of Charleston; Harlan Greene of the College of Charleston's Special Collections; and Celeste Wiley and Molly Inabinett of the South Carolina Historical Society. Nic Butler at Charleston County Public Library knows, I do believe, pretty much everything there is to know about historic Charleston, including which roads were cobblestone and which were sand. He took time to explore several issues with me, including whether or not there were any Quakers left in Charleston by 1822. Karen Emmons of the Historic Charleston Foundation (HCF) was so kind in helping me pursue details on Tom Russell and figure out where to find other answers. Karen dutifully informed me of a late-breaking discovery by an HCF summer intern that Tom Russell, weapon maker of the Vesey revolt, may have been owned by a Sarah Russell other than the one married to wealthy merchant Nathaniel Russell of what is now the Nathaniel Russell House Museum. Of all the marvelous historical tidbits she provided, this one alone was too late to change—so we will chalk that up to artistic license.

Dr. Elizabeth Ammons of Tufts University was my dissertation adviser during my own doctoral process (although in English literature, not history like Kate Drayton's degree), and Dr. Julian Ammons in this book is named in her honor, although he is depicted as considerably more gruff than she ever was in her gracious patience with me. She, along with Dr. Carol Flynn and Dr. John Fyler of the Tufts English Department, set a memorable example of scholarship that does not lose touch with social justice and compassion.

Thank you, too, to those who've read earlier books of mine and in some cases chose them for the Common Book at your university or for your book club selections or for your classroom reading. I am picturing your names and faces as I write this and am so grateful for the fine and fascinating people I've been privileged to meet through the books we've read or written.

Some of the books that have been helpful for background research include those listed below, in no particular order. My thanks to the authors and editors of the following titles:

The Classic Slave Narratives edited by Henry Louis Gates Jr.; Bernard E. Powers Jr.'s *Black Charlestonians: A Social History, 1822–1885*; Mark Perry's *Lift Up Thy Voice: The Sarah and Angelina Grimké Family's Journey from Slaveholders to Civil Rights Leaders*; Charles Johnson's *Middle Passage*; William H. Pease and Jane H. Pease's *The Web of Progress: Private Values and Public Styles in Boston and Charleston, 1828–1843*; Charles Johnson, Patricia Smith, and the WGBH Series Research Team's *Africans in America: America's Journey Through Slavery*; John Hope Franklin and Loren Schweninger's *Runaway Slaves: Rebels on the Plantation*; David Robertson's *Denmark Vesey: The Buried Story of America's Largest Slave Rebellion and the Man Who Led It*; Douglas R. Egerton's *He Shall Go Out Free: The Lives of Denmark Vesey*; Lacy K. Ford's *Deliver Us from Evil: The Slavery Question in the Old South*; *The Trial Record of Denmark Vesey* (introduction by John Oliver Killens); George C. Rogers Jr.'s *Charleston in the Age of the Pinckneys*; Robert Rosen's *A Short History of Charleston*; John Michael Vlach's *Charleston Blacksmith: The Work of Philip Simmons*; Alphonso Brown's *A Gullah Guide to Charleston: Walking Through Black History*; Tom Blagden Jr.'s *Lowcountry: The Natural Landscape*; Charles L. Blockson's *Hippocrene Guide to the Underground Railroad*; Anne Sinkler Whaley LeClercq's *An Antebellum Plantation Household: Including the South Carolina Low Country Receipts and Remedies of Emily Wharton Sinkler*; David Doar's *Rice and Rice Planting in the South Carolina Low Country*; Gerda Lerner's *The Grimké Sisters from South Carolina: Pioneers for Women's Rights and Abolition*; Vincent Harding's *There Is a River: The Black Struggle for Freedom in America*; Elizabeth Fox-Genovese's *Within the Plantation Household: Black and White Women of the Old South*; Eugene D. Genovese's *Roll, Jordan, Roll: The World the Slaves Made*; *Sarah Jane Foster, Teacher of the Freedmen: A Diary and Letters* edited by Wayne E.

Reilly. I also stumbled upon Rebecca Lee Reynolds's article in *Slate* on the *Places with a Past* exhibit at the 1991 Spoleto Festival, which was a helpful piece in providing Kate Drayton with one of the clues to her mother's past.

Thank you also to my mother, Diane Jordan; my brother, David; his wife, Beth; and their kids, Chris, Catherine, and Olivia, for their kindness and encouragement and for never betraying when they asked about this book's progress that it had been way too long in the making.

Last but so completely not least, I want to thank my husband, Todd Lake, and my kids, Julia, Justin, and Jasmine Jordan-Lake, for their unflagging love and enthusiasm on this long, hard slog of a book—from solely a historical novel to solely a contemporary story to a dual timeline to an already-complicated story that now needed to include a devastating recent tragedy. Through all the twists and turns of this book's formation, they shared an admiration for this history and these people with me. They made me laugh, inspired and encouraged me, painted pictures of Charleston, walked every block of the historic district in the searing summer heat with only a small bottled Coke as a reward, and kept me (marginally) sane. I am grateful beyond words for who they are and for the great gift of their lives.

Author's Note—and Some Background on the Writing of the Book

First, please let me say thank you for the chance to talk with you about how I came to write—and be obsessed for years by—the story of 1822 and present-day Charleston, South Carolina, and why this story, for me, is one that needs to be told: how the historical characters have changed the course of American history and why their message still matters today, particularly in a cultural moment in which people of common goodwill but different racial and ethnic and political backgrounds and perspectives are trying to hear and understand one another—and move forward together.

This is a work of fiction, which, contrary to what any reader paying attention to recent events might assume, I began writing more than twenty years before its publication. It has been a most unusual journey.

Before I tell—briefly—the story behind this novel and the remarkable people who inspired it, let me add that while this novel does feature some real people, places, and pivotal events, they are handled in a fictional manner. My intent is not only to tell a story worth reading but equally—or, to be honest, more importantly—to honor the memory of those in nineteenth- and twenty-first-century Charleston who have set an example of courage, conviction, and a spirit of love far stronger than hate.

In the late 1990s, twenty years before this book was published, I was a young PhD student living in Boston, and though I'd grown up in the South and loved American history, I'd just learned for the first time of the Denmark Vesey slave revolt and of the white abolitionist Grimké sisters of South Carolina—and I was more than a little rattled that I'd never even heard of these people or events before. I was supposed to be continuing research for my dissertation, but as I slogged through archives of writings by formerly enslaved and slaveholding women, I found myself taking more notes for a novel I'd like to write than for my dissertation. So I packed up my eight-month-old daughter and my ever-up-for-adventure husband in our tiny Dodge Colt and drove to Charleston, where I fell hopelessly in love with a city: the way the past bleeds through the present at every corner—as one character in this novel says, like a camera shutter left open for two hundred years. I was hooked by the Low Country's beauty, its charm, its turbulent and often horrific history, and its complicated present that in many ways represented to me the racial landscape of America: painful, often raw, yet also living proof of real transformation and hope and a hard-fought, still-in-progress unity.

I should probably mention at this point that I am white and grew up in a nearly all-white small town in the East Tennessee mountains, so I ought not even be a candidate to tell this story. But please let me add that my very first memory as a child is of my mother sitting on our living room floor, rocking to and fro and sobbing in front of the television news: Martin Luther King Jr. had been shot. Her reaction then and a hundred other such moments taught me early that the color of your own skin ought not to be the thing that determines what shatters your heart.

If you and I were sitting over coffee together, I'd like to tell a few stories, like another childhood memory: my family being stopped at a KKK roadblock on the back side of our mountain, and how one of the men wearing a bedsheet tapped with a rifle on the driver's-side window, poked its muzzle inside the car, thrust a KFC bucket at us, and asked if we'd "like to donate." And how the Klan rocked the car back and forth so violently we were sure it would flip, and how, even though in my seven-year-old mind at the time we were clearly about to die, how comforted I'd been to know for certain what my father would say before he said it: *No. We would not like to donate. And, no, we do not need to reconsider the answer.*

I could go on and on, including the story of my teenage friend Shyama Haniffa, a Muslim from Sri Lanka who'd moved to our all-white town, and the cross burned in her yard, but let me skip ahead to my early twenties, not long before my first trip to Charleston. I'd come to share a friendship with a couple my husband had known since his first year at Harvard. Gloria and Ray, both medical doctors and both ordained African Methodist Episcopal ministers, had been mentors for him and quickly became that for me, as well. With multiple graduate degrees from the finest universities and a vast circle of influence, Gloria and Ray were (and still are) among the first people the *Boston Globe* called to find out "what African Americans thought" about any given issue—which they chuckle over, as if two people could speak for a diverse community of perspectives. But one Saturday when we'd sched-uled to get together on a rare morning off for all of us, Gloria showed up dressed immaculately from head to toe. In a ratty sweatshirt and jeans myself, I teased her about trying to show the rest of us up. She replied simply that she'd had to drop by the hospital to get a quick head shot made for an ID. When I laughed that surely a head shot didn't require this level of sleek and polished gorgeousness, she let me know bluntly, matter-of-factly, that, yes, if *I* were to show up in a ratty sweatshirt and jeans, hospital personnel would assume I was a doctor on my day off. But if she, as an African American woman, showed up in the same clothes, the same people would assume *she* was a maid.

It was not the first or the last time I'd been caught up short by my own shortsightedness, but it's a moment I use to challenge my students when they push back at me or at another student that *white privilege* is just a term tossed around by liberals and academics.

Through the next several years, between finally finishing my dissertation and teaching classes and publishing other books, I returned—now hauling three children and a still-willing husband with me—for more research on the Charleston novel, which had come to include Emanuel African Methodist Episcopal Church on Calhoun Street, where Denmark Vesey and several of the slave-revolt strategists had been leaders. The church, I learned, had suffered incredible racial violence in the nineteenth century, including many of its members being hanged and its building being burned to the ground by an angry mob. From the beginning of this novel's historical story line, the church appeared in several chapters. Similarly, when about three years ago I began weaving a present-day thread into the novel, the now-rebuilt Emanuel AME Church appeared as a key element in the story, and as I chose from among prominent Charleston family names, I gave one of the main characters the last name Pinckney.

Not with any particular political strategy, the protagonists that emerged from the two story lines were a black male and a white female. The world of the white female doctoral student, floundering and confused, I could easily create, partly from recent memory. The world of an enslaved black male two hundred years ago was the work of imagination and research and compassion—like any writer, trying to see through a character's eyes and feel what he feels.

When, early on the morning of June 18, 2015, as I was slipping down to the kitchen from my attic office, where I'd been working on final revisions of this dual-timeline Charleston novel to send to my agent, my older daughter hurtled down the stairs to tell me that "something terrible had happened in Charleston," Emanuel AME felt like a part of my own life that had been attacked. The very date of the shooting, June 17, was the 193rd anniversary of Denmark Vesey's 1822 slave revolt, moved up to begin at midnight of June 16, 1822 (so essentially the early morning hours of June 17), because an informant had leaked the original July 14 date.

With the rest of the world, I followed the unfolding news with horror, including that the church's pastor, the Honorable Reverend Clementa Pinckney, had been among the victims.

On that morning of June 18, the morning after the shooting, with tears streaming and the *New York Times* in one hand and my cell phone in the other, I e-mailed my agent to say I didn't know how I could *not* include these events somehow in this novel. But that I'd no idea how to do that in a way that honored the victims and retained the hopeful note the novel had ended on before.

And then, over the next several days, the people of Charleston themselves provided the ending that to me is the true one: full of outrage and pain and horror but also of love and unity and jaw-dropping forgiveness and strength.

In the 1822 story line, characters based on actual historical figures include Denmark Vesey, the multilingual and charismatic leader of the planned revolt; Tom Russell, its weapon maker; Mayor James Hamilton; Governor Bennett; Colonel Drayton; Vesey's lieutenants, including Mingo Harth, Gullah Jack, and others; Penina Moise, a Jewish hymn writer and poet; and Angelina Grimké, who is only seventeen in the novel but who would grow to become a leading abolitionist and spokeswoman for women's rights—and early on, demonstrated an intellectual and theological inquisitiveness that led her to reject her comfortable life in a culture based on slavery. In early nineteenth-century Boston, the Haydens did run a clothing shop that distributed abolitionist propaganda by slipping pamphlets into the clothing they sold, as mentioned in the book. Dinah's escape in the novel is based on that of Ellen Craft, who disguised herself as a wealthy Spaniard with a wounded neck and managed (along with her husband, playing the part of her slave) to reach freedom in the North.

In the 2015 story line, the majority of the protagonists are purely works of fiction. Included in the story line, however, and handled in fictional form, are those involved in the Emanuel AME shooting:

Sharonda Coleman-Singleton, a minister, high school track coach, speech pathologist and mother of three; Cynthia Marie Graham Hurd, a public servant, lover of books, and manager for the Charleston County Public Library's St. Andrews Regional Branch, renamed in her honor; Susie Jackson, a grandmother of eight, church choir member and trustee; Ethel Lee Lance, matriarch of a large family and the church's sexton who for three decades took pride in keeping sparkling clean the very room where she died; DePayne V. Middleton, an ordained minister who was the mother of four daughters and also a school administrator and admissions coordinator at a local university; Clementa Pinckney, father of two daughters and Emanuel's pastor as well as a South Carolina state senator and the youngest African American elected to his state's legislature; Tywanza Sanders, a recent college graduate, poet, and entre-preneur who tried to reason with the killer and died attempting to save the life of his great-aunt, Susie Jackson; Daniel Simmons, a grandfather and retired but still-practicing minister who served in Vietnam and was awarded the Purple Heart and who died attempting to save Clem Pinckney; and Myra Thompson, a mother of two and a gifted Bible study teacher and an AME minister who had renewed her pastoral license only a few hours earlier. The more I read about these individu-als, beloved by their families, colleagues, and community, the harder it became to try and sketch out the tragedy in the basement of Mother Emanuel. They deserve far more than these lines to describe the breadth and depth of their lives and the many, many others they impacted. In the wake of the tragedy, their families continue their legacies of love and strength.

The survivors of the shooting, victims in their own right who must now deal with the harrowing memories of June 17, 2015, include Polly

Sheppard, Felicia Sanders, and Sanders's granddaughter, who was eleven years old at the time of the atrocity, the age of my youngest child.

I have been humbled and inspired—and am still regularly brought to tears—by how these people, together with their loved ones and the wider population of Charleston, including its police force and its long-time, marvelous former mayor Joe Riley, have set an example for our nation and for the world of a community drawing together in grief and horror after an atrocity, with renewed efforts to connect peacefully and authentically across lines of race and income and religion and to seek justice and fairness and safety for all. Out of respect and admiration, a portion of the proceeds of this novel will go to a foundation set up and administered by Mother Emanuel to serve the families of the victims.

I'm grateful to have gotten to explain at least a part of this novel's peculiar journey. I'm a writer because stories have shaped who I am and continue to challenge and change me. In a cultural climate all too prone to shouting and insults and refusing to hear one another, and a climate in which talking about race is risky, I believe *not* talking about race is far more dangerous still. It's my hope that this story of tragedy, brutality, beauty, and courage across two hundred years might be at least a small part of that conversation.

I also hope that if the reader takes anything away from spending time in the pages of this novel, it would be a sense of awe for the kind of courage that is willing, in the words of the Honorable Reverend Clem Pinckney, to "make some noise" on behalf of those whose voices aren't being heard and a sense of hope that there is, in fact, despite all the evidence to the contrary, a way to live out a kind of love that annihilates hate and that always, in the end, gets the last word.

—Joy Jordan-Lake

Reading Group Questions for Discussion

1. Have you ever been to Charleston, South Carolina, and if so, what were your own impressions of the way the city approaches its history?

2. How much—if anything—did you know about the Denmark Vesey slave revolt of 1822 before reading this book? From what you know of him from history and through this book, what arguments can be made for his being a revolutionary for freedom along the lines of those who fought in the American Revolution just a few decades prior?

3. Had you ever heard of the Grimké sisters of South Carolina, and if so, what did you know? Angelina, a character in this book, and her sister Sarah were among the few Southern slave-holding women who took a public stand against slavery. What do you think made them willing to differentiate themselves from their family and the culture that had raised them? Have you had times in your life you felt called upon to stand up against the culture around you? What happened? Have there been times you wish you had spoken out but failed to?

4. Emily Pinckney chooses a different road from the slaveholding women who did nothing to assist suffering slaves, but also a different road from her more politically engaged friend Angelina

Grimké, who would go on to become the first woman ever to address a legislative body in the United States. What do you think of Emily's decision, and is it admirable or a cop-out?

5.   *A Tangled Mercy* interweaves the stories of two different time periods and two different sets of characters. Which time period and which characters did you find more engaging? Can you talk about why? Did either of the time periods help bring to life the other for you?

6.   If you had to choose a theme for this book, how would you phrase it?

7.   Do you remember where you were and what you were doing when you first heard or read the news about the tragic shooting at Emanuel AME in Charleston? Has it blurred together with other recent tragic events for you, or has it remained distinct in your mind—and why?

8.   In the wake of the shooting at Mother Emanuel, much has been written about forgiveness versus an understandable rage at injustice, discrimination, and violence. Do you think these things, forgiveness and unity versus a demand for justice, are properly balanced in our culture? How can we promote healthy, respectful conversations about these things among people who might disagree?

9.   One of the family members of one of the AME victims in 2015 said candidly that she had not been able to forgive the shooter yet but that, given her faith, she knew she had to be on the road to forgiveness—that it is a process in some cases more than a moment in time. What do you have to say about the giving or receiving of forgiveness in your own life? In what instances has it been a moment in time, and when has it been a long, hard journey?

10. Which character in the book, historical or fictional, do you most admire and why? Which do you find most despicable and why?

11. What is it that enables Kate to move beyond the walls she's set up in her life to protect herself emotionally? Based on what you know of her now, will she choose to become a professor of history or a working artist or both—or something else? When in your life have you put up these sorts of walls or faced these sorts of professional pulls in very different directions?

12. After the 2015 shooting in Charleston, thousands of residents and people across the globe made a point of crossing racial, economic, or other cultural lines to show they cared and wanted to help. How can that sort of spirit of unity and desire to connect be fostered on an everyday basis, not just in the wake of tragedy? If you have a place of worship, does that faith community contribute to racial justice, compassion, and unity? If it doesn't contribute to racial justice, compassion, and unity, why not?

13. What practical steps might you take in your own neighborhood or workplace or through a group to which you belong to promote greater understanding, respect, admiration, and cohesion across cultural lines?

About The Author

Joy Jordan-Lake has written more than a half dozen books, including the novel *Blue Hole Back Home*, which won the Christy Award in 2009 for Best First Novel. The book, which explores racial violence and reconciliation in the post–Civil Rights South, went on to be chosen as the Common Book at several colleges, as well as being a frequent book club pick.

Jordan-Lake holds a PhD in English, is a former chaplain at Harvard, and has taught literature and writing at several universities. Her scholarly work *Whitewashing Uncle Tom's Cabin* draws on the narratives, journals, and letters of enslaved and slaveholding antebellum women, research that led her to the story behind *A Tangled Mercy*. Living outside of Nashville, she and her husband have three children. To learn more about the author and her work, visit www.joyjordanlake.com.